Praise for M.G. Vassanji's
The Magic of Saida

An Amazon.ca Best Book of 2012

"Vassanji is at his best writing about how history affects at a micro level, isolating details whose implications spread in concentric circles."
—*The Gazette* (Montreal)

"In [Vassanji's] hands, the material of encyclopedias and non-fiction tomes becomes the vital particulars of life. . . . *The Magic of Saida* is the sort of novel that, upon finishing, one wants to immediately read again, to examine, to study just how Vasssanji works his narrative magic, and to allow oneself to savour it just that little bit longer." —*The Globe and Mail*

"Vassanji manages—elegantly—to evoke both loathing and sympathy for the colonizers and for Omari, who turns out to be more pragmatist than poet. This section becomes the book's anchor, illuminating the depth and complexity of identity in Tanzania—and in all humans."
—*Maclean's*

"A gripping narrative . . . [Vassanji's] material is so compelling that he needs little more than to adopt the role of a chronicler." —*National Post*

"The novel is a sensitive examination of love, loss, and homelessness resulting from necessary shifts in cultural environments. Kamal has no control over his life: he can only react and try to make the best of choices others have made. As he reviews his life and wonders if it was worth all the suffering experienced by him, his family, and friends, I think it's impossible not to feel enormous sympathy for a man who overcomes so many hurdles except that of his own humanity. For creating this character, M.G. Vassanji must be thanked." —*The Vancouver Sun*

"Vassanji employs dense yet splintered prose to mirror the dense yet splintered identity of his multicultural/multiethnic protagonist. An ambitious, passionate work about racial identity, deracination and the unsolvable mysteries of the human heart." —*Kirkus Reviews*

ALSO BY M.G. VASSANJI

FICTION
The Assassin's Song
The In-Between World of Vikram Lall
When She Was Queen
Amriika
The Book of Secrets
Uhuru Street
No New Land
The Gunny Sack

NONFICTION
A Place Within: Rediscovering India
Mordecai Richler

THE MAGIC *of* SAIDA

Anchor Canada

THE
MAGIC
of
SAIDA

M.G. VASSANJI

LIBRARY AND ARCHIVES CANADA CATALOGUING IN PUBLICATION

Vassanji, M. G.
The magic of Saida / M.G. Vassanji.

ISBN 978-0-385-66715-9

I. Title.

PS8593.A87M33 2013   C813'.54   C2012-906664-8

The Magic of Saida is a work of fiction. Names, characters, places and incidents are
products of the author's imagination or are used fictitiously. Any resemblance to
actual events or locales or persons, living or dead, is entirely coincidental.

Cover and text design: Terri Nimmo
Cover image: © STR/Reuters/Corbis
Printed and bound in the USA

Published in Canada by Anchor Canada,
a division of Random House of Canada Limited

Visit Random House of Canada Limited's website: www.randomhouse.ca

10 9 8 7 6 5 4 3 2 1

*To the poets of old,
the washairi*

· CONTENTS ·

THE MAGIC *of* SAIDA

prologue

He came to my notice quite by accident one afternoon, when I overheard a nurse tell the receptionist at the city hospital about a curious patient who had been brought in in a state of delirium early that morning. He had been ranting all sorts of crazy things, the nurse put it, adding, "This one's headed for the madhouse, for sure."

What sort of crazy things?

"Eti, a poet was hanged in Kilwa, after he wrote a letter to Mecca, and—you will like this—there is a lover, *beautiful* like a mermaid, called Kinjikitilé . . ." High laughter rippled merrily down the hallway on this otherwise depleted Sunday afternoon. I happened to be visiting an old colleague of mine, and on my way out had paused at the station to make an inquiry. And this bit of hospital gossip awoke some nerve in me—and not because Kinjikitilé, as every child in school learns, was the name of a man, the prophet who inspired the great War of the Waters against the Germans in this country a century ago. It was the reference to the poet that had caught my breath. He could only be Mzee Omari Tamim, one of our preeminent bards, found hanged from Kilwa's equally famous mango tree, sometime during the 1960s. The townspeople, not satisfied with the police verdict of suicide, engaged a renowned sorcerer to solve the case. The verdict: murder by a djinn. I happen to know that the case was deemed politically embarrassing to our young nation and was hushed up.

I am a publisher by profession, and in my field discoveries are what one lives for. It was also through casual hearsay that some years ago I discovered the manuscript of a Swahili novel, possibly the first one ever written. For me, a sensation; a financial failure nevertheless. But it's what I do, nosing around after stories, from Oyster Bay to Kariakoo, Dar es Salaam to Mwanza. In that pursuit, I admit, I sometimes forget the occasion. "Take me to this curious patient," I told the nurse.

He was called Kamal Punja, the nurse informed me on our way to his room. That Indian name belied his appearance when I saw him, which was very evidently that of an African. He was a big man, lying on his back, his hair partly grey. His breathing was quick and audible, his pallor a deep ashen, and his lined, fleshy face had the look of a man worried by his sleep. A young man and woman sat beside him, the one towards the middle, the other at the head, and turned out to be his son and daughter. I assumed it was they who had brought the expensive roses by the window. I felt sorry for them. The girl was as thin as a reed, the boy big boned and muscular; in their North American accents they were attempting to convince Dad that he was not well and should return home to Edmonton to be looked after. It occurred to me briefly that they were not used to such unhappy scenes; they were in their early twenties. There was one other person in the room, a young woman present in a consular capacity, and she left as soon as I arrived.

Visiting time was over, Sister Felicity announced, and the girl and boy left, promising to be back the next day. The nurse, with a knowing look at me, also departed, closing the door behind her, and I was alone with the patient, who had turned his head and was staring at me.

"Hello," I said and stepped closer to his bed.

"Who are you?" The voice fragile, the look tired. The large eyes alarmingly bloodshot. There was a small growth of beard at the chin, and the nose, I noticed, was fleshy without being broad.

"I am Martin Kigoma, a publisher. I am visiting a friend here and I heard about you from the nurse. You seem to have had a wild experience."

Having pulled up the chair vacated by his son, I watched him somewhat warily. I had already been apprised by the nurse that he was a medical doctor from Canada, and had been flown in from Kilwa in an emergency. He had been pumped for an overdose, based on the diagnosis that accompanied him. He needed help, that face seemed to signal, and it was not just of the medical sort—and, I hasten to add, this was not the opportunistic observation of a predatory publisher with a need to make a comeback.

"How do you feel now, Doctor?" I asked with concern.

"Woozy," he answered, and twitched an arm in an attempt to raise it. "Confused. You see, I've been poisoned by a mixture of hallucinogenic drugs . . . plant extracts . . . make you talk and talk . . . make you see things . . ."

I noticed from his accent that he must have left these parts a long time ago. At this time I also had the feeling that he seemed familiar, and I'd seen that face in perhaps its younger days. This happens sometimes, with people showing up on our streets after long absences abroad. And so my empathy for him was all the greater.

"The nurse said—" I began, then switched tack. "What took you to Kilwa? Did you go on a holiday?"

He didn't reply. A deathly quiet descended upon us, in that bleak, spare cubicle. His head had fallen back and his eyes were shut, and it seemed that in his struggle with himself he had lost consciousness; but after some minutes as I prepared to leave he suddenly spoke, as though in his sleep.

"Kinjikitilé. I came on a mission, to find her . . . to keep my promise. I told you I would return, and I came. It's not too late . . . not too late."

I stood up—Sister Felicity was at the door with a firm look, bidding me to leave. I put my hand on his arm and asked him, "Shall I come to see you again?"

"Do," he said, turning ever so slightly towards me now. And to my great surprise, added, "Please. I need to find out . . ."

"I will return," I assured him, kindly. I turned to go, and as I reached the door, he said, "Martin . . . that's your name . . . do you believe in magic?"

I don't know, I would have told him; yes and no, but probably no . . . He wouldn't have heard me, for he had drifted off.

I left the hospital deeply affected. It is rare to be provoked to such pity, and to such a sense of mystery. As I drove along Ocean Road in my old jalopy, the beach to my left crowded with visitors this bright late afternoon, expensive leisure vehicles parked to either side of me, I wondered at the nightmares of the man I had just left in his sickbed. An African with a very Indian name, a look of utter desolation on his face, making obscure historical references in his ravings while admitting to a drugged state. Calling on a woman with an impossible name. *Do you believe in magic?* Many people do, to this day.

Some instinct drew me back to the hospital late that night on my way home from a party, to discover that the patient's condition had worsened. His son and daughter had been called and were waiting outside his room in the open corridor, sitting on the floor, leaning against the wall, looking lost and dejected and half asleep. Inside, there was some commotion, which seemed the louder for the utter stillness all around, against the background of a cricket chorus in the garden before us and the gentle wash of the ocean tide coming in across the road from the hospital.

"What happened?" I asked.

Before they could answer, the medical resident and a nurse emerged, and I repeated my question.

"He has high fever," the doctor said. "He should be all right. We're running tests."

"Can he go back to Canada for treatment?" the daughter asked.

Both the kids had now stood up.

"He can't be moved until he's stable," the doctor said testily, then went on kindly, "He will be all right. This is a modern hospital, and we have the most qualified staff. It is likely that your father has a tropical malady, for which this would be the better place for treatment."

He turned to me for confirmation and I nodded briefly.

I stepped inside the room. Kamal Punja lay on his bed breathing deeply and looking ghastly, the dim overhead lamp having rendered his sweat-drenched face weirdly electric, like that of a lit-up zombie. A nurse stood by the bed working with an IV drip. His daughter behind me gave a sob and I put an arm around her. There we left him, and I drove the boy and girl to their hotel, not far away, where we all had some tea in the bar. They became chatty and talked about their father and their life back in Canada.

"It's hard to imagine him here," said Hanif. "Like I can't believe that he grew up here in these same streets."

There was a silence, before his sister Karima looked up. "Yes, I find it hard too."

"Did he often talk about his childhood?" I asked.

They nodded.

"Especially when we were little," the girl said.

"How could he leave, just like that?" the boy responded, slowly and bitterly. "Abandon us and everything . . . Now this . . ."

It took him a week to recover. He was treated for malaria, finally, the two attending physicians disregarding the previous diagnosis of a drug overdose. There was malaria parasite in his blood, and who was to quibble; no point in reporting to the triumphant medicos the patient's own corroboration, albeit made in a confused state, that he had been poisoned with drugs. His deliriums had become rarer and then gone away altogether. But once when I sat alone with him, he startled me by suddenly turning on his side and looking straight at me with wide open eyes. "A girl called Kinjikitilé—you find that strange, don't you?" "Yes, I do," I said. "It's not commonly used, that name. Who was she?" He kept quiet, turned away, and went back to sleep.

A few days after that, Hanif and Karima departed for Canada, leaving him, they said, in my custody: "Martin, he's in your hands." Kamal was sitting up on the reclining bed as they embraced him and took their leave. It was a sad moment to watch, but the parent and the kids had had a talk and apparently come to an understanding.

"Don't you want to return home?" I asked him once we were alone.

We exchanged a look, and he replied, haltingly, in a low voice, "I must find out first. I don't know . . . I don't know what happened . . . I don't know if I've seen her . . ."

I did not need to ask who.

Over the weeks that followed I saw him regularly, and he seemed to welcome my attention. He was a lonely man, and not only in this city, where he knew no one besides me and an old schoolteacher; a lonely man anywhere, who had after three and a half decades come back in search of someone he had loved once. What he discovered was his nightmare. It had left him with a dreadful uncertainty. What exactly had he seen and heard during that bizarre ordeal? How much was true, how much, simply, hallucination? He wanted to talk, I was there to listen. I was his comfort, his sounding board, his nurse—not the first publisher, surely, to find himself in such a role.

Her actual name was Saida, he informed me. He knew her until age eleven, when his mother sent him away to become an Indian. He said this as casually as if it were the most normal thing to do. They were from Kilwa, the coastal region to the south whose recorded history and culture go back a thousand years and more—John Milton's "Quiloa"—though recent neglect has seen it waste away into the dust of obscurity. They were an African boy and girl: their single mothers were like sisters; her grandfather was the beloved poet Mzee Omari Tamim. Their companionship had been accepted, even encouraged. He thought he would marry her. He could never understand why he had been led on, to follow his fool's path and love her, only to be sent away to pine for her.

It was to find her that he had returned.

A successful and driven doctor in Canada, he had reached a stage in his life of material abundance, in which however—as he obliquely put it—his personal ties had weakened. And so one day he stepped off the treadmill, allowed an old regret to awaken, and suddenly set off to find the girl he had known as a child, keep his promise to her that he would return. That there was more to his urgency, I could guess. Wearing round his neck a tawiz, a Quranic charm given him by her when they first parted, he took a flight to Dar es Salaam. From here he took a bus to Kilwa. It was burning hot in December, and despite some talk of bandits on the way, this is what he preferred, travelling over land—the sight of each bush, each blade of grass, each tree so loaded with sentiment as to grip the heart of the returning native.

Thus he arrived in Kilwa.

One

❧

the boy, the girl

Kilwa was all history, Kamal said. The past haunted from the ruins and graves; it was there in the references to the Germans who had ruled here once, and the slaves who were sold here; he heard it in his mother's tales and he heard it recited—majestically—by the old poet, Saida's grandfather.

Kamal was nine years old when Mzee Omari began his final work, his magnum opus, with much fanfare. It was to be called *The Composition of the Coming of the Modern Age*, and it would relate how we came to be what we are on this eastern coast of Africa.

Mzee Omari Tamim returned from the mosque as usual that Friday afternoon. He wore his embroidered kofia and a crisp, pure white kanzu, and this being a special occasion, he wore also a black vest. On his feet were his old leather slippers. The skin of his face despite his age was a smooth dark brown like polished wood, the lines on his forehead feather-light. He was a man of medium height, with a slim and compact body. There were people standing on the porch whom he greeted as he passed. He paused at the entrance; the corridor was also filled with well-wishers, who hushed upon seeing him. His grand-daughter Saida came and took his hand, guided him through the crowd to his room. Mzee Omari entered and sat down on his haunches upon the mat, which was spread close to the back wall. On the coarse whitewashed wall in front of him hung a couple of ancient photographs inside their unfinished wooden frames, approximately aligned; a side wall carried a framed certificate in the strange letters of the German language; otherwise the walls were bare. In a corner was his rolled-up bundle of sleeping mat and thin mattress, and beside it his precious portable writing desk.

From where he sat the old man looked towards the open door and commanded his wife, who stood in the corridor with others, "Mwana Juma, bring me my table for writing"; Mwana Juma went and picked up the small portable desk and handed it to him. "My son, Shomari, hand me the fine paper from Syria"; a young man in his twenties came in through the doorway with a sheaf of notepaper, which was actually bought from a local Indian store. In olden times, it was said, the poets always preferred the fine white paper from Syria, which was excellent for calligraphy. "And my little granddaughter," continued Mzee Omari, "you, Saida, bring me my pen from Europe and the ink from India—and the boy, Hamida's son, Kamalu, can come with you." Kamal followed the girl as she gave her grandfather the ink bottle, and he handed the old man the long pen. Mzee Omari waved both hands in the air to dismiss them all and they, having indulged him in his beginning of his grand project, a poetic history, retreated.

Mzee Omari then looked up in front of him and called upon his djinn. "Idris, my friend and servant, fly me to days past, so that, looking down upon this land, I can see again what transpired and complete my verses about the coming of the modern age, when the European met the African, and how people followed their leaders and like the wind fighting the ocean took up arms against the Germans, and each time fell to the *pe-pe-pe!* reports of the machine guns."

In Arabic letters, in the Swahili language, Mzee Omari began to write.

Outside the room were heard cries of "Subhanallah! God give him a long life. A safe journey." There was some clapping. Then the people departed.

But Mzee Omari was near blind. How could he see clearly the dots and curves of his script? Distinguish *te* from *nun*, or *be* from *ye*? Didn't his lines run into one another? It was widely believed, it was said with awe that his djinn held his elbow and guided his hand steadily as he wrote. And so those four-line verses, those utenzi, had power, they had truth.

Having been treated to a mandazi and a shot of kahawa by the poet's friends sitting outside on the front porch, and taking one steaming roll of mandazi for his mama wrapped in a newspaper scrap, as he rounded the house on his way home Kamal decided to take a peek through the old man's little window. Perched with both legs on a stone lying next to the wall, hanging on by the single window bar, he peered inside and stared at Mzee Omari scribbling slowly and intently on the paper with nib and holder. No djinn there. Suddenly Kamal felt a stinging slap on the side of his face and went flying to the ground. He stood up, eyes teary, and picked up the mandazi and dusted it with his hand. There was no one around, but he knew it to be Idris the djinn who had so violently slapped him.

Kamal never peeked through that dark little window again. But he would listen to the old man recite his verses to listeners outside on the porch, or at the square on the beachfront, seated on his favourite tree trunk; and once the Tanganyika Broadcasting Corporation came and recorded him, and the following Sunday his voice was heard on the radio to great acclaim throughout the town.

· 2 ·

He had returned. But the Kilwa that Kamal saw, as he stepped off the bus at the busy crossroad and looked around, wrung his heart. It was to see a beloved again, now aged; a mother, a lover. Every eye was upon him, it seemed, as he abruptly sighted then took the few steps to the old German monument around which he had played as a child. It stood now forlorn amidst a dump and parking space, a tall white stone memorializing two foreign gentlemen, Herr Krieger and Herr Hessel, who had died in 1888, both in their thirties. They had meant nothing to him. That they were beheaded in Kilwa, during a brief insurrection against its colonization, he discovered much later. He turned around and walked across the road to the tea shop, sat down and ordered chai rangi—black tea—and mandazi and steeled himself. Calmer, he strolled to the end of the road, turned at the boma, the great fortress and administrative headquarters of former times, now, he saw, a hideous ruin of exposed brick punctured with gaping holes. He came to stand at the edge of the town square overlooking the sea.

Try to be cold, objective, he admonished himself, things change, you've changed; but he couldn't stop the images flitting through his mind, couldn't suppress the outrage. This plaza would fill with people come to relax and catch the breeze on an evening or a Sunday afternoon. Vendors went around selling goodies to eat. In the morning, the sun just peeping out from the horizon, the town's Indian men came in their singlets to do their exercises. Some evenings Mzee Omari would sit on a tree trunk (Kamal couldn't see it now) and recite to an audience of rapt admirers in the dark, a solitary lamp beside him. This sanctified ground, now brutalized by encroachment: a cow pen, a bar, a government shed built centre stage at water's edge so as to steal the sea view . . . five minutes from what had been his home, a short walk along the creek from the lagoon where he would meet her, where he last saw her. What hope could it give him, this memory's violation? We leave so many things behind, why not this one, why not her? Why relive the guilt? Did he want to take this road, wherever it led to—disappointment, heartache? But he was already on it, he had waited a long time.

The town had long possessed him, he mused; always known as a home to spirits, it let loose a spirit to come and haunt him. As he stood looking out at the ocean, the Island, Kisiwani, loomed distantly to his right, its ancient ruins a dim blur. On a school trip to the Island once, they had been met by a short, bearded white man, Mr. Archaeologist, who had shown them around the ruins and attempted to narrate the Island's history to them. Once upon a time there was a great city on the Island, known all over the world, he began, and gave up right there, wistfully watched the oblivious boys racing away screaming in all directions. What did they care about the past.

Now it was he who had come from abroad to search for a past. Kilwa had called and bid, and now he was here at the "*pays* of my haunting, to feed my obsession." He had left half a lifetime ago, more; he had made a life elsewhere, planted roots there; and still Kilwa haunted. He had headed out, he said, when there was the world to see; he had seen it. When there were triumphs to achieve, he'd had his modest ones. "I'm a rich man," he said to me in a tone I could not quite place. He was not boasting; I wished he were, then I could have judged him. I did feel a twinge of envy. It occurred to me that there were many here in this city, in this country, who would have killed to be in his shoes. In Edmonton.

A haze drifted over the shimmering sea, lending to the far distance a myopic vagueness, an impression that a mere lens would suffice to sharpen the horizon; closer at hand half a dozen small dhows were beached, their sails down, waiting for the tide to rise. A covered cart loaded with salt, perhaps, creaked its way across the wet sand to meet them. The clean, regular beat of a hammer on the woodwork stitching its way to the land. Come evening the dhows would rise and sail, for Zanzibar and Pemba and Mafia. Kamal looked around desperately. This is my place, my little town where I grew up, how can I reclaim it. Where are you, Saida, who called me? I'm here, come find me. And we'll sit here and watch the sea return, and stroll by the creek, we'll sit down at the edge of our secret lagoon, hidden by a curtain of fronds . . . and you will recite?

When God expelled Adam from Paradise, writes Milton, the angel Michael took him up the tallest hill and showed him the world of his dominion, which included "Mombaz, Melindi and Quiloa." Paradise lost, paradise regained?

Literature was Kamal's favourite subject, and history; how could that not be, growing up in this ancient town, under a poet's shadow? In high school he had produced plays and written stories. You will be wasted in medicine, said Mr. Fernandes, the English and history teacher. And Kamal had replied with a schoolboy's passion, "How can you be wasted as a doctor, attending the sick, sir? When we have fewer than fifty doctors for a population of ten million in our country?" Easy, as he was to discover; by going abroad, and attending to the rich.

He turned around and slowly walked back to the tea shack, where he had left his luggage.

"This region has a bright future, sir."

It took Kamal a moment to realize that this hope, expressed in English, had been articulated outside of his musing. He turned his head towards the genial face at the next table, belonging to a rather large man, who was wearing the traditional white kanzu and kofia.

"You are here to buy property, sir? Are you on business? I can help you."

No, Kamal told him, he was here simply on a visit, and received a doubtful but benign look in return, from someone who knew better. "But I can tell, sir, you have come from abroad."

He was originally from Kilwa, Kamal persisted. "My mother was Bi Hamida—perhaps you heard of her?" Why would he, he's not old enough. No point telling him either that he had lived with his mother just off the street known as the "one behind the Indian shops."

"No, I have not heard of her."

"You must be a teacher," Kamal told him politely.

"A businessman," the man said, then pointing to his attire, explained, "I have just returned from prayer. But I can be your guide. I know a lot about this place. All its history."

"I'm not sure I will need help . . . but if I do, I'll find you. You live around here?"

"Yes. I'll be happy to be of service. I used to guide the archaeologists. Now I also guide developers from Dar. They want to know the history, the geography, even which places are haunted—I can tell them. Nobody knows Kilwa as I do."

"Really!"

"Yes!" the man replied with equal emphasis, and they laughed.

They came out together on the street.

"Who's buying the property?" Kamal inquired.

"Tanzanians like yourself who went away are looking for places to retire."

"All the way here?"

"What better place? And Arabs," he said softly with a glance sideways, expecting who knows what. "Mafia," he added, a shade more softly. "Cosa Nostra. There is offshore oil and gas. The Aga Khan is interested. A Serena perhaps, like in Zanzibar."

Kamal informed him that he was booked at the Island View Hotel.

"In Masoko?"

Kamal nodded. Masoko, twenty miles away, was the town the colonial district administration had favoured over Kilwa because of its deep harbour and had summarily moved there. Even during Kamal's days, old Kilwa had begun to look defeated. There were no hotels in Kilwa.

"You can take a taxi," the man said. "They all go to Masoko." He put his hand to his heart, made a slight bow of the head. "Sir. Please call me when you need me."

"I will. And your name?"

"Lateef," he said. "Well, goodbye, kwa heri ya kuonana, see you again." He gave a wave and headed off, and disappeared into the side street.

· 3 ·

There were actually three Kilwas: the Island, called Kisiwani, the ancient stone city now a collection of ruins; Kamal's Kilwa, which saw its heyday in the nineteenth century trading ivory and slaves; and Masoko, the Markets, having all the look of an afterthought, scattered about the main road to the harbour. The taxi dropped him off at Stendi, the depot in Masoko, from where he took a bajaji—an Indian-made autorickshaw—to his hotel. The road was deeply potholed and muddy, and twice Kamal almost flew out of the bajaji, luggage and all. They finally reached the hotel gate, which was opened for them. An unpaved driveway led directly to the steps of an oversized circular hut with a high thatched roof and a low enclosing wall to let the breeze through. There was not a soul in sight, but there came a faint and distinctive tinkle of glassware.

He went up the steps and inside, relieved at the sudden coolness of the shade. A large, imposing bar stood straight ahead, facing a dining area, both looking out at an empty beach. There was a back entrance at the bar, opening to a patio. The tide was still out. He saw no reception desk, therefore he headed for a table to sit at and paid off his awe-stricken driver, who still could not comprehend how an American bwana had spoken Swahili to him, and so familiarly at that.

A burly, red-faced Englishman stood at the bar lecturing the barman, leaning forward, perhaps raining spit on him. Evidently the manager, or owner. "You keep your eye on his glass, my friend, and don't pick it up without asking first, 'Another glass of the same, sir?' I'll bet you even money, our visitor will say yes. Hakuna mtu who says no. And you keep a plate of the salty peanuts beside him, to keep him thirsty. Ume elewa, John? You understand? It's the liquor that keeps us fed. He can afford it. Or you're out of a job and back to Nairobi, and I'm out of a hotel and back to nowhere."

"Yes, bwana," said John.

Now the barman came over, a dark and hard-featured man in a server's white jacket.

"I have a reservation," Kamal said and handed him the printed confirmation.

"Yes, sir," said John. "We have a room waiting for you. Would you like a drink first?" The thick accent very much Kenyan.

Kamal ordered a gin and tonic, though it was too early. The man at the bar flashed a knowing grin.

"The name's Markham," he said, shuffling over, breathing quickly. "Welcome to Island View. We also arrange tours."

"Thank you. I'm Kamal Punja."

The man before him was dishevelled and shapeless, with baggy linen trousers and an undersized blue shirt barely covering his stomach; there was a white stubble on the patchy red face and a crown of wispy white hair on his head. He could be playing a role, but then he could have grown into it, the lonely white Conradian exile at an outpost. And he was going nowhere from here.

"Edward Markham," he leered. "Looking for property? Or have you come to sightsee? You don't look like a government chap."

He irritated. These colonials never learn, Kamal thought, and was immediately surprised at himself. This is not me at all, it's what I might have said in my youth, and even then, not with conviction. Times have changed. It's the new century.

Markham shuffled back to the bar, brought out a register from a shelf, and returned. "Here, we'd better check you in." He sat down and flipped open the oversized book.

Sixty, Kamal guessed. More.

"And you'll be staying for . . . ?"

"Let's say a week."

The face lit up with a grin. "A week in the sun, then. Why not, it's unspoilt and it's got the ruins. You'll be paying in dollars, then?" he asked, having noted the Edmonton address Kamal had supplied.

"Yes. You'll take a credit card?"

"Cash better, but we'll work it out, old chap. I'll give you a good rate." He looked towards the bar and called out, "The same here, John—and put both on my tab."

"No, put them on mine," Kamal protested, as he knew he must. "I insist."

"That's decent of you. What kind of doctor are you—if you don't mind my asking?"

"General practice."

"I see. And you're staying a week—perhaps more?"

"I'm not sure."

"If you want to take on patients while you're here—"

"I'm on holiday. And I'm not licensed to practise here."

That earned him a look of mild disdain, and Kamal turned away to gaze towards the sea. Two motorboats were moored in the shallows, rocking on the waves of the fast-approaching tide; in the distance loomed the Island, flat and faint as a pencil sketch. His attention was caught by a boy walking on the beach, carrying on his shoulder a tray of something to sell, something to eat, bringing back a sharp memory. Kamal followed the child's listless walk, his hopelessly searching eyes upon the few people he passed. Why isn't he calling out? Who's going to buy your stuff, child, when they don't know what you're selling? You've got a thing or two to learn, young fellow. And your mother's waiting for the money you bring to buy the flour tonight . . .

He came to, to see Markham's hairy face fixed benignly on him.

Could he ever guess? Could this discarded English specimen possibly see him in that boy outside?

Markham stood up with a heave, hobbled over to pick up Kamal's suitcase. Sciatica, the physician diagnosed; bad heart, high blood pressure. What else?

"Don't worry about that," he said, rising, and he took the suitcase and shoulder bag and let the man escort him to his cottage, past the patio and straight down a planked corridor.

"Sorry, no television in the room," Markham said as he opened the door, turned on the light. The room was spacious, though filled with a strong residual odour of insecticide. There were two beds, with nets, and a small table and chair. The bathroom was tiled and clean. "Anything else you need, say so. Keep the door closed always—mosquitoes." With that advice he left, closing the door behind him.

Through the gap in his window curtain Kamal briefly glimpsed the man wending heavy-footed back to the bar. What could have brought him here, Kamal wondered, to sink every penny of his savings? We all have our secrets, lives unlived . . . He fell on his back on the bed behind him; it felt firm, and cool. The sheet had been washed many times. The pleasure—or ache—of travelling was this feeling of being precisely nowhere. Like Zeno's arrow. Was this nowhere, or back home? What was he doing here? Here, staring at the lizard on the ceiling. Was he real? Was this a dream? Had he died and woken up somewhere . . .

He felt utterly desolate. Not a soul to tell his story to, explain why he had come, why he must see her. Tears rolled down his cheeks onto the sheets. Have pity on me, someone. Must be the gin; the heat; the jet lag. He was ready to admit defeat—confess to the pointlessness of his venture, its vanity; his ingratitude for all he had been able to achieve in life starting from nothing. If Shamim had come that moment, he would have let her carry him off back to the prairies of Canada, back to the certainty of their luxurious suburban home. He fell asleep.

When he awoke, it was dark, quiet. In a panic, he ran towards the door, groped around for the light switch, flicked it on. The modest furniture, the chemical odour reassured him. There were sounds of people somewhere. He washed his face and came out, cast his eyes on the dark, silent sea for a moment, and the sky, noting that the constellations were indeed different from what he was used to. There was no moon, instead a close bright object hanging low like a lamp that he surmised was a satellite, perhaps relaying at this moment millions of phone calls and text messages to people everywhere in this part of Africa. Cell phones were the big thing, that's what he had learned the few days he had already spent in this country. A gust of wind hit him. He hurried down the dark corridor towards the front. Dim, romantic lights, music. Two people at the bar with John, several diners at the tables. The clink of cutlery.

The waiter pulled a chair for him and Kamal sat down, ordered a drink, paid heed for a moment to the faint cheerful strains of African jazz from the bar. Then he pulled out his cell and dialed. "Hullo, is that Lateef? This is Kamal, whom you met this morning—in Kilwa, at the tea shop. Yes, I am at the hotel, it's comfortable . . ."

It turned out that Lateef was in Masoko, sitting down to dinner at a local joint not five minutes away; he could join Kamal later; no, it would not be too late.

Lateef came an hour later, transformed, having changed into a pressed white shirt over smart black trousers, though still wearing the kofia, which gave him the look of a respectable Muslim and earned him the deference of the waiter who brought him over. As he sat down, he said, leaning forward, "Sir, you mustn't consume that."

"Come again?"

"You must not drink alcohol."

Kamal looked at him, feeling silly and suddenly elated, because this situation was so palpable, down to earth. The man was playing a role too. The waiter had stopped to observe them with a smile.

"Why not?" Kamal asked.

"It is haram, sir. Alcohol is forbidden to we Muslims. But it is your wish."

He sat back.

Dinner had been fish fried crisp, with rice, meat curry, and chapati. And, of course, soggy chips, the side dish of choice of the modern upwardly mobile Tanzanian. Earlier, the chef had come over and asked Kamal if he had a special request for the days he would be staying, and Kamal said could there be more vegetables on the menu, even spinach, which he liked very much. The chef looked disappointed, but said he would be happy to oblige.

When the waiter came to refill Kamal's glass, he declined out of consideration for his abstemious guest, who smiled his appreciation. At the bar once more stood Markham, in a black shirt for a change, and looking very gratified at this scene of happy consumption on his premises. He turned the music loud to enliven the mood even further.

Lateef's family had lived in Kilwa for many centuries, he said. They had come with the first sultan from Persia, Ali bin al-Hassan. Some of his ancestors were buried on the Island. They had been imams. What business did he do? He did not reply, glanced around mysteriously. He wanted to open a touring agency, he said. Life was hard in Kilwa, but the government had promised new development. This region was Tanzania's unexploited gem, its best-kept secret. After all, the Comoros were only a short hop away; so were Maputo and Durban. And from Kilwa, tours could go to the Selous National Park. Offshore gas had been found, and was already being pumped away north. But so far the locals had received no benefits; they had their ruins with new plaques donated by the United Nations. And they had the sea and the fish and the beach. Jobs would surely come. Bwana Markham was no fool, he too was awaiting the inevitable tourist boom. But Bwana Markham was not so young, and he did not look well, Kamal wanted to tell him. He desisted.

"There."

Lateef gestured with a brisk nod at the table behind Kamal, who turned around to see. Two young Europeans sat in a cheerful group with three youths who looked like Filipinos.

"Surveyors," Lateef explained. "Their boat is anchored at the harbour—with all the machinery. You can go and see it." Kamal had hardly taken this in when Lateef leaned forward and said, "Behind me—those two."

Kamal observed a well-groomed man in a goatee, dressed in designer safari, sitting with someone older and very evidently a local.

"What about them?"

"Hunters," Lateef said, taking aim with an imaginary rifle.

"They can hunt here?"

"In the national park. With a licence. Each licence twenty thousand dollars. They come with machine guns, from the Middle East—pa-pa-pa-pa-pa!—lions, buffaloes, rhinos. They come in planes, but this one"—his gesture indicating a beard—"must have missed the plane or wanted to see the country. They come with bodyguards."

A troupe of beautiful women in colourful attire arrived in the company of two men. As the music turned louder, the men and two of the women paired up to dance. One of the prospectors briefly took the floor. Kamal declined, as Lateef readily took on a partner. One hand behind her in a slow dance, he was suddenly clutching one plump and willing buttock, Kamal observed of the strange Muslim teetotaller and descendant of imams, who continued to dance in this manner as if it were the most natural thing.

"You don't dance?" Lateef asked, back at the table.

"I can't." How he'd tried, in senior year of high school, it was a way to get close to the girls, in a once-every-blue-moon party. He'd had to give up. And got teased: What kind of African are you if you can't dance? An Asian African. A chotara.

"I am looking for a woman," Kamal said at length. Lateef's face lit up and he opened his mouth, but Kamal hastened to explain. "Not like that. I am looking for a particular woman. I knew her as a child. She was my friend. Here, in Kilwa. She would be the same age as me. Her name is Saida, and her mother was called Bi Kulthum. Her grandfather was Mzee Omari bin Tamim, a famous poet."

"Ah, Mzee Omari."

"You know about him?"

"Famous poet of Kilwa—everybody knows about him. But sir, shairi is not popular these days. People prefer Bongo Flava—have you heard it? Hip hop, Swahili style." He paused, went on. "Mzee Omari's family, they have a shop in Kilwa. But I have never heard of this girl, this woman called Saida. You must tell me more about her. Then I will help you find her, wherever she is."

He nodded, his eyes fixed on Kamal's, ready to do the big favour.

What to tell him? Just that, there was nothing more. But of course there was more. There was a whole lot more.

Lateef told him he would inquire about Saida, then left. Kamal stayed in the lounge a long time, long after everyone else had gone, wary of being alone in his room. He had brought reading material, but the lights here were dim; he might have to use his flashlight. It might be a good idea to start his day early so he could end it early, that's how it was done here. Evenings emptied the streets, all life disappeared, only the spirits were about. He glanced towards the Island. He listened to the waves and the wind, the odd voice in the dark; revived his memories of his life as a boy here, as he drank the tea the waiter had brought him in a very English service, only for him.

· 4 ·

Kinjikitilé, the jingle of a dancer.

One morning while their mothers organized how he could help her with her lessons, he showed her his mother's anklets. Mama did not dance, they were her mementoes from another life. What was he thinking? He took the anklets from their place on the shelf and jingled them in his hands, and grinned at her; showing off. The girl took them from him, started rhythmically to stamp her feet, chanting *o-o-o-o* like a traditional ngoma dancer, but softly so as not to provoke the mothers. Jhun-jhun . . . Kinjin-kinjin is how he would recall that moment. Kinjin-kinjin, she took up his challenge. The innocence. The mischief. The provocation. Without a word spoken, or even the thought articulated, he was hooked on her. He was hooked on that look, that manner, that moment in their lives. It was to see that face again, howsoever ravaged by age, that he would travel thousands of miles, abandon his practice.

"I want this Saida to be a madamu, a teacher," Bi Kulthum, her mother, was telling Mama.

Mama and Bi Kulthum were as close as two sisters, and unlike as any two women could be in Kilwa. Both were without their husbands, Mama's, an Indian doctor who had absconded, Bi Kulthum's, a trader who had died of fever. Bi Kulthum shared a house with her parents, Mzee Omari and Mwana Juma. Like most Swahili women she came out in a black diaphanous bui-bui, full length over her dress, only her long face exposed; Mama wore a dress always and used a colourful khanga to cover her shoulders and head when necessary. She was the modern one. But now both had their heads uncovered, as they sat in the front portion of the room that was the entire house, Mama on the broken-down sofa, Bi Kulthum on the chair opposite. The barred window in the front was wide open, looking out upon the tree.

"Mwalimu, eh!" Mama exclaimed approvingly. A teacher! Well indeed! "And she will stand up straight and command with a ruler." She laughed gaily at the thought, gave a clap of the hands. "Weh, Saida!—do you listen? That would be very good. Then, my sister, my son Kamal will be very happy to help her."

This was the request Bi Kulthum had come with. Saida should be a teacher, with Kamal's help, and God willing. Saida's schooling thus far had been sporadic; she had attended when she or her mother had felt like it. Now Bi Kulthum had been struck by this whim, this ambition for her daughter. She said to Mama, "Your son is a gift to you from Allah the Merciful, even though he does not have a father."

"Truly," replied Mama and made a brief gesture of spitting on the floor. Bi Kulthum followed suit. It wouldn't do to invite ill luck.

He enjoyed watching them this way, so much at ease with each other; it gave him pleasure, and a sense of comfort. The world was a glad place. Mama husky-voiced, and strong; fleshy in a nice sort of way; darker. Bi Kulthum angular in face, like her daughter. Her eyes fascinated him, more flashing purple than black. Her speech was more formal: she would say *Allah* to Mama's *Mungu*.

After three decades, these scenes came vividly to him.

He was a lonely child, I observed to him.

Yes, he admitted, though he did have companions to play with. But essentially lonely and very attached to his mother. They were a unit— Hamida and her son Kamalu. He had often wondered, what did people say about Mama and him behind their backs? The abandoned twosome. When will Hamida forget her Indian doctor and accept one of her admirers? A woman needs a man, whatever she says.

And then came Kinjin-Saida into his life. Before, they had hardly spoken to each other; now she came to see him, with respect, to learn from him.

She came on Sundays, around eleven, having completed chores for her mother; she would be washed and dressed up, her hair combed neatly into braids. But barefoot. They would sit down on the floor, the linoleum from his father's time with its pattern of overlapping squares long having lost its gleam, and he would try to teach her English and arithmetic. He found it hard going; she was easily distracted by the sounds on the street outside, or by his mother working in the other end of the room. Often they got stuck on some simple problem whose concept would simply not penetrate her head.

"Why should I do it like that?"

"Because that is the way to do it."

"Let's play. Tucheze," she would say in a small pleading voice, having already given up in her mind. The gleam of hope in her eyes, the puckered lips ready to smile. The little sorceress.

"To play? What? Tucheze nini? Sit down and do the sum!"

Mm-mm. No, with a shrug, the Swahili way. Mm-mm. Aa-aa. She'd push the notebook away, he'd raise a hand to threaten her, and she'd pull the book back to her. He was not a good teacher, he couldn't have been at his age.

"Mama, do I have to teach that girl?"

"Saida? No, you don't have to. She doesn't have the brain for it, does she? I'll tell Bi Kulthum."

"No, I'll teach her."

She threw an amused eye at him. "You like her?"

"She's only a girl," he replied scornfully.

She quickly looked away, but not before he caught the edge of her little smile.

Mama liked to tease him. He was her little husband. He watched her as she finished hemming the cloth in her lap, cut the thread with her teeth, squeezed the needle into the reel and placed it on her little table of sewing things that stood by the window. She turned to look at him and he could sense her eye caress his face. Then the anxiety overcame her, like a shadow. There were only the two of them, and they had long stopped waiting for his father to return. Dr. Amin Punja had abandoned them.

As you've done your children.

That persistent, wifely voice in his head, relentless, all the way here, even after the separation.

They're adults, for God's sake!

You are going back to the witch and you'll never return.

For a few weeks, he had told her. He would go away for a few weeks. But then single-mindedly prepared to go away not knowing when he would return. Or if.

And his own father, what did *he* say before he left his wife and child and never returned? What destiny called *him*?

As an adult, did he ever try to find his father?

Yes, he said, and left it at that.

And his mother? Where was she now?

He didn't know.

"Your father came from seafaring merchants," Mama said proudly. Masultani, mabalozi, waarabu! They were sultans, ambassadors, and nobility, and he did not have the heart to call her exaggeration. Perhaps it was her eyes that betrayed her, that quick glance that shot away. The meagre story that he gleaned from her over their years together was that long ago in the previous century one Punja Devraj, a Gujarati from India, came as a trader to Zanzibar. He became known for his business acumen and honesty, and one day the sultan sent him to Kilwa on a mission. In those days Kilwa was an important place. Caravans arrived all the way from Zimbabwe in the south; from Bagamoyo and Zanzibar in the north; and from as far away as Congo in the west. Ships took away slaves and ivory, gum from the ground, and grain, and even wild animals, for in Europe they liked to look at our animals. Here the story became weak. She couldn't say what Punja's mission was, and she couldn't say for certain whether his family accompanied him to Kilwa. Sometimes yes, sometimes no. If yes, what happened to them? They left after he died. Then he died in Kilwa? How did he die? Where is he buried? She didn't know. "I wasn't born then! Why do you have to ask me of days long gone?" "*You* began it, *you* told me about my ancestor!" They quarrelled.

One day Punja's grandson, a well-mannered, quiet, and dignified man called Dr. Amin, arrived in Kilwa to look at the place where Punja had died, and to say a prayer, a Fatiha, for his ancestor. The doctor liked the town and stayed on and opened a clinic. He married, or kept as common-law wife, a woman named Hamida, whom he trained as his nurse and dispenser. But one day when the boy was four the doc upped and left.

There was that picture, the telltale snapshot that he left behind, evidence of his fall from Indian respectability—having gone local, fathered a half-breed, an outcaste whom he could never call his own back in Gujarat. He appeared very fair in that photo, sitting stiffly on a chair, and he was short, with his hair parted in the middle. He wore a Western-style double-breasted suit and tie. Beside him stood Mama, solemnly staring straight out at the camera, in a khanga dress with a headpiece. Between them—he could sense her pushing him towards his father—stood the boy, wearing awkward, extra-large shorts. Looking rather lost—or did he project himself as he looked at his own photo?

He didn't recall posing for it.

"What about *your* family, Mama?" he asked her.

"Hamna kitu," she'd say impatiently. Nothing to speak of. What did she hide?

Kamal begged her for her story, perversely as he later thought, for he had guessed somewhere deep in his mind the reason for her reticence. She was from slaves. But the Devrajes, his father's folks, yes, she would tell him about them. They were his people. The sultans. The ambassadors. From India.

"But I'm an African," he protested with vehemence. Ni Mwafrika! "I don't speak Indian, I don't eat Indian! They eat daal and they smell!"

"Mhindi, tu." An Indian. That's what she wanted for him. But why? So he too could be a sultan. Once when he pestered her for details of that phantom figure Punja Devraj, his great-grandfather, she told him, "Ask Mzee Omari, he knew him."

He knew him! But how to ask that fearsome poet, with that lout of a djinn hovering about him?

When he asked her about Punja's grandson, the daktari, his father, she said he was a steady man. "Did he love you, Mama?" She smiled to tease. One day he brought up his father when Bi Kulthum happened to be visiting. And Bi Kulthum voiced boisterously, "Your father! The doctor! He was a generous man! A lovable man!"

Later, Mama said to Kamal, "Don't mention your father in Bi Kulthum's presence." There was mischief in that admonition. "Eti, she fancied she would take him away from me!"

There lay a story, the precise nature of which remained a mystery.

Kamal could never get the African out of him, even when he washed himself with bleach to get his muddy brown out. That was in the future, when Mama sent him away to claim his father's heritage, become an Indian.

"Listen to this," Kamal said to me. He read out:

"'In November 1776, French ship owner Captain Morice arrived at Kilwa and signed a treaty with Sultan Hasan bin Shirazi by which every year he would take away a thousand blacks, for twenty piastres each, men or women; he was granted exclusive rights, and the treaty was valid for a hundred years.'"

A hundred years later, in 1878, an Englishman, Capt. J. Frederic Elton, departed from Zanzibar on Her Majesty's service to inspect the towns along the east coast of Africa for slaves owned by the Queen's Indian subjects. All along the coast in the trading towns he freed the Indians' slaves, the majority of whom opted to stay with their former masters for wages. The Kilwa–Dar es Salaam route was busy with slave traffic. Elton described an encounter: "One gang of lads and women, chained together with iron neck-rings, was in a horrible state, their lower extremities coated with dry mud and their own excrement and torn with thorns, their bodies mere frameworks, and their skeleton limbs slightly stretched over with wrinkled parchment-like skin. One wretched woman had been flung against a tree for slipping her rope, and came screaming up to us for protection, with one eye half out and the side of her face and bosom streaming with blood."

In Kilwa, the roads upon which the crooked black lines of slaves passed were called the "places of the skulls" by the locals. The beach was strewn with skeletons. In the preceding two months, wrote Elton, at least four thousand slaves had been trafficked north, and he freed fourteen hundred who were owned by Indians, who used them as concubines, their womenfolk not having joined them, and as servants, and they sold them to pay debts.

That was the pain and humiliation concealed behind Mama's silence about herself, Kamal explained. Her mother had been used for pleasure, had been traded by men. And she herself, Hamida, his Mama, had been as easily abandoned by her husband. She must have been barely thirty, as he recalled her, yet to him she was as ancient as the continent.

All those years while he practised in Edmonton, Kamal had collected a small library on the subject of Kilwa, all that could be possibly known, expecting that one day, like many an immigrant whose past is slipping away from him as he grows older, he would write it all up for his children. A family history, and a people history. His bequest to them. And surely a tribute to his own mother and his African past. His children would know where they came from, who their ancestors were. His passion started with a visit to a used bookstore in Toronto, where he bought a cheap library discard. It was the memoirs of a district commissioner who had spent some time in Kilwa. Imagine his delight to see his hometown described in a modest chapter, illustrated by a couple of line drawings. He waved it at his family, took it to work. "Look—this is where I was born. This official was in my town when I was running around in shorts! I must have seen him! I *know* I saw him—there was only one white man there—in the boma, the old fortress! Here—he's drawn it!" Kilwa had an actual existence outside of his memory. Later, during a visit to London, he embarked on a frantic treasure hunt, visiting the antiquarian bookstores, and spent a small fortune. Then there came the Internet. A bit of Kilwa here, a bit there, bought at a steep price with the click of a mouse.

His wife Shamim had been wary of this new African obsession and his outbursts of euphoria, which she would counter with unnerving silences. For a brief period his children had indulged him, calling him Ancient Mariner, and paused to humour him whenever he emerged beaming from his study with an old book in his hand. And then—what came over him?—he had brought out his one and only family photograph, of himself (in those awful shorts), Mama, and his father. The shock on Hanif's face—he was eleven then—was cataclysmic. "Me, African? That black woman in that weird outfit, my grandmother? You're lying. No way." Utter rejection by his private-school son. And

Kamal had not brought up the slave ancestors yet. Who wants to be reminded of that? The kids had their own battles to fight, as children of immigrant parents, who could blame them from shunning this rather iffy connection? "But give them hip hop any day," he observed wryly to me, "they'll gladly spit rhymes about the Detroit projects."

And so in the interest of peace in the household, he shelved his ambition to write a family history and restricted his hobby to the confines of his private study, far from everyone else, obsessing over bits of information like a stamp collector over postmarks and perforations. Shamim would not hear or speak of Africa unless it was expedient—once a year she ran for the benefit of AIDS victims in Africa. His negroid features were already an embarrassment to be explained away. He fought off a suggestion to lighten his skin and straighten his hair.

· 5 ·

Some nights as he lay on his mat in the dark, listening to the mango tree rustling outside, he would think of his father. The tree was ancient, gigantic, easily shading two houses on either side of the road. The barber, Bakari, sat on the ground under it during the day, next to a rickety chair for customers' use and a mirror hanging from a nail in the scraggy bark; a vendor came by at noontime every day to sit down for a breather on the other side of the broad trunk, and there would follow a chatter, a soga, that was part of the day's noise and ambience. But at night the tree stood by itself, its waving branches echoing the distant waves of the sea. Kamal imagined the Indian man of the photograph, the doctor with the parted hair and double-breasted suit, picking him up, putting him on his shoulders and carrying him outside to watch the sea and the waves, the dhows anchored, the fishermen drying fish or repairing nets, the occasional mysterious steamer in the distant mist. Once a manwari—a man-o'-war—had anchored, a grey ship of iron far in the distance, where the ocean was deep, and the town had started a celebration for the sailors of the British Navy, who arrived on shore in boats with plenty of money to spend. There was music and food and a football match. But when he was older Kamal could never tell how much of this scene was real, or whether it was simply his fantasy given wing by his desire to have a father. He didn't even know when his father had left for India. Perhaps Baba had perished at sea, on his way back? He imagined a ghost emerging from the sea's depths, riding the waves, wading to the shore carrying a chestful of treasure, returning home to his son. No, said Mama. Perhaps he will return, but not as a ghost. Perhaps he will send for you.

She knew even then that she would send him away?

Sometimes at midnight footsteps could be heard shuffling softly down the streets. They belonged to an evil. She even had a name: Mariamu. People smacked their slippers on the ground when she approached, shouting, Weh, Mariamu! God curse you! and the steps ran away, but no one had actually seen Mariamu. What did she come for? It was said that she dug holes for little children to fall into, and came by at night to collect those young ones she had caught. In German times she would pick off corpses hanging from trees. Shouldn't the sheikhs speak with her? Couldn't the district commissioner drive her away? When he suggested this to his mother, she got annoyed. "You'll bring bad luck here, why do you have to talk about shetani?" But she reassured him that before his birth the town had been swept of all evil by the famous sorcerer Akilimali, so the old hag could do no harm.

Kilwa is a thousand years old, a haunt of spirits. All those who died and never made it to the house of God, all those suicides and all those murdered and the infant deaths; the djinns who accompanied the Persians and Arabs who came here long ago. The first sultan of Kilwa was Ali bin al-Hassan, the Shirazi. He made his city on the Island and it had mountains of riches, so they say. They say London in those days of zamani za kalé long ago was like Kilwa is now—nothing. But Kilwa then: big mosque, big castle. Houses of stone and marble—no bandas like this one where I live with Mama, making a racket when it rains and leaks through. Ai, but we are poor! But Kilwa of old! Gold from Rhodesia! Silk from India! Perfumes from Arabia! The white men are now digging up treasure from the old city and shipping it away to London. Gold coins. Bi Kulthum has seen one. Arabic coin with the name of Sultan Ali bin al-Hassan. There was that time the police came searching houses, beating men black and blue, searching for coins stolen from the white men's iron safe in their ship. The police came out empty-handed, and how people laughed behind their backs! Then the district commissioner offered a hundred shillings for each coin. A hundred shillings! And afterwards you could pick out a hundred-shilling man walking a little too stiffly on the road—wearing brand-new leather shoes, or brilliant checkered socks, or a stiff-collared white shirt—having turned in a stolen coin. Thieves are rewarded and the Indian in his shop makes profit selling shoes and socks, Mama said, while we honest people burn our bare soles on the hot earth.

His night thoughts made him so excited he would be breathing hard. In his nervousness he would edge closer to Mama, sleeping beside him on the mat, her deep, even breathing a comfort, her body radiating a delicious warmth.

One day Saida brought him an old coin. "Here," she said shyly. "Take. I have brought you a present." Perhaps she was hoping he would make the lessons easier. It was a small black disk, inscribed, "1 Heller. Deutsch Ostafrika. 1908." He smiled, patted her woolly, oily head. But the next day she came back sobbing, her calves beaten red with a broom. Bi Kulthum could be hard. With a heavy heart Kamal returned the German coin. It belonged to Mzee Omari, and she had pilfered it. Mzee Omari knows about the Wadachi. They say he went to a German school. Those pictures on his wall are of him standing with Germans, and that certificate with weird letters, that too is German. He has many stories about the Germans. How they came from Berlin in the land of the Kaiser to dominate this land. They were fierce but they were just. But most of all, they were unbeatable. Brave men had tried to fight them, their reward only a hanging from a tree. And they were called mkono wa damu, hand of blood, for they wielded the whip hard!

He knows dawn is approaching when from the mosques one after another come the calls to prayer: Hayara sala! Who has the time but the old men. They walk silently to go pray, if you listen carefully you can hear the shuffling of feet in the distance. And then comes the Shamsi Indian going from house to house waking people up to go to pray. Once he wandered by on this street and Mama shouted at him: "Go wake up your brothers, don't bother us!" After the Shamsi disappears, the Banyani start singing in their temple, and the sound is sometimes like kinjin-kinjin . . . Kinjikitilé: is she awake, that one?

Should I marry her when I grow older? But first she must act more like a woman, she is too much a child.

Bi Kulthum wakes her up early to fetch water, and help fry vitumbua. The Swahili from the mosque will buy them. The Shamsi and the Banyani will buy them. And Khalid Restaurant, too, from which shortly blares out the radio. Quran.

Mama gets up, picks up the sheet from her mat and says her prayer. She never demands it of him, but gives him a look and sometimes he joins her. Side by side, they pray, he following her motion: on the knees, prostrate, straighten up, hands to the ears.

Kamal says to his mother he wants to have vitumbua this morning. "Go," says Mama, "go and buy three from Bi Kulthum, while I make the tea." She strides off to the backyard to light the fire.

He ambles along their narrow street that's just waking up, people standing or crouching outside, brushing teeth with miswaki, spitting on the ground, the litter on the road more exposed at this hour. The smell of woodfire. The early goat out rooting. As he crosses a street, a breeze from the ocean wafts over him, sudden and reckless, pungent and deliciously cool; he shivers with pleasure. The pounding of the waves in the distance, Indians standing at the square, watching the sea. Bi Kulthum's house is across the main road, beyond the monument. As Kamal arrives, outside on the porch sits Mzee Omari, in kanzu and cap; he must have returned from prayer.

"Shikamoo, Mzee," Kamal says in polite greeting, I touch your feet. He takes the old man's hand in a formal gesture of kissing it, bowing to it, and Mzee Omari responds by saying, "Marahaba." But Mzee Omari does not let go his hand, keeps holding it firmly, and gazes at him with half-seeing eyes, and Kamal awaits the inevitable list of formal queries, and responds as required: I am well. And my mother, too. We both are well. Thank you. Studies are good, thank you. Yes, I have come to get vitumbua. They are sweet. Yes, I am well. Released, finally, he scampers off inside the house, down the long dark corridor, on either side of which are the rooms, to the backyard where Bi Kulthum sits on a low stool, her face glowing before the fire. Opposite her sits Saida, staring intently at the sweet vitumbua frying. She looks at him and smiles. He's her teacher.

Three little woks filled with oil, into which Bi Kulthum pours the batter, which sizzles and puffs up into the sweet little floating tummies, the vitumbua. She prods them with a long metal rod. When cooked on one side she turns them over using two rods and there they are, enticingly golden brown, Kamal's mouth watering. A man stands to the side, also staring at the spectacle, awaiting his batch. He leaves, then Saida leaves with her full tray to take outside and sell on the street, and then Kamal puts his thirty cents into Bi Kulthum's hand and takes away three vitumbua wrapped in a newspaper.

Outside on the porch Mzee Omari is still seated, now with a cup of tea, staring straight ahead, chatting with a man in the house across. His ears perk up as he hears Kamal come out.

"Umevipata, Kamalu?" Did you get your vitumbua?

Kamal hesitates, says, "Yes, I got three . . . ," and holds up his package and waits for the inevitable farewell process. These old people are all for slow formality.

"Good," says the old man. "What class do you study?"

"Four."

"You study English, sio? Good. Very good. You will go far with English. The language of the rulers. I studied too, you know—in Deutsch—German."

Kamal stares in silence. German is from another age, though he is aware that some among the old ones know it.

"Sprechen Sie Deutsch?" asks Mzee Omari, his sardonic smile broadening only a little. "Go then with your vitumbua. My salaamu to your mama. Auf Wiedersehen!"

"Ahsante, Mzee. Thank you! Kwa heri!"

"He teaches English to our Saida," Mzee Omari explains to the man across. And as Kamal speeds away, he hears Mzee Omari say, warmly, apparently for his benefit too, "Anampenda." He likes her! "A Majnoon, that one. A Romeo. He's an Indian, but . . ."

He doesn't hear the rest. On Khalid's radio, on the way back, the news booming out, receiving all the town into its intimacy.

What a joy when the town awoke!

And the news? *Yesterday, speaking to the Legislative Council, the Governor of Tanganyika Mheshimiwa Sir Richard Turnbull said that Tanganyika's peaceful struggle for self-government should be an example to other African countries. And Bwana Nyerere, our leader, said, Tanganyika will never be like Congo, from which dreadful stories of killings come every day. We are peaceful and we are united.*

Something like that. A new governor had arrived, and the country was headed for independence. After the Arabs, and thirty years of German rule, and forty of British, this was the time of the African. We will now rule ourselves; tutatawala.

But there were others who went around saying, We will possess the Indian shops and send them back to Bombay, we will move into the European houses in Dar es Salaam. We will marry Indian girls.

"Mama, will I be chased out of the country because I am an Indian?"

"Not at all! Who told you that? You are an African."

"But you call me an Indian every time. Everybody calls me an Indian! Except the Indians themselves."

"That is because you are an Indian who is more African than all these Africans walking about. And a better Indian than all those Banyani shopkeepers. Remember that."

"Are you telling me a riddle now, Mama?"

"Enh-heh. You find out the answer when you grow up, not before."

The riddle of his life, that's what she had casually thrown at him. It meant nothing at the time.

· 6 ·

The old men would gather for poetry, sometimes on an afternoon
outside somebody's porch, or under a tree, consuming kahawa, a boy
vendor going around with his charcoal warmer and decanter, serving
the arabica in delicate little cups; and sometimes in the evening,
almost in secret, in a corner of the town square facing the harbour,
breeze blowing, the hiss of waves breaking upon the shore, the distant
echoes of mundane life. All would sit on the ground facing north.
The proceedings would begin, someone would come forward to
recite a verse from the Quran. Following this, a few amateurs stood
up one by one to be indulged, and rendered the occasional poem
they happened to have written—on the occasion of Eid; or giving
thanks to the Prophet for bringing God's message to Arabia, from
whence it came down to the coast of Africa; and once, to much
approbation for the vulgarity of the subject, praising the skills of the
footballer Salum Ali. But Mzee Omari was *the* poet, he was the one
awaited. He would stand up from the first row, assisted by his son
Shomari, if he was there, or someone else, and step forward. He
would go and sit on the tree trunk. With his barely seeing eyes he
would look up, and then, the audience hushed, begin. His high,
trembling voice would rise and fall, but never to extremes; it was
the same shairi tune that came over the radio, that others used too,

but in his voice, as it was said, a steel wire ran through. In spite of his age, it had a toughness, a flexibility, the cool glisten.

He always began with a minor preamble, as though to provide a transition from the amateur displays that preceded. In one preamble, he advised "our young brother" Julius Nyerere from up there in Uzanaki, near Lake Victoria, to engage against the British with care, for we your fathers already saw how useless the struggle can be against the wazungu, the white men, when our own fathers failed against the Germans with their machine guns that spilled out pellets of death like rain; another sent blessings to our Kikuyu brother Jomo Kenyatta in a British jail—palé Kenya, there in Kenya, as the refrain went. Then he would continue where he had left off previously, reciting his utenzi, the long poem that told the stories of zamani za kalé, the history of our Kilwa and of our precious Swahili coast. It was the one he had begun some time ago with fanfare, invoking the djinn Idris, and was called *The Composition of the Coming of the Modern Age*. It would contain a thousand verses when finished. These old men sitting before him mesmerized were the witnesses to its birth.

—Go on, Mzee Omari. Recite.

—Recite what? (A purely rhetorical retort.)

—Where did Idris your servant take you? What did that djinn show you of the past?

—Sing, Mzee Omari. Tell us about the war.

—That I will, but can you bear the truth?

—Who can't bear the truth?

—Sometimes I can't.

—Ah, Mzee Omari! Stop playing with us! Go on, tell us. Tell us, we are all ears. Tell us about our mababus, the grandfathers; tell us about how they lived. Tell us about their bravery. Our ears burn to hear praises of our people; our eyes are ready to shed tears when we hear from you of their forbearance in the days of kalé.

Silence. And it would seem that Allah's entire Creation waited, under the swaying branches and the stars and the moving clouds, for that voice to cut its sonorous way through the frivolous night breeze and silence the crickets and configure from the vacuity of the retiring night the events of the hazy past, lend them coherence and bring them to life.

When Mzee Omari recited, he became a different man, as if in a trance, standing upright but not rigid, his near-blind eyes staring in front, the words emerging steadily from his mouth as if some spirit inside him were sending them forth into the world where they became real and permanent. When a verse was recited, it had received birth. It was a bead to join a rosary of beads, its four lines artfully constructed in that unforgettable rhyme, *aaab*, to please the ear and the mind, and also to instruct.

I begin in the name of
the Kind and the Merciful One,
our Mola and His servant
our lover, the Habibu . . .

On a day of Ramadan
When war loomed from the West
The sultan of Persia put to sea
Seven princes to head south.

They landed at different ports
Ali bin al-Hassan at Kilwa the Island,
which he purchased with much cloth
enough to circle the Island.

Hidden among the night shadows, Kamal sat a few paces behind the attentive men, when a pebble hit him sharply, from somewhere in the dark. He winced, tried to pay attention, when another pebble hit him, from the opposite direction. Then a sharp pain in the back, where a bigger one landed, and he stood up to go. He didn't have to think who it was harassing him from all sides. But then Mzee Omari came to his rescue, stopping his recital abruptly to sternly chide his djinn, "You Idris stop harassing the daktari's boy and sit down!"

He waited for the audience to settle down again. When silence fell, the poet opened his mouth; but instead of resuming, he said, "That boy who sits quietly there listening, know that his grandfather Punja has sent him here to listen. Yes, this Punja was a lion. His tale too belongs to this composition, and I will get to it! I will get to it, and then you will see; to everything its time."

"Yes, Mzee, without doubt. The Indian's time will come. Pray, go on. Continue."

Mzee Omari continued. But Kamal heard nothing now, the rich voice only the background, in his mind the words repeating, "Punja was a lion . . . Punja was a lion . . ."

A lion of a man. Mzee Omari knew about him. Kamal wished he could sit with the old man and ask questions. Yet how could a boy ask questions of a venerable mzee, a man of such skill and wisdom that he could compose a thousand verses and recite them without looking at a paper? And who had his own personal djinn?

The evening would end suddenly. Mzee Omari would pause and say, "Here I end my recitation today. Now to praise the Maker, Ashahadun la ilaha illallah . . ." They would all repeat the prayer with him in a chorus, then get up to go, the more knowledgeable among them ready to discuss the fine points of prosody: the subtlety of a rhyme, how the Arabic pronunciation lengthened a vowel, how a German word had saved the integrity of a line, and so on. The men would disperse into the darkness, head for their houses in Kilwa's dark streets. Mzee Omari would walk slowly home in the company of his son Shomari.

Some nights another strange being would be haunting these gatherings, lurking among the shadows. He was Salemani Mkono, the one-armed beggar. At the end of the night's proceedings he would slink off into the shadows, observed only by one person, Kamal.

"Don't go to the seashore at night," Mama warned, when she found out about Kamal's nocturnal jaunts. All the time she had thought he was out at play down the street.

"Why?"

"Don't go when those old men gather there. I am telling you."

"I'll go."

"Thubutu! Don't you dare!"

"But why? I like to listen, Mama. I like the stories—they are like cinema!"

The only film he had seen was a Laurel and Hardy clip on a screen set up in the backyard of the Shamsi jamatini, the large prayer hall. He and a few other boys had gathered in the alley outside and climbed up on stones and boxes and craned their necks over the wall to watch, but created such a noise that they were allowed in and told to sit quietly at the back. After that the Shamsis showed their films inside their jamatini. But Kamal knew about movies from the notices in the papers, and from listening to Indian boys talk about them in school, having seen them during holidays in Lindi and Dar. And so he knew about Raj Kapoor and *Shane*. His dearest desire was to see a Tarzan film. But Mzee Omari's stories were exciting too. His heroes were Africans like al-Bushiri and Makunganya and Kinjikitilé of Ngarambe. And Punja the Lion.

"Don't go, I tell you," Mama said. "There are djinns there, by the sea, in the trees. That Mzee Omari, he attracts them. He has no fear of anything, that old man. Don't go there, did you hear? Some shetani-djinn will get inside you."

"Thubutu! That Idris tried to chase me away one night, and what a chiding Mzee gave him! In front of all."

"I told you!"

He couldn't keep away. One way or another he would find out when a recitation was scheduled, and he would sneak off and find his place behind the rows of sitting elders. One evening Kamal sat mesmerized, listening to the poet, when Saida slid down beside him, silent, panting. She smelled of pee.

"Mama, she does not wear knickers. I can see her uchi sometimes."

This happened when they were sitting on the floor, studying. His mother looked strangely at him, then looked away.

But Saida got her knickers, she showed them to him proudly when she came for her lessons, in one quick flick of her dress, when Mama was not looking. Red and yellow checks, the kunguru design, coming up to her belly button. Mama had stitched them. Kamal was pleased with himself too. He had got his first Y-front from the Indian store. The problem was when it was in the wash. "I'm saving," Mama said,

"I'm saving for the next one. Meanwhile keep your thing discreet. Don't let the bwana peep out or flip-flop about."

They had a long laugh together.

"Mama . . ."

"Mmm. Nini, sasa." Stitching buttonholes for the Indian store. She wore glasses now. "What's it," she said.

"Mama, sikiza!" Listen!

"Now what, my son?"

"Mzee Omari's ancestors were Arab."

He sat down beside her, on the broken-down sofa.

"Who told you that?"

"Even he said that—they came from Baghdad!"

"What are you saying?"

With that tone there always came a glare. He didn't like to make Mama angry. It was so much nicer when they were friends and she looked after him, when they laughed together. Seeing her mood suddenly scorch unsettled him. But he couldn't help it. He had discovered a point of argument.

"Mama—can anyone be more African than he? And yet his ancestor came from Baghdad."

"Don't trouble me." Then she reached out and drew him up close. She laughed, and his heart relaxed with joy. There were only the two of them then, the third one mere memory, an imprint on their existence, slowly fading.

He had heard about India in his school, and he had read about Baghdad in a storybook. In his class, which contained all Indians except for him, a teacher came to instruct the boys about their culture. Every time he came he would tell a story. Kamal would be asked to sit in the last row during this lesson, but he paid attention, and that's how he learned about his father's country. In India there was a king called Rama who had a wife called Sita. The teacher held up pictures of this couple; they were similar to those in the calendars in the Indian shops. Rama and Sita were white people and had four hands. Rama held a bow. Their friend was a monkey who stood tall on two feet, looking very serious. This monkey was a fundi, an engineer. Was his own father, the doctor who had gone away, white? Did some Indians look like monkeys? If so, then he begged Allah that they did not include his ancestors. Among the Indians in town there were one or two men who would definitely fit that description, he thought. And in Baghdad there was a powerful sultan called Harun Rashid. There was Aladdin who had a lamp with a djinn inside it. No surprise that Mzee Omari, whose ancestor came from that city, had his own djinn too. Did Mzee Omari keep the dreadful Idris in a bottle? Did he come out of it like a blue puff of wind as in the storybook?

· 7 ·

During the month of Ramadan, early in the evening, when the day's fast had been solemnly broken in each Muslim home, Kamal would emerge into the streets with a sinia, a round tray that he would balance carefully on one shoulder, holding it against his neck, heaped with diamond-shaped kashatas, pink and orange coconut brittles, sweet. Barefoot, the imported, England-made Y-front his only, though hidden, privilege. "Kashaataaaa! Five cents a piece!" he would call out proudly in a high pitch as if calling the azan—there was no shame in doing business. "Weh kashata!" would come a cry, calling him over, for in the parlance he was identified with the product itself, and he would go and ask the customer, "How many?" and collect his money. From such origins to medical school. From there to Edmonton.

With his laden tray he would first meander towards the monument on the main road and linger, until her high, thin voice rose and she appeared from the opposite side, calling out, "Ee-eeh taaambi!" Fried vermicelli. They would sally forth on the street of the Indian shops, separating to compete for customers, then on to the street of the large Indian stone houses, which had a few shops too and the large prayer house, outside which the kids played. They were the best customers. The two vendors would rendezvous for a break to give their throats a rest. At one of the shops they would get a drink of water. "How much did you make, Kamalu?" "Fifty." "Me, sixty-five!" "Go on, eti!"

One last round as the streets turned dark and they would part company at the monument.

They never spoke about each other, they just were, the two of them, a conspiracy together. An implication.

During Ramadan the stores stayed open late, for it was the month of shopping, with money saved, money borrowed. Even the poorest needed new clothes for the Eid celebrations at month-end. Groups of women fluttering out in bui-bui, trailing sweet perfumes, children wailing for the toys displayed so cruelly in the stores, tailors on sidewalks, their machines grinding away creating dresses and shirts, beggars unrelenting. Night fell, the lamps would come out, the shops began to close. The Indian boys and girls would be outside playing in and out of the shadows. Their fathers sitting around in groups drinking kahawa and playing cards by lamplight.

Among the beggars was the despicable Salemani Mkono. Not with an enlarged foot, or leper's hands, or unwieldy scrotum, not old and covered in poxes. He was just a purple-skinned beggar, with a short, scruffy beard and an idiot's grin on his large round head. And a bad, motionless left arm at his side. He wore the same soiled clothes for months, a checkered cloth round his waist and a torn T-shirt, until someone gave him a new set, and he might appear suddenly in green and red instead of red and black. Come Friday morning and he would be out, hand outstretched, and the faithful could not very well deny him alms on this day, even if it was a cent or a heller. Sometimes the kichaa hit him, that fit of madness, and he would march up and down the street of the Indian shops like a soldier, a stick on his shoulder, kids following, teasing him, calling after him, "Generali, generali"— the general. To their utter delight he would come to a sudden stop, shout a hoarse "Halt!," then turn around and scream, "Achtung!"

One Ramadan evening he approached Kamal as the boy paused on the street with his tray. Eh Kashata! "Come see this miracle, young man," the grinning Salemani said, and foolish curious Kamal followed him open-eyed into the shadows, where Salemani turned around suddenly and lifted up his loincloth to reveal his prodigious penis.

Kamal stared at the monstrous piece of flesh, his heart thudding inside him, walked away, as Salemani called after him, "Feel it, hold it." At home he couldn't eat that night, his heart still pounding, and he went outside and vomited in the yard.

A few days later, walking with Saida, still during Ramadan, he turned sharply away as Salemani approached. The girl snickered. "If you go with him, he will show you his mshipa!" she said, shocking him.

"Who is this Salemani?" he asked his mother. "Why does he have such bad manners?"

One look at his face, and she knew. "Salemani the shameless. Eti, he showed himself to you?"

He nodded, tears in his eyes.

"That bastard, I'll teach him manners!" She picked up the broom and stormed to the shopping street, rolling her wonderful haunches. "Where is that shameless fellow?" she demanded, until she found him slinking at the refuse dump on the main road near the monument, where she flew at him with the broom. Bystanders joined her in the abuse and the beggar was pelted with pebbles and anything else possible. Hamida's fury was well known. Don't toy with her or her son. Ni mama na baba huyu, she is mother and father, now that her man, the Indian, has absconded.

Sometimes the Indian barber gave Salemani a haircut, shaving his grey head completely, and the boys would jeer at the bald, shameless general. He trimmed his own beard at the dump, using an old knife or a piece of glass, appearing on the street bleeding and shocking.

But who was Salemani? What did he want? Why did he beg? And why did he act crazy, when all the town knew that he wasn't?

One day he and Saida strayed away from the square, took the path alongside the creek, an inlet running north from the harbour through a wall of mangrove forest. It was noontime, just before lunch, nobody was around. The tide was low, the creek depleted of water. A salty stench hung in the air. Walking side by side in this private moment, holding hands while pretending not to, what do you talk about? "When I grow up I will buy Mama the best dress from a shop window in Dar es Salaam. Or from Nairobi—they have the best shops there."

"How do you know?" "Some Indian boy told me." "You will go all the way to Nairobi? Where is that?" "It is in Kenya Colony, where Jomo Kenyatta is in prison. What will you buy your mama?" "I will have a husband," she says, "and he will buy me a dress."

So simple. Recalling that moment so many years later, when he, now a doctor, was back in Kilwa inquiring about her, he was moved by his desperation to utter: "I will buy you your dress, Saida, where are you? . . . I'll buy you a house!"

At the German cemetery, where they arrived, the two youngsters strolled about among the graves, the empty grey beds of stone under which rested the remains of dead white men of long ago, and eventually as they sat down on the ground with their backs against one of them, suddenly there was a murmur among the bushes down towards the creek that startled them; but when the sounds seemed human they crept stealthily closer to peer at the source. Male and female voices and a thrashing in the bushes. They looked through leaves and branches, saw an Indian girl lying down, the boy kneeling over her. Together they pulled down her knickers. He lowered his trousers.

Kamal and Saida stood away.

"He's fucking her," she said matter-of-factly. Anamtomba.

"Ah, Saida! Don't say such bad words! Who taught you to speak like that?"

"Mm-mm."

That surely linked them, this knowledge. And he looking at her like the girl she was; a female. She looking back at him, wide-eyed and innocent.

And how old were they? Perhaps ten and eight. Even now, he said, that image in his mind, the memory of that primal revelation had the power to chill the heart. There was something about what they saw, where they saw it. Some days after that incident, he would hear of a violent ruckus in the Indian community, involving a girl and a boy, and that the girl had been sent away.

We were sitting, Kamal and I, on a bench at Dar's Oyster Bay; before us, on the beach, young men playing football, a couple of hawkers vending coconuts, and young teens in uniforms, fresh out of school.

Behind us a steady traffic. This area in colonial times was for Europeans only. Our previous governments, against advice from bankers, kept it free of development and tourists, so that now we can come and enjoy the beach unimpeded. Until the developers, someday, win.

He had rented a furnished flat in the Asian area, in one of those new eight-storey affairs built on two-storey former foundations and a prayer (his word). He enjoyed the crowded ambience of the neighbourhood, though not the cars parked thick on the sidewalks so you couldn't enter the building easily. To keep fit he jogged, early in the morning. And he gave free medical advice, while he bided his time.

A ship appeared in the far distance and he gazed at it intently—an understandable obsession if you've lived by the sea. Soon the ferry from Zanzibar came speeding along, headed towards the channel into the harbour, and Kamal turned to me with a grin.

For decades he'd had this story to tell, and now he was telling it.

"It just happened," he said. "We would meet at the shore and hold hands and walk by the creek."

Impulsively he would wander off by the creek and wait; it would be after the noon hour, and she would be there or soon appear. There was an illicit feel to their trysts, they both knew that, without knowing quite why. Perhaps it was the secrecy that made them so. They would stare out at the dhows, watch them being loaded, painted. They would imagine spirits haunting the tall, mysterious deep-green forest of mangrove that sheltered the harbour. They would race to the German graves and play there. Near the bushes where they had discovered the Indian couple, they had found a shallow lagoon protected by overgrowth, with a narrow sandy clearing around it that was like a beach. She would remove her dress, enter the water and splash about in it. He would do the same in his shorts. It was here that she once immersed herself in the water and did not emerge for what seemed a very long time; he could see her clearly, looking flat and ghostly, and he got worried and called at her. When finally she emerged, she said, "I am Kinjikitilé." The magician of Ngarambe, who went by that name, had also immersed himself in water, before emerging to inspire men and women to make war against the Germans.

One day from the mud near the bushes she picked up a piece of white rock. "It looks just like you!" she said and giggled nervously, holding it forward. Not a rock, but part of a skull. He picked up something else to beat her with for the insult, and she ran off, throwing down the skull. Then he saw that what he was holding was a bone. A broken tibia. He dropped it.

She came back. They concluded that these bones were the work of sorcerers, those of the evil sort who sometimes killed people and dismembered them. Ate the parts in order to gain strength. Used the brain to make medicine. So much for wandering off by themselves. Their sin, unarticulated, instinctive, against the modesty required of them had received an admonition. They stopped their outings together.

But it was their secret place, this lagoon, its compact beach; for one day she would arrive there again to meet him. But that was later.

When he told Mama about the bones on the beach, and his explanation, she cut him short. "What do you know? Witches go to the forest, not to the sea, out there in the swamp!" He was shocked by her unexpected sharpness and turned to go, but then she said kindly, "Come here, you. So the two of you went out for a walk together?"

He did not reply.

"The sea holds many secrets, you understand? Kilwa is an old town. Slaves were brought here, from the south. Many died. Others?—sent off to Zanzibar, Bagamoyo. Arabia. India. Know this. Those are the bones of our ancestors."

So she told him. Know this. Eyes fixed into his. But before she said "India," she had drawn a long breath.

There were African slaves in India? Slaves everywhere?

"Mama, what is your tribe?"

She eyed him angrily.

"Mama, were you a slave?" A mtumwa.

"Do I look like a mtumwa to you? Whose slave, eti—yours? Do you see chains on me, like this—?" She circled her neck with her fingers, making a funny face, tongue sticking out, then clutched at her ankles, pretending to cry out. "Do you see minyororo on me—clinking, cheng-cheng, cheng-cheng?" She looked at his hands. "Where is your whip, you Swahili?"

He slapped her behind, and they burst out laughing.

"You want to know my tribe."

"Tell me, Mama!"

"I am a Matumbi. You want to know how. Do you know the Matumbi? The bravest of people, who live on those hills in the distance. Once upon a time in the days of kalé they defeated the fierce Ngoni warriors who had come from all the way in the south. The Ngoni. Even now they think they are something. How did the Matumbi defeat the Ngoni? They set bees upon them. Don't laugh. The little people find all sorts of ways. And later they defeated the Germans. Now you ask, how could they defeat those white men with their guns. I am telling you. When the Germans came with their askaris carrying bastolas, the Matumbi rolled pumpkins on them from their hills. Those Germans!— I'm telling you they didn't come back soon.

"You have heard of Makunganya. Also known as Hassan bin Omari. He was of the Yao people, and a wealthy businessman. Compared to them these Indians of Kilwa are nothing. His agents went to Dar es Salaam; they went to the south; they went into the interior of the country where the barbarians lived. They brought gold, they brought ivory. But they also captured slaves and sold them at the market, here in Kilwa. One day his men captured my grandmother, who was a Matumbi. Makunganya sold her to an Indian.

"And God knows the rest. I am not going to tell you more. Go away."

He was a descendant of a Matumbi slave. Did the African genes call out in his children's interest in African American pop culture? He laughed at his own question. Of course not. The whitest Canadian kid blared out rap from his car.

I reminded him that rap was ubiquitous, you have it everywhere in East Africa too, even among the Asians.

In spite of his evident African features, there was no way he could make his wife, Shamim, acknowledge his Matumbi origins. "Why do you want to bring this hypothetical connection into our lives?" she asked bitterly. The very thought caused her anguish, and he could well be guilty of mental cruelty. "The kids have enough handicaps as it is without your Matumbi complex."

After all their training in violin, voice, and piano, it was not Bach or Beethoven but 50 Cent and Beyoncé they went for, and he had muttered cynically that that surely was the subversive Matumbi gene wreaking havoc on a mother's ambitions.

That day, when Mama informed him of her Matumbi origins, he had surreptitiously examined himself in the mirror. Nothing different. What did he expect? Something else in the nose, the lips? And after that argument with Shamim he would see her examining the children for any vestiges of Africa.

It was easy to get sentimental and recall those drawings from the histories and see your mother's grandmother chained in a train of slaves, then in the market picked by an Indian merchant. Your great-grandfather. What does it matter now? Go and make your future, as Mama said. And he had made it. Do we owe anything to the past? A silly question?—the past is over—or a profound one?—we are part of a continuity.

I would have given him a publisher's answer: it's important if it's interesting, and you have made it so.

I was of course keenly waiting for him to get back to Mzee Omari the blind poet, our historian.

· 8 ·

He had been drafted to be her teacher, the mwalimu, superior and domineering, who was privileged to go to the Asian school. He had agreed to share with her the precious knowledge he himself received, with which she could hold her head up with pride in that world away from the humble Swahili quarter of Kilwa, on the other side of the German monument. She could become somebody special, just as he would become. Over the months they'd become friends; her former awe and respect had yielded to a certain kind of familiarity. But he had ruefully come to accept that she was not very bright, her interest in his lessons limited, often feigned and fleeting. There were weeks when she did not show up. And when she did, the sessions on the floor ended at times in their moments of amusement. Her nickname for him was Bwana Hodari, Mr. Clever.

But one day she surprised him, and all his fragility was exposed. All his orphan shallowness, his want of inner anchor. He would often wonder how much smarter she was than him; surely she had toyed with him even at that young age. But never out of malice, only mischief; and humility.

They had gone over the silly line "A man, a pan, a man and a pan," from her English reader, over which they had had many a laugh, she mangling it in her African accent, "A many and a pany and a many and a pany" in the nasal voice that he could always recall. Wasn't his own accent the same as hers, that way of saying *ende* for *and*? It must have been. Now he gave her a division problem, 9999 divided by 11, which impressed him no end about his own capabilities and terrified her by its monstrous morphology. While she was attempting this impossible sum, he helped his mother pick an egg from the vendor. There was a science to picking a good egg: you dropped it into a pan of water; if it sank, it was bad, if it floated, it was good. The puzzle was that intermediate case, hanging undecidedly, between here and there, and he would help her guess. There was no money-back guarantee, of course. There were women who had run chasing after the vendor, cheated by an egg. As Kamal and Mama debated the buoyancy of eggs, from behind them came Saida's voice, low and irresistibly sweet. Absorbed in herself, she was singing a verse.

"Weh Saida!" Mama shrieked. "Who taught you that? And beautifully too!"

"My Bibi . . ." Grandmother.

Mwana Juma herself, as everyone knew, was a poet's daughter from Lindi.

"Sing that again."

And Saida sang:

Negema wangu binti
mchachefu wa sanati
upulike wasiati
asa ukazingatia . . .

Come near, my daughter,
listen to this advice
young as you are
pay close attention

Later he could not recall the words exactly, he had to find them in a book, the first lines of a famous poem written by a woman from Lamu called Mwana Kupona.

Kamal and Mama standing at the door with the vendor, a stained egg half-floating in the bowl of water in her hands, Saida's voice delicate and soft, the words clear, the modulations beautiful; in that moment there was not another sound in the world, not a stray thought, his heart had stopped beating. And he felt cheated.

"Weh shetani, weh," Mama said simply. "You little devil. What do you hide in that head of yours?"

He could not believe she was that same girl—his pupil, whom he had considered inferior. All the while she had been playing dumb. She had a depth he was not aware of, a dimension hidden from him. He did not know her after all.

He kicked her in the shins. She went home crying. And Mama punished him by beating him on his calves with a stick. He cried. He cried because he had hurt his only companion besides Mama; he ached because he felt so alien. She was a proper Swahili, an aristocrat, granddaughter of two poets; he a chotara, a mixed-blood, as he was called in school.

The next week she was back, sent by Bi Kulthum. Kusoma—to learn, she admitted shyly. A many and a pany. The two of them went around in circles laughing, chanting, A many ende a pany, a pany ende a many . . .

"Sing!" he would command. "Mm-mm." No. Her grandmother Mwana Juma had forbidden her to sing. She was not ready. But she wrote for him the Arabic alphabet, told him how to read the letters and the words.

Mwana Juma was a mysterious one. Small and dark with staring eyes, she did not leave her house often. And she was devout, and did not like Mama, because Mama was modern and assertive, was not in the care of a man and did not drape herself with the black bui-bui—even though she covered her head when appropriate.

Mama did not send Kamal to the madrassa to learn Arabic and Quran, because his father had wished him to study in the Asian school. English and arithmetic, geography, history of India and England. He had to go far. But now, after he learned the rudiments of Arabic writing from Saida, he went and bought from an Asian store the Juzu, the elementary Arabic reader, with its cardboard cover and thin, flimsy pages, and he read it with Saida. After "a many ende a pany," they went, "an-fataha-tin, in-kisira-tin, un-zamu-tin . . ." An *alif* with two strokes above it becomes *an*, and so on.

A new world—an inkling of another world—was offered him in this strange, sensual script that he could now falteringly read. It was the physical face of the Quran. Laying out these wonderful magical letters, the tall *alif*, the *lam* like a reflected L, the *mim* like a tadpole, and so on, Mzee Omari wrote his poetry; it was these that Gabriel commanded the Prophet to read, in the name of God—*iqra bismi rabbi-ka*—thus revealing to him the Book. It was what the other African boys read in the madrassas, sitting on the ground in their kanzus and kofias, chanting. These new wonderful letters, written from right to left, in books that began at the back made him feel a part of a world he had been denied.

Mama was aware of his new learning, and that sometimes her teacher son became the pupil, but she seemed not to pay any attention.

Kamalu and Saida grew close; he was kinder to her than before, more caring and tender. If she was not quicker on the uptake, at least she tried harder—or feigned better. Her affection for him was implicit in her mischievous smile and easy amusement, her yielding to his attentions; the way she leaned forward, as he bent over a piece of paper to do a sum or read to her, to flick a stray thread from his shirt or blow a something from his hair with a quick puff from her lips. They were growing older. The poem she had recited, Mwana Kupona's advice to her daughter, indicated that she might have been made more aware of her role as a young woman.

Once he composed some lines for her, mimicking Mwana Kupona's advice, encouraging her to study: *Sikiza sana Saida / a many ende a pany / jifunze kiengereza* . . . Listen well, Saida, teach yourself English. And she corrected him, "Not *Saida*, but *Sa-i-da*!" The lines had to scan properly.

When her lesson with him ended, she returned home, and he set off to play. Sometimes he accompanied her partway, to the monument; a few times they wandered off from there, past the boma to the shore. Once, with the money Mama had given him to buy a

packet of sugar, he bought a coconut and they drank the water together. Mama was furious when he returned without the sugar and
told her that instead he'd bought Saida a coconut. He went to bed in
tears and without food, until Mama woke him up and fed him some
hard maize meal.

· 9 ·

After a light rain in the night, the morning appeared fresh and clear. Harsh new sunlight streamed uninhibited into the hotel lounge. It was the third day since Kamal's arrival. Today he would begin his search proper. He was the only one present for breakfast. The prospectors had left at dawn, all five of them; the two hunters and their invisible body-guards had driven off the previous afternoon in their mammoth Land Cruiser for the joys of the chase and the kill. The morning flight had brought no tourist. News was that the rain had been heavy upcountry, part of the highway from the capital was unpassable, and some guests had to spend the night on the road.

Kamal asked only for tea—he would be having breakfast later in Kilwa.

"Ah. Going native, are we," said Markham, shuffling over from the bar.

"Yes, we are."

"Well, we'll have a brand-new mosquito net waiting for you in your room when you return. Look."

On the floor in front of the bar, under the watchful eyes of barman John, lay a pile of pure white cotton nets like a heap of fresh snow. They all stared at it as though at a miracle.

"Brand-new, arrived this morning," Markham explained. "The entire town is getting them, free of charge."

"Oh yeah? From where?"

"Courtesy of a certain Millicent Cole, American actress. Recently our great leader announced to a world conference in Singapore that we are so poor, we cannot afford mosquito nets. Voila—here they are. Ms. Cole, all by herself, has donated nets to the nation. How gracious of her."

"And how beggarly of us?" Kamal replied, provoked by the oozing cynicism in Markham's voice.

"You object, Doctor?"

"Surely the nation can afford mosquito nets. And there are enough wealthy people locally, if a donation were required?"

"In Africa, Doc, you don't look a gift horse in the mouth."

Seeing me smile as he related this to me, Kamal admitted, "I know, I know, I'm outdated. And who am I to come here and judge, having gone away and made my life elsewhere in comfort? Still, let me express a thought. Weren't we *exhorted*, as the future generation of this country, Help yourself, we are not beggars? Be proud? Where's all that pride gone?"

He had put his question mildly, even excusing himself as he did so, but he waited for my answer. It is a touchy question, especially to those of our generation here, and we talk about it rarely, but when we do, always after a sufficiency of drink late in the evening, we go on and on.

He was, as he confessed, out of date in his concern, and out of place. But he was right too. Where indeed has that old idealism, that uhuru spirit, gone?

The answer is that it didn't last long after he left. That idealism and pride, the hope of independence that some of us remember so wistfully as the heyday of uhuru, was taken to ideological extremes that finally brought us to this state. All this bustle that you see in our capital, the wonderful dollar consumerism, runs on the rails of foreign aid. I could have told him my own personal truth—that I happen to be one of those ideologues who railed in the past against capitalists and imperialists. Even in those shrill days my publishing business could survive only on foreign generosity, and it's still foreign patronage that keeps me in comfort. That's what became of our pride. We swallowed it, along with all the gifts we received. An Oliver Twist nation: Sir, can I have some more?

All I said was, "Times have changed, my friend."

He nodded as though he understood. But his new net was welcome, he told me; the old one had a hole in it and was spotted with bloodstains.

Later that morning Kamal met Lateef at Kilwa's taxi stop at the monument, from where they walked to a chai shop on the former street of the Indian shops. The menu, written on a board, was extensive and hopeful, but there were no other customers around. The oil-painted cement porch and walls were a leftover from a previous, more prosperous era; this had been an Indian establishment once, selling bhajias and samosas. The two men sat at a table on the porch, looking out on the street with their chai and mandazi, objects of curious, passing attention.

Across from them was the market, looking desolate, three women sitting idly before their meagre heaps of mangoes. It had thrived once, with varieties of vegetables, fruits, and grains. Next to the market a small and crowded store purveyed Islamic music videos. On their side of the street, next door, was a Sufi madrassa. Two smiling little girls, heads modestly covered, entered the establishment, as a chaotic high-pitched chorus let loose inside. Kamal had noticed that he had hardly seen a woman wearing the traditional black bui-bui, of the kind Bi Kulthum and most other Muslim women used to wear; the fashion now was a coloured chador, wrapped tightly round the face and draping the shoulders, over a long dress; it was what the girls in the imported music videos across the street wore (he'd had a peek), what the girls next door in the madrassa wore. The other style was still the khanga going over the head when desired, the way Mama used to wear it.

He realized he did not feel alien—he spoke the language like a native—but was a returned native nevertheless, and he surely must look alien to an extent, with his grooming, the design of his shirt, the leather in his track shoes; merely from his bearing. Everyone knew everyone else here; he knew not a soul, except Lateef. This had been his haunt, his place, his front yard, where he used to roam around with his kashata tray, she with her tambi. They would sit outside that market to rest during their rounds. He had known everyone here, every shopkeeper, every boy at school, every man and woman sitting outside on their porch. He had returned to it like a ghost.

"Let's go see the family," he said to Lateef.

Mzee Omari's descendants ran the little medical shop two doors away, on the other side of the madrassa. The painted sign over the open serving window named Ali Hasni as the proprietor and gave a postbox number. A poster on one side of the window displayed a happy young couple and recommended a single partner as a preventative against HIV; on the other side some organization extolled the virtues of solar power. This place had been the site of the tailor's shop, which had supplied Mama with piecework.

They had been expected, for as soon as she saw them, the woman at the window came out, adjusting her scarf, and went around to the back of the shop, then immediately returned. A man, who seemed to be in his fifties, wearing a cap and his shirt flopping over his trousers, followed her and came to stand with them outside the shop. He was Ali of the nameboard.

"Ali will help you," said the woman.

After the greetings, Kamal said, "I am from these parts, Bwana Ali—I was born in Kilwa. I used to know Mzee Omari."

Ali said nothing, wiped his hands in his shirttails.

"I used to hear him recite. He was a great poet. Was he your grandfather?"

"We don't have any of his things," Ali replied. "No papers, nothing." He paused, then inquired: "Are you from Dar es Salaam?"

Kamal nodded.

"Others have come before you, searching for his papers; white people have come too, from overseas, and I've told them we have nothing here."

"I just need information, Bwana Ali. I don't seek papers or anything else. Mzee had a daughter—Bi Kulthum. Did you know her?"

"Kulthum died a long time ago."

His manner clearly indicated that he had better things to do inside.

"She had a daughter, called Saida. Did you know her, Bwana Ali?"

There followed a silence, during which Ali threw a long look at the young woman, who muttered something about people digging the dirt on other people.

"That Saida," she then spoke up, "just went away. I didn't meet her, but that's what I heard."

"You don't know where she went?"

"We don't know where she went. No news at all." And then, "Jé, you knew her?"

"Yes, I knew her when we were children." Kamal turned back to Ali. "Did you know me, Bwana Ali? I was the son of Hamida."

Only now Ali permitted a wry smile to steal upon his face. The woman was watching. She smiled too.

"I remember you now. Didn't you go to the Indian school? You are the son of the doctor, aren't you?"

"Yes. And you are the son of . . . ?"

"My father was Shomari."

Shomari, hand me the fine paper from Syria . . . Kamal recalled that memorable afternoon when Mzee Omari sat down to begin his magnum opus and commanded his son to fetch his writing paper. That was the time when the djinn Idris had slapped him.

"And Saida?" Kamal pleaded.

"She went away," said Ali.

"Where did she go?"

"Don't know."

"We don't know," reiterated the woman, a little too forcefully.

Ahsante, thank you. How could that be? They didn't know where she went? Saida was Ali's cousin. Surely news arrived, so-and-so is at such-and-such? They were holding something back, he was certain. Now what?

"Don't worry, sir," said Lateef as they walked away. "We will find her."

"How? Is there someone else who can tell us?"

They went the short distance to the main road, where the taxi touts—muscular young men—bantered with each other, occasionally looking up to call out. Signboards on either side where they arrived exhorted you to buy tomorrow's bus tickets today, for Lindi and Dar. Here Kamal left Lateef to go for a walk.

He strolled past the boma, turned into the plaza, came to stand at the harbour, as he had done so many times before. This was a scene that brought back not just the near past of his childhood but also the more distant past of Mzee Omari's history. At night it was the venue of that history's narration: how easily he could imagine the audience of old men sitting here quietly on the ground as the poet recited. Now the tide was partly in, a boat was heading out to the dhows. He turned around. On the right-hand corner facing the sea had stood the town's new clock tower. How could a clock tower disappear without a trace? Straight ahead of him had been the little house and consultancy of the district medical officer—his father. When Dr. Amin's term expired, he departed by himself, and Hamida moved with Kamal to the African quarter four streets away. Not surprising, some might say, why the town square by the harbour had such a magnetic pull on the son.

Crossing the plaza, Kamal continued for a while on the path that ran by the creek—partly a stinking refuse dump now—then he cut back across a field, passing by a school, behind which was the old German cemetery. Exhausted from the heat, he sat down on a grave, wished he had a bottle of water with him. He reflected on the men buried all around him. Did they have descendants in Germany, did anyone remember them at all there, where their mothers had pushed them in prams, where they had gone to school and college and gotten married? And went away to build an empire. Saida once said a Fatiha here, the prayer for the dead. She had learned this from her grandfather, who stopped here every month to visit one particular grave. He stood up, looked around until he found it: *Hier ruhet Carl Schmidt. 1865, Waren; 1904, Kilwa.*

He walked tentatively towards the creek, came upon a dense overgrowth. A path from here had led down to the lagoon, their secret place. It did not seem safe to go farther, and so he returned to the cemetery.

"Do you want to see another cemetery?"

Kamal looked up. The boy who had spoken to him had apparently walked over from one of the houses a few hundred yards away across a clearing, where a street came up from the town centre and terminated.

He might have been eleven, was barefoot, and wore a T-shirt and shorts with an elastic waist.

Kamal thought for a moment, then said, "Yes, show me."

They walked on a winding path further away from the town, cross-ing a long, grassy plain, staying fairly close to the creek. Kamal remem-bered this area, was thrilled to discover it again. The scene was as green and idyllic as it had been and fairly deserted. Saida and he had come running here and played on the grass. The path wound past a salt works before arriving at some bushes, behind which were the graves of the Sharrifs, the holy men no one recalled even in his childhood. The inscriptions on the stones were in Arabic. Here too Saida had recited the Fatiha. One of the smaller graves, she showed him, marked by a stone tile inscribed in Arabic, belonged to Mzee Omari's brother. What was his name? Karim. He died in 1326, she read the Arabic. 1908.

He had never given it a thought, until much later. Mzee Omari had an older brother. Of what consequence are the dead to a child who's not known them? He could not find the grave now, where he thought it should have been.

The boy with him was called Fadhili, and on their way back they chatted, sort of. Fadhili was in Standard Four. Did he want to go on to secondary school? No. He would go to madrassa—which was prob-ably what he could afford. Would he like to have a soda? Mm-hm. They stopped at a little store and had their sodas. Then they parted.

The street was an extension of the street of the Indian shops. Arriving there, Kamal took a cross street and found the one on which he had lived with his mother. He choked when he saw the old mango tree, staid, dignified—as he imagined it—the lonely sentry of his nights' imaginings. It looked strangely forlorn; why wouldn't it, with its old friend gone. He went and stood under it; almost shyly put a hand on the trunk. Bwana Mwembe, do you remember me? Can you tell me things? The house in which he had lived had been built over. Three women sat at the porch, chatting, and he greeted them. "Jambo Mama, how are you. There was a woman here who was called Hamida, do you remember her?" "No . . . how many years ago?" "Forty." They gaped at him. "Do we look like grandmothers, then?" They laughed, and he smiled and walked back to the main road.

It had been a disappointing day, he thought, marked by that perverse silence at the medical store, the deliberate refusal to *say*—anything. His walk through the streets of his childhood had depressed him. How could an established, historic town so completely lose itself, become a nothing place? Still, his walk with young Fadhili, that small communion, had gladdened him; the sight of the old tree had clutched at his heart. The tree could not talk, but it was as if in Bwana Mwembe he had met someone who had known him intimately, who was a witness to his memories. Surely, slowly, he was arriving?

He would not give up. Saida, I will find you.

· 10 ·

On the last day of each month, in the afternoon, Mama would stand in a long queue at the post office, Kamal by her side, to withdraw a fixed sum from her account. This money augmented what she received from her tailoring jobs. During month-end or on the eve of a festival there was a pile of clothes to work on from the Asian shops. Kamal would thread her needle and stitch on buttons while she darned the holes and turned in hemlines. It was understood that it was to help the doctor's half-caste son that his mother received the work. During Ramadan or Christmas or when the crop season had been good, a shopkeeper called her to work on one of his sewing machines. Sometimes Mama had her entrepreneurial brainwaves, as when she rented an old ice cream maker. The venture proved disastrous, because for one thing few people could afford the ice cream; and then the ice, milk, and sugar had to be purchased in advance. If that were not enough, neither she nor Kamal was adept with the leaky gizmo. She gave it back.

The post office money was what his father had left for her, with clear instructions that she faithfully followed. She would withdraw not a penny more nor less, not a day sooner than mwisho mwezi, the end of the month. All her major shopping was done this day, whatever was needed that they could afford. Soap, maize flour, tea, and sugar to last as long as possible. And only once in a rare while, something to wear. The shops were full, the shopkeepers inviting you in with smiles as you passed, Karibu kijana, Karibu shoga! Starehe, would reply Mama, and hesitate outside, before stepping in. You had to be alert for those Asians, smooth as butter and sweet as honey, even their children, they would not let you leave without a purchase. But there were no returns, of course, the smiles would turn into scowls—honey into salt, as Mama said—were you to dare to bring something back.

After the shopping they visited the market, and then they would treat themselves to a lunch of pilau, which had in it a bony piece of meat for each of them, and a curry of spinach or beans, followed by a dessert of an orange or a mango. Late in the afternoon she would allow him a stick of muhogo—cassava—from a vendor at the seashore.

And when the two Eids came! They were the happiest times of the year, the first one marking the end of the Ramadan fast, the other, Abraham's sacrifice and the season of haj. In the morning, wearing his bright white kanzu and hand-stitched cap, Kamal would hurry off to the big mosque for the communal prayer where many of the town's men and boys also came; most would be barefoot like him. After the prayer he would return home, greeting the elders and anyone else he met on the way with cries of "Idi Baraka!" He would kiss Mama's hand and tell her, "Idi Baraka, Mama. God give you a long life!" And she would reply, "You too, my son," and he would receive a thumuni, a fifty-cent piece, from her. To be put away with the coins he occasionally received in his sanduku, the savings box, like a stingy shopkeeper. Mama would laugh at this, saying, "Just like his father," though it was she who encouraged him to save. Then the two of them, Mama in a brilliant khanga with the latest design printed on it, and smelling of Bint el Sudan, would go off to visit the house of Mzee Omari, taking a plate of tambi for them. Upon arriving at the porch where the family would be gathered, first of all Kamal would go and kiss Mzee Omari's hand, saying, "Idi Baraka, Babu," and receive a thumuni. Then he would greet the others, Mwana Juma, Bi Kulthum, and Saida, and whoever else was there. Saida, in a new dress, wearing slippers, her hair braided neatly, would receive a thumuni from Mama and do a kind of curtsy Kamal never understood. After a round of kahawa and some sweets, during which the adults would chat, they would depart, his mother and he, and have an Eid lunch, just the two of them. And he would give her the thumuni he had received earlier.

"Why don't you have brothers and sisters, Mama?" he asked. "Why don't I have uncles or cousins, why don't I have brothers or sisters?" And she said, "Just the two of us, we have no one else." "And if I die, Mama?" She drew a sharp breath. "Thubutu! Don't you dare."

One memorable Eid—it was Mzee Omari's final one—the old man, having called Kamal over, put into his hand not a thumuni with the head of the Queen or King on it but a pale little silver coin. "Take this," he said with a smile, and he covered Kamal's hand with his. When he let go, Kamal saw in his hand an Indian anna. He gazed at it with devotion. It had a head he did not recognize, and the writing on it was Indian. "You like it, yes. It's from your country, after all. From kwenu."

Startled, Kamal said, tearfully, "Kwangu ni hapo, Mzee Omari." I am from here.

Mzee Omari looked at him, the grim smile back on his face. "You are from here, but your grandfather was a Mhindi."

"Did you know him, Mzee?"

"Yes, I did. Punja was a good man. I was a little boy and he gave me sweets to eat in his shop. And one day he gave me this coin."

"He was a lion!"

"A quiet lion, yes. This coin belonged to him. It was blessed by a saint, there, in India, and brought him good luck."

"Ahsante, Mzee Omari." Thank you. "Idi Baraka!"

Mzee Omari said, to Mama, "Your boy will go far, Hamida. You are bringing him up well."

"That I am," Mama replied.

"But it's also the baraka of his ancestors, all their blessings."

"Both the Indians and the Africans, my father," she said to him. "And the blessings of the Rabbi, and His Prophet."

And they all said, "Alhamdu lillahi rabb al-alameen." Praise is to Allah.

· II ·

The Composition of the Coming of the Modern Age.

Bismil, I begin in the name of the Kind and the Merciful One, to whom there is no equal, whose praise is always an auspicious start; and I recall His beloved servant our lover, the Habibu, and Ali the wielder of Dhulfikar and Fatima the mother of Hasani and Huseni . . .

If you listen, my brothers, you will learn of the wonders that took place, in the past among our fathers, and this knowledge will keep us wise.

The priests of the Kaiser in his city Berlin approached his presence and gave him khabari that great calamity had been foretold to befall on Ujerumani. How did they come to know of this misfortune, the great king, the Kaiser, asked. They told him, Bwana, we have studied Torati, the book of Moses, and Injili, the book of Jesus, and Zaburi, the book of David; and the books of the Infidels too. Those who worship fire and their prophet Zarathustra. And we have learned. Evil times will engulf our land. These wise men all beseeched the Kaiser that another land be sought for their people. A land peaceful and fruitful where men did not lust for wealth and could toil on Allah's earth in peace. A land beautiful and near the sea so that the people can trade in the necessities and the luxuries required

of civilized people. The blessed Kaiser gave permission for this land
to be sought. The Kaiser's ministers interviewed the merchants
and sailors of their land, who knew the geography of the world,
and these men spoke of Azania, which is our land of Africa in
the east, the Swahili coast from Lamu and Mombasa to Tanga
down to Dar es Salaam and Zanzibar then to Kilwa and Lindi
farther south. And so there arrived in Zanzibar, in the year of
the Christians 1885, a German prince called Peters, but his
intentions were the darkest. Like Iblis deceived our mother Eve,
Peters deceived Bargash, and using low tricks and lies he
accepted the thumbprints of foolish leaders of the coast, showing
them papers written in his language which they could not read,
and thus he planted the flag of the Germans on the ancient
lands of the tribes. All the land of the coast and that of the
washenzi in the interior, which we call Tanganyika, that land
the German Peters stole from us in the name of his Kaiser. He
brought soldiers from Sudan and gave them guns. He carried a
whip and he used it at will.

Among our people, when visitors came to our land, they
brought presents of beads, cloth, metal things. Now these white
men came as our guests, but they demanded work, and payment.
Instead of sitting and talking they brought guns and shot at us.
Where we planted grain, on our stolen land they planted cotton,
and told us, Work. They brought foreign askaris to beat us. They
broke the rules of our elders, our sharia. For disobeying which, the
kiboko, the whip. For this misdemeanour, the khamsa-ishirin, for
that one, the same. The twenty-five, referring to the number of
lashes, delivered so hard they made you bleed and weep like a
woman. Not for nothing we remember the German as mkono
wa damu; the hand of blood. As the song says, the Arab put us in
chains, the German whipped us raw, and the British sucked
our blood.

And so we Africans made war. From Tanga down to Pangani
and Bagamoyo, from Kilwa down to Lindi, we made war. And the
tribes, the Ngoni and Matumbi, the Hehe and Yao, they too made
war. Bushiri bin Salim and Mwana Heri, Hassani Makunganya and

Chief Mkwawa all made war. Kinjikitilé of Ngarambe through his water magic and his spells inspired the people, and they brought out their spears and went to war. That was the great War of the Waters, known as Vita vya Maji Maji.

"Say, Doc, how about giving me a checkup for a day's rent? You give me a clean bill of health, I write off a day from your bill."

Beneath the crude humour Kamal discerned a lurking fear. But he declined Markham's offer.

"I've stopped practising, Ed. And I am not licensed here."

Yes, he'll have coffee with his breakfast, he said to the waiter, who left with the order, and Markham continued,

"This is Africa, Doc. Two days' room and board?"

"Aah," he waved away Kamal's demurral, and confided, "I think my prostate's killing me."

The red face, the yellow teeth, the hard breathing, the silver stubble. The acrid odour. Kamal was not about to physically check the man's prostate, and gave him a look to say exactly that. "You could get a blood test, Ed," he suggested. "The local medic will have the equipment."

But Markham too was medically equipped. He hobbled off and brought back a cardboard box.

"I'm not licensed," Kamal repeated, his attention drawn by blister packs of antibiotics and other medicines in the company of a fat paperback handbook. He noticed the blood pressure kit and instinctively pulled it out, and began taking Markham's pressure. Then he took the pulse.

"Just as I suspected, Ed. Not good."

Markham put on a rueful face. "Your advice."

"Less fat, less salt," Kamal recited the mantra. "And exercise. Or one day soon you'll drop dead, like that. Or you'll suffer a stroke, and John will not be your nurse for long. And the prostate—get it checked in Dar. Soon."

By this time there was a queue of five people, all the kitchen hands and John the barman, waiting for the doc, grinning sheepishly, sleeves rolled up.

Sulking, Markham was at the bar helping himself to a whisky.

Having checked the blood pressures—all excellent, Kamal reassured his five patients—he made to attend to his breakfast. Just then Lateef arrived, and stumbled on a chair as he dramatically raised a desisting hand.

"You are not to eat that!"

Kamal was halfway into getting to his mouth a morsel of sausage, cut from one of the two on his plate that the waiter had enticed him with, having arrived on the morning's flight from Dar.

He looked up at his friend, dressed today in a kanzu and cap. He must have been to prayer.

"Why not?" Kamal asked, knowing full well that it was not the cholesterol value that had drawn the objection.

"Daktari, it is pork." Nguruwe. Haram.

"Perhaps."

"It is not good, sir. Daktari, you have fallen from your ways. How can I help you this way?"

"I don't know, Lateef."

He was not the man he was, yes. He couldn't be. Then what was he doing here? Did he have a right to return and interfere with lives with which he had lost connection? What would Saida expect from him? She had called him, a part of him believed that; she must have called him over the years. These thoughts and their many elaborations would torment him later, tortures designed for his particular insecurities, but for now they fleetingly made themselves felt as he surrendered the two sausages, putting them on a separate plate that Lateef delivered hastily to the kitchen, where presumably the staff ate them.

Lateef returned, puffed up with satisfaction. "Good, sir. You are a good man."

The waiter soon brought a tray for him, and Kamal felt the odd wave of pleasure watching him fall to it.

Lateef had come especially to condole with him regarding the previous day's disappointment. He already had a solution. Ali's father's sister, Mzee Omari's daughter, lived with him behind the medical shop. It was to her that Kamal should talk. He would go himself and arrange a meeting with her. That would be just wonderful, Kamal told him. All he required was one piece of information.

The rest of that day Kamal spent by himself. To begin with, after breakfast he chose to sit at the beach with a book, under an umbrella. The sky was perfectly clear, the breeze delightful. But he was not used to such idleness. The life he had left behind had been hectic and crowded. He had patients at three clinics, he managed to visit two of them every day. Now, sitting here and waiting, he felt listless. Everything proceeded slowly in these parts, he reminded himself; he would have to be patient. Bado kidogo, wasn't that what they said?—not yet, there is still time. A fisherman came by, holding in both hands a large fish for sale, and one of the kitchen hands hurried out to negotiate the price and buy it for dinner. The sun was gradually rising over the ocean, glistening over the wavetips; a few dhows were out. Kamal dipped into his book, an anthology of Swahili verse he had brought with him, in which however Mzee Omari bin Tamim was represented by only one entry. He had heard the poetry of his mother tongue all his young life, but it was only much later, as an adult and when he had gone away, that he had taken the pains to learn all about it: its history and tradition, its rules of prosody, its noted practitioners. How different, the dignified and elitist concerns of that poetry, and how naive, compared to the mischievous rap—the Bongo Flava—that the youth delighted in now. Every instinct, fed by such observations, told him he was on a quixotic, hopeless quest—every instinct but one: that Saida had called, Saida to whom in a passionate moment he had promised that he would return for her.

In the afternoon, after a simple lunch in Masoko, at a restaurant recommended by Lateef, he strolled over to the harbour. The prospectors' ship, a small, squat steel vessel with a square bow, was busy receiving attentions from its crew; one of the Filipino crew waved at him. Kamal had had a chat with the two Dutchmen and learned that their work was done and they would be flying off to Mombasa, the ship to follow at some lowly speed. An idle motorboat was ready to take Kamal to the Island to see the ruins. As soon as he had bargained the fare and sat down inside, the boat filled up with passengers who had been waiting under a tree for a dhow to take them across. Now subsidized by his fare they would pay nothing, or only a token. He didn't mind. The sea was choppy and the ride took ten minutes.

He had not been to the Island, Kisiwani, ever since that day he had come on a school trip, when they had met the bearded archaeologist. The ruins of the ancient sultanates were now a UN Heritage Site, as a sign proclaimed. There was nobody else visiting, and Kamal meandered through the site by himself, noticing that the newly posted descriptions—of the Big House, the mosques, the graves—seemed to have been taken directly from a book he had in his possession. It was impossible to imagine, he mused, a different form of life here, with luxurious houses of stone, containing baths and recreation rooms, and mosques with multiple domes and columns, when there was leisure and wealth to create beauty. He wondered where the slaves—the ones the French captain Morice took annually—were kept: here on the island, or on the mainland? In later times, when the Island kingdom was long extinct, it was to Kilwa the slaves were taken and sold.

A gang of small boys followed him at a distance, and when he paused for them and greeted them, they walked with him, past an immense baobab tree to a small settlement where he sat down and asked for tea. The houses were of mud and thatch, and there was no electricity, and no employment that he could see.

On the way back to the shore he came across a solid brick building, above the entrance of which was a sign indicating a madrassa. He stepped in, and was met by a polite man in kanzu and cap, who was the teacher. There were sixty-three students, the teacher said, when Kamal inquired. They were all boys and came from all across the southern region of the country. All were on scholarship and boarded here. He showed Kamal the weekly schedule of classes, written on a blackboard. The instruction available was Islamic and in Arabic, but there was some English and math too.

Kamal phoned the boatman on his cell and was picked up. Back on the other side, the water having risen, he had to take his shoes off to wade to the shore. It was no longer easy, he discovered, to walk barefoot on the pebbles.

He sat at a table at the hotel's small patio overlooking the sea, musing to himself, waiting for the chef to sound the dinner gong, which he always did with much gusto, bringing sudden life and cheer to the place. It was dusk, the hour of mysterious portents. Where he sat, the beach was empty, though from somewhere came the disembodied voices of two men out on a stroll. Earlier, on his way back from his Island tour, he had splurged on several newspapers at a vendor's stand in Masoko. The stand had appeared like a miracle on the roadside; he had not seen it before. Nobody read newspapers in these parts, as far as he could tell, or anything else. In Kilwa he had looked foolish merely asking where he could buy one. He thought about the sign he had noticed behind the vendor—painted in crude caps on a board nailed to an electric pole, advertising the services of a mganga, a traditional doctor, for problems of love, sickness, business, virility. A mobile number was provided. Perhaps that might be his last resort? How far was he willing to go in his search for Saida?

The dull drone of an outboard motor, a thread of sound in the pitch-darkness of the sea, drew him away from his consciousness, until Lateef had arrived and rescued him.

"Sir—you think much," Lateef said, sounding cheerfully solicitous beside him. "It must be about this woman, Saida. Tell me about her. Eti, she was a good woman?"

"She was my friend when we were children. We played together. I taught her English and math, and she taught me Arabic writing. Our mothers were like sisters. Then we got separated, and now I want to find her."

"You came from Canada to find her."

"Yes."

"Enh."

He had been asked a half question to which he gave a half answer, and received a grunt of approval. He had come all the way just to see this local girl with whom he had played. Lateef was impressed.

"Sir—tell me about Canada. Does it have the sea, eti?"

"Yes, it does. You have seen the map of America? And it has the sea on both sides?"

Lateef agreed.

"Well, Canada is just to the north of it, you see. It too has the sea on both sides—Atlantic Ocean and Pacific Ocean." And it has a sea on top, but he didn't say that.

"It's big then."

"Yes, it's big—like from here to Nigeria," Kamal said, taking a wild guess.

"The marvels of Allah never cease." Ya Mungu ni mengi.

Lateef became thoughtful; he looked around and glanced behind him into the bar. There was only John there, standing idly at his post. Finally, in a somewhat muted tone, Lateef said,

"They have agreed, sir. Saida's family have agreed. Ali's younger mother, Fatuma, will talk to you. I explained that you are one of us and a daktari, and she was impressed. Here we worship doctors. We will go and see her tomorrow."

"Thank you, Lateef. God bless you."

"You are welcome, bwana."

"You came all the way here—you could have phoned me, Lateef."

"I was in the area, bwana. I thought I would come and see how you were doing."

He had a soft drink and left.

Watching him go out past the bar and through the dining hall, returning greetings, Kamal had the distinct feeling that he was still under observation; the door had only been partially opened to him. But what could there possibly be to hide or hold back? Why had his simple search become such a runaround? He knew this for certain: if he had not put aside the two pork sausages that morning, he would never have had a second chance with the family.

The gong had already sounded, and he went into the dining lounge.

That evening, sitting in the lounge, Kamal put himself to duty writing letters. Markham was alone at the bar, chatting with two customers, the reverberation of his drawl like the rumble of very distant thunder.

Candle lamps flickered on a few random tables and the dry, acrid smoke from a mosquito coil swirled up from the floor somewhere, thinly tainting the evening air. Music played as usual in the background, and from somewhere came the sound of a soccer commentary. He felt strangely calm and contented. This was his escape, this lonely tropical night, the insistently quick guitar twang in the background only serving to sound its emptiness. It could have been terribly romantic, with the right companion. A good wine, the medium-bodied Chianti he liked, sinful lamb or rabbit, espresso and cognac; slow adult sex. But with the right companion, there would be no limbo, there would always be that preordained ending. The return ticket. As it was, this loneliness should be relished. There was no war in Iraq or Afghanistan, the Dow Jones did not exist. The media did not snipe at you with shock and awe, breaking news every minute; hucksters didn't pop up all the time, with promises of better life, endless life, more money, more erection and more sperm; the phone rarely rang. Of course he was connected, but that other world was a long way away, on another planet, its signal dim.

He wrote to his son, Hanif, and to his daughter, Karima. Platitudes. What else but suggest bounds you expected them to transgress, provide a superego or an elastic band of safety. In his childhood there were no bounds, just obligations and love. His one fear in life was that he'd lose his mother, the dearest thing to him. He lost her. But to his Canadian kids and their cohorts such fears were entirely alien. What they knew was want, that fuel of the consumer index.

He decided he would not mail the letters after all. What was a letter but a strong signal? He did not need to send one of those now. He did not want a reply. He would remain silent as an unknown planet, going about his business somewhere. The kids were taken care of, wherever they were.

Across the channel, the Island lay like a shadow, two dim pinpoints of light visible upon it. The twenty-first century, and still no electricity there. Where I come from, on that planet we leave lights on casually, cities light up the sky, and we contrive to feel cold in the summer. The sea was calm, black and receding. The lounge had emptied, the few other guests retired. At the bar, without turning to look, Kamal sensed Markham's presence. Another escapee from out there, come to eke out the remaining years of his life. There was perhaps fifteen minutes of probing silence between them, before Markham shuffled over with two drinks and sat down. Kamal said thanks.

They spent a few more quiet minutes, each to himself, before Kamal ventured, "What brought you to these parts, Ed? Not business, surely. Where were you before you came to Kilwa?"

Markham shook the ice in his glass, the tinkle startlingly eloquent. "I came to East Africa in 1965," he said. "Nairobi. The days of Kenyatta. Happy days, generally speaking."

"And never went back?"

"Once—for the World Cup in sixty-six."

"England won."

"They did. Beat the Krauts and that made the win sweeter."

He had worked as a book salesman initially, got to travel around East Africa, but mainly the three capitals. He took a car dealership in Kampala, in Idi Amin's Uganda, slipped out in time and became hotel manager and owner in Arusha for many years. Serengeti, Ngorongoro, and all that. A salesmanship for Land Rover enticed him to Dar, disappointed him, and he returned to Arusha to manage a hotel.

It occurred to Kamal that the Englishman had spent more time in the country than he himself had, yet he thought of him as a foreigner. Markham spoke familiarly of events and conditions that happened long after Kamal was gone.

"All South Africans there now, young chaps," Markham was saying, "can't bloody well understand them half the time when they speak."

"South Africans? Where?"

"Arusha. Ran the hotels when I was there."

They had fired him. He came to Kilwa.

"To the end of the world."

"The end of the world."

They clinked glasses.

Markham had come to Kilwa once in the 1980s with a group of archaeologists; that was when he decided it might not be a bad place to retire in.

What had he left behind in England? What part of England, for that matter? Had he married, did he have children somewhere? Kamal dared not ask.

It was while he looked pityingly at the man that the thought came, Shamim came, intruding once again,

Is this what you want to become. A wretched old stinking bag of an exile dying unnecessarily in a tropical hole.

To which, riled, he replied as viciously as he could,

That's one way to think of it, from where you are in your sanitized world. He'll be buried next to the ocean that brought him here, and you'll lie embalmed under several feet of snow in the middle of a continent you don't quite belong to.

· 13 ·

The Composition of the Coming of the Modern Age.

They had come in their manwari warships from Berlin, bearing instructions from their Kaiser, full of guile, eager to make war and acquire territory, and they coerced the Sultan in Zanzibar to yield them Tanganyika's coast, the home of the Swahili. In Tanga, Sadani, Pangani, Bagamoyo—great markets of the north—they alighted from their boats and haughtily put up their flags; they shot at the people with their rifles and stormed into the mosques in their boots. The leaders of the coast refused to lower the Sultan's banner and declared a jihad. They won great victories, but finally their strength was found wanting against the might of the foreigners and they lost. Bushiri bin Salim, the leader of Pangani, was hanged and the people were disheartened. Mwana Heri, the leader of Sadani, fled into the hills.

In the interior of the country, Mkwawa of the Hehe, the bravest of warriors, whose equals you will look for in vain, also fought. A great fortress at Iringa was his lair. To crush this hero, the Germans sent Captain Zelewsky, the warrior who had defeated Bushiri and was known as Nyundo, the Hammer. This Nyundo met his death at Mkwawa's hands. The furious German government, vowing, Mkwawa we will crush! Nyundo we will avenge! sent the soldier von Prince to do battle against the Hehe. After a long and hard war of seven years, Mkwawa was betrayed where he was hiding, but when von Prince found him, he had taken his own life. The German cut off the chief's head and sent it off to Berlin for the Kaiser to look at this African who had resisted him so fiercely. And so the Hehe were left without a head and dispirited.

When we display ignorance of the world and take up battle against greater forces, it's a bitter lesson we learn.

Kamal sat silent on the grassy verge behind the elders, mesmerized by the world that Mzee Omari had wrought. A gust from the sea shot a shiver through him; the branches overhead swished and swept at the air, as if by this show of force echoing the poet's last words. A hush had fallen on the scene, and the oracle himself sat still on the tree trunk, a white-clad figure outlined by the night. Kamal could imagine the German askaris—the Somali, the Sudanese, the Zulu— Mzee Omari described them all, with their backpacks, their thick boots, their long rifles at their shoulders, cartridge belts at their waists, pounding the earth, trampling through the jungle, hacking through the bushes as they tracked down Chief Mkwawa of the Hehe, who awaited them. The drum belting out its boom-boom-boom, the men singing hoarsely, "The Hammer will be avenged! Oyé, oyé, Nyundo will be avenged!" All these details Idris the djinn had conjured up for Mzee Omari. Kamal looked around nervously for a sign of that malignant spirit. He stood up, for the men were dispersing, and walked back slowly home in the dark. In the far corner of the square he spied Salemani Mkono the one-armed beggar slinking away into an alley like a rat.

Why would Africans fight fellow Africans on behalf of the Germans, the boy wondered. And now, as we sat together in Dar's Asian quarter eating bhajias at a vegetarian joint, tormented by an army of flies, discussing distant historic wars and the poet of Kilwa, Kamal said, "What a defeatist message, that one: 'a bitter lesson we learn.'" I replied the obvious, that many African peoples, having tasted heavy defeat, took the prudent decision to cooperate with the Germans. Thus, the next time around, in the great Maji Maji War, the Hehe kept quiet for the most part, as did the Swahili.

We were approaching the real story behind Mzee Omari and his muse, the djinn called Idris.

"Where were you?" Mama asked severely, when he returned. "So now I have to leave my work and go looking for you!"

"I was playing."

"Playing what?"

"Gololi"—marbles—"with the Indians."

"Wewe . . ." She heaved a sigh. She didn't believe him.

But he could catch a whiff of Bint el Sudan on her, The Beauty of Sudan, the thin, dark bottle of which stood on her table. She had on a new khanga, a white, black, and bright red wraparound, which he did not recall her buying. She too had been out. At such times, when he knew she kept a secret from him, he felt depressed, he couldn't sleep. She knew his hurt, he could see the sympathy in her eyes. That night as she lay on the mat facing away from him, she muttered, "I am doing all I can for you." Why wouldn't she? She was his mama, and he would buy the earth for her, just let him grow up.

Meanwhile he would get her a present. During mwisho mwezi, the month-end, one or two Asian stores brazenly displayed ready-made clothes on racks and shoes on stands outside their doors to entice customers; so easy to steal. One day he made a resolution. While out selling kashatas, Kamalu hovered outside the shops, wandered by the clothes racks and shoe stands, made his choice. Just as he was about to pick off a pair of bright new plastic sandals for Mama, he became aware of two sharp eyes watching him: a boy his age sitting quietly at the store's threshold, a comic book on his lap. Pretending to look casual, Kamal wandered away with his tray, bleating, "Kashaataa!" These Indians always had someone watching their goods; to them every African was a thief. They had no right tempting people, especially boys with mothers and no fathers.

But he had gone to steal, hadn't he? If that Indian boy had not been there, watching, Kamal would have become a thief. He felt ashamed of himself, for the way he had been anticipated. How lucky that boy.

What fears could he have? Did he ever go without food at night? How far apart their worlds were.

The Composition . . .

Each time he continued with his composition, Mzee Omari began with an altered invocation.

> To start Bismil I invoke / the blessed name of He / the Merciful and His servant / Muhammad the honest one / and the blessed Companions . . .
>
> In Kilwa Kivinje too, and in the nearby towns, they resisted the Germans, not having learned from the defeats of the others.
>
> The trader and warrior Hassan bin Omari, the giant in white kanzu, famously known as Makunganya, celebrated even in our day, began to gather weapons and men. A thousand strong warriors rippled their muscles, hungry for battle. When these majitus stood up in a straight line, a wall of shields and spears extended as far as the eye could strain to see, their voices rose like thunder in the sky and this land called Tanganyika itself trembled with pride. Makunganya vowed to chase out the foreign devils from Kilwa all the way up the coast to Dar es Salaam and there cut off the head of Wissmann, the governor, and to put all the Germans who remained on a ship back to Berlin to the Kaiser. And so when the German force was away fighting Mkwawa of the Hehe, Hassan attacked the Kilwa fortress. The surprise was great, victory was but a breath away; Makunganya's spies had done their work. But the German commander Schmidt who remained behind was prepared; he too had been listening. And the spear and the shield were no match for the hidden guns that rained bullets. Makunganya escaped. When news of the attack reached Bwana Wissmann in Dar es Salaam, this furious German sent a shipload of his soldiers to Kilwa. Capture Makunganya, he thundered. I will despatch the chief to his God. On the Lindi road, that obstinate chief fought valiantly against the soldiers, until he stood alone against them all. But they would not give the warrior his death. He was captured and brought to Kilwa. Wissmann himself arrived

in his manwari warship to put Makunganya and his collaborators
on trial. Boats rowed the German and his men from the warship to
the shore. Fierce in his moustache, wearing helmet and boots, his
legs apart and arms akimbo, he stared up at the boma in which the
prisoners were kept: thus Wissmann the warrior governor. Show
me Makunganya, he said.

The trembling voice proceeded in the night narrating events from
a distant, hazy past in short, rhyming lines of a slow rhythm, in a
poetic, archaic Swahili with Arabic gutturals and stretched vowels not
always easy to comprehend . . . And Punja the Lion, Punja the Lion,
when would the poet's words describe the deeds of Punja, Kamal's
great-grandfather? In the dark Kamal sat waiting anxiously for his
ancestor's turn to come, when he heard a stirring to his side and saw
one-armed Salemani Mkono crossing the square, approaching the poet
and his audience of old men with an evil grin.

"And weren't you his slave, you Omari bin Tamim?" The beggar
sneered, his voice rough and bitter as a rotten cassava. "Didn't you
sing praises to the German? Wasn't the white man your master? Didn't
you betray your own blood—"

At which point Salemani, approaching Mzee from the side, spewing
forth his venom, felt a push from the djinn Idris and stumbled back,
then recovered himself and departed, to jeers and abuses from the
assembly.

Polé, Mzee Omari's companions said, Polé, Mzee, the man is no
good. Laana to him!—may he be cursed, that beggar, the son of Iblis,
beloved to none!

Mzee Omari stood up and left, his hand on the shoulder of Saida,
who had accompanied him that night.

Kamal went home crying.

Mzee Omari, the most venerated of men, pious and gifted, the town's
own poet and historian, had suffered an insult. How could that be?
His face had clouded, and for the briefest moment it seemed to fold
and he was someone else. This was too much. But the next day all
seemed normal; those who knew, knew. Salemani continued to hover

about town, despised as always, but Mzee Omari's night recitals stopped. He is not ready, it was said, he is composing. When Kamal contrived to go and buy vitumbua from Bi Kulthum one morning, Mzee Omari was at the porch as usual, having kahawa by himself; his greeting was elaborate as always, but the hand was limp, the voice was from somewhere else.

It was as if the Mzee Omari he had known was gone.

He had asked his mother about it the morning after the incident.

"Mama, that Makunganya—he was a great man, a jitu, who fought the colonialists—sio?"

"Eh," his mother agreed. "That he was. But he was also a slaver who captured and sold my grandmother. Or it was his men who did that."

"Could he be my ancestor, eti?"

"Maybe."

He took a little time debating with himself whether to tell Mama about the previous night. She would be angry. But he had to tell her. It was too important.

"Mama."

"Naam?"

He told her, and her response, which he expected, was, "Didn't I tell you not to go listen to those old men at night?"

"But Mama—why did Salemani say that?"

"That fool says anything that comes to his head."

She was busy ironing, and they both were quiet, he watching her. If she got tired or had something else to do, she would ask him to take over the chore.

Finally she said, "I will tell you. This is only what I have heard.

"Long ago Salemani was a pupil of Mzee Omari in the German school. One day after the Maji Maji War, a German bigwig came to Kilwa by steamer from Dar es Salaam. A great public meeting took place outside the boma, right there where you say that crazy man insulted our Mzee, and there Mzee Omari recited a poem in this bigwig's honour. The next day in class Salemani taunted him—just as he did last night. He was punished. He was given the khamsa-ishirin—twenty-five strokes of the whip—and then sent off north to work on the railways. He returned many years later with only one arm and a little crazy."

"But why did Mzee Omari honour the German?"

"Eh? He was young. And what would you do when the man holds a whip and your job in his hand?"

Salemani's language was coarse, his intonation different from that of most men of the coast. He evidently came from somewhere else; possibly he was a Nyamwezi from near Tabora. Some years ago, the District Commissioner had him dispatched to Dodoma, to the big hospital for mad people. He had returned crazier than before.

"Poor man," Mama said. "But he doesn't behave himself. Now these school clothes—you iron them."

He took over from her. "And if I burn them?" He smiled slyly.

She eyed him. "Then you don't go to school. You work as a servant for the Indians."

"Did you also go to the German school, Mama?"

"I was not born then! Do I look as old as Mzee Omari?"

No she didn't. Which was why the suitors came, and why, whenever she went to the Indians' stores, she took him along as her chaperone, for he had heard her complain that some of them were lechers, sitting in their shops in their loincloths, looking out at the women and scratching their balls.

· 14 ·

"Hamida, my sister—we are defeated. That is what I have come to inform you."

Bi Kulthum made her dramatic announcement as soon as she had sat down and taken a moment to settle. She had on, as usual, the flowing black bui-bui over her dress, revealing only her long face and her rather beautiful hands.

"What now?" replied Mama, sounding amused. "What has defeated you, my sister? And it's you who always cheers us up."

"We have discovered that our daughter is not capable," Bi Kulthum said, more calmly. "She will not make a teacher. And so Kamalu will not have to knock his brains out trying to teach her. Eh, Kamalu?" She looked at him.

Saida, sunk quietly beside her mother on the broken sofa, both her hands stylishly on one knee, cocked her head and gave the barest smile at Kamal that only he could sense, that said, Now how will you deal with this. He had been playing outside when they arrived and he had followed them in. He went to the back to bring water for the guests.

Mama gave a hard look at Bi Kulthum. "Dada'ngu, my sister, are you sure? Have you thought carefully? Is this your own or someone else's thought you are telling me?"

Obviously Mama suspected Mwana Juma, Saida's grandmother, behind this change of heart. But Bi Kulthum reassured her otherwise.

"My own, in truth," she said. "I have observed this girl of mine, and I tell you she is not capable of learning complicated subjects. Better she be instructed in what will make her a good Muslim wife."

"You will teach her, then," Mama said, with mild sarcasm, "the etiquette befitting a good Swahili wife."

"Enh. It is time, my sister."

Bi Kulthum was wrong about her daughter. Saida was not dull, she simply was not very keen to divide and multiply numbers, or to read and spell English, or know who was the prime minister of England, or what was the capital of Norway. The kind of knowledge Kamal could rattle off with ease. What she possessed instead was something else, that captivating innocence and joy that was a different knowledge. What she decided to learn she learned easily.

The two mothers were both looking at him where he had come to sit, on the floor at the outside doorway; he could sense Saida's eyes upon him too, that mischievous gaze. What will you say to my mother? It was Saturday afternoon; outside, the street had turned quiet. He wanted to tell Saida's mother that they would work harder, Saida would for sure learn from him and become a teacher. She should give Saida a second chance.

As he was thinking this, Bi Kulthum said, "Tell your mother, am I saying the truth, Kamalu? Eti, can you make her a teacher of English?"

Kamal said nothing.

Bi Kulthum smiled slyly at him, as though having read his heart.

A kahawa seller came by outside, briskly rattling his cups together to announce himself, and was called—"Weh, Kahawa!"—by Bi Kulthum and entered the room and filled out four little cups of coffee, sprinkling them with ginger powder from a shaker. Mama, having hers, met Kamal's look through the swirl of vapour over her cup. She turned to Bi Kulthum, who had just finished with the vendor.

"In that case, Kulthum, let me teach the girl some sewing. That will be of use to her. It will bring her extra cash when she is older. We women always need it."

Bi Kulthum's eyes lit up and she leaned forward. "Do that, then, sister. Do that. I will send her to you as usual and she can learn sewing instead. What more does a girl want to know about numbers, as long as she can count her money? Who needs alithimetiki—" she pronounced the word derisively in the Swahili manner, "—who needs it? And we won't need English either when the British go. Eti, who speaks German now, besides the old ones?"

"To each his aptitude," Mama responded philosophically, not wishing to argue. Then she added, scanning Saida with a kindly glare, "Your girl will soon be a young woman."

Much was implied in that statement.

"I tell you," Bi Kulthum agreed. "She is going to cost me." She perked up and smiled. "But she has a gift, Hamida—she knows the magic of the Book. You bring her a shida, a problem that's ailing you, and this girl will find a prayer for you."

"W'allahi! I will try her skill, then."

And that was that. Mama and Kamal did not exchange a word on the new arrangement. Saida would arrive Sunday afternoons and do some stitching. Then Mama would tell her, "Before you go, Saida, do a little studying." And add an afterthought, the same one each time, "Don't speak to your mother about it."

Saida would come and sit on the floor with him and struggle with the math or a reader for some time. Sucking on her pencil. She would tire and he would bring out his Juzu and read a page or two of Arabic with her; then he would write something and she would check it. Sometimes they did the puzzles and coloured pictures in the *Sunday Standard*'s children's section, presented by "Uncle Jim." He read old news to her—the papers came from Dar es Salaam and sometimes were months old, Mama occasionally buying them in bundles from a vendor who came by. Sometimes he read to Mama, too, in English and Swahili. She did not know English, but it gave her pleasure just to hear him speak it.

"That's what she was," he said softly to me, "Mama'angu . . . my mother. She could feel my aches even before I did. She read in my eyes that morning my worry that, if Bi Kulthum had her way, Saida would cease coming, and so she arranged something, right then and there. Which is why I could never understand . . . why she . . ."

"She what?"

"Abandoned me," he said.

When she heard him read in English, did she see the foreigner he would become? The man who, walking the streets he occupied in his childhood, would get followed by kids shouting "Mzungu!"—meaning not white man in his case but foreigner, perhaps American. If she had sent him to a madrassa he would have sat on the ground with other little boys wearing kanzus and caps, chanting their lessons like automatons. They would have made fun of the stern mwalimu and feared him as well. He would have made friends with some of the boys. Would he have been better or worse off than what he became?

A well-known and affluent doctor in Edmonton: the thought came to my mind just as he asked, "What do you think?"

"I don't know, really. One of those hypothetical questions, isn't it?"

The instinct was to say he would have been better off back home and rooted among his people, but on the other hand, more rationally, surely the opportunities he had had could not be so easily dismissed. I couldn't help thinking of the American rock idol Madonna's adopted African child. Surely he will do well?

"I think you've done well," I said. "The rest is hypothetical."

In the comfort and freedom allowed us nowadays, it's easy to be cynical and harsh: those who left us for abroad during our worst times under a suffocating bureaucracy, when we had to queue up for a loaf of bread or half a kilo of sugar, and suffered the tribulations from our war with Uganda, when we rightly threw Idi Amin out, deserve no sympathy from us. But this man before me demonstrated how complicated a real life could be in our times, how painful the idea of belonging. I myself am attempting to send my youngest child away for his education, and I worry, Will he return? As what?

When did he know he *loved* her?

On Sundays he would join a few Indian boys from his school who gathered to play on the grassy plain at the edge of town, past the Germans' and on the way to the Sharrifs' graves, a path he had taken with Saida during their noontime outings. He got along with all the boys, though their nickname for him was the diminishing Chotaro, half-caste; he laughed it off, most of them had a nickname, some much worse than his. The local fat boy was called Moon. Kamal was no good at cricket but he could leave them helpless and paralyzed with his speed and moves with a football. One Sunday when he arrived on the ground, he saw to his horror the boys encircled around a frightened Saida, taunting and trying to push up her dress. With an angry shout he had run into the fray to rescue her. And got beaten up, for he was one against seven or eight of them. He was thrown to the ground, Moon was brought to sit on his face and pound him. But Saida escaped. That's when he knew he loved her. Kamal could have brought his African friends from the neighbourhood to beat up the Asians; the next day in school he sensed their nervousness, as they tried to patch up. Why did he not take his revenge for the humiliation? He could not say. Years later, he met Moon briefly in Edmonton, when he tried to sell him a life insurance policy; they pretended never having met before.

That day of the fight, when he returned home dusty and bleeding, there was a man in the house. He was one of the several polite gentlemen who had recently come courting Mama. She always told them that she was married but her husband had gone away. Perhaps he was lost at sea, like Sinbad, but until she was certain, she could not remarry. She told Kamal now to go to the back and clean himself and return, which he did, and then she introduced him to Bwana Bakari, from Lindi. Bwana Bakari was a tall man in bush shirt and neatly pressed trousers and a cap. He had a pleasant voice and manners to match. Kamal got to share with the two adults a cup of tea and biscuits—a rare treat, brought by the visitor—and he had to report on the fight. Bwana Bakari was impressed, though he said fighting Indians was easy.

Kamal had heard it said to Mama that a woman without a man was a nobody and always at risk, like a warrior without a shield. A mumé was necessary. And Mama would reply that she had her mumé, he was none other than her own Kamalu.

One day Bi Kulthum had come visiting with another woman, perhaps having brought a proposal. In the middle of their conversation, she leaned forward and said something in a low voice to Mama and sat back in triumph; the other woman gave a laugh and clapped her hands once, loudly, in approval; their looks declaring, QED. You have no argument, Hamida.

Mama threw a glance towards Kamal and said, "I don't have the urge."

Did she really believe he was all she needed? Did she have plans for the two of them, a future for him in which she would also be around? What made her give them up, give *him* up?

He had said it was Saida who had called him back, but it was very obvious to me when I heard him speak of his childhood that he came also to confront his mama, even if that meant only to return to his birthplace and recall her in his mind.

15

"Welcome," called out the young woman from the medical store as they arrived, sounding distinctly friendlier than before. Lateef proceeded with an elaborate greeting, rather obvious in its flirtatiousness, during the course of which she laughed rather pleasantly. Kamal had learned that she was called Amina. "She's waiting for you," Amina said, stepping out of the shop, and led them by a side alley into a yard at the back that was shared by several houses. The house behind the shop had a cement porch, on which sat three middle-aged women around a fourth and much older one seated on a stool. A wooden post behind her supported the metal roof that gave the porch its exclusive shade; the rest of the yard bathed in a brilliant glare. The older woman was wearing a black bui-bui, her forearms lay on her knees, the hands joined in front. She had the demeanour of a judge, and she'd been waiting for them. Only the skin near her eyes indicated her age; and her hard stare.

Ali, her son, walked in, and stood with Amina.

"Bring them chairs," the woman commanded, and Ali went inside one of the rooms and brought out two chairs. The three other women had already got up and disappeared into their houses.

"How are you, Mama Fatuma?" said Kamal, and she murmured, "I am well," throwing a distracted, dismissive glance to her side.

Not the most amicable of circumstances.

"Thank you for seeing me, Mama," Kamal continued.

She turned to Lateef. "So this is the daktari?"

"Yes, he's the doctor," Lateef replied. "The same one I told you about. His name is Kamalu. He grew up here in Kilwa, then went overseas to America. He's one of us."

"That's true, Mama Fatuma," Kamal said. "I am from these parts."

"Nzuri," the woman said. "Good . . . Sometimes my stomach hurts." She pointed briefly towards the area.

Is this what she had expected of him—a consultation? Had she misunderstood his purpose? He didn't think so. She had yet to look directly at him. He was the foreigner, whether born here or not, everything about him suggested that to her, and he was well aware of that. But she could use him. Kamal glanced at Lateef, who came immediately to the rescue.

"Bi Fatuma, the daktari will examine you some other day, if you want him to. You know some women don't want men doctors to examine them. But if you wish, he will look at you another time. He has a question for you. It is very important to him—he has come all the way from America to ask you."

Outside on the street a customer was demanding service. "Weh Amina, are you closed or what? Why is no one here?" Amina hurried out to the shop. Water was brought by Ali in a jug. Kamal and Lateef exchanged another look. This was not a time to refuse water, to tell the watchful hosts that only bottled water would do for the daktari's delicate stomach. Kamal took his glass and drank quickly, curry aftertaste and all.

"I am looking for a woman called Saida," Kamal began, hiding a grimace. "Her mother was Bi Kulthum, and her grandfather was Mzee Omari the poet."

"Mzee Omari was a teacher," Fatuma corrected him. "You know we don't have anything from him. No papers, nothing of the sort. Now what do you seek from Saida?" This time she looked at him.

Kamal hesitated, concerned that there should not be a wrong impression. He could say they were like brother and sister; but that was a lie they would see through, and it would make him suspect. He could not understand this reticence, this cloak of secrecy about Saida.

This whole elaborate performance for a simple question: Where was she? Was something wrong, or did they simply intend to squeeze some benefit out of him?

"Our mothers were like sisters. The closest of friends. I want to find out what happened to her. That is the absolute truth. I swear to you by God."

"And you want to help her?"

"Yes . . . What help does she need?"

"And how can you help us?"

She looked away, with the flourish of a chess master having made a decisive gambit. Was she expecting money? Her arrogance amazed him; where did it come from? What made her feel so superior—that someone like him had come to beg at her door?

"Now look," Lateef scolded. "Stop harassing the doctor. He's a Swahili like you and I. Why do you have to try to extort from him?"

"We all need help," Fatuma replied, unfazed.

"He'll look at your ailment, he said. If you want."

"Can't he talk for himself, if he's a Swahili, as you say?" she retorted. "I have yet to meet a Swahili who can hold his tongue."

Kamal laughed out loud. "I will examine you, if you wish, my mother. But please help me. I beg of you." *Tafadhali. I have come a long way for her.*

It appeared that he had been tested, more or less, and had passed, because some kahawa was brought for them all. And he discovered over kahawa that Bi Kulthum had been Fatuma's older sister. He could have wept with joy.

It was, said Kamal to me later, despite the suspicion and the runaround that preceded it, a most significant moment. Before him sat the old poet's daughter, no less; Saida's aunt. I've done it, he murmured to himself, I've discovered her. I'm back. He grasped the tawiz around his neck. His pleasure was so radiant on his face, the other three people on the porch all smiled back at him.

"What have you there?" asked Fatuma.

"A tawiz," he replied, clutching it again. "Saida gave it to me . . . when I left."

"Show it to me."

He handed it to her, and she held it in her palm, gave it a quick look before handing it back.

"Where is Saida?" he asked. "What happened to her?"

"That, we don't know," Fatuma said and looked away again, almost casually. Taunting him. And all his hope and joy turned to ash.

"You don't know? You don't know where your child lives—the daughter of your sister? How can that be, Bi Fatuma?"

She looked straight at him and said, "Then how come you don't know, you who claim to care? We don't know where she is, I tell you."

Why the change of heart—for so it seemed? Was the knowledge so precious that—just like a child—she could not bear to share it?

Kamal stood up, his dejection as evident as his pleasure had been a moment ago. "Could you inquire with any jamaa, any relatives, if they have news of her?" he asked her desperately.

"I will."

As Kamal and his guide reached the door, Fatuma called out, "Daktari, I'll come and show you my ailment."

"You are most welcome," Kamal replied.

This wasn't the end of the matter, he was certain. There were a few moments in that backyard when the tension had eased, and there was a willingness to talk. Saida had been there. He had found her. But where was she?

Lateef left him at the taxi stand, joining there a rough-looking man who had been waiting anxiously for him, and together they hurried off towards the harbour. From what Kamal could overhear, a ship had been loaded and the captain needed some money.

It occurred to Kamal that he knew next to nothing about the man who had devoted himself to helping him.

16

The Composition of the Coming of the Modern Age.

By now the Germans had vanquished the Swahili coast. They had hanged Bushiri bin Salim in Pangani and Hassani Makunganya in Kilwa, together with their allies and companions. They had defeated Mwana Heri in Sadani. And many others too. They had defeated proud Mkwawa, chief of the Hehe, who chose to take his own life. With arrogance and verve they cut his head off and sent his skull to Berlin. Our lives had changed, we were the subjects of the Germans, to do as they commanded. We grew cotton where we had grown maize and millet; we paid taxes and learned their language; we were sent north to carry lengths of iron and build the railways. We cleaned their houses and carried their women, who were too precious to touch our earth. We bowed, accepted the yoke, and became their slaves. Like a shetani they stole our spirit. Like a worm that enters the body and eats you from inside, draining your strength, they turned us weak and helpless.

Now in the land of Matumbi, in the place known as Ngarambe, rose a wizard, a mganga from the waters, who was known as Hongo, who was called Kinjikitilé, who called on the people to come to his kijumba-shrine and take the magic water, the maji, and beat the war drum. They came in their hundreds from all around singing their woes and their hopes and brought their offerings, and he said we must repossess our land and he sprinkled them with the magic water. Go, he said, with this magic water on you, and the rifles of the Germans will turn limp like the penises of old men, their bullets will fall like water from your bodies. The ugly German will become weak like a fish. We are sultans; we are the Sultan of Zanzibar. But for this maji to work you must follow instructions. You will not loot. You will not eat meat. You will desist from relations with your women. And word spread through the country like the whisper of the wind that the white man could hear but not discern. Have you heard? There is a mganga in Ngarambe. This is the year of war. We are suffering, and there is this fundi in Ngarambe called Kinjikitilé who has the medicine.

The people made war; they uprooted cotton and threw it on the ground, and thus they declared war. With their spears, their bows and arrows, they attacked the towns; they set the shops on fire. Planter and overseer, askari and jumbe, all these they killed. All over southern Tanganyika the cry of Maji! rang with a roar, the Germans trembled. Then the government came with their foreign troops, with guns that rained bullets without end. But it was not a rain of water, it was a rain of steely death. Kinjikitilé was captured and hanged. Elsewhere the fighters were defeated and hanged.

Following the defeat of the warriors, the Day of Judgment came, Jehanna arrived on this land, and the archangel was the German; grief and hopelessness, drought and starvation befell the land; poverty and hunger was the lot of the people. The Germans, like God's angels when in His fury He sent them to punish the Egyptians, scorched the farms and forests to deprive the warriors of food. They burned granaries, they destroyed huts and villages; people slept in the forest and were devoured by lions. If you asked a beggar in Kilwa or in Dar es Salaam, Where do you come from? he would tell you, I come from a place that does not exist. I have seen it and played in it, my ancestors' spirits lived in it, but it is now smoke and ashes. I am but nothing.

———

The Maji Maji vita—the War of the Waters—was called a rebellion in our schoolbooks; the image cultivated was of gangs of half-naked, chanting, superstitious Africans foolishly pitting their spears and bows and arrows against the most modern machine guns. Now we are told that the uprising involved large swathes of the country; as many as three hundred thousand Africans—some ten to fifteen percent of the population—perished from the scorched-earth tactics employed at the direction of the governor, von Götzen. Fifteen Europeans were killed. A genocide, as some call it? Perhaps not. But that's only a word to allocate a star to a measure of destruction and death. Now, a century later, a modern German government acknowledges the atrocities of a predecessor.

Meanwhile we in this—and other—nations must face a conundrum: how do we accept those who collaborated with our colonizers? Worked for them; put on boots and uniform and took up arms on their behalf against fellow Africans. Were they traitors or simply practical and realistic? This was the dilemma put to me by Kamal. It is the shameful part of the history of any nation that is often glossed over in silence. The policemen who brought down their sticks on the skulls of Gandhi's followers were fellow Indians; those who hunted the Mau Mau in Kenya and the ANC in South Africa were in large numbers fellow Africans.

How to judge, then, the poet who yielded, who took up his pen and praised our oppressors, and gave them legitimacy? To resist was heroic, but was it better for some to create, to record, to learn and to survive?

"As a boy I was moved by Mzee Omari's stories of resistance," said Kamal. "Mkwawa. Makunganya. Kinjikitilé. These were the heroes. How could you not be proud of them, when we were on the verge of our independence? When our own flag now flew outside every shop and house. There were processions, meetings, songs, poetry; the radio was listened to avidly, just to confirm, yes, freedom was coming, we would have our own prime minister! And so how to explain the old man's pride in his association with the German colonizers? He was a man of great dignity, much loved. It was impossible to imagine that under that venerable, ancient exterior of our poet-historian there lurked something else, so fragile—and guilty?"

In the anthology of Swahili poetry which had become Kamal's faithful companion during this visit to Kilwa, and which he had possessed for many years now, there was one short poem by Mzee Omari and nothing else by him. Other poets in the book had written touchingly about their loves, and about aspects of their faith. Mzee Omari's poem was about the German governor. It was distressing to read.

The German Bwana is fair
He looks after us
But he is strong, watch out
If you are thinking mischief.

He watches us, the Governor
Bwana Schnee in the European city
Called Bendaressalaam to our north
As beautiful as Berlin itself.

This wise sultan from Europe
Governs the coast of Swahil
From Tanga in the north
Through Dar essalaam, Pangani,

Our Kilwa Kivinje and
Down to Lindi in the south;
His manwari steamers
Prowl our ocean with canons.

How different the tone, the message of these abject lines compared to that of his majestic, upright utenzi, the magnum opus, *The Composition* . . . ! According to the book, the eulogy was written in 1907, when Mzee Omari was a young teacher at the German school in Kilwa. It was for reading such lines in public in honour of a German official at the town plaza that Salemani Mkono had taunted him, at the very same venue fifty years later: "Didn't you sing praises to the German?"

Yes, he did, and Kamal had seen that flash of pain cross Mzee Omari's face when he heard that stinging taunt. Couldn't the editors have picked a better poem than this for their anthology? They had included a short biography of the poet, which read:

> Omari bin Tamim, a.k.a. Mzee Omari, was born in Kilwa
> Kivinje c. 1880, according to von Rode, German Commissioner
> in Kilwa, 1905–1910. It is likely that the poet witnessed the
> suppression of Hassan bin Omari Makunganya by the Germans
> and the punishments inflicted on the rebels, including hangings
> at the "Hanging Mango tree." It is certain that he witnessed the
> Maji Maji war. It is not known when he attended the German
> school but he was a teacher when von Rode commissioned this
> poem, which was later included in a collection sent to Berlin
> and read to the German parliament. Omari's older brother,
> Mwalimu Sheikh Karim Abdelkarim Qadri, was also a poet.
> As the last name indicates, the older brother was a member of
> a Sufi tarika. He is known to have been involved in the Maji
> Maji uprising. Sheikh Abdelkarim was tried in 1909 in Kilwa
> for conspiracy against the government and hanged. None of
> his works have survived.

Sitting in the quiet refuge of his study in Edmonton, Kamal had often contemplated this summary of a life which had touched him so deeply as a boy, and tried to understand it. Carl Schmidt's grave was in the old German cemetery that he and Saida would visit during their escapades. Mzee Omari, she had told him, stopped there regularly to pay his respects and recite the Fatiha; Kamal had stood beside her as she too recited that Quranic verse for the dead German. They did likewise at the grave of Mzee's brother Abdelkarim in the cemetery of the Sharrifs farther up the road.

One day Bi Kulthum told Mama that Mzee Omari was behaving strangely. He had stopped writing. He had run out of paper, and ink for his pen, and said rather obtusely that he had no money with which to replace them. He slept badly and was quarrelsome at home. They could even hear him abusing his djinn in his room. Mama said she had a solution. She sent Kamal over to the old man with a sheaf of papers the two of them had torn out from an old exercise book. Kamal also took along a pencil and an eraser.

It was Bi Kulthum who met him at the door and sent him to the old man's room. For a long moment Kamal stood nervously outside in the dark corridor of the Swahili-style house. Then timidly he knocked on the warped, wooden door. Mzee Omari surprisingly heard him and opened the door, saw him with his dim sight, and asked, "What have you brought for me, child?"

Bi Kulthum had already informed him that Hamida's son had arrived bringing an offering.

"Paper and pencil and eraser," Kamal replied. Karatasi na kalamu na raba.

Mzee Omari accepted them and thanked him gracefully; then, as if in afterthought, he bade Kamal come inside and sit next to him on the mat, behind his writing desk. Kamal went in and sat down at the spot as told. He could smell a faint odour of agarbatti in the air. A block of sunlight streamed in through the window behind them, dust motes dancing in the morning's golden rays. Opposite them on the wall, the two faded photographs; on the right, the certificate. Nothing else but the mat and the desk, and the rolled-up bedding in the corner. He turned nervously towards the poet.

Mzee Omari leaned forward and brought out from under the desk a sheet of paper and placed it on top.

"Can you read Kiarabu?" he asked.

"Yes," Kamal replied, then hastily added: "A little—only a little." Saida came home only occasionally now, and practice by himself was not so compelling. Besides, reading the big and bold Arabic letters in his Juzu was different from the script placed before him, which looked like a shaky trail left by a crab on the sand.

"Read this, then," Mzee Omari commanded, pointing a finger at the page on the desk. But the page was upside down, and so in a barely audible voice, Kamal inquired, "Can I turn it . . . ?"

Mzee smiled and turned around the paper himself.

All Kamal could recall reading from that page that morning was the first word, *auwali*, "in the beginning," which much to his lasting shame came to him after some effort. When he finished the verse, with not a little assistance from Mzee Omari, the elder smiled and said, "Nzuri, you have done well . . . you have read the mwanzo, the beginning." He picked up the paper and put it back under the desk. Then he picked up a small sheaf of manuscripts from his side and made as if to read the top one, and recited a verse. Then another, and another in that steel-edged, sinuating voice that grabbed your insides. And Kamal's own heart pounding. But did he detect the slightest tremor in that throat? Kamal glanced around. He should have been proud of this privilege, being sung to by the town's eminent poet and elder, yet he felt oppressed, felt an intense urge to dash out of that bleak, empty, and haunted room echoing with the poetry that he normally so much adored.

Mzee Omari stopped reading and said, "Go then. Nenda zako. Come back when there is more paper. God will bless you . . ." He kept muttering as Kamal left the room. As he hurried out into the corridor, he felt someone trip him: it could only be the jealous djinn, Idris. Kamal swore at him in Arabic, *naalabuka, kilbvahed,* "Your father's arse, you dog," having learned the curse from the Indian boys at school.

The boy started collecting paper for the old man, pages donated here and there by classmates. But he never delivered them, never again entered that sanctum, the bare imposing room with the desk and mat, the testimonial and the photographs.

It was when he first read in the anthology that brief biography of Mzee Omari, together with his eulogy of the German Governor, that Kamal began to grapple with the mystery of Kilwa's poet laureate and the dark side to his career. And one night as he recalled those privileged, though nerve-racking moments he had spent in Mzee Omari's room, as he mused over the verses that Mzee Omari had recited for him, a few broken phrases began to come back to him. One of them was, "barua kutoka Makka tukufu," meaning, the letter from Holy Mecca. Much later he would come to know it as the infamous Mecca Letter of 1909. Mzee Omari, Kamal realized, had been attempting to recite to him the khatima, the end of his history, when Kamal betrayed on his young face his desperation to escape.

It began to seem that all he had to do was rub a lukewarm bottle of Tusker or Serengeti, or merely ask John the Kenyan barman, "What's in the cooler today?" and Lateef, his own djinn, appeared, admonishing forefinger raised against imbibing. But it was pleasing to see him. It was the afternoon following the impasse with Fatuma. He had read. He had reflected. He had decided against an impulse to visit Kilwa. And reluctantly he had given medical advice to a relative of a kitchen hand. All this while he awaited news from Lateef. Perhaps he should have rubbed a beer bottle sooner.

"What are you reading today, bwana?"

Kamal showed him the page. Lateef leaned forward, read a few lines slowly. Kamal inquired, testing him, "Why do you think Mzee Omari would praise the Germans after the Maji Maji War?"

"The German was powerful," said Lateef, straightening up. "It made good sense to flatter him. If you misbehaved, it could be the kiboko, the whip." He made a gesture, flicking his fingers. "You know, bwana, we Africans have had to be cunning."

"Yes," agreed Kamal, and recalled his mother. "Do you know how Mzee Omari died?" he asked.

"Yes, bwana."

Kamal was surprised. "Were you born by then? How old were you?"

The man looked down and said, "I heard."

"Do you know why he died?"

Lateef looked up and smiled sheepishly, which could mean anything.

Then he said, "Sir, I am still talking with the family about this woman Saida. They are very nervous."

"Nervous?"

"Enh." A heavy assertion.

"But why? About what?"

"They do not say, sir."

They eyed each other briefly as the barman brought Lateef a soda.

"You know, Lateef, I've been thinking. Perhaps they are the wrong people to talk to. Isn't there someone else who can give me the information?"

"These people know something, sir."

What do *you* know that you are not telling me?

"You think they want money."

"It could help."

Kamal gave him a few American bills and he left, saying he would be away on business the next day and would call or visit when he returned. He must have seen the desperation, the doubt on Kamal's face, but this time had no cheer to offer.

· 17 ·

He said—continuing from where he had left off—he said, speaking quietly in response to something earlier, "When I think of my life changing, so that I am what I am now, a medical doctor and returnee from abroad talking to you, instead of a local businessman or civil servant, it always begins dramatically, with the sound of running feet. Bare feet thumping the ground, a multitude of them, approaching. That thunder reverberates in me even now, it would come to torment me in the comfort of my study in Canada . . . and awaken the most painful memory."

It could have been a thief getting chased. Not an uncommon phenomenon; the fellow would get caught, beaten up, and taken to the police station in a raucous even joyful procession. It was fun to watch, though in retrospect not so much for the unfortunate thief. Such was the frantic roll of running feet outside their house early one morning, heading towards the main road. Kamal ran out with curiosity and after a moment's hesitation he too took to his feet. What boy could resist? The crowd, mostly men, kept up a pace, but no thief was in sight up ahead. The boy realized that this was not some fleet-footed shoplifter they were chasing, and where were the shouts of Mwizi! Mwizi! anyway? This was some other chase. But nobody had answers, everybody was running. And so he ran and he panted, until he arrived where others had stopped, at mwembe kinyonga, the hangman's tree. He pushed through the crowd, even as he overheard the disturbing buzz: The old man's hanged himself; Mzee Omari has taken his own life. Astaghfirullahi. Allah forgive him.

He reached the centre of the gathering under the old mango tree.

A few shehes, venerable old men, were tending to the body of Mzee Omari, as it now lay, flat on the ground in a muddy white kanzu; a noose lay beside him, having been removed from his neck, which was bruised red. His face was firm as always, his eyes were closed; on his feet, the ancient leather slippers. Beside him, his tasbih, the beads, and his embroidered white cap.

As Kamal gaped at this nightmare, all the time from behind him came the muttered prayers, Astaghfirullahi; adhubillahi shetani rajim . . . W'allahi karim.

He stared and he stared, his hand now clasped in someone else's next to him, a small, clammy hand, and he heard a sob, and felt a tug and glanced sideways to see that it was Saida. She started wailing softly, crying, "Polé Babu, Babu amefariki," and he wept with her, repeating her words, Grandfather has died, and then they slowly made their way home.

The streets were quiet that day, which was a Friday. Mzee Omari had chosen his day well. A light shower fell, though it was sunny, a sign from the heavens, for sure. People stood about to talk, and asked the same question, Why would a great man like Mzee Omari take his own life? If our spiritual leaders lost hope like this, what about us ordinary folk? He was a saidi, a man of God and descendant of the Prophet. Teller of our history. The azan from the big mosque was loud and clear, at noon and again at four. People went in numbers to pray.

The following morning an inspector of police, named Mwanga, flew in from Dar es Salaam. A stocky man with a bureaucrat's belly, wearing a long-sleeved bush shirt, Inspector Mwanga interrogated those who had found the body. Mzee Omari, he heard, had been found hanging from a thick branch of the famous mango tree, and a few men of the town had cut him down. Having heard the witnesses, the inspector was driven to the site in the government Land Rover, accompanied by the District Commissioner, and followed on foot by a crowd. The great tree, which had stopped bearing fruit many years before, stood by the roadside near the hospital. The two men walked towards it, the inspector in front. "So this is mwembe kinyonga," Inspector Mwanga exclaimed, "from which our heroes of the past were hanged!" He went forward and embraced the tree trunk. The onlookers found this behaviour amusing from a government man. The inspector walked a few times around the tree, deep in thought. The fat branch from which Mzee Omari had been cut down was cracked and split, it hung crooked. It was the same strong branch, the inspector was informed, which had held the weights of the old warriors. "If it could only talk," said the inspector. "This tree bears witness to our history." He walked back with the DC to the vehicle.

Inspector Mwanga departed early the next morning. Having spoken to witnesses, and examined the knot on the noose, he had determined that Mzee Omari had hanged himself. This was the conclusion he had reported to the DC and it spread through the town.

Mzee Omari was buried that day. His body, which had been kept at the hospital, was brought to the town in a procession, borne on the shoulders of men, a few of them walking with it all the way, while others waited on the highway to give it their shoulder when it passed. Kamal and Saida waited at the monument, and when the body arrived, they accompanied it home. The prayer ceremonies were brief and the corpse was taken in another procession to the cemetery behind Kamal's house.

The inspector's conclusion confirmed what most people had believed anyway, until it began to be whispered about that nothing had been found that Mzee Omari could have used to climb up to the height of the noose. Besides, the man was almost blind. He could not have hanged himself.

Evidently some menace had come to lurk in the town; who knew what else it was capable of? Stories of evil deeds of the past were recalled, and Mariamu the witch was remembered, who had only recently stopped stalking the streets at night. Finally some of the town's influential elders held a meeting outside the big mosque on the Friday following the death and came to an agreement that what was needed was someone who could root out and neutralize the evil. Such a man was the sorcerer, or mganga, Akilimali.

Akilimali was a native of the Kilwa region and the nation's most celebrated mganga, renowned for his ability to counter evil and discover hidden truths. His method was to use secret medicines. Recently he had garnered great fame by solving two cases which had stumped the police. In one of these, which happened at a sisal estate up north, a newborn baby belonging to a European couple was kidnapped; the police dragnet yielded no result, and witchcraft was suspected. The couple's plight drew great sympathy, and Akilimali was finally called as a police advisor. The mganga determined that the baby was alive and the kidnapper was none other than another European woman, from a neighbouring estate. The case made head-lines throughout East Africa.

Some years before Kamal's birth, Akilimali had been called to rid Kilwa of its evil spirits, which he claimed to have accomplished, sprinkling every corner of the municipality with a secret medicine. Now the town was ready to redeem his warranty. A messenger was sent to him at his home outside Dar es Salaam.

The day before the mganga arrived, three assistants came in a bus and went about snooping all over town, asking questions. The next day in the afternoon Akilimali himself appeared, riding up the main road on the back of a pickup, the sun like a bright halo behind him. The truck was bedecked with his witching paraphernalia—gourds, pots, bottles and pouches of medicines, strange-looking rattles, small drums, their grating jangle amply announcing his arrival. He sprang down in front of the monument, holding up his flywhisk, and instantly the crowds gathered, and watched from a good distance, awestruck. So this is the man. The mganga was a short man with surprisingly soft features, and he had an amused, enigmatic smile on his face. A smile to be feared, not answered. Like the grin of a leopard.

Having cast his gaze all around him, he was met by his three assis-tants, and went along with them, taking long jerking steps as they escorted him to the house which had been readied for him.

A kind of unease had settled upon Kilwa, a dread brought on by the uncertainty and doubts concerning Mzee Omari's death. An evil spirit was harassing the town. In the evenings, a couple of times, Mama took Kamal to the small mosque down the street, where they sat outside with other women and heard the men inside go "Allahu! Allahu!," chanting in unison and swaying back and forth, in the form of mystical prayer called dhikri.

Kamal asked his mother, "Mama, this Akilimali is a Muslim?"

"He sure is," she replied.

This was when they were returning from a sitting outside the mosque.

"Then why doesn't he ask Allah to give him an answer instead of using magic?"

"Maybe Allah doesn't give him the answer."

Mama had had their door bolt repaired against possible evil, though she said that with people down the street chanting Allah's name, no shetani could beset them. Besides, what was a mere bolt in the face of real evil?

On his first night in Kilwa, Akilimali stayed inside, in his allotted house down the street from Kamal and Mama. A hush fell on the neighbourhood. People didn't call out and there were no children outside. But the mganga had a quiet and steady stream of visitors who brought presents along with their shidas, difficulties to be resolved. Mama said that the sorcerer made a lot of money this way. Some of the sorcerer's visitors were Indian shopkeepers. "You ask me why they with their strange ways would appeal to African magic." He hadn't asked, but he listened to her answer. "Well, if it works, why not?"

In the morning, stories went around of the miraculous powers which Akilimali had demonstrated to his petitioners the previous night.

The second night, based on his interviews and investigations, Akilimali summoned a number of people to join him for a truth session under the hangman's mango tree. When Akilimali summoned, you went. If he didn't, you kept well out of the way and counted your luck, even as you waited impatiently for the outcome. It was not widely known who among the townsfolk had caught the mganga's attention, but secrets were about to emerge, chief among them the solution to the mystery of Mzee Omari's death. From Bi Kulthum, Mama learned that her mother Mwana Juma had been called. It was from Bi Kulthum that Kamal and his mother heard the details about the proceedings.

Akilimali gathered twelve nervous people of the town under the hangman's tree. Among them was Salemani Mkono, the one-armed. The sorcerer bade all but one of them, Mwana Juma, to sit in a half circle before him on the ground. With him facing the half circle were his three young assistants and the diminutive Mwana Juma, also seated, privileged to witness the truth emerge about her husband's death. There was a small lamp present, along with the mganga's paraphernalia. The master and his assistants began by performing a short dance, beating their drums, banging on a tambourine, and singing. Abruptly, using his flywhisk the mganga went around sprinkling liquid from a gourd upon his guests; it tasted like honey water. Outside this gathering all was quiet and deserted. The hospital nearby was covered in pitch darkness. The music and dancing stopped, and Akilimali went around peering at all those assembled. He acknowledged each of them, then he sat down and started to speak. Akilimali's expression did not waver as he spoke. He maintained a mild and brisk manner and that mysterious smile that seemed to probe their thoughts. His voice was pleasant and high in pitch, and he terminated his sentences with his characteristic raised inflection that Bi Kulthum would later demonstrate with gusto.

"A strange event, an ajabu has occurred in this town, Kilwa Kivinje. A great poet and scholar, Mzee Omari, he was found hanging from this tree—this ancient one, this one which has seen our warriors hang. The police have come and gone. He hanged himself, they say. Then how did he reach the noose, up there? I ask. My powers of seeing have shown me, my hidden eyes have told me—some agency put him there. Each of you has been called here, under this ancient tree, where the old man hung, why? Because you have something to reveal. From what you say, I will conclude. Yes, my friends. Now each of you will drink this uji. You may choose not to drink this porridge. We live in a free country, we are told, a democrasia, they call it. But then I will draw my conclusions. But if you drink it, your spirit will talk. And I will listen. And this mama will listen, whose husband, a great man, was found hanging from a noose."

It was a long process. In such sessions, the guilty party took the medicine in the belief that refusing to participate gave them away; if the guilty party was a sorcerer or sorceress, they hoped by their own powers to defy the mganga. In the other of Akilimali's famous cases, a coven of sorcerers had murdered a young woman by slitting her throat and dividing up her body. All were present and rendered powerless at the truth session that exposed them.

Akilimali's powers were such that sometimes he had grasped the truth from your mouth before you even uttered it. Bi Kulthum demonstrated this by grabbing at the air before her face.

"Didn't his boys go nosing around town?" Mama asked. "That would tell him secrets."

"Yes," Bi Kulthum agreed, "that would help him."

"Suppose he made up his own truth," Mama wondered, "suppose he—"

"Watch what you say, Hamida," Bi Kulthum interrupted. "That man is powerful."

That night at the hangman's tree there was one obvious suspect, Salemani Mkono, who had hated and derided Mzee Omari, had a long history of antipathy towards him. Nothing significant emerged from any of those who drank the uji before him. A woman confessed to adultery; an old man to theft; another man to lewd thoughts about a boy. It was just before dawn when Salemani took the cup.

Yes, he said, he had despised Mzee Omari, whose cronies the Germans sent him to the work camps in the north where he lost one arm; the teacher Omari sat with them sipping tea from their dainty cups and sang their praises, and made himself into a German, when his own brother had hung from this same tree under which they were sitting now, from the same branch where Mzee Omari had finally hung. That was justice. No, he did not touch Mzee Omari! But early in the morning before sunrise, as the azan was given at the mosque, and the Banyanis were getting up to go and sing at their prayer house, he woke up where he was sleeping outside a shop and saw Mzee Omari walking on the long road, his head bowed. And then ahead of the old poet, almost hidden by the darkness, Salemani saw a shadowy figure in bui-bui, covered head to toe. They both were walking slowly, keeping the distance between them. After waiting for some moments, Salemani followed in their direction, until he saw them come to stand under this tree. They seemed to wait. Salemani watched. Then suddenly—he did not know how! he swore—there had appeared a noose hanging from the tree branch, and a stool under it. Salemani ran away towards the town as fast as he could. He ran until he had no breath left. He almost died.

Akilimali departed Kilwa with fanfare, having first gone all around the town with his flywhisk and rid it of any residual malevolent spirits. He took with him the considerable payments and presents he had received: bundles of cloth, a cage full of chickens, a goat, and an amount of money that could only be guessed at. The pickup had arrived earlier. Before getting on, the mganga and his assistants did a small dance. Then Akilimali got in next to the driver, the assistants climbed in the back to join the chickens and goat, and they drove away.

What truth did Akilimali uncover? He had made his report to the town's elders and to Mwana Juma, and then the rest of Kilwa heard it. It came out that Mzee Omari had caused his own death, having constantly called up the past with the aid of a djinn. Now the poet had reached the end of his utenzi, he had no further need of his djinn. But you can not so easily dismiss a djinn. Out of spite, the jilted Idris poisoned the poet's mind and led him to the mango tree and there caused him to hang himself. And then the djinn went away to seek another home. The past is a dangerous business, warned Akilimali; it is best to keep it buried.

And so Kilwa came to terms with its poet's death.

Mama acted strangely, suddenly took to advising Kamal about the ways of the world, matters he didn't wish to care about. Always pretend you don't really need it when you go to buy something, umesikia Kamalu? Do you hear me? That way you'll keep the price down. As though he cared. Did he ever go shopping by himself? No. Remember, these Indians can be nice; they have values too. Why would he argue with that? Wasn't his father one? But his father had gone away, never written a letter to him. And Kamal had never been to an Indian home, never had an Indian friend. So they had values. He noticed too that Mama was avoiding physical closeness with him. Before, she would often draw him into her bosom; now, when he embraced her she would turn stiff. It was hurtful. There was still that sideways glance of before as she sat down with her needle and thread, watching him, but without the caressing smile and the twinkle in her eyes. She spent more time away from home, ostensibly on some errands; she would sit outside on the porch, casually chatting with the barber under the tree, or a neighbour, or a passerby when Kamal sat inside studying.

Saida had stopped coming home altogether, and he didn't find her at the seashore, or out in the streets vending something, or loitering outside her house. Bi Kulthum did not make vitumbua any longer; his breakfast on a good day was now a slice of bread or a mandazi.

Sometimes while playing outside, he couldn't help glancing down the street in case by some miracle Saida had turned the corner and was on her way, shuffling along as usual.

Once, out walking at the shore, he saw Mama seated on the grass verge all by herself, looking out to the sea. He went and sat beside her. "What a beautiful world God has made for us," she said after a while.

Recently, visitors had come to their home, first two Indian men and then one African, and later a woman accompanied by Bi Kulthum. Each time the adults waited for him to depart before conversing. He had assumed that they had come with proposals, which his Mama would reject. Mama fretted because there was no money with which to buy biscuits to serve her guests. "W'allahi, we are that poor," she muttered in despair.

"Mama, I will open my sanduku," he offered his savings box, but she refused.

One morning on a Sunday, when he was especially listless, Mama said, "Do you know that Saida solves shida? She is a big girl now, and she's gifted, they say."

"Eh—what shida does she solve?" he replied angrily. "She knows nothing! How can she solve shida?"

"We'll go there and see."

That afternoon they went to Bi Kulthum's house, and entered through the backyard. Bi Kulthum was not around. Mwana Juma welcomed them and after the greetings invited them to go inside to see Saida. There were four people waiting for Saida in the corridor outside one of the rooms. A teenage girl sat with her mother on a short bench, and a boy of six sat with his mother on the ground. Mwana Juma brought Mama a stool and she sat down facing the other four visitors.

"Is it the girl—what ails her?" Mama asked the first mother.

"She is pregnant."

There followed a silence, as Mama turned away, before the woman spoke again, rather peevishly.

"My girl has not known any man. It is a shetani that's possessed her. The mganga can remove him."

What did Saida know about removing spirits from people?

The little boy with his mother was suffering from lethargy.

Kamal stood there beside his mother. This long corridor had always been quiet; he had stood here last waiting to see Mzee Omari in his room, to make him an offering of writing paper, pencil, and eraser. He had sat inside with Mzee Omari, read to him and heard him recite. And now? What had happened to Saida, this girl who not long ago had cried for her grandfather, who had held his hand? Had she become someone else? How did she become a mganga? Had she completely gone from his life?

The last time they were together, and he had patted her shoulder and wiped away the tears from her face, he had felt the first stirrings of something. He didn't know what it meant, exactly. In school, boys talked about things, and he read comic books about young men and women in love. They were white people, and the English words were sometimes difficult, but he understood enough and he wanted to be in love. The taarabs, in Swahili, too sang about love, as did the Indian and English songs on the radio. You didn't have to understand the language to know it was love.

Their turn came, and Kamal and Mama entered the room. It was an ordinary bedroom, at the centre of which, on a mat, sat Saida. In front of her was a thick, ancient-looking leather-bound Quran. She wore a new dress and her hair was combed neatly. He and Mama sat before her on the ground and exchanged greetings. Mwana Juma stood at the door.

Mama said, "Tuna shida, eh Saida." We have troubles.

"Did you bring a gift?" asked Saida shyly.

Mama put a coin before Saida, who said, "Tell me your shida."

"Tell her your shida, Kamalu," Mama said.

Kamal looked at his mother. He could not think of a shida; if it was anything, it was to ask Saida why she had disappeared.

Saida said, as shyly as before, "Bi Hamida, I must hear his problem alone. Please." She sounded very adult.

Surprised, Mama said, "All right," and got up.

"Na Bibi," Saida invoked, looking at her grandmother, who took the cue and also left through the door.

"Why haven't you come, Saida?" Kamal whispered. "Did you fall sick? Eti, what kind of mganga are you?"

"Sijui." I don't know. "They told me to sit here."

"Aren't you going to come out, Saida? Will you always hide yourself here? Don't you want to go about?"

At this point Mwana Juma looked in and asked, "Has he described his problem? Give him the response."

Saida said to Kamal, "Say the Sura Fatiha. Seven times."

"You gave the same verse to the other two," said her grandmother.

"And the same one to Kamalu. Seven times."

"Goodbye, Saida," Kamal said. "And I will say the sura seven times."

Then Mama went in, and emerged after a few minutes.

"What shida did you have, Mama?" Kamal asked on the way back.

"No need for you to know," she replied, but with a smile. Then she asked, "What did she give you? Sura Fatiha?"

"Yes," he replied.

"I don't know what kind of mganga she is. It is always difficult to know, but there is no harm in trying. What kind of shida do you have?"

"I have no shida. I only asked her why she doesn't come out."

They walked home in silence.

There she was, the next afternoon, at that hot, sultry hour, watching the waves in the harbour, waiting for him. Joyfully he hurried towards her.

"So you came."

"Mm-hm."

He noticed that she wore a khanga over her shoulders now, to be able to cover her head when required. At first they simply stood there, exchanging news. Then gradually they ambled over to the path by the creek and made their way to their little lagoon and sat down there.

"Saida—eti, how did you become a mganga? A djinn came to you?"

"My grandfather."

"Mzee Omari himself? He came to you?"

"I dreamt him. Three times."

"Three times! Your luck. What did he say? Did he recite to you?"

"He told me to help people."

"Help people?"

That thin childish voice tugged at him, he would never be able to forget it. He sensed a helplessness to her. She was told that the old man had chosen her, and she could help people solve their problems by telling them what suras from the Quran to recite. She should open Mzee Omari's old Quran at random, and wherever it opened would be the sura to prescribe. Sometimes she forgot to open the Book, and simply told them to recite Sura Fatiha.

"Saida—let's get into the water!"

"No . . . I don't want to."

They walked back to the square where Mwana Juma found them and took Saida away.

They met again a few days later. This time, sitting in their hideaway at the lagoon, he asked her, "Saida, can I put my head on your lap? So I can see the sky." Of course it was too bright to see the sky. But she agreed, and he had to cover his eyes with his hands against the glare. Soon she said, "We must go." But before they parted she gave him the hand-wrought, silver box with the flutter inside. The tawiz. "You must keep it with you," she said. "It has a dua." A prayer. "A dua?" he asked. "What kind?"

She ran and he chased her, back up the path before they slowed down, panting, and parted, he clutching the tawiz in his hand, she with the khanga pulled over her head.

So she knew that day that he was to go away. He didn't.

"I always imagined," he said to me, "that the prayer inside the tawiz was something she had herself written down. Why would I think that? I don't know. That little flutter inside the box . . . that little heartbeat was an intimate reminder of her. It was her prayer for me. Later I began to wonder if perhaps it was not Mzee Omari who had written the prayer and put the paper inside the box before it was sealed."

"Or someone else could have written it?" I posed.

He turned thoughtful, and at once I picked up the trail.

"Do you still believe," I asked him, "that when the half-seeing Mzee Omari wrote, the djinn Idris guided his hand? You are a rational man, Dr. Kamal—do you actually believe there was an Idris?"

He smiled, sheepishly, I think, and said slowly, "It was a comfortable belief to have, which I clung to for many years, without actually confronting it rationally. Everyone believed there was Idris—his personal djinn and assistant who in the end turned on him and killed him. This neatly explained the mystery of his death. Idris was a part of my life. He had assumed a personality for me. He was the one who slapped me, and tripped me, and threw stones at me." He became silent. Unconsciously he had gripped the front of his shirt, under which the tawiz hung. He turned to meet my look and said, "If there was no Idris, why did Mzee Omari invoke him as his muse when he wrote those long poems, the wonderful utenzi? That history of the 'coming of the modern age' in our country? If there was no Idris, how did Mzee Omari die?"

"And . . . ?"

"The revelation dawned rather slowly."

The discovery of the truth did not follow a chronology, coming at the end of painstaking research; it did not come as an explosion of light, lux and veritas. Bits of Mzee Omari's story had already tantalized him as a child; he was a curious boy, often to his mother's exasperation. After he left Kilwa he learned the story of his own Indian grandfather. His later obsession with rare books that had anything to do with the town of his birth revealed to him a patchy history of a backwater belonging to the farthest fringes of mainstream interest. But it was his.

Is it too precious to draw a connection between a middle-aged doctor in the wintry isolation of his study in suburban Canada, carefully turning an illustrated page of a rare book, and the boy sitting quietly on a tropical shore at night listening to a verse recitation of a history? On a couple of occasions of conference travel he had entered the hushed preserves of colonial archives. His revelation is what he arrived at gradually, a story of Kilwa. It begins in the distant past and ends with the death of the poet.

We have agreed that this is the best juncture at which to place it, at the end of his own story in Kilwa. It is told in his own words.

Two

❧

...of the coming of the modern age

· 19 ·

It was suddenly revealed to young Punja Devraj, as he sat partaking of a communal meal at Sidi Sayyad's shrine in Singpur, India, that he should go to Africa. It was summer, sometime in the 1870s. A wish had been fulfilled, a goat had been slaughtered.

Singpur was a long way from the port city of Verawal on the Arabian Sea, in the province of Gujarat, where Punja had come from, walking part of the way on the forest roads and catching rides on farmers' bullock carts at other times. Africa was not entirely foreign to the western ports of India; since olden times ships had plied the ocean between the two continents, carrying a small but steady trade. More recently an increasing stream of adventurous souls had departed from the port towns to go to work or trade in Africa; those who had returned had acquired conspicuous wealth, and moreover spoke a foreign tongue bizarre enough to brag about. But Singpur, lying in the hinterland, had a different connection to Africa. It was home to the Sidis, the dark people whose ancestors had travelled the other way, from Africa to India, some centuries before and never returned. Their saint, Sidi Sayyad, was known widely for his magical powers. Upon advice, Punja had come to supplicate this saint with a wish. Go to Sidi Sayyad in Singpur and ask, he had been told, ask with open heart and promise him a gift and you will obtain your heart's desire. And so Punja had brought with him a can of the purest ghee as a gift, and his earnest wish: that he be accepted by the family of a certain pretty and wonderful girl of Verawal, whom he desired for a wife.

When Punja arrived in Singpur, a noisy festival was in progress. There were black folk, the Sidis, everywhere and there was the sound of drumming the like of which Punja had not heard before. It came from the location of a prominent white dome, at the end of the main street, where a frantic crowd had gathered. He assumed that the dome marked the famous shrine. As he approached it and asked some loitering boys what was going on, he was told that a maanta, a special rite, was in progress. He hurried forward, and reaching the gate of the shrine he threw off his slippers next to a pile of footwear and pushed his way into the crowded compound.

A chaotic procession was heading towards the entrance of the small square building with the dome that was the shrine. This melee was led by four dancers, a lithe bare-chested youth, two older men, and an old woman; behind them came two drummers, one of them lean and with a blind man's stare. The short black woman in front moved as though in a trance, her feet following the rhythm of the drums in slow dancing steps and her body swaying likewise as she meandered forward. The bare-chested youth leapt about, from side to side and forwards and backwards, collecting the donations of coins thrown down generously by the crowd.

It was a wonderful, magical sight: a procession of black folk, a dance so unlike the ones performed by his folk in Verawal. Behind the dancers and drummers followed a black goat, wearing garlands of bright yellow marigolds, its sides daubed with coloured flour, and goaded forward by two young boys.

What kind of maanta was this?

It had been requested by a family from Junagadh, the nearby princely capital. The belief was that if the saint accepted the maanta, he would fulfill the supplicants' wishes; to signal this boon, the decorated goat would climb up the steps into the sanctuary of the mausoleum and greet the saint. This was exactly what the goat, shy and confused as a bridegroom, proceeded to do, to much applause, and as was the custom it was taken away to be slaughtered for a communal meal of biriyani.

As the supplicants came away and the mausoleum emptied, Punja entered the small room where the raised grave of Sidi Sayyad lay, covered with a mound of coloured cloths and flowers. A sweet perfume hung heavy in the air. Punja stood humbly before the grave, eyes lowered, hands raised in prayer, and said, "Pir Bawa, if it is your wish, let Sherbanoo's father and her elders change their minds and accept my proposal." He put his can of ghee on the floor and departed, with prayers on his lips and making sure to step respectfully backwards as he left.

Punja came outside into the compound and joined a circle of men seated on the ground awaiting the meal. They were of the supplicating family, and it turned out that the elders among them knew his father, Devraj Madhvani of Verawal, the ghee merchant. Punja learned that the maanta had been requested in aid of a child who lay sick at death's door in Junagadh. The holy Sidi Sayyad had given them hope.

Punja heard it said that the ancestors of the dark curly-headed folk of Singpur had come originally from a wonderful island called Jangbar in Africa. It had a forest denser than the Gir, and lions more fierce. But in the island's city there was wealth for the asking. You could trade in spices, cloth, beads, ironware, and, if you possessed the means, in ivory and slaves as well; communities of Khojas, Bhatias, and Shamsis were already thriving in Jangbar. Potmakers, shoemakers, and barbers too had set up there. Food grew plentifully, droughts were unknown, and a dhow could take you there in a few days. The ruler was an Arab sultan, who desired Indians to come and do business in his domain. You returned in a few years, a rich man, speaking a secret foreign language called Sawahili. But the wonder was that here in India the Sidis themselves had forgotten their Sawahili; they spoke only Gujarati and Urdu.

It was as he heard these tales of the spice island of opportunity and its friendly sultan, away from anything he'd known, that the revelation struck Punja: he need not marry Sherbanoo at all, if her folks were against him; they had called him too unsettled, and they were right. He would go to Jangbar. The Pir of Jangbar, Sidi Sayyad himself, had beckoned him. This is what he would always relate. Sidi Sayyad had sent him to Africa to take his greetings to his people.

It turned out that Sidi Sayyad also fulfilled his original wish, for Sherbanoo was given to him in marriage before he sailed away by himself on a dhow bound for Jangbar, which was also known as Unguja and Zanzibar. Sherbanoo would follow him when he was settled.

A spice-filled fragrance suffused the evening air as they approached the island, grabbing them all in its cloying, clammy embrace; the Muslims among them heeded the evening azan, called by a fellow passenger, and facing north they said their prayer. There followed a farewell meal of fish broth, vegetable curry, and pilau, which was easily the best of the entire journey, incorporating in its tastes all the exotic richness of the surrounding air, after which a drumbeat started and singing began. Finally the immigrants lay down on their mattresses and slept the sleep of the drugged, each to entertain his or her own fantastic dreams of the future. In the morning, smiles accompanying the hot tea after prayer, the *Khadija*'s sails puffed up as the salty sea breeze blew across the bow, and the boards of the ship cracked their joints as if it too had awoken and welcomed the sun, and the palm-fringed tip of the island appeared as in a dream under a light blue sky.

The sight of Zanzibar harbour, where a few dhows lay anchored and smaller vessels of various sizes scurried to and fro, a steamship or two waiting in the horizon, was one to set the heart of any young man on fire who had come to seek a destiny here. Punja alighted on the jetty and pushed through the throngs of porters and people come to receive the passengers. He had no one waiting for him, but he had the address of a merchant, a member of his Shamsi community, who could not possibly deny him assistance, and so he made his way there.

Men of all races mingled in the streets of Zanzibar; you might see a European in white shirt and trousers and white helmet out for a walk, a stick in hand that possibly concealed a blade; a fair-skinned Arab lord in white robe and embroidered vest, and a turban, carried in a litter or out for a walk with a retinue; Sikh policemen in khaki; Baluchi soldiers; Gujaratis and Kutchis from India, in their white dhotis or in trousers and various headgear; Arab or Swahili womenfolk in veil. There were the Africans, some lordly in demeanour and dressed like the Arabs, others mere servants; and crooked lines of slaves in chains, miserable men and women kidnapped from the mainland, already shorn of all human dignity, scantily dressed, heading towards the market to be sold and transported to wherever fate took them. In this entrepôt there was no pity; you made of your station what you could; those who could help you were your kinfolk. Everyone had a community, except the slave.

Most men who arrived in Zanzibar went onward in due time to the mainland, where they settled in one of the port towns, in Dar es Salaam, Mombasa, Malindi, Bagamoyo, Kilwa, or Lindi, where opportunities were greater, for the city was small and crowded. From the port towns the braver souls headed farther inland into the interior, to live and trade in isolation and gradually start new communities. Punja, whose family were dealers in ghee back in Gujarat, found a job with a merchant of spice and grain. He knew his weights and measures, kept abreast of market prices, could go to the port and negotiate duties on Indian imports.

One day at the harbour, awaiting the release of a newly arrived consignment of goods for his employer, Punja ran into the customs master Tharia Topan. The tall, pale-skinned Tharia in his Khoja turban always cut an imposing, severe figure abetted in its effect by his grey eyes and trimmed beard; he was one of the richest and most powerful men on the island; no ship docked at the harbour, or departed, without his say-so. The sultan, it was said, always owed him money, as did a lot of the city's traders. Tharia was on his way to board a dhow and noticed his assistant missing. He turned and glared at young Punja.

"Here, take this notebook. Do you know how to write?"

"Yes, Ji, I can write very well."

"Can you count?"

The young man nodded and rolled his head side to side: of course.

"Whose son are you?" Tharia demanded. Punja explained his background, and was abruptly told, "Let's go. Come with me. Get on the boat, we're going to check out that dhow from Kutch."

When Punja's story would be related many years later, it was always to present him as a simple yet independent soul, who left all and went away to seek a destiny in Africa. He was an ordinary guy, capable but not especially brave or pious. The moment he met Tharia Topan his course, set initially for him by Sidi Sayyad, was further directed as by a firm but friendly wind; the great man offered him employment as a clerk. Some years later Punja Devraj was Tharia Topan's chief assistant, an influential man in his own right, and as incorruptible as his master.

Down the street from his house, as a grateful businessman, Punja endowed a mosque in honour of Sidi Sayyad of Singpur. It came to be called the mosque of Saidi Puri, and on the special day of that saint, a goat was slaughtered and cooked for a feast. On that occasion, Punja might say to his friends and neighbours that Saidi Puri had returned home. He would relate his oft-told story of his journey on foot through the great Gir forest to pay homage to the saint; he would relate the miracle of the goat; and embellishing a little he would tell of a strange incident involving a lion from the forest. The story went as follows. On his way back home from the shrine of Singpur that fateful day, as evening fell, Punja sat by the roadside under a tree to say his prayers and eat what remained of his roti and pickle. He was nervous; all was quiet around him save for the whisperings from the swaying branches overhead. Suddenly Punja heard a roar that startled him—and saw in the near distance the silhouette of a lion, its face turned directly towards him. Terrified, Punja first called on the name of Imam Ali, whose symbol was also a lion, and then he took the name of Sidi Sayyad. The lion gave another, gentler roar and walked away into the dusk. Who could it have been but Sidi Sayyad himself come to wish him bon voyage! Punja Devraj stood up and resumed his journey without fear.

One afternoon, some fifteen years after Punja's arrival in Zanzibar, he was summoned to the palace. Upon arrival at the royal house, which looked out at the harbour, he was made to wait in the cavernous lobby, before being taken upstairs to the receiving room to see the sultan. The room was on the front side of the building. Said Bargash, whose father had moved the capital of his Arab empire from Oman to Zanzibar in 1837, was seated on his upholstered chair, making use of the carved armrests. On either side of him stood a Baluchi soldier. The other notables, sitting before the king in two rows, discreetly stood up and walked away outside to the corridor to murmur among themselves.

"Punja Devraj, I have a mission for you," the sultan droned after the greetings, in a toneless, tired voice, and flicked his prayer beads as he did so. He was dressed in a black outer coat over a white frock, with thin gold embroidery running down the front, and a green-and-black turban with specks of gold. His ceremonial dagger was tucked in at the belt. His eyes probed the Indian who stood before him.

Punja Devraj was a small, thin man still in his thirties, dressed in European-style trousers and a white linen coat, with a black fez on his head. Along with other island notables he had been in the sultan's presence during the annual Eid and Maulidi festivals, close enough on a few occasions to bow before him.

"I am your servant, Your Highness," he replied quickly to the sultan.

Punja was a nervous man at that moment. A sultan was a sultan, no matter what; he deserved loyalty, especially from a Muslim. He was a commander of the faithful and his name was invoked at Friday prayers. But he was of a family that were a breed apart in every way and full of intrigues and whims. For the most part they left you alone to do your business, and to run your private life. You were advised to let it stay that way. The men were arrogant; their women haughty—and diverse, and beautiful, Arabs, Africans, green-eyed Circassians. When they passed you on the streets, in their gleaming silks, their faces covered, attendants by the side and behind them, you respectfully but hastily greeted them, and the slaves bowed down to the ground. A man could be stopped and whipped on the spot on the mere suspicion of disrespect. The princes were often at daggers drawn, moreover, when you avoided them and their worthless hangers-on even more. Bargash himself had not long ago attempted to wrest the throne from his brother Majid, and when he failed he was forced into exile in Bombay. Tharia Topan had accompanied him. But Tharia was a powerful man.

"Tharia recommended you as trustworthy," the sultan continued, "and I trust Tharia."

"I will be happy to serve, Your Highness," Punja replied.

The sultan's eyes fixed thoughtfully upon Punja, while the brown beads in his hands clicked their uneven beat.

"The matter is urgent," Said Bargash said finally, with an ever so slight change in the voice. "And it is secret. We cannot play our hand openly—or else Allah knows what will be this island's fate."

Punja was well aware of the king's troubles, as who was not, even the lowliest servant on this island. They were of concern to the town's eminent citizens, the businessmen, who worried about its future and their fortunes, and they were the talk in the gatherings of immigrants in their temples and mosques. Zanzibar was in the midst of a crisis, your barber would tell you that. The way of life long known on the coast was under threat because a different and powerful race of people, hitherto only casual visitors in these parts, had arrived in numbers, bearing arms and with intentions. The once energetic sultan, who had returned from exile with ideas of greatness, was losing control to Europe. While Punja had been waiting downstairs in the lobby, a tall, bearded Scotsman, as well known to all Zanzibaris as the palace building itself, had come down the stairs from the royal presence. On his long face was the genial smile that could have said anything. Dr. John Kirk was the British Consul.

Yes, Sultan Bargash had his worries. The grey in his full beard was of recent vintage, as were the bags under his eyes that gave him the rather mournful new look. Now his sister Princess Salme was in town, and five German warships had their guns trained on the palace.

Two decades ago, the princess had had a scandalous affair with a German businessman; bearing his child, she had escaped in a British ship to Europe, where she had become a Christian and married the man, called Ruete. On her native island she could have been executed on two counts. Now she was back to make demands upon her brother, protected by the warships. Dressed like a European, the woman walked about freely and arrogantly, accompanied by her half-breed, gawked at by the public. There were factions in the palace and among the clergy who demanded Islamic justice for her adultery and her apostasy. The sultan could do nothing. It was likely that Dr. Kirk had come to discuss these developments regarding the princess and the warships.

The sultan said, "You saw the mzungu, Kirk, walk out of this hall as you came in. He is our protector, as you know." He paused. "But beware when a wolf appoints himself your protector."

And beware when a sultan tells you secrets. Due to what was he, Punja Devraj of Verawal and now of Zanzibar, a trader of modest achievement, privileged to hear politics from the sultan?

"The Europeans have their eyes on our territory," Sultan Bargash said. "The whole of Africa Masharik. Like bandits they have swooped down upon us. The mainland, all along the coast from Mombasa down to Kilwa and Lindi, and way into the interior up to Tabora and Ujiji, has been under us, the Omanis. But the Europeans have the guns. They will take it. I have been assured that this island will not be touched, and perhaps the mainland coast. I want to send you to Kilwa, my friend. I want you to reassure my subjects in Kilwa and the coastal regions to the south that their welfare is very much upon my mind. And I want you, Punja Devraj, to be the new ambassador and customs collector in Kilwa. Will you leave Zanzibar and go to Kilwa on my behalf?"

So this was it. Not a question but a command. A promotion and a trust, but also an exile.

"Yes, Your Highness," Punja replied. "I will go on your behalf and reassure your subjects. And I will collect customs duties. Rest assured that your flag will keep flying high on the coast."

"As God wills. You are a good man, Punja. I can see that. I will have a letter prepared for my Vali in Kilwa. He may be forced to return to Zanzibar—for a short time, if God wills—but you should remain. And shortly I will also send an eminent man to see you. He will tell you of matters that I cannot know about."

As I gather and construct this history of my shadowy ancestor, I cannot but be awed by the prospect—how precarious yet true it appears, how necessary it is. My life as a child had begun and ended with my mother, whom I lost, who would occasionally release to me tantalizing snippets of information, always ending with the formula "And God knows the rest." My father's antecedents she had turned into characters out of the *Arabian Nights*. Only Mzee Omari, the poet, had hinted at Punja Devraj's life and activities in Kilwa, but that story was tied into a knot involving the poet's own shame, and he was not going to reveal it all. That so much of our history lies scattered in fragments in the most diverse places and forms—fading memories, brief asides or incidentals in books and in archives—is lamentable, but at least they exist. All we need do is call up the fragments, reconfigure the past.

Once on a visit to Los Angeles, at a literary soiree of East Africans—a gathering where the samosas and chai were as important as the book reading—I came across a Zanzibari instructor of Swahili at the university, who happened to be a descendant of Tharia Topan, the customs master who had summarily hired my great-grandfather at the docks and later in all good faith had him sent to Kilwa to meet his fate, and make mine. Thus our scattered selves—precious and rare like the rarest of stones.

The man who came to see Punja Devraj at his home was a tall, charismatic figure in the crisp white kanzu and white kofia of a pious Muslim. He was more African than Arab, with a rich and scraggly glistening black beard that rather became him; he spoke in a full voice, and his pleasant smile revealed an attractive set of even white teeth. His name was Wasim, and he was a follower of Sheikh Ayesi of Somalia. That sheikh was a Sufi teacher worshipped by many in Zanzibar. Every time he arrived on the island, his followers received him with much ceremony and bore him away on a palanquin, singing, playing music, and bearing flags. It was in one such procession that Punja had seen Wasim, striding cheerfully alongside his master's lifted carriage. The Sufis achieved their piety through devotion to their sheikh and following his teachings. They met in the evenings for their dhikri, or chanting sessions, during which they invoked the name of God. The power of that holy chant, *La ilaha illallah*, recited in ecstatic unison, was mesmerizing, and often just enough to attract many to these mystical orders. But in these dark times, Wasim told him, the aim of the Sufi orders in Africa and in India and in the Middle East was also to preserve Islamic ways from corruption by the Europeans, and therefore to take measures to throw off the yoke of foreign colonialism, and moreover to spread Islam in regions where it had not taken root.

Even the sultan, said Wasim, was a follower of Sheikh Ayesi.

"I hear you," said Punja. "But what can ordinary folk like us do who do not bear arms or have the ear of sultans?"

"When you get to the mainland," said Wasim, "be sure to give support to our people who are resisting the white man. This is a jihad. Soon we may be able to drive the infidel out."

Punja said he would do all he could to support the cause of the sultan.

By this time, Punja had two wives. His Indian bride Sherbanoo had followed him to Zanzibar, bringing with her their young son. Meanwhile, in the manner of other men, he had also married a second wife, a local Arab woman called Zara. By these two wives he had a total of six children. He left all of them in Zanzibar to set himself up in Kilwa.

· 20 ·

It was a placid little town that suddenly appeared in the distance edging a harbour, embraced from the left and right by dark green forests of tall, slim mangroves. As the kidau, the small dhow, sailed in, the white seafront shimmered against the morning sunlight, the building to the farthest left much bigger and higher than the rest, evidently the administrative quarters, the boma. The dhow anchored, and Punja alighted onto one of the boats which had arrived to row the passengers to the shore. As he came ashore and climbed up to the landing at the town square, a thickset figure stirred from amidst the waiting crowd and pushed forward to greet him. The man looked eerily familiar.

"Punja Devraj," said the man, "welcome to our town. God bless. We have been eagerly waiting for you."

They stared at each other, a twinkle in the other man's eyes.

Punja returned the greeting, then asked: "You wouldn't be . . . you were not at . . . ?"

"Singpur!" they shouted at once then burst out laughing. What a coincidence!

Kassu Ghulamu, for that was the man's name, had been present that day many years ago at the shrine of Sidi Sayyad in Singpur, a younger member of the large party which had come to seek help for their sick child. Punja had observed him at the communal meal as one who had stayed in the background and kept silent. He had seemed the same age as Punja was. The sick girl was healed and was now the mother of his five children, Kassu proudly informed Punja.

"You were not expecting me, by any chance?" Punja asked. "Or do you go to greet every dhow that arrives?"

"Word travels, but we also come to greet new arrivals. And besides, a certain Sufi has spoken well of you."

"His name wouldn't be Wasim?"

"He comes by."

Kassu too had resolved that day in Singpur to go to Africa. "When I saw your interest, Punja Bhai," he said, leading the way into the town, "when I saw the light shine in your eyes as you heard of this place called Zanzibar, I knew right there that you were headed for Africa. That resolve came to me too, but slowly."

"That day I saw my calling," Punja repeated his oft-told credo. "Sidi Sayyad instructed me to come to Africa."

"He instructed both of us."

Kassu had followed two years later. It was surprising they had not met in Zanzibar, because Kassu had stopped on the island before heading off to the mainland. He looked bigger than Punja remembered him—more than fifteen years had passed—and in the manner of a provincial was dressed informally, his large shirt hanging out and his slippers ploughing a trail in the sand.

Beyond the harbour, the streets were beginning to stir: a couple of men emerging at their doorways still in their nightclothes; the smell of woodsmoke; a woman's voice singing inside a house—life tucked away at the side, in the bagal, of the continent, whose vastness and reserves were awesomely apparent to the visitor as he looked away from this coastal coziness to the beyond. The casual spread of the distant hills seemed to know no boundary; the sight of the green, extending in wave upon wave of limitless landscape into the horizon, brightened in inches by the rising sun behind him, was enough to take the breath away. Through all that vastness ran the routes along which the caravans brought back the ivory, which was taken to all the ports of the world. Not many years ago the routes had also brought back slaves, before the British warships put an end to the trade. And into the interior went cloth, metalware, beads, and jewelry. This was his new home, this small but ancient entry point into the continent, he the appointed gatekeeper. He had sold all he had accumulated in order to settle here. His prospects, from what he had gathered from his mentor, Tharia, were good. A trader was a trader, said Tharia, whatever else changes.

Behind the seafront was a row of large white stone houses where the Indian traders lived; here a shop and house had been arranged for Punja, who also had an office in the boma as the customs agent. All arrivals were reported to him; sometimes he went to meet them. All the exports and imports were entered into his ledger and appropriate duties collected. A monthly tax was collected from the traders. From the treasury a few policemen and a peon were paid. From what remained, Punja gave a percentage to the Vali, the sultan's local governor.

But Punja's official status did not last long.

Late one morning, three months after his arrival in Kilwa, a few boats were sighted in the harbour, heading towards the shore. People stopped to watch. There was something special about them, the way they stayed together. Two Germans landed, accompanied by armed askaris and much baggage. Showing the Vali, who was among those who had gone down to greet them, a decree in Arabic, the two men instructed him that they had the authority to take over the administration of the town. The sultan's green flag was thereupon brought down by their soldiers and the German eagle went up the flagpole outside the boma and was saluted. All the bystanders were commanded to stand still, at the point of the askaris' rifles, as one of the two white men stood to attention and, his eyes raised to the flag, solemnly sang an anthem. It was the day of Eid, the morning prayers had not begun.

The Vali left the next morning by dhow. And Punja had no more business at the boma. When he vacated his office, the Germans did not prevent him from taking his ledger and the sultan's cash with him. We do not need your sultan's money, they said, our Kaiser is a rich man.

In this manner the Europeans annexed East Africa, having conferred among themselves around a table in Berlin and carved out much of the continent for their colonization. The mainland north of Tanga and Kilimanjaro had been declared a British colony, where white governors ran the country, and white families with children had begun to arrive to settle and farm and be served by African retainers. The territory to its south, long under the loose influence of Zanzibar, became a colony of Germany, the takeover effected by means of its warships' guns trained on the Sultan of Zanzibar's palace, the British Consul's exhortations to the sultan to acquiesce to the brazen threat, and the prior machinations of Karl Peters, who had gone about collecting signatures from ignorant chiefs on treaties they could not read, in which they ceded territory to the German East Africa Company.

But this takeover of the mainland did not go without resistance. The coast, from Lindi in the south to Mombasa in the north, long a cultural and political extension of Zanzibar, was burning with a fury that the island itself could not show openly.

From Tanga news arrived that the townsfolk had fought daringly against the foreign occupiers and locked up the German officials; Bagamoyo, directly across the channel from Zanzibar, took up the call, as did Pangani, to its north, under an Arab called Bushiri bin Salim. One Captain von Zelewsky was captured and then expelled from the town with jeers and abuses, but only after the Germans had paid a ransom. Arriving in Zanzibar, Zelewsky was heckled further. A short sail up from Bagamoyo, in Sadani, a Swahili called Mwana Heri was in charge of the resistance. And so on, down to Kilwa and Lindi, and in the interior. The news looked good; the people may have been divided, but there was a common enemy, the white infidel and interloper with the gun and the warship.

The two administrators in Kilwa who had taken over from Punja were called Krieger and Hessel, and were about the same age as he. If they had shown due diligence and gone over the Indian's ledger book they might have noticed the arrival, in a few shipments, of a suspicious number of knives and arrowheads and a few rifles. A discrepancy between monies collected and at hand in Punja's cash box might have been attributed to misappropriation or—Punja was an honest man—to certain discreet disbursements. They might perhaps have discovered that a distinguished-looking passenger had accompanied one of the arms shipments and stayed two days before departing; he was called, simply, Wasim.

One late afternoon on a Friday there ensued much commotion in the town. Kassu Ghulamu came over to Punja's shop and told him grimly, "They have done it."

"What have they done, my brother? And who has done it?"

"They have slaughtered the two Germans."

"They have killed the two Germans?"

"Cut off their heads."

"By God, now what."

An armed gang had attacked the boma; the two soldiers on duty were overpowered and killed. Then the Germans were attacked and beheaded, their heads displayed on poles. The remaining soldiers disappeared and the bodies of the Germans were hastily buried. War had been declared by Kilwa. Consequences would follow. The town waited with trepidation for events to unfold.

Chaos ruled on the coast for a year. But there was no stopping the aliens, with their warships, their soldiers, their superior weapons. The German chancellor von Bismarck sent his friend von Wissmann to quell the insurgency. Von Wissmann arrived, having recruited hundreds of Sudanese mercenaries, and went down the coast in a warship from town to town stamping out the "Arab Revolt," as he called it. Tanga was shelled and reoccupied; Bagamoyo was burned to the ground. Pangani was captured and Bushiri bin Salim hanged from a baobab tree along with others. Mwana Heri of Sadani escaped into the hills.

In Kilwa, von Wissmann arrived with three boatloads of troops. It was May 1890. As they landed, a few men took shots at them with their rifles, wounding a soldier, and were immediately chased and shot down; their bodies were displayed at the fish market across from the boma. The soldiers then went searching house to house for more rebels; they entered the mosques with boots and guns; finding no rebels they rounded up all the adult males they could find to attend a meeting at the boma.

Von Wissmann, impressively cut out with a neat moustache and smart uniform, stood on a crate and sternly addressed the crowd in a mixture of Swahili and German. It was useless to resist, he warned. The sultan himself and the chiefs of the tribes had placed the country in the able hands of the Kaiser, the king of Germany. The Kaiser's name was

Wilhelm. He was a just and benevolent ruler; under him the country would prosper and become modern. But if defied, his retribution would be swift. Those who resisted would be punished severely.

The two murdered Germans were buried properly, a short distance from the boma, on the main road leaving the town. The site of the graves was marked by a mound of rocks, to await a proper monument. Von Wissmann left behind two new administrators with a contingent of armed soldiers.

And so was established Deutsch-Ostafrika. All homage was now to be paid to Kaiser Wilhelm, whose chief representative, the governor, sat in Dar es Salaam, his commissioners running affairs in the districts. There was another language heard in the country, German; there were new laws and customs, there was new punishment and fear. And the air and the sun and the seasons seemed suddenly different.

But the warships had no reach in the forests, and back in Iringa, Chief Mkwawa of the Hehe gave the Germans a resounding defeat. Zelewsky, "the Hammer," was killed during an expedition to defeat the chief. And down south Machemba of the Yao would not surrender.

From Zanzibar, news came that the new sultan, after only two years on the throne, had died of grief. But the jihad must go on, said Wasim.

Punja was now a man of the coast, a respected Indian trader and honorary Swahili who was convinced by now that Sidi Sayyad of Singpur had sent him to Africa with a noble purpose: to help his people, the Africans, resist the onslaught of the Europeans. He gave himself a place name, in Indian fashion, so that he was now Punja Devraj Sawahil. He was that saint's emissary and gift to his ancestral homeland. He would do all he could to help resist the invasion of his adopted land.

Punja's great-grandson, a century and some years later now, wonders whether Sidi Sayyad, if we grant him his supernatural powers, lying in state in Singpur under a mound of fragrant flowers, was aware of this singular irony, that those leading the fight against the foreign invasion on the east coast of Africa were eminent traders in slaves too; that it was slavers of this ilk who had brought at least some of his people all the way to India, there to subsist in the back of beyond in Gujarat as one of the lower castes. And what was Punja's reaction upon seeing the heads of Messrs. Krieger and Hessel displayed on the poles outside the boma? Was the hatred against the white men so absolute that there arose for them not an ounce of pity or compassion in the townspeople? Were the Germans so irrevocably alien that no empathy was possible? That the situation was capable of evoking complex emotions and contradictions we know, because they managed to entangle a local poet.

Briefly, very briefly in the year 1890, a teacher appeared in the Kilwa region called Sheikh Muhammad Aleta Baraka, the bringer of blessings. He couldn't have come at a better time with his message, the coast being caught up as it was in chaos and war following the German takeover. In these troubled, bewildering times of violent changes the charismatic, soft-spoken Sheikh Aleta Baraka promised his followers a life of spiritual happiness. The key to his teaching was devotion and gratitude to Allah, expressed in observance in prayer and the ecstatic dhikri-chanting of His name at evening gatherings; he exhorted modesty, charity, and honesty from his followers. I will be your doorway to Allah, he told them, I who come from a long line of teachers, beginning with the incomparable and beloved Muhammad His Prophet, and Aly His favourite, and down the blessed lineage through Sheikh Abdel Qadir Gilani of Iran, and Sheikh Ayesi of Barawi and Zanzibar, who made me his khalifa and representative. Follow me and I will guide you. Change your ways and obey the One, and the German foreigner and unbeliever will disappear. God knows best.

A young man called Muhammad bin Tamim, son of a poet and eminent teacher now dead, and himself an aspiring poet, was greatly moved by this message. Wistful of the piety of the beloved Prophet and his Companions in Arabia, their honesty and compassion in victory and their courage and fortitude in persecution, about which his father had written some lovely utenzi, and about which he himself had attempted his own verses, he grieved in his heart at the iniquity and sin all around him and the breakdown of order. Ah, to live in those times, witness the honesty of the Prophet! The courage of Hamza! The purity of the desert!

Sheikh Aleta Baraka accepted him as a disciple and named him Karim Abdelkarim.

Not long after his arrival, having set up his centre and new mosque in Kilwa, Sheikh Baraka set off to proselytize in the interior of the country, many parts of which the message of Islam had yet to reach. Karim Abdelkarim stayed behind and ran the madrassa at the centre. He was also the guardian of his younger brother, Omari.

Thursday nights being holy to Sufis, the new adherents to Sheikh Baraka's order would stay behind after normal prayers to conduct dhikri. Other townsfolk, including Indians, joined too, this being a more rewarding pastime than playing cards or bao or smoking. It was at a dhikri session that Punja Devraj first paid notice to the tall, noble figure of the young teacher as he stood in the front row, swaying side to side in a gentle ecstasy like a young tree seduced by a sweet breeze, repeating Allah's name. Punja's two wives had joined him in Kilwa by this time, with some of the children, and Punja enrolled two of his younger boys with the teacher.

One evening after dhikri, Punja asked Abdelkarim if he would come to partake kahawa with him. They picked up Kassu Ghulamu from his shop and the three strolled over to the town square at the seafront. There was no moon and the night was dark; a cool wind blew as the waves washed noisily upon the shore. Behind them to the right loomed the boma, draped in darkness; farther to it was the compound where the Germans lived. A kahawa seller went around with his urn serving all the men who sat on the square in small groups chatting quietly. The two Indians asked the young poet and mystic whether he didn't wish to see the infidels driven out from the land. Abdelkarim agreed with all the vehemence his gentle nature would allow him. "I would like nothing better than to see this country subservient to Allah's will, guided by his representative the Caliph."

Gradually the two older men made him understand that even though the last insurgency in Kilwa had been quashed by that devil Wissmann and his African mercenaries, and resistance in other places was meeting with defeat, there were those who believed it was still possible to make life difficult for the Germans. Did he understand? Could he keep secrets? There was a certain movement of concerned citizens. It involved eminent people here on the mainland coast, and in Zanzibar, and was known to the sultan, and it was providing support to the fighters who were resisting the iron hand of the Germans. None of them here were fighters—they laughed at the thought—neither Kassu Ghulamu nor Punja, nor indeed the pious Abdelkarim. But there were ways to help. At present the movement needed a secretary versed in Arabic and Swahili and other local languages.

A plot against the Germans was soon taking shape in Kilwa: the plan was to attack the boma, the German headquarters, then spread the resistance northward up the coast and finally capture the governor in Dar es Salaam.

Arms and ammunition continued to be smuggled in from Zanzibar, and were put away in storage behind Punja's shopfront. Every few days the young poet and teacher Abdelkarim came and spent some time in the shop, where he had been given a small table and a ledger. He updated the inventory of weapons and the list of sympathizers, writing down what and how much each had received, thus creating in his beautiful poet's calligraphy a topography of the coming revolution. It was kept in Punja's safe. The scribe wrote and received messages as well and recorded minutes of the secret meetings that took place at Punja's house late in the night.

Among the plotters, in addition to Punja Devraj and Kassu Ghulamu there were three other Kilwa Indians, Moloo Kanji, Kassam Peera, and Muhammad Suleman. There was a specialist in cutting telegraph lines, called Mkasi, and a spy called Jicho. Always accompanying Abdelkarim on his secretarial assignment would be his younger brother, no more than ten, called Omari. The boy would sit on the threshold of Punja's shop while his brother worked inside. Punja would give the boy a sweet to eat.

During the secret nightly meetings Omari would be curled up on a mat in the shop, fast asleep. One evening the boy woke up to see a short, thickset character in a white kanzu standing a few feet away, addressing a group of diverse men who stood before him. He had just been handed a rifle. His voice was thick, his skin a deep black. He was the famous Yao chief and trader, Hassani Makunganya, possibly my mother's grandfather through a Matumbi slave his men had captured during a raid. For more than two years Makunganya, using this *matériel* from the town, attacked German settlements around Kilwa, looting and burning down the businesses, cutting telegraph lines, waiting for the big chance to expel the Germans once and for all, for his revolution to happen.

One night, when the sea was raging, a boat heading towards the shore, having received passengers and weapons from a dhow, overturned at the edge of the harbour in the shadow of the mangrove swamp. A few bodies were discovered the next day; what goods could be recovered were done so early in the morning before the incident got reported. Some months later, Commissioner Carl Schmidt wrote about this incident to his sister Katrina Maria in Tübingen:

". . . but for us the capsizing of the boat was a Godsend. Among the dead were a tall handsome man held in much awe among the locals, Wasim by name, and one of the sons of a local shopkeeper named Punja. A rifle was discovered at the site at lowtide. This is when I began to suspect that the mild-mannered Indian Herr Punja was involved in the intrigue . . . It is indeed astonishing, my dear sister, how the uncivilized will resist our mission to lead them out from the darkness, and more so how ordinarily peaceful and God-loving folk will give support to terrorists . . ."

Circumstances brought Makunganya his chance for the big attack. The spy Jicho reported that the soldiers had been paid in advance and were buying supplies, including tobacco; they were getting drunk and visiting women; there was talk and boasting. It was apparent that soon they would be off on a long march inland to fight Mkwawa of the Hehe, still very much a headache for the Germans. Early one morning a company of African soldiers under their German commander went marching smartly down the main road and out of town. A military band led the way and the German flag was held up high at the back and front of the troop. The townsfolk came out to bid them goodbye and godspeed; some even accompanied them past the hangman's tree and wished them never to return. God keep Mkwawa even if he was a pagan. Left behind was a small contingent of soldiers under Captain Schmidt.

Hassani did not attack the town immediately. Instead he raided a village nearby as a diversion and allowed one of his men to be captured, who reported in his confession that Hassani was wounded. Captain Schmidt was not quite fooled. Early every morning, heading out to the boma from his little bungalow, the short, bearded German would make a detour and stroll through the business street, tip his hat to the shopkeepers and inquire after the townsfolk. He would come upon the boy Omari, in the typical white cotton collarless tunic over a wraparound msuri, sitting huddled at a corner with a tray of vitumbua for sale. Captain Schmidt would ask for one to be wrapped in a paper for him. And he would ask mischievously, "Is it today, Omari? Will Hassani strike today, do you think?" Playing along, Omari would smile and reply with a little nod, "Yes. Today is the day. Ni leo tu." But one day, when the captain repeated the question to the boy, the youngster drew a sharp breath and said nothing. The German gave him an extra heller and quickly departed, to prepare for the attack that he felt certain would come later that day.

Could such a simple ruse ensnare a child's life forever? That is what Omari bin Tamim would always believe.

A fierce and long battle took place that day, beginning at the outskirts of town, where the soldiers waited in ambush, as hundreds of warriors approached, most bearing spears, a few with rifles, and none carrying a shield. After the first skirmish, the outnumbered soldiers fell back to a position outside the boma and continued to engage, while others fired down on the swarming warriors from the windows above. Hassani Makunganya was defeated, though narrowly, and retreated to the forest to regather his forces and plan anew. The Kilwa boma had proved impregnable, though no doubt with the aid of a betrayal. Another such chance would never occur, and the chief resorted to hit-and-run in the outlying area, until the exasperated governor, von Wissmann, put a price of a thousand rupees on his head and sent more troops on a ship from Dar es Salaam.

Hundreds of soldiers combed the area for Hassani the Fearless, as he was called, tracking him from place to place. In the final battle, on the road to Lindi, facing a bevy of machine guns and rifles, as his warriors fled his hideout and disappeared, he emerged into the open, wielding a knife, daring the soldiers, "Makunganya does not fear death! Come and get me!" The soldiers didn't shoot him, they fell on him instead and took him in chains to Kilwa.

Von Wissmann himself came down from Dar es Salaam to pronounce judgment on the fighters, bringing the rope with him for the hangings. A call went out in town: "Tomorrow all assemble at the boma. Makunganya will get his justice, Bwana Wissmann will deliver his hukumu. You must come and witness." Early the next morning the people came and sat outside the boma and watched in awe as the smartly attired von Wissmann, with a sword and a pistol at his waist, arrived in brisk military steps accompanied by his officials, including Captain Schmidt the Kilwa commissioner and two German translators, and sat down before a table. Makunganya and seven others were brought in chains and presented to the court; then the five Indians were brought, and the hearings began. Witnesses included the soldiers who had captured Makunganya, Captain Schmidt and others, including the chief's own men, one of them his disgraced witch doctor who had selected the fateful day of attack. Makunganya and his men were all sentenced to hang, upon hearing which the people bowed their heads in grief and shame, murmuring exclamations to Allah. Astaghfirullahi. We have become women; if the Dachi—the German—can get Fearless Makunganya like this, to tie him up like a goat, who else can fight them?

The turn of the five Indians came to face the court. Accused of aiding the terrorists, all pleaded not guilty, upon which a commotion arose. Captain Schmidt strode off to Punja's shop along with some askaris and returned with a suitcase containing papers incriminating many people and the book in which the poet and scribe Abdelkarim had meticulously written down details of the plot. How the captain learned of the suitcase never came out; perhaps someone had bargained with him. Punja Devraj, calling himself Sawahil, was sentenced to be hanged. Captain Schmidt pleaded on behalf of the four other Indians, who were consequently sentenced to pay a heavy fine and to go to work on the Tanga railway line in the north.

As von Wissmann stood up, he glared witheringly at Makunganya. "Hassani! You are finished, do you hear? I have defeated you and you will hang." Then he turned to Hassani's grieving supporters and told them, "Women, all of you! Why do you weep now? Isn't this what you asked for?"

A camera had been set up and photographs were taken.

· 22 ·

Early the next morning, four of the Africans and Punja Devraj were marched off in chains along the main road to the hangman's tree, where von Wissmann and the other Germans had preceded them on mules. The hanging had not been announced publicly, and young Omari and his brother, Abdelkarim, were among the handful, scattered across the road and partly hidden by the grass, who watched the proceedings. The brothers saw mighty Makunganya, his eyes covered by a white cloth, his demeanour as defiant as always, accept the rope and swing from the hefty branch until he became still; whereupon a murmur of the shahada erupted from the grass: There is no God but Allah. Whatever his folly and cruelty, he was a man of Kilwa. He was ours and his motives were right. Angry looks from across the road restored stillness once more. The brothers watched the chief's war minister, his spy, Jicho, and his telegraph saboteur, Mkasi, do likewise. But their hearts were heaviest when they watched the small figure of the man they had come to know well, the Indian Punja, also walk to the gallows, where he removed his black fez and handed it to a policeman before accepting the rope.

After the hangings, a few soldiers under the command of a German superior carted away the bodies to be buried in secret. Governor von Wissmann and the other Germans rode their mules back to the boma.

That afternoon, the governor inspected a guard of honour of the troops, after which, tables having been laid on the ground outside the boma, he and his fellow Germans sat down for tea and, it was thought, liquor. Finally, his boat ready, von Wissmann waved to the assembled crowd as he was rowed away to his ship. The four remaining guilty men went with him in a separate boat to be hanged in Lindi, to set another example.

Omari watched this impressive finale from the edge of the town square in the company of his mates; like them he'd been awestruck by the might and panache that the Germans had displayed over the last few days. How foreign they looked, with their pale skins and cat eyes, their helmets, their moustaches; and yet there was not a trace of the uncertain about them, not a doubt to their rightness. How deliberately they moved and acted; no element fazed them. They were always prepared. Their men, the Sudanese, the Somalis, the Zulu, were like an army of fearsome djinns under their command. Whereas the Swahili walked about barefoot on the hot ground, these soldiers, rude and ill behaved, speaking no Swahili, came out in clean clothes and boots and carried rifles, trampled through the forests, fearing neither man nor beast. They marched with authority, all as one, their commander's sharp calls as clear and precise as a whip, and when they stopped their boots hammered the ground like the rumble of a terrible and ominous thunder. The boy could not help but come to a secret conviction: the methods of the old men had proved ineffective. As he would say many years later, when he himself was an elder, Learn the conqueror's language. By learning the German ways and language, he himself would survive and succeed.

His brother, the austere and pious Abdelkarim, who—when not chanting the name of Allah—preferred more than anything else to sit in silence and compose his poetry, was of another mind. He prepared to leave the town and follow his spiritual master to the interior, to see the country and spread the message of their order. Omari stayed behind; as soon as his brother left, he accepted work as a servant for Captain Schmidt in exchange for a place to stay and lessons in German.

British East Africa and Deutsch-Ostafrika were finally subdued and became established as two more European colonies in Africa. The former would become Kenya, the latter, Tanganyika, or the mainland of the future Tanzania. The German Kaiser being related to the British Queen, the boundaries were soon redrawn to give Kilimanjaro to the Kaiser. Chief Mkwawa had been defeated at Iringa, his skull dispatched to Berlin to receive a standing ovation in parliament; in the south, Machemba of the Yao, weary of resisting, escaped to the territory called Mozambique, ruled by the Portuguese. And the British bombarded Zanzibar for forty-five minutes from the sea, in what was, as they would proudly proclaim thereafter, the "shortest war in history," though it was a one-sided affair undertaken to ensure that it was their man who acceded to the sultan's throne.

At the age of eighteen, Omari bin Tamim, as he styled himself, graduated from the elite German school in Tanga, where he had been sent by the government. He returned to Kilwa to work as a teacher, and always comported himself about town with the utmost dignity. He was almost as tall as his brother, though less lean, and in his demeanour Abdelkarim's influence might have seemed perceptible. Like his brother and father he too was a poet, though perhaps not as gifted; in Tanga he had published a poem in the school magazine, *Kiongozi*. It was one of his German teachers who had encouraged this interest, and had sent along that poem, an homage to the Kaiser, to Berlin to be published in an anthology of Swahili verse. By coincidence, his Tanga teacher and patron was none other than Hans Zache, one of the two translators who had accompanied Governor von Wissmann to Kilwa to assist with the trials. The other translator had been Carl Velten, who had returned to Berlin and was the editor of the anthology. These two Swahili enthusiasts had stood to attention side by side, their hats in their hands, as one after the other the Kilwa conspirators were brought forward in front of them and hanged from the projecting limb of the mango tree, the last of them the Indian Punja. That memory was forever carved into young Omari's mind; he had trembled and cried as he watched the lives thrash out of the warriors, his brother's arm tight around his shoulder. That scene would play out in his mind, he would visualize it on the blackboard every time Herr Zache, known as Bwana Saha, stood before the class in Tanga and gave his lesson.

Then why that poem, why such abject flattery of the Bwana Mkubwa, the German overlord? Every such falsehood he wrote and uttered was a betrayal of those Kilwa warriors and all the others who had hanged for resisting; it was a betrayal of his language and its beautiful poetry, so much so that it embarrassed; it was a betrayal of his people. Omari knew all that. But he had resolved that there was no alternative to bending to the new order. Who could deny its superiority, its achievements, its strength? Instead of fighting it blindly and arrogantly, and be vanquished, why not take from it? Why not learn to recite a few lines of Bwana Goethe, appreciate the German lied? And as for telling the truth, surely there would come a time; there would come a time to explain, to revoke this Faustian pact. After all, how could a subject's simple-minded homage to the Kaiser be taken at face value?

When obliging a request for a poem on the occasion of the Kaiser's birthday, how could the young poet laureate tell his king that his rule over the African was symbolized by the cruelty of the khamsa-ishirin, the twenty-five lashes of the whip; or by taxes and forced labour in the farms; or by abject humiliation, as when a German child was carried in a palanquin by four conscripted barefoot Swahili elders? That a frequently used moniker for the German was mkono wa damu, hand of blood? A poet had first to survive: to eat, yes, but also to witness. There would come a time to explain.

Abdelkarim on the other hand continued his exile in the interior, where he travelled extensively. Occasionally the Kilwa Sufi centre had news of him. Omari himself was by now aligned to the more orthodox and mainstream Muslim community. That pleased the new commissioner in Kilwa, Bwana Rode, who was made uneasy by the secrecy and close camaraderie of the Sufis. Captain Schmidt had succumbed to malaria and been buried at the local German cemetery.

Omari was eager to see his beloved elder brother, yet he knew he was safer at a distance. News about Abdelkarim sent a tremor through him, of joy and concern, of fear. There was a fragility to Abdelkarim, a fineness; he was in search of the impossible, had always been oblivious to the world around him that was cruel and crude. They had met once, two years after his departure, when Abdelkarim appeared mysteriously in Kilwa in the cover of night to take part in the Maulidi festival on the Prophet's birthday. Tall and handsome, he had walked in the procession during the day, chanting with the others and holding up one end of their master Sheikh Aleta Baraka's green-and-gold banner. In the evening during the dhikri session, in his beautiful rich tenor Abdelkarim had recited several devotional poems, including, modestly, one of his own. After the dhikri the two brothers met in the house of an elder for dinner, and there, while partaking of kahawa, when Omari, barely thirteen, expressed an admiring opinion about the ways of the Germans, showing off his acquired language, the older brother had admonished him with a resounding slap. Abdelkarim slipped away into the night before someone reported him to the authorities.

That was the one meeting of the two brothers, since Omari had gone to the school in Tanga, and by the time he returned he had moved even closer in his German affiliation. Outwardly confident and successful, a teacher respected by most, but at heart a grieving young man. For to add pain to his memory of the hangings—that tableau of events under the mwembe kinyonga in the quiet of dawn—there gnawed in his breast the guilty knowledge that it was he who was responsible; he, however witlessly as a boy, who had betrayed the Kilwa warriors.

· 23 ·

Some ten years after the Kilwa hangings, a rumour began to be heard: There is this man. In the Matumbi district, *eti*. In a village called Ngarambe. He entered the water for a whole night and when he came out he was possessed by the spirit. Kinjikitilé. Enh-heh, that's his name, this mganga. He is the one with the dawa and the spell. Bokero, Hongo—these are also his names. He will spray you with the magic water with a branch; or he may make you drink it, or pour it on your head. He will tell you what to do. And then? These Germans—nothing. They will go. How? Their guns, their bullets—nothing. How, nothing? They will fire, *pe-pe-pe!* but their bullets will turn to water with this magic. Soft as rainwater, and then we will fight them. But the time is not now. The water is travelling through the country.

In large numbers pilgrims went to Ngarambe, some fifty miles from Kilwa, to hear the mganga Kinjikitilé speak and to make him their offerings. From tribe to tribe the whisper of war spread, as the agents of Kinjikitilé brought their water and performed their ceremonies. Do not look behind you, those who received the water were told; do not enter your women, don't spill the water; abstain from meat. Do not loot when you fight. Finally, in upper Kilwa, in Matumbiland, the people went and uprooted the dreaded German cotton fields, where so many of them had been forced to work under the whip;

a settler named Hopfer was killed; towns were attacked; Indian shops were sacked.

Thus began the Vita vya Maji Maji, the War of the Waters. It was July 1905.

Kinjikitilé of Ngarambe, the prophet who inspired the movement, did not himself go to battle. He was the spirit of the resistance, its inspiration. He raised the possibility, he offered the method. In August, however, two thieves went and robbed his shrine, then betrayed him to German forces. Kinjikitilé was hanged. But the whisper, the water, and the fighting spread like a wildfire across the country, to the south and west and thence back up north, attacking German stations, planters, missionaries, and collaborators, from Kibata and Nandete to Liwale and Masasi, and on to Songea and Kilosa, involving a good swathe of the country, thousands of fighters everywhere, using bows and arrows and rifles.

The Germans did not take the outbreak lightly. Warships were called; more soldiers arrived and set off to the south and west, into the forests and along the coast; settlers organized militias. Gradually, from region to region the insurgency was quelled, the better weapons and training prevailing, as rattling machine guns mowed down close-packed formations of chanting men who had believed themselves protected by the dawa of blessed water. In the mopping-up that followed, villages and farms were scorched by the troops, and granaries were confiscated or burned down to starve the people into total submission. The policy had worked wonders in Southwest Africa. As Captain Wangenheim, a German commander, reported, "Only hunger and want can bring about final submission." Finally, after two years, in August 1907 the war ended. Much of the country in the east and south lay wasted and starving; the devastated area in the hinterland became the Selous National Park.

During much of the war, Omari lived with the constant dread that one day he might see his brother marched up to Kilwa by the soldiers and hanged from the mwembe, the mango tree, along with others. He, Omari bin Tamim, now a head teacher and man of family, would publicly have to acknowledge his brother as a traitor, and then bury him. Intermittent news of Abdelkarim had come from Kibata and

Samanga, close by in Matumbiland, and later from farther away, Kilosa and other places where the Maji Maji resistance was pronounced; there were rumours of a certain mwalimu, a tall and enigmatic man from the coast, who gave the most potent magic water to fighters while reciting from the Quran; and it had become obvious to Omari that his gentle brother, the poet and mystic, the lover of God, was involved in the Maji Maji movement as a recruiter of warriors. Omari did not approve of the movement. Chanting "Death to the Germans! Cut their stomachs open!," these so-called warriors, drunk with the sounds of their own voices, set off to attack, only to meet their own deaths in a hail of machine-gun fire. Madness, blasphemy, suicide! What was the good of that? What had got into his brother?

When the war had just about ended, early one afternoon a young stranger in traditional Muslim garb confronted the teacher Omari on the street and told him in a low voice that a certain relation of his was living in Pembeni, a small settlement a few miles up from Kilwa on the coast. It could be reached by donkey in approximately three hours, and he was requested to bring provisions with him when he visited. Omari nodded that he understood. Early on Sunday morning, modestly loaded with provisions, Omari set off on a hired donkey called Fatuma to seek his brother. The village called Pembeni was on a track that ran over rough terrain some two hundred yards inland, and consisted of a few houses, a defunct shop, and some fishing boats on the shores of a narrow creek. He had been seen approaching, and his heart leapt as he sighted a tall figure, standing at the point where the track forked, waiting for him. Omari got off his donkey and walked the remaining way to go and kiss Abdelkarim's hand.

"How are you, my younger brother?"

"I am well, my older brother. Praise be to God."

"And your work is going well? I see you are in the family trade of teaching."

"It is going well, my brother. And yes, my brother. And you, are you keeping well?"

"For which thanks are due only to the Merciful One."

They walked to a small, shambling house, the crude wattle frame exposed where the outer mud wall had broken off. At the doorway

Omari unloaded his parcel, which a young woman came and took from him with a curtsy, and he tied up his donkey.

Inside, at first the brothers sat on a mat in an awkward silence; the room was dark, but for a few thin rays of golden sunlight shooting through the roof, forming a somewhat catching display where they crossed in midair. It made for the only ornamentation in the room. Omari leaned over and handed his brother the manuscripts he had left in his custody when he first went away. "These have been with me a long time," Omari said. "I have treasured them and learned from them." Abdelkarim looked at them with a smile. "I do not remember them," he replied. "They are all a young man's compositions. But I can see that you must have improved them." "I took the liberty," Omari told him, "using what you taught me of composition. You will see that I have copied them on better paper too." "I see that," nodded his brother. "Well, keep them until I call for them. And I have more for you, copied on extremely poor-quality paper such as was available to me in my travels."

Abdelkarim had married a woman from the interior, the one who had accepted the provisions from Omari at the door. Her name was Zaynabu, and she could barely speak Swahili. There was a child, a girl. Zaynabu brought the men kahawa, which was too strong. Then they had a meal of ugali, which was too dry and grainy, and fried fish.

"My dear brother," Omari said as they sat eating this coarse meal, when some time had passed, "you should return to the comforts of Kilwa. You should teach there. The German commissioner Bwana Rode takes an interest in our poetry and language, and he will appreciate you."

Abdelkarim said only, "Hmm." Then a moment later he said in mild admonishment, "Omari, chatting while eating is a white man's habit." Thereafter they ate in silence.

Afterwards as they sat, it was Abdelkarim who spoke first, looking away from his brother. His knees were raised, where his hands met, the long slender fingers intertwined, and his long back curved like a bow. He looked like a sculpture.

"I have seen much in the forests. Enough for a full lifetime. I have seen terrible things, my brother. I have seen men cut open and left for the hyena, and I have seen men in the hundreds fall to the bullets just as . . . when a swarm of locusts rushes in and razes a field in moments. I have seen hunger and grief. There were unbelievers who showed the utmost courage, took steel in their chests, and believers who betrayed them to the German's mercenaries. It was too much to take, but events led from one to the next. Our Book tells us to resist oppression; but there comes a time to submit and leave the fighting to Allah. He sent us the plague, as though we were the Pharaoh, when in reality it is we who are the slaves. But He knows best. It seems to me now, my young brother, that the path you chose to walk in life was well considered and had its merits. There is no harm in learning new ways, even if they are of the oppressor; the Quran exhorts us to be curious. And so, my brother, forgive me for the harshness I showed you when you were only a boy."

"My brother, you shame me," Omari protested. "It was your love truly that has inspired me."

"Still, I must walk on the path that I took," came the quiet reply. "There was no other way for me. And I must live in hiding now. I dare not show my face to the Germans or their askaris." He paused, then added, "It is Allah's miracle surely that two brothers so close to each other can also be so different."

Omari had brought with him some Indian sweets, the round ladoos the two would eat in Kilwa together, and as he unwrapped the package and placed it on the floor between them, the brothers exchanged a look and held back their emotions. Time and absence from each other had created this gulf, across which they could signal their feelings only in awkward gestures and formal speech. Omari told Abdelkarim about his own life, his wife who was called Halima, and his three children, and his work in the school under a woman called Frau Schwering; he spoke of his schooling in Tanga, a town of great charm, with its promenade and large buildings. He described the white people he had seen in all their finery, doing their pumzika, relaxing outside a hotel. The women looked like angels. He described his stopover in Dar es Salaam, also beautiful, but bigger, with two big churches, bigger than any mosque he had seen. He had been shown where the governor Bwana Goetzen lived, but it was a forbidden area. They said Dar was as big as Berlin.

"Yes, the Germans are a people of achievement," Abdelkarim admitted.

He had not been to Tanga or Dar, but he had seen much of the country. It was vast, endless, people after people, tribe next to tribe, the number of languages spoken without number; but people in the villages everywhere were beginning to speak Swahili now. Soon the entire country would speak this one language, their language, of the coast.

"And your former patron?" Abdelkarim asked, finally. "What happened to him?"

"Bwana Schmidt. He died of fever," Omari said.

What does he know, Omari asked himself, how much does he suspect of my betrayal of Makunganya and Bwana Punja and the others to Bwana Schmidt? The German always paused to speak to me outside Punja's shop; and that day he gave me a heller—Abdelkarim knew that. Could that be why he left, so he wouldn't have to confront me?

Omari prepared to depart and took the fresh manuscript his brother gave him, along with the pages he himself had brought, wrapped in a newspaper. They walked outside. There, at the point of bidding farewell, he turned to Abdelkarim. Shame-faced, he made a request: "My brother, please sing a shairi in your voice, which I have not heard in a very long time. It is a voice I recall as beautiful as our father's. By reciting for me you will be giving me two rewards."

Abdelkarim said nothing for a long while, apparently recollecting. Then he cleared his throat and sang a few verses, beginning in a very low voice until it became full and steady, and the notes became clear, strong and vibrant, as tears ran down Omari's cheeks. It was the last time Omari heard him recite. Zaynabu and the child—her name was Aisha—had come to listen.

Omari presented the child with two candies, which happened to come from England, each wrapped in shiny foil, and gave a five-rupee note to Zaynabu for the household. He kissed his brother's hand, and then slowly rode home on the donkey.

· 24 ·

A year passed, in which Omari did not see his brother, though he sent him provisions every few weeks, whenever Abdelkarim's secret messenger arrived bearing good wishes and an empty basket. Abdelkarim was not in a position to earn a living, but he managed to grow vegetables. Omari sent him rice, oil, and maize flour; some European medicines; on rare occasions, meat. A few times Abdelkarim had sent him some pages of poetry, each of them written neatly in four columns of stretched Arabic script as was his style. To have his brother so close yet inaccessible, and in such pathetic straits, saddened him. The messenger was therefore a welcome arrival. Catching Omari's eye on the street, he would follow him home and have the basket filled. He would accept Omari's heartfelt greetings for his brother and leave. What made these furtive rendezvous risky was that Omari's house was one of a row that the government provided for its prized employees and was close to where the Germans themselves lived.

It was as the next great festival of Eid al-Fitr approached, a time for families to get together, that Omari decided to pay his brother a visit. Early on the morning of the Eid, after attending the public prayer, he set off. When he arrived at the house in Pembeni, he discovered from Zaynabu that Abdelkarim had gone away to celebrate the festival with his master, Sheikh Aleta Baraka. Zaynabu gratefully accepted his presents of new clothes, and presented him on behalf of Abdelkarim a beautiful Quran from Turkey. Omari took the midday meal with Zaynabu and Aisha, then departed. My brother knew I'd come, he reflected on the way back; Sheikh Baraka is more important, understandably; but Abdelkarim trusted me to come, and I came. What stronger bond can there be between brothers? And yet, anxious as I was to meet him, am I unhappy to have missed him? He is strong medicine, is my brother . . . and now I have stolen his art; I have passed off his work as mine. How do I explain myself to him? Will he understand my reasons?

When he reached home, Omari was reminded by his wife that he had missed the affair organized by Frau Schwering, a luncheon on the occasion of Eid at which Commissioner von Rode was to be present. Omari hurried up the road to apologize to Frau Schwering, at whose house however he met the commissioner, and gave them the typical servant's excuse that an older aunt was sick and he had gone to see her. He had a kahawa with them; he could tell by the whiff of European spirits that was in the air that the Germans had been imbibing. The commissioner's boisterous manner only confirmed this.

"We should organize another recital of poetry, Mwalimu Omari," blustered the commissioner, his face completely red in the afternoon heat. "We've not had one in months. And have you composed any new verses for us, O Goethe of Ostafrika?"

"A few, bwana. We can have a recital whenever you say so."

Omari disliked the recitals, which the previous commissioner, Captain Schmidt, had initiated as a gesture of goodwill towards the town. They were held on the public square on occasional Sundays, in the late afternoons when it was shady and cool outside. At these meetings the commissioner would also make public announcements. The officials, and sometimes a family or two of German or Greek farmers from nearby, would sit on chairs; a few elders and the poets would sit to a side on benches. A small public sat on the ground to face this distinguished group, and one by one the poets would step forward and recite. Most were rank amateurs and beginners, their quick, formulaic compositions praising the government, the governor, the commissioner. Omari bin Tamim was the star and he too had praised Bwana

Mkubwa, the governor, and the reliable virtues of the colonial government. His praises were evidently superior to the others', and in appreciation the commissioner had awarded him a prize consisting of an illustrated book on Germany. Once, however, Omari deviated from his subject by reading from an utenzi narrating the Prophet Muhammad's exile from Mecca, telling how while escaping to Medina pursued by his enemies, he had sought refuge in a cave, where a spider had woven a large enough curtain in front of him to hide him. It was one of Abdelkarim's compositions and told a well-known story, but with such clarity and emotion as to move his listeners to sighs and tears. Omari had read it perhaps with his brother's own exile at the back of his mind, and that exile was perhaps also why Abdelkarim had composed it.

In his mind Omari was only giving the composition an airing, an audience. The poem was admired immensely, by those who knew about prosody and those who didn't, and he was pleased for the praise on behalf of his brother. On another occasion he read another of Abdelkarim's compositions, and thenceforth he was trapped. Omari bin Tamim became known as a formidable poet, to be matched by only a few on the entire East African coast. At every recital he had to match his previous achievements, and therefore was tempted to include more of Abdelkarim's superior poems, which he sometimes amended. Perhaps a time would come when he could reveal the truth. Meanwhile he was exposing his brother's talent, bringing admiration to his compositions. He was only the messenger, the mouthpiece. But because he could not name the author as someone other than himself, he knew that the praise he received was stolen, and he was ultimately a thief.

One day Abdelkarim's messenger, after receiving provisions from Omari, shoved upon him a piece of paper. "Your brother says you must copy this letter many times—in secret. It must spread like the wind and it will bring change to the country."

Omari went inside and read the letter. It was addressed to the faithful and spoke about the coming end of the world. Those who followed the true path would be saved. Those who deviated and took on foreign ways would be punished. The infidels would be destroyed. There was no signature.

Who had composed it? Not Abdelkarim, Omari concluded from its brittle language, although the writing with the peculiarly stretched characters was his. Surely any message circulated in secret would be considered criminal, especially after Maji Maji. And this one was openly subversive, even though it did not call for violence. Why would Abdelkarim involve him in this new business? Hadn't he retired from his activities against the Germans? Didn't he say it was time to submit and leave the rest to Allah? He had a wife and a child. And the Germans were here to stay, they were going nowhere. It must be that he believed strongly in this message, wherever it originated, and he needed a scribe and a postman to help distribute it. And in his isolation he was going mad. Omari hid the letter in his Quran and did nothing about it.

One morning as Omari was speaking to his class, Commissioner von Rode entered unannounced with two askaris and said, "Mwalimu, with all due respect, I must take you to the office for questioning."

It is over, Omari thought. What I knew had to happen has happened. All my reputation, my status, in the dust. All because I have a brother, Abdelkarim. And perhaps because it was ordained to happen. A thief's punishment.

"But it needn't be that way, Mwalimu," exhorted the commissioner back in his office. "I know you are a good man. A good subject of the Kaiser. He has heard your praises of him. That is why you must give up your brother. Tell us where Abdelkarim is hiding. He is no good for you, Omari. You have much to achieve in your life."

That the commissioner even knew Abdelkarim was his brother gave Omari a jolt. But the serikali's memory is long, the government never forgets. And it has eyes and ears everywhere.

"Bwana . . ." Omari did not know what to say, what lie to give. "The letter was thrust into my hands—"

"The man who gave it to you—he has been known to us. He's escaped. But we know he came from your brother. This was not the first time, Mwalimu Omari."

Omari wanted to weep, he felt so helpless. Ya Karim, Ya Rabbi . . . Allah, where to go? Abdelkarim, why did you drag me into this?

Simply because I was your little brother? Allah's miracle, two brothers so close to each other . . . yet so different. Like you said.

"Mwalimu," exhorted the German again, jolting him back from his thoughts. "You are a man of the people. An admired man. A respected man. Do you want to be known as a traitor—to your students, to your children? Do you want to be known as someone who received notes from a known agitator—who assisted Makunganya and his gang—we know that too—and one of those who spread the Maji Maji water? Do you, Omari bin Tamim, wish to be known as someone who received poems from his brother Abdelkarim and passed them off as his own? It is known, Mwalimu. We Germans are not just fools and drunkards."

Shame and destitution, that was the threat. Where would he go? There was nowhere he could hide. No one would want him, German or African.

He looked at the whiskered, red face of von Rode and slowly nodded.

Abdelkarim was captured by the troops at his home in Pembeni at dawn. He had no time to flee. At his trial in Kilwa, Omari testified that he had received the Mecca Letter—as that infamous pamphlet came to be known, having been discovered in many parts of the country—from a messenger sent by his brother Abdelkarim; he had been instructed to make copies and spread the message; he confirmed that his brother had worked as a scribe for the Indian Punja Devraj, who had been convicted of collaborating with Hassani Makunganya in his plot against the government in 1895. Another witness testified that during the Maji Maji disturbances, this Abdelkarim had sprinkled the magic water to a group in Samanga, of which he had been one. They had all stood under a tree and received the water. He asked forgiveness for his own crimes.

The trial took place in the boma, inside a room that was the court. The judge had come all the way from Dar es Salaam; he was Werner Faessler, a plump man with a thin moustache and neatly parted hair. Abdelkarim stood diagonally across from the judge, tall and implacable in kanzu—he had to remove his cap—arrogant and silent.

Abdelkarim was found guilty of conspiracy against the government and, further, of recent sedition for having copied and distributed the Mecca Letter. He was sentenced first to be whipped twenty-five times and then to be hanged. Early the next morning he was taken to the site of mwembe kinyonga, the hangman's mango tree, where, with his hands tied in front of him, his kanzu removed and wearing only a msuri round his waist, he bent against a barrel and received twenty-five strokes from a cane. And then he was hanged from that infamous tree, which had seen the demise previously of Hassani Makunganya, Punja Devraj, and so many others who had resisted the Germans. After the hanging, his body was cut down and given to the care of his brother Omari, who washed it and draped it in a white sheet for burial, and recited the Fatiha over it at the cemetery, where most of the townsmen, from fisherman to sheikh, came to pay their respects, including Commissioner von Rode.

Born from the same womb, he'll die with you. Words of that proverb came to mock Omari bin Tamim. But I chose their side, not yours, my brother. I chose to survive. If I had not cooperated, wouldn't they have found you anyway? Why do I reason with myself? I must bear the burden. Each of the twenty-five wounds is lashed upon my heart. And I will carry them the rest of my life.

That evening the Sufis of the town held a special ziara at their centre for Abdelkarim. His brother Omari bin Tamim was turned away.

"Karim Abdelkarim was destroyed. It is a pity that evil can come to reside in the heart of the handsomest of men. Corporal punishment prior to the execution was a necessity . . . Examples have to be made. Insurrection must be crushed in such a way that not even an atom of defiance should remain in the African mind."

So wrote Captain Faessler from Dar es Salaam in his journal, *My Colonial Days in Africa.*

25

When the Great War of the Europeans closed its East African chapter, the Germans having been ejected from all the territories they had colonized, Omari bin Tamim, teacher of Swahili and German, had but scant knowledge of English, the language of the new rulers. Omari found himself without employment for a few months, until he was hired in the post office, situated in a ground-floor corner of the old boma. One morning, having sorted out the day's incoming mail, while he stood behind the counter attending the odd customer, still confused by the new postage stamps, a note arrived requesting his presence in the district commissioner's office.

"Mwalimu Omari," the DC said, having offered him a chair, preferring himself to come forward and stand, looming awkwardly over the poet, "I was not told until yesterday that a poet of your eminence lived in our town—and was working just two doors away from me at the posta!"

Omari bin Tamim smiled ironically. "Who would tell you?" he murmured.

The DC's hair was a startling mop of fire that drew your eyes away from his face; he was a big man somewhat dishevelled in appearance and known as Bwana Kendrick. Omari liked his respectful manner and noted that his Swahili was spoken in a sharper accent than that of the Germans he had known. Like theirs it was clean—too clean, like a house that is swept every day but not lived in. The European officials learned the language well. The trouble was they learned it too well, diligently noting down rules and expecting them to apply everywhere. But there was the language of the poet and that of the street and that of polite discourse; there was the language of Kilwa, and of Zanzibar, and of Lamu. The white man's consonants, too, were hard and angular. Swahili was soft and pliable. That was its beauty, its fun to the poet, its lover.

Omari had hardly composed any poems in recent years. His heart had turned cold to the art: when he wrote, his sentences came out stiff, suitable to speak only to the tone-deaf; it was as though he were laying bricks or arranging sticks in a row. During the last weeks of the war, he had written for the German commissioner of Kilwa one verse on the hardships of war and another on the bravery of soldiers, the second of which he had been asked to recite when a company departed from Kilwa to go and fight the British Army. They were casual verses, nothing he was proud of. In one line he had mentioned the African soldiers on the British side, but Herr Buler, the new German commissioner, had asked him to remove that reference. "Mwalimu," he had said, "you are German, and they are British, you have to remember that. The old alliances are gone." And now the Germans were gone.

"Mwalimu," DC Kendrick now said, "they speak well of you in Mombasa, where I was posted before the war. They say you are a poet of substance. I want you to teach in the government school here in Kilwa—you would bring it honour. You should impart your knowledge and wisdom to the young ones."

"I will do that if you give me the job, bwana."

It has been a long time, Omari thought, sitting in the DC's office at the boma, where he had previously met Captain Schmidt, Bwana von Rode, and Bwana Buler, a long time since my boyish, nonchalant shrug sent a signal to Herr Schmidt, five men were hanged and my life changed. My elders fought to bring back old ways and they were thrashed by the new dispensation. I had to point a finger at my brother and he was hanged. The German was here to stay, and he wore a heavy boot. But he too is gone, his stay now only fragments of stories for memory to prey upon, and now we have the Biritishi. He treads lightly. But beware the mouse who caresses you as he gnaws.

"Do you want me to write a poem to the King?" Omari asked. "But I have forgotten his name, sir."

Bwana Kendrick threw back his red-mopped head and laughed heartily. "Only if the poem comes truly from moyoni, from the heart, Mwalimu," he said, beating his breast stoutly. "The King's name is King George the Fifth. Meanwhile I would much appreciate hearing the poem called 'Buraq.'"

"You know it, bwana?"

"My German predecessor, whom I happened to meet in Dar es Salaam recently, told me about it. He felt grieved to have lost his copy during the war. But he failed to tell me that your home was here in Kilwa. I wonder if that was deliberate. To tell you the truth, kwa kweli, I am jealous of the Germans for having known you first."

Omari Tamim laughed politely, but he felt trapped. The poem was his brother's, inspired by the blessed journey of the horse Buraq, who carried the Prophet on his journey from Jerusalem to heaven on the holy night of Miraj. Omari had emended it, transcribed it for von Buler in Arabic script. Bwana Buler had then transcribed it into the European script, but the process was not accurate; much was lost, and Omari had not liked the result. Why change the script? How can Arabic accents and elisions be copied? But that is the script of our nation, Bwana Buler told him; it can be adjusted for new sounds.

Bwana Kendrick was looking at him eagerly, and Omari relented. "Yes, I will read the poem to you, bwana."

When DC Kendrick introduced him at the school assembly at the beginning of his employment, he begged Mwalimu Omari formally to step forward, cast modesty aside, and recite from his repertory. Omari stood up and, as he had promised, read verses from "Buraq." In his reading he could no longer identify his own emendations to Abdelkarim's poem. His editing had been informed by his firm belief that Abdelkarim too had been carried by Buraq to heaven that fateful morning. He knew that poem so well, he read it as his. A renewed fear gripped him as Bwana Kendrick stood up and bravoed his recital and all those present followed suit; as elders of the community took the opportunity now to praise also the exemplary fortitude and wisdom he had shown over the years; and as a few others recited their humble verses to praise him. They were all honouring him, and not Abdelkarim, the hero, the genius and patriot, the man of God. He had ingested his brother. No one spoke of Karim Abdelkarim; they knew only Omari bin Tamim, the poet and teacher.

Over the years Omari bin Tamim's eminence shone like a star over Kilwa, bright and steady, not extravagant. A teacher in the government school and in the madrassa, an august man with experience and apparent influence in the colonial administration, a poet who could be relied on to come up with something appropriately edifying for an occasion—the King's birthday, the sacrifice of Abraham, the birth of a son—without taxing the mind. His renown among the aficionados of poetry all along the coast, from Lamu in the north to Lindi in the south, was of course due to that one famous poem, "Buraq." Like an unclaimed child it haunted him, for he could hardly now deny that it was his, and it was partly so, in any case. Letters would come by post congratulating him for his genius, or seeking some explanation, always inquiring about his more recent work. He replied diligently, thanking the writer for the praise, explaining a choice of word or an apparent deviation in meter. No, he would conclude in his replies, I have nothing of substance that is recent, the muse has abandoned me for the time being; but if Allah wills . . . and so on.

Each letter and reminder a pang of guilty conscience, a prod to the wound, to be borne patiently. Finally these letters of praise and acknowledgement stopped, the past was ready to let him go, and he it.

The Germans were long gone, the gutturals of their language now only distant echoes, riding the waves of a fast-ebbing tide. The terrible wars of the past were forgotten, their heroes consigned to a few paragraphs of the history books. There was stability in this land, now called Tanganyika Territory, one of a triad of East African countries, its symbol the placid and enigmatic giraffe. Life was changing apace; the developments taking place in the country would have been beyond imagination only a few years ago. There were now already those too young to recall days without an automobile or bus on the road, the telephone at the post office from which you could place a call to Dar es Salaam or Arusha, a camera to capture events and people on a piece of paper to show around and keep as a memento; when English was not spoken. Once in a while you might see an airplane, constructed of iron and bigger than any bird, flying in the sky, carrying people inside its belly. Watching one drone overhead against the glare, he was led to wonder, Truly, could this overwhelming force of destiny, could this storm of progress and change have been stopped? Surely it was God's will, even the pain and humiliation? It was Allah, after all, who had sent the flood upon the earth when He thought it appropriate, and all sorts of plagues. Wasn't his gentle brother, Abdelkarim, his most dear companion once and a father to him, in error when he challenged this dispensation? And yet Omari couldn't forget that hanging, the tall lean body of his brother stretched from a rope, the look of physical pain borne without a sound . . . when the life left him there was not the slightest twitch from the body, it was as if a saint had died; the caning that preceded . . . the punishment so drawn out as though the clock had slowed . . . the skin flaying . . . Shouldn't there have been some among the onlookers to register protest at such humiliation?

Omari's wife Halima had died, having given birth to two sons and two daughters. Together they had buried a boy and a girl while still young. He had seen a lot, like his generation. His second wife Mwana Juma was a much younger woman, a somewhat perky daughter of an eminent sheikh from Lindi who also fancied himself a poet, and naturally therefore she could read and write. One day, having peeked into the sanduku of manuscripts which had been used as a table in their home, she asked him as he came in the door from work what these shairi were, who had written them and when. Angrily he shouted at her and beat her. "They were written by a djinn!" he said angrily. "It is not your business to know!"

It was time to shed this last burden of guilt and reproach, this physical reminder of his brother, this temptation to steal a look at the contents of those curling pages of poetry and marvel at their skill and poise. And so one night with determination he took the sanduku of manuscripts, put it upon a donkey, and silently set off. The moon had just sunk into the forest ahead, a dim silver glow emanating from that direction like an inspiration or affirmation; night calls rang out, strange and familiar, disembodied; hyenas emerged from the shadows then slunk off to root; probably towards the forest a lion or leopard was lurking. Witches came out to at this hour to plot their nefarious acts, search for herbs or a grave to desecrate for their medicines and powers. He himself was a sinner, a fratricide, his load the sacred, intimate words of his dead brother, whom he had betrayed. What curse might not spring from those pages? All the way to his destination the poet repeated the names of Allah and of His Messenger, and recited the auspicious Sura Yasin of the Quran to ward off the evil spirits.

He arrived at the old mango tree. He stood in silence for some moments and then in a low voice said the Fatiha for his brother's soul. The ground was hard under the tree, thick roots creeping out from the surface. He found, however, a soft grassy patch nearby, the soil newly damp, and dug a hole there and deposited the sanduku inside. He covered it up to look undisturbed and left. Although Abdelkarim was buried in the graveyard on the other side of the town, Omari had always imagined his spirit haunting this mango tree. Now Abdelkarim was united with his brilliant compositions. The air in this place will be hallowed by his words and phrases, thought Omari, they will float in the air like the smoke of incense and make it sacred. Transported by his sentiments, heavy in the heart—and he thought he was shedding his burden—Omari bin Tamim turned to go, patting the donkey to trot on ahead.

When he arrived home, Mwana Juma was waiting for him. "Where did you go?" she asked suspiciously. "I went out, that's all," he replied curtly.

But she glanced at his soiled kanzu and hands and knew that he had taken along a spade. She's a smart one, he admitted to himself not for the first time as he slowly turned away from her quiet defiance. He already regretted marrying a much younger woman, and daughter of a sheikh.

26

He had only fooled himself. Gradually and inevitably the doubt crept upon him that he had not freed himself from a burden at all but had actually betrayed his brother's trust. Hadn't Abdelkarim of his own accord sent him his manuscripts for safekeeping? Hadn't he allowed Omari to make copies and add his corrections? Now they were buried somewhere: all those testimonies to the beauties of their mother tongue, all that history told and all those stories of Islam and the Prophet retold with such cleverness and precision, such honesty and piety. When he visited the hanging site again, a week or more had passed; it was day-time and the sun was shining; there were people about. The place had changed, as though someone had erased a picture and painted a brighter one in its place. A vegetable plot had sprung up, and beside it stood a makeshift hut used by a vendor. He couldn't tell where exactly he had buried the trunk; and anyway, he realized with despair, the ants and the rain would have got to the papers by now. He imagined them rotting away in their dark prison.

He had acted impulsively. But whom did he have to talk to, take advice from? He had only himself, with his gnawing guilt.

Lines from those buried compositions came back to haunt him; fragments of his brother's poems that he had copied with devotion on good German or Syrian paper in his best writing and recited to himself with admiration and joy, were resolved to torment him in his night-mares. They came twisted and stretched, hairy snakes and scorpions with big grinning mouths, laughing and taunting, nipping and sting-ing, always beyond his reach. How he wished to get his hands on them, turn them around, join them, reshape them into poetry; or to capture them and beat their heads in and throw them away by the roadside like vile, dirty things.

So you thought you would bury us, ha-ha-ha Mwalimu! jeered the snake.

What is written is never erased, didn't you know that, Teacher? retorted the scorpion.

Kilichoandikwa hakifutiki, ha-ha-ha!

What is written has a soul, ha-ha-ha!—it never dies!

Although he taught Swahili and not English or arithmetic or geog-raphy, subjects that held more prestige in the territory, Omari had enough of a standing by himself to have been named vice-principal. He was comfortable. But now the nightmares came. They were not frightening but wounding, so that he would wake up full of regret and guilt, and he would cry out. He became depressed, listless; thoughts of suicide came. All this began to show in his demeanour. He looked dishevelled and talked to himself when alone. It was evident to all those close to him that he had become possessed. He was given a leave of absence from school, and Mwana Juma kept him at home as much as was possible. Traditional doctors—the mgangas—came occasionally to exorcise him, using prayers, rituals, and medicines, but the tormenting spirits would not leave him.

One afternoon Bwana Kendrick—who had long since transferred from Kilwa—was travelling in the area. He came by to visit Omari and his wife, wearing the Englishman's long flappy shorts and white shirt with a hat, followed on the street by a trail of boys. He was given water, which he accepted gratefully. And then the two men were left alone in the house.

Bwana Kendrick was aghast upon hearing of the fate of the manu-scripts, which he still believed were Omari's own; he was unconsolable. "I cannot believe it, Mwalimu. I cannot believe you would do such a thing." He got up in his agitation and took a deep breath, and almost in tears walked out of the house for a few minutes, then returned.

"You should be able to recall them and write them down again carefully," he said calmly. "After all, Mwalimu, they are your own words. Could you do that?"

"I have forgotten much," Omari mumbled. "And my mind is giving troubles, I am haunted by spirits."

"I have heard," Kendrick said. Omari described his torments and Kendrick, turning thoughtful, simply said, "Those poems are calling you, they want to come back, don't you see? They want to live!"

The Englishman wrote a letter referring Omari bin Tamim to a doctor friend at the government hospital in Dar es Salaam. "You should see this mganga, Mwalimu. He is an English medicine man, but he can help you with your problem. Currently I am travelling on behalf of the government, but if I am in Dar es Salaam during your visit, I will come to see you and show you around."

In about a week Omari set off on a ship bound for the capital, accompanied by Mwana Juma. In the city they were put up in a room in the grounds of the hospital, a large, sedate two-storey white building from German times, close to the sea. They were told they would have to wait a few days; Dr. Jennings, whom they had come to see, was busy. And so while they waited they went about seeing the sights. The city had changed much since Omari had last seen it two decades earlier as a trainee teacher. Beyond the peaceful tree-lined avenues and the beautiful European houses, and the Government House where the British governor lived, thrived a teeming city where they could wander around and shop among people like themselves.

What impressed Omari the most during their jaunts in Dar was one prominent addition to the landscape since his previous visit, a statue of the African soldier, the askari, in the centre of the town, situated such that cars went around it all the time like a train of ants. The askari wore a uniform, with cap, boots and puttees, and stood poised with his rifle and bayonet, ready to charge at an enemy. The resemblance to the soldiers Omari had seen long ago in German times was uncanny. Omari and Mwana Juma would contrive to pass by the statue every day. It had a hypnotic effect and they couldn't help staring at it until they had passed it. One day Bwana Kendrick joined them, and as they stood together at the roundabout under the statue he explained to Omari that the memorial celebrated the courage and endurance of the African askaris who fought in the Great War between the Germans and the British, on either side.

"It is a generous tribute," Omari said, adding, "I have often thought, the war was not the Africans' war, we had no quarrel with each other, and yet these soldiers killed and were killed by their brothers."

Kendrick smiled. "Tell me what's on your mind," he said quietly.

They had come to sit at a shed to have tea. Mwana Juma, too embarrassed to be seen beside the white bwana, sat by herself on the ground at a distance until she found someone to chat with. That she was talking about her husband and the white man, Omari could tell by her occasional glances towards them.

Omari said, "When the Germans came, there were wars that were our wars. We lost them. But there are no memorials, no statues to honour those dead warriors. Only the old mango tree stands as witness."

"Write about them," said Bwana Kendrick. "String your utenzis, Mwalimu, and in them make the people see and remember those warriors who died." He became thoughtful, before continuing. "Listen, here is what one British poet wrote about that same war." He recited haltingly in English, then translated.

When Dr. Jennings saw Omari he asked him many questions. He wanted to know the exact descriptions of the snakes and scorpions of his nightmares, and exactly what they said. He wrote everything down patiently, a process that enervated the patient. These white men want to capture our everything, even our thoughts, even our spirits; what will we have then? When the doctor asked Omari about his brother, Omari clammed up. Aa-aa, don't go there. The doctor then questioned Mwana Juma. Finally the doctor spoke to Omari and Mwana Juma together.

"Omari bin Tamim," he said. "Mwalimu, you are a learned man. What you have not learned in school you have learned from life itself. It is evident to me that you have seen much. You should confront what's tormenting you. Face up to those spirits that haunt you. Even by refusing to speak to me about your brother, you are confronting something in your mind. That is good. Tell me, have those snakes and scorpions come to pester you during your stay in Dar es Salaam?"

"No," said Omari. "But they are lurking somewhere, I can sense them, somewhere close behind me in the air."

"They are afraid of the English mganga," put in his wife. "Enh." She nodded confidently, then kept quiet.

Jennings said he would send a report to Bwana Kendrick.

Back in Kilwa, Omari's condition improved, though it remained somewhat ginger, as he thought of it. It was a matter of treading softly so as not to provoke the devils. Bwana Kendrick had given him some paper and a pen and ink as gifts, but these remained on a table waiting to be picked up.

A few months after the couple's visit to Dar es Salaam, Bwana Kendrick came to town, while on a tour of the area by car. He paid a brief visit, gave them news that he had been sick and that his father had died in Scotland, and left. Some days later there came news at the district office that there had been an accident on the bridge over the Rufiji River, and Bwana Kendrick had died in it.

The following Friday, after the midday prayer at the mosque, Omari was invited to speak, and he spoke about the death of the Scotsman and how much grief that caused him. Bwana Kendrick had been a good man, a friend of the African. His birth was his fate, but he had earned his worth by his own deeds. Surely he would be welcomed by the angels and at resurrection earn his deserved reward in paradise. Later that afternoon Omari went and paid his usual respects at the grave of his brother, stopping briefly on the way at the German cemetery. On his way back, his head bowed in contemplation, he felt a gentle shove from behind him against his right shoulder. A voice spoke, "Samahani, excuse me." Omari turned but saw no one. He was in the grassy stretch of land between the two cemeteries and it was very quiet. Dusk was approaching. He became wary, but he was not afraid. He could deal with spirits.

As he walked on, the voice said, "Your brother forgives you."

Omari looked up and then around him in annoyance.

"What do you know? Get away! And who are you, you barbarian?"

"I want to help you."

"Help me? Help me to do what?"

"You yourself know what. Help you to pick up your pen and give life again to your brother's work, and to your own skill. Don't demean it."

"And your name?—laana on you if you come from Satan."

"I am Idris, your faithful servant."

The next morning, having had his tea and mandazi, and taken his bath, Omari bin Tamim sat down on a mat and formally asked his wife Mwana Juma to give him his paper and his pen. Happily she obliged. She also lit some incense and then left him alone in the room.

Omari wrote, Bismil,

I invoke Him the Merciful
to begin thus being auspicious
I pray to Him the Creator
that I succeed instructing you

For "merciful" he had deliberately used "karim," thereby placing his brother's signature in the poem. It brought him joy, to begin thus.

As he contemplated his strategy on the page, he asked himself why it had not occurred to him that Abdelkarim was always merciful, had always understood and forgiven him.

Omari bin Tamim composed several long poems in the utenzi form. These include, besides the well-known "Buraq" and the narration of the Prophet's exile, the story of Adam and Eve, an account of the Prophet Moses' humbling adventure with the ascetic Khizr, and a dialogue between Muhammad and the angel Gabriel about the future of the world. His last work was the historical magnum opus, *The Composition of the Coming of the Modern Age*. Of which of these utenzis he was the sole author is impossible to say. None of them survive except as subjects of hearsay, or in memorized fragments. A few corrupted verses of the celebrated "Buraq" were recited to a German student, Gudrun Eberhardt, by an Indian car parts dealer in Dar es Salaam in 1994. In an interview with the same researcher, an aged Mwana Juma binti Nassoro, widow of Omari and a resident then of her native Lindi, affirmed having knowledge of these and other poems:

"I heard him recite them to himself. Yes, he liked to recite."

"You yourself can read?"

"With these eyes I cannot read. But my father taught me to read."

"You didn't read your husband's compositions?"

"No. Once I read them and he scolded me bitterly. And then he went and threw away the papers. A whole sanduku-ful of them. That is why you will look for them but won't find them."

Her last answer is not quite accurate, as we know. The trunk that Mzee Omari buried in the ground beside the mango tree contained the older compositions, and obviously not those he began after his consultation with Dr. Jennings and his encounter with the djinn Idris. Omari's final work, *The Composition . . .* , must have ended abruptly, after describing the conclusion of the Maji Maji War. I recall sitting beside Mzee Omari in front of his portable writing table, as he showed me the last page he had written up to then, in which he mentioned the Mecca Letter. Frightened, I was anxious to escape. And many years later, caught in the grip of nostalgia and the need for answers, I would be possessed by this other guilt, that with my child's insensitivity I could not give comfort to an old man when he had turned almost completely blind and needed it most.

It was a short time after he had showed me that page that Mzee Omari hanged himself from the mango tree.

"It was time for him to die," Mwana Juma said in her interview. "He was possessed by his old madness. It would not leave him. His time had come."

"I don't understand," Gudrun Eberhardt responded adroitly to this ambiguous pronouncement. "If he hanged himself, someone must have collaborated?"

"It was that djinn Idris only."

The researcher knew better than to question the existence of djinns in a Swahili home. But if it wasn't the djinn who assisted in Mzee Omari's suicide, it must have been a person. There was one person who had confessed at the sorcerer Akilimali's truth session that he had been about at that ungodly hour, adding moreover that he had seen Mzee Omari on the main road walking towards the mango tree. He was Salemani

Mkono, Mzee Omari's accuser. The truth, writes Ms. Eberhardt, seems remarkably simple and obvious. Salemani himself must have assisted the poet in hanging himself, and then successfully conned the sorcerer with a tall story about having seen a djinn in a veil following the poet. What bargain these two old antagonists made was one of those secrets forever buried in he past.

What Gudrun Eberhardt did not discover, apparently, was that the sorcerer Akilimali had the reputation of being able to divine an answer from a drugged witness before he or she even spoke; as my mother had remarked astutely, this raised the possibility of planting an answer. And this too seems to have escaped the otherwise intrepid Ms. (later Dr.) Eberhardt: there was one witness under the tree that night who did not sit with the others in the circle to receive the sorcerer's truth medicine: Mwana Juma.

It was Mwana Juma, perhaps to put the old poet out of his misery, who encouraged his ironic exit, with the assistance of the one-armed beggar. The sorcerer became instrumental in the cover-up.

Three

⚜

golo

· 27 ·

"I had returned after thirty-five years," Kamal told me, "a respected doctor, fortified with vaccinations and prophylactics. I took care with food and drink, used insect repellent, slept under a net. Every means to protect myself from the ills of the tropics in which I was born. Yet I was horribly sick."

It was that one exception he had allowed to breach his armour, the single glass of water he drank at Fatuma's—and Africa invaded him, reclaimed him once again. To get to Saida he could keep no defences— he knew that when politely he sipped the ill-tasting clear liquid behind the medical store.

Gripped by bouts of fever, attacked by diarrhea, hammered by head- aches, now it was he, not his innkeeper Markham, who was the stinker, too weak for a bath, with no appetite but constant thirst. And fever led him back to revisit his childhood Gehenna, to resuffer its torments in the loneliness of his hotel room. A nightmare within a nightmare.

In his later life, in the comfort of wealthy suburban Canada, he had occasionally dreamt about his abandonment, though in his dream he would see his trauma transferred onto some other tender thing—a child, an animal—and woken up shaken but in the safe surrounds of a delicious climate-controlled certainty. He never expected he would relive his hell. He never believed he would return.

We were visiting Zanzibar, the two of us, in the vague hope of finding there some trace left by his ancestor Punja. We found none. It was Kamal's first trip to the island, and we sat in the lounge of the plush Serena Hotel, where he wished to drink coffee of a quality closer to what he was used to. He could afford it, I mused, as I watched the wealthiest of tourists relaxed in their various outfits, some in almost none, and he described the most traumatic and pivotal moment in his life. Pivotal, yes, because he was forced brutally to shed the life he knew, moult and step away from one existence entirely into another.

"Mama, don't let me go! Usiniache! I don't want to go. Mama don't throw me out, usinifukuze!—I will be good, Mama . . . what did I do to offend you?"

"You have to go, my son. Your father has arranged it."

"And you? And you . . ." In his bed in Markham's hotel he found himself clutching at his fever-wasted sheets.

What do you do when your world suddenly comes to an end, when those tender insecurities, those delicious fragile times of temporary want and despair, those moments of pure laughter, those minutes of mysterious poetry, those timeless delights in your mother's bosom are all of a sudden torn away from you? You stare ahead at a frightening wasteland without love.

Mama, don't let me go. Usiniache. How could she, his mother, simply tell him, Go, there is no choice.

He never forgave her.

Even if maybe she had no choice?

He shook his head, slowly, tenderized by his reborn grief.

She did not even prepare him.

On a Sunday morning, she woke him up, told him to pack the trunk, he was going on safari. What safari? Did they have money for a safari? School was not out yet.

"Stop harassing me now," she said. "Pack."

They packed the trunk with his things, but not hers.

"Are you not coming?" he joked.

"No," she said. "I am sending you away to become an Indian, to your father's family. And you must be good. Remember, I have taught you adabu, and religion, and respect for elders. You are going to the world to become a big man."

His eyes widened with disbelief, with panic, for she was not joking.

"What kind of big man? I don't want to go."

"You are going to your relatives' home in Dar es Salaam. They are Indians and they are now ready to receive you and prepare you for the world. I cannot give you anything. I have nothing, but these are the socks I have bought for you, and these the handkerchiefs, and this shirt—"

And Kamal was staring at Mama as she coolly counted out these things.

A man came in through the door, one of the Indian men who had come a few days before to see her, a short, stocky man, who said, "Is the boy ready? The bus leaves in a short time."

And that was when a huge wave of realization crashed upon him, and Kamal cried, "I don't want to go, Mama, don't let me go, please!"

On his sickbed in Kilwa he was weeping as Lateef's voice came at him, "Daktari, you must drink this soup."

And Markham was gruffly saying, "A spoonful of whisky will revive him."

And Shamim put in her bit, *You never told me this, all these years of marriage and you never said how you came to Dar.* And he replied, *What could I say, that my mother abandoned me and broke my world?*

A porter carried his trunk and the Indian man walked beside Kamal, his mother watching from the doorway, murmuring, "Kwa heri, mwa-nangu . . . ," Goodbye my son, we'll meet again, God willing. And suddenly Kamal made a dash for it, as fast as he could, the fastest boy in his school, and a voice shouted, "Kamata mtoto!" Catch the boy! and feet came thumping after him but could not catch him, the onlook-ers watching, some encouraging him, "Raise the dust, boy!" He fled down the street and across the main road, raced past the German memorial and towards Saida's house, saw no one there, and he turned around, raced past his two pursuers and the monument again and back into his street towards—of all places, but understandable, surely—his own house and into his mother's arms—which handed him over to the Indian. His name was Samji, and holding Kamal firmly by the wrist he took him to the waiting bus, sat him by a window and planted himself next to him.

"You, Kamalu, now don't give me trouble," Samji said as the bus filled up and then groaned away onto the highway. "I am taking you to your father's family. They are watajiri, people of means, and they will give you a good life and a future."

The world of his familiarity, the parallel streets leading carelessly in from the main road, the white memorial stone, the boma, and the town plaza at the harbour, the chai shop at the crossroads . . . there a sheikh in white kanzu and cap strolling, there a woman in black bui-bui, there the orange-seller and the fish vendor . . . all pulling away behind him, never to be seen the same way. People watching him, knowing his plight. Kamalu is being sent away. Kwa heri, Kamalu! And then he looked behind one last time and saw her, standing by the memorial, her small figure dwarfed by it and getting smaller and smaller, gazing in his direction. Kwa heri, Saida. He clutched at the tawiz she had given him.

It was a long journey north. They passed the land of the Matumbi, his African ancestors, and the Ndengereko and the Zaramo. The bus had originated in Mtwara to the south and had people with all sorts of features. There were two Masai with spears and gourds and a distinctive odour; there were several men and women with tattooed faces, the women with black buttons stuck to their upper lips, making them look grotesque. They were from the Makonde people. The Makonde make good watchmen, explained Samji, but watch out for the Zaramo with the kumi-na-moja sign of eleven on the sides of their heads. They are thieves, every one of them, and will have their hand inside your pocket in no time. When the bus stopped at a place called Handeni, Samji came down with him, and they peed by the side of the road in the bushes. The Indian bought him maize from a road vendor and from an Indian shop a Coca-Cola, which Kamal had tasted only once before. Mama had bought a bottle once as a treat for them both, and they had made it last two days.

As the bus left the village, it ran into a patch of deep mud and tilted alarmingly to one side while attempting to run through, until finally having dug in deeper it gave up and stopped. They all got out again.

Kamal could have run off into the jungle or hidden behind bushes or climbed a tree, and taken a bus back home afterwards. In the months ahead he would regret many times not making the attempt. Years later he would ponder over his reluctance. Partly, he thought, it was the sheer shock that his mama had let him go, and the awareness that he always obeyed her, that made him accept his fate, whatever she had decreed. She was sending him into the world. He had to be good.

That world began with Dar es Salaam, the European city as beautiful as Berlin, according to Mzee Omari's account. He was curious about his father. Why had he gone away? He asked Samji, "I will see my father in Dar es Salaam?" "No," Samji said. "Where is he, then? Is he dead?" "I don't know. You will stay with your uncle, his name is Jaffu Punja. He has a shop. Everybody knows him." Why had his mother not been asked to go too? He would tell his uncle, Jaffu, it was all right, he did not have to worry about him. He, Kamal, could manage with his mother. He did not need help. He would help Mama, he would grow up and find work and get her a small shop of her own.

That had always been his dream, to get his mother beautiful clothes, to get her a shop of her own.

Dar es Salaam, as they entered early the next morning, was disappointing in its familiarity. Not the London he had seen in the books, and he was certain it was not like the Berlin of Mzee Omari. It looked like Kilwa, only much bigger and busier; there were people already on the streets, the shops were opening, and the number of vehicles dazzled him. But the familiarity also comforted him. So this was Dar es Salaam. The bus stopped at a noisy, crowded station, and as he and Samji waited for his trunk to be handed down by the man on the roof rack, he was told to watch out for pickpockets. With his flashlight Samji peered at all the luggage that landed on the ground. When Kamal's small trunk finally appeared, they got into a taxi and were driven on a long and busy street to a small cross street near a big yellow building with a clock tower. There, outside one of the shops, they got off and entered. An Indian man sat motionless on a chair in the middle of the shop, looking out, his open shirt revealing a heaving, hairy chest over a bulging stomach. Kamal went up and in a nervous low voice greeted him respectfully.

"Shikamoo, Bwana Jaffu."

"So you have arrived. Welcome."

His uncle had a stiff manner. He rarely showed emotion, as Kamal was to discover, and his throaty voice rarely altered its pitch. He was not a big man, and he had a scar over his left eye. His right leg twitched constantly as he sat.

"Your relative has arrived," Samji announced. "And don't think he came willingly. We had to chase him through the alleys of Kilwa." He broke off into Kihindi, the Indian language, which Kamal of course did not understand.

Jaffu Ali Punja grunted and eyed his nephew with interest. He said, "Your mother has no need for you now. She will get married and go to live with her husband in Lindi."

In Lindi.

"You are now a Mhindi, an Indian, and will live like a Mhindi. You will go to a good school and you will learn. Your father wanted that. Forget about the past. It is over." Yamekwisha.

The boy started to cry and was taken upstairs to the family flat.

"Why did she abandon me?" he pleaded in his North American inflections to the red, hairy face of Markham looming over him.

Markham had him lifted by the head and poured a shot of whisky down his throat.

"Bwana Markham," came Lateef's reproachful voice, "you are giving forbidden substance to this sick believer! Haram! Shame on you!"

"A little Scotch never harmed anyone," came the gruff reply.

"Sir," pleaded Lateef to Kamal, "please let me give you a bath."

"No," Kamal said. "I will do it myself. Though I'd appreciate clean sheets." He turned to Markham.

"Clean mattress, Mr. Markham!" demanded Lateef. "This man is paying you dollars!"

Later Kamal went out to sit on the patio outside the lounge. The sun, the salty breeze, the booming crash of the waves; here they were again. He'd been out two days, it seemed an eternity. Those nightmares. He had not for a long time recalled his childhood trauma so vividly, so precisely. Over time his mind had blotted out the details, so that what he ever recalled were abstractions, bloodless events in the resumé of his life. His dreams about that parting became fantastic allegories. Now in his recovery he had all his pain back again.

He looked around at the three men who had tended to him, John and Markham standing at the doorway, Lateef hovering beside him.

"It's the water I drank at that Fatuma's shop," he explained sheepishly, "that surely did me in."

The warm water with the greasy aftertaste. The thought made him shudder. "Perhaps they put a spell in it—to give me nightmares." He attempted a laugh.

"You said it, bwana, you've hit the nail," Lateef said.

"But I was only joking."

"Ah no, bwana. They wanted to look into your heart. They wanted to see that innermost self that resides there."

"Who? You mean that Fatuma?"

"They put a medicine into the water."

They put a potion into a doctor's drinking water. Some truth drug. Some doctor.

"And now they've seen into my heart?"

"Enh-heh. With the help of a mganga."

"What mganga?"

What nonsense, he thought, but he couldn't help feeling a certain trepidation. He turned gratefully to the tray of tea and toast that John brought for him. "I want to thank you all for looking after me," he said. "Really, I am touched." "It was nothing," Markham growled and disappeared inside.

The rest of the day Kamal spent outside on the patio and later on the beach. There was hardly anyone around; a few tourists set off for the Island in a motorboat; a fish vendor came by with a late catch; a group of youths strolling. He napped on the beach chair, too afraid for now to go and abandon himself back to his bed. He read from his anthology, though fitfully. There was in him that pleasant feeling, as he lay exposed to the elements of his childhood, that awareness of a gently throbbing but not unbearable wound. He had been transformed somehow, born again by his experience. By reliving the angst of his childhood, he had arrived in Kilwa shorn of foreignness. He had made his confession. Was this pure fantasy? Had he come under a spell? Did he believe in spells?

No. Not any more.

But he was back in Kilwa. And in the Kilwa he knew there was always magic. That thought was perturbing.

28

Sometimes we African sophisticates of a certain age, well travelled in the world, at ease even at a Stockholm reception on a winter's night, having raised ourselves from the primitivism in which we were born—and I don't mean this negatively—find ourselves pushed back onto our heels by the occasional eruptions of barbarism on our home ground. It is as if an uncouth elder, dishevelled, incoherent, unclean, shuffles in from the inner room where you would rather keep him to the cocktail party in progress in your drawing room. Incidences of magic are such. Simple magic is understandable—it is of the order of superstition. Even American presidents, we are told, consult the stars. But what of cannibalism: making stews out of murdered humans expressly quartered for the purpose, and using them as tonic to bring on strength and vitality? I have in mind the recent murders and mutilations of our albinos for purposes of witchcraft. In a macabre twist, the police recently exhibited in Dar es Salaam an albino human skin to discourage such atrocities. That they felt the general public needed discouragement is a backhanded admission, surely: more people than would care to admit believe in the efficacy of magic. If a potion works, why bother where it comes from? Still, call me an apologist—and those convinced of my provenance on a tree will sneer—I am firmly of the belief that not much separates humans from each other, wherever they come from, nor humans from the bestial. History shows amply that it is not only Africans who are capable of grotesqueries.

Of course Kamal was horrified by the grotesque examples of magic he had heard about upon his arrival. And yet—especially as a doctor—he seemed a little too sanguine about the potion he himself had been—or might have been—administered so that his heart could be peeked into and his nature revealed. I am one of those who get embarrassed about and angry at such beliefs. Surely they keep us back. But Kamal was desperate: if the potion took him closer in his quest, so be it.

Sorcery being the subject of the day, John the barman had informed Kamal why Markham wouldn't venture out to the beach at night: He could be mistaken for an albino and murdered, his precious body parts used to make potions to give strength to some sorcerer's client. They laughed. A potion could cost you two thousand dollars American, John added calmly, and Kamal looked at him in surprise. Was the man serious? The thought occurred to him that Markham was red, in any case; his fear, if real, was surely irrational. Where did one find such sorcerers? he asked John. Mostly in the west of the country, the barman said, but if you looked hard enough, you would find one even in these parts. You needed an agent.

Relating this conversation to me much later, during one of our tête-à-têtes in Dar, Kamal said he was surprised at himself, at the calm manner of his discussion with John. "It's surprising what begins to seem the order of the day, even a joke . . ."

"And remember," I told him, "it's not just albinos these devils kill, as you must know. Trade in body parts goes all the way up to Congo, to give strength to the militia leaders there."

"Well, something surely gives those monsters the strength to keep feeding on their people," Kamal replied.

He recalled a time, when he was little, when Mama would not let him out of her sight. There were people about who could take you away and use you for magic.

When he had his serious bout of malaria, Mama sat on the floor beside him, keeping watch, eyes wide with anxiety. Breathing deeply so he could hear the catch in her breath, a short, high-pitched squeal.

She gave him fever pills from the Indian medicine shop, but sparingly, and therefore ineffectually. She gave him compresses, and she boiled roots in water and made him drink it; perhaps they were medicine from a mganga, he'd never know. She brought prayers from Mzee Omari to recite over him and strips of cloth on which he had written formulae to tie to his bedpost. And waited for the miracle. She believed some evil spirit was possessing her son, but she also knew his sickness could be the work of mosquitoes. You could not live on the coast and not get homa from those devils at least once. And so it was spirits or mosquitoes, you took medicines against all. Anything that promised to work, you took.

"But you yourself don't believe in magic and prayers as medicine, do you, Doctor?" I probed.

"It's not what I believe to be true that's important, but what people believe for themselves, isn't it?" he replied musingly.

"Then if you believe a dawa works, it works, and if you believe the bones and skin of an albino—"

"That's extreme, and I didn't quite say that. But you have in mind that dawa, the medicine that Fatuma put into my water, don't you? It could actually have contained a compound to make you hallucinate and remember. That's possible."

"An African truth drug."

"Yes."

I thought he slipped out of that snare too easily.

29

The European town of Dar es Salaam that Mzee Omari had described in his verses was the older, picturesque section that lay by the seashore: the yellow Lutheran church with its square tower, the Roman Catholic cathedral with its silver spire, the broad, low white buildings with arched verandahs and, farther along, the Government House in its large grounds from where the German and British governors once ruled, and now—when Kamal arrived to live with his uncle Jaffu—the residence of the prime minister. A block in from the shore ran the elegant Independence Avenue, lined by acacia trees, its shop windows brazenly displaying items only to be gawked at by the native. Prominent at the centre of a traffic island stood the Askari Monument, memorial to the fallen soldiers of the First World War, which had so awed Omari bin Tamim. At its far end, the avenue abutted the Gymkhana Club and its golf course, in an area of small, shady side streets with beautiful bungalows.

Beyond this European town, once admired as the Berlin of Africa, lay the crowded, bustling Asian town dominated by the Shamsi khano, the prayer house, with its chiming clock tower; here Jaffu Punja had his shop, at the bottom of a two-storey building overlooking the narrow, potholed Jamat Street. The family residence was in one of the flats above. Of a race of seafaring merchants, as Mama had described them, every morning Uncle would sit on his chair close to a table, shirt open, making cryptic phone calls or vacantly staring out, picking his crotch, awaiting his cup of kahawa from the vendor; at lunch hour he would go upstairs to eat, take his nap, then he would return to the shop and await his afternoon kahawa—as placebound as anyone could be. His cropped hair was already greying; he was a man of few utterances, which he would emit in the form of throaty commands and concise opinions. In the evening, just after six, as the singing from the Shamsi khano came loud and clear from a loudspeaker, transforming the mood of the neighbourhood from one of commercial bustle into one of a complacent piety, Jaffu Punja had his bath, put on a plain loose shirt over freshly pressed cotton trousers and strolled over to the prayer house just as other men did. He would return and eat dinner with the family, then, having changed into a pyjama, go back downstairs to sit outside on the cement porch of his shop under a light and play cards and chat with the other shopkeepers.

Asians loved to play cards. In Kilwa too they would sit outside their shops, or on the town square at the seashore, and play. And eat snacks, and drink tea or kahawa. Now Kamal realized that of the Asians who all seemed the same, some were Shamsis, others Ithnasheris, and still others Hindus, which was why there were several prayer houses in the neighbourhood. But in Kilwa there were no Kalasingas, the Sikhs with their turbans and full beards, as there were in Dar. He, Kamal, had to become a Shamsi. A singing Indian. He did not know how.

His aunt, Zera, was a fair-featured, curly-haired and kindly woman considered generally to be a bit daft. She spoke rapidly and earnestly, often repeated herself, and as she spoke, she would stare into your eyes and was likely to make a grab for your hand or arm and start fidgeting with it, until you pulled it away. When Kamal first arrived, she had hugged him to her bosom, then handed him a container of Vim detergent, instructing him, "Wash with this soap, wash with this when you take your bath—it will make you white, you know, white—like me, look!—like a European." She had meant well, of course, but Kamal's skin had chafed and flaked, and bled, and Uncle had yelled at Auntie the only way he knew, acerbically, his crackling voice rising only a pitch.

His aunt and uncle had three kids of their own, two girls and a boy, the youngest and the darling of the home. Living in the typical

Asian style, repeated flat after flat, from building to building in the neighbourhood, the family shared two bedrooms on the second floor, one for the kids, the other for the parents. There was a small sitting room, and a dining area next to the entrance, attached to a window-less kitchen. His new home was crowded and noisy, and confusing, because he had to relate to so many of them, including three Asian females. He had never spoken to one before. But the meals were filling and satisfying. Communication was an ordeal, often an occasion for mirth, when he misspoke or misunderstood, or utter bewilderment, when he was caught in a crossfire between several voices babbling loudly in Kihindi all around him. Only Uncle spoke Swahili fluently, the way Kamal did; the others spoke the Indian variety, hearing which sometimes he in his turn couldn't help but break up into laughter.

At the raucous dining table, sometimes, as he watched the family members in their closeness and comfort and belonging, tears would roll down his cheeks. During one such moment, he asked his uncle, "Where is my father? Is he alive?" There was a sudden silence at the table, and then his aunt fluttered over to comfort him, herself breaking into tears. "Aren't we your parents? Isn't he your father?" She pointed to his uncle, who got up from the table without a word.

One day Kamal wrote a letter to Mama and told Uncle he wanted to post it. His uncle said, "If your mama had wanted to keep in touch, wouldn't she have written herself? And did she remind you to write her a letter? But go and post it, if you want to."

He did, and the following days after school his uncle quietly handed him the postbox key, so he that he would be the one to pick up his mother's reply in case it had come. His disappointment was bitter; his uncle was right. But Kamal had become the family's postman now, in charge of their Independence Avenue mailbox, bringing home let-ters from India, and from Kenya, Uganda, Congo, Madagascar, Zanzibar, other parts of Tanganyika. But not one from Kilwa.

Slowly, slowly he learned to bend his tongue to utter Kihindi. He could never call it by its Indian name, Kutchi; to him it was always Kihindi. The language of *kin ai*, and *thik ai* and *kem chhe*. He spoke it with a certain lilt, a musical accent, and he would tend to put vowels at the end of the words, the Swahili way: *mamedi, booti, foulo*. This manner of speaking, his dark brown skin, and his curly hair set him apart in his new, Indian environment. He was the local chotaro, the half-caste.

Everyone had a nickname in school, and his was Golo. It was friendly; even to this day, Kamal said, some of his friends knew him as Golo. It meant, in its original sense, servant, or slave. In a strange way, he was proud of it. There was nothing to be ashamed of, he was living in Africa, his continent. And later, it was just a moniker.

Later in life, in Edmonton, his wife Shamim would detest it. *How could you allow yourself to be called a* slave. *Where is your pride?* Once she had told off a friend who was in town and had enthusiastically called and asked to speak to Golo.

But that's what he was in Dar es Salaam: Golo, the African; the chotaro, the half-caste Indian; mouthing Indianisms with increasing fluency, occasionally stumbling.

Mama was the ache Kamal brought with him to Dar. Often he would recall their life together, the way they laughed and quarrelled, her constant struggle for money and the look of worry on her face, her drawing him close . . . but the image that overcame all, what could suddenly draw up a sob from deep within him, belonged to that morning when she just let him go. That expressionless face. Don't bring shame upon me. How could I, Mama. Lying in bed at night, as his childhood in Kilwa returned to him, as he pictured the streets, the houses, the shops, the ocean and the beach, he would also think of Saida, his companion and friend. His pupil. A many and a pany; a bad learner she was; he would smile in the dark. But she taught *him* how to read, she showed him the secret of the Arabic script. And like a nightingale having just found its song, suddenly she could recite poetry. You're a devil, Mama said when she first heard Saida recite. He recalled every significant moment of their time together, their meetings at the square, their walks along the seafront. Their secret place below the German graves, the lagoon. Saida, can I put my head on your lap . . . And Mzee Omari, who showed him his manuscript pages and asked him to read, shortly before he died. Shikamoo Mzee, I touch your feet. Why, Mzee, why did you have to hang yourself and die?

What would become of Saida? Did she remember him? He was not sure. Lately she had become a mganga of the Book. A girl with responsibility, who earned for her family. Who had no time to play. People came to see her with problems. She did not need school or English anymore. After he wrote to Mama, he wrote to Saida, a short letter in Arabic script, which would surely delight her, and this letter too he sent care of the Kilwa Post Office, as Uncle advised him to. But at his Dar post office portal, no sign from her either.

And so the years passed.

30

Here he was now, back in Kilwa, having tea at the crossroads chai shop, taxis and buses waiting for passengers, touts hanging about—strong men with gleaming biceps and predatory stares, evidently among the few who looked like they actually ate well. Did they meet to work out somewhere? Across the street, partly glimpsed behind a pickup, was the German monument. It was at this site that Kamal had come running that morning, in his wild bid to escape from the man Samji who had come to fetch him. It was from here that the bus finally dragged him away to Dar es Salaam. He had looked back just one last time and seen Saida standing in front of the monument. Watching.

He had never stopped to ask himself—until now—if she had ever received his letter, or if Mama had. Perhaps they hadn't. But as Uncle said, if Mama had wanted to stay in touch, wouldn't she have done so? And Saida was in the clutches of her family, consulting the Book she didn't understand and giving advice.

"You are dreaming, sir," Lateef said cheerfully, walking in from the sun. He ordered a soup, which arrived immediately, a large, meaty bone inside it. Another one of Kilwa's few hearty eaters.

Lateef had not shown himself the previous day, but now, unasked, obliged an explanation—"I was called away"—that was not one at all. What work does he do? Kamal watched him attack the bone with gusto. Taking a moment to look up, he ordered an extra mandazi. Kamal ordered a chai just to keep him company.

At this moment two women who had long stood uncertainly outside the entrance drifted in and stopped before him as the manager scowled and grumbled about unwanted beggars.

"Daktari . . ." the older one said.

"Yes?" He feigned sternness, their plaintive tone provoking his formal response.

"The girl is sick."

He took the younger woman's hand, acknowledged fever, then told the two to go to the town hospital. He had discovered that there was a physician in residence, whose name was, curiously, Dr. Engineer. They had spoken on the phone.

"We have no money, Baba . . ."

"Tell the doctor I sent you. Now go." He quickly, almost furtively, put some money in her hand. "Buy the medicine with this."

He glanced guiltily around him, at Lateef slurping his soup, at the glowering manager, at the cluster of touts gathered outside.

Even in charity you feel dirty; it's so easy it's not right, to give away a cure, possibly a life, just like that. And when you give, the word spreads, a provider has come, a donor is here, and a long line awaits you, the outstretched hand of Africa.

Later he would recognize this episode as his second turning point, the first one being his illness, possibly aided by a potion. He was a doctor, after all. How many sick people there must be like this girl. He did not even know her name.

He sipped his tea, met Lateef's eye.

"Any luck about Saida?" he asked.

"Not yet. Give it time, bwana."

How much time? Time for what? The matter was exceedingly simple: he needed to find Saida; she had relatives in town who knew something but were keeping mum.

A faint azan rose up from a mosque nearby, insinuated itself into their silence. Kamal watched Lateef become still, pay heed.

"Come, sir, let's go to the mosque," Lateef said.

Kamal pushed his chair back and they set off.

The mosque was around the corner, on a side street. The structure was imposing and seemed new, though the whitewash had long faded. There was an open space in front of it through which the street passed. Some eight or ten steps, built against the wall, reached up to the landing and the dark opening that was the door, a thin steady stream of men going inside. It was Friday. Kamal had not been to a mosque, not prayed in decades; had prided himself in being a man of reason and consequently an agnostic.

"You go," he said to Lateef. "I'll wait for you."

He wandered off, strolled up and down the streets, exchanging greetings with people outside their houses, pausing at the medical store, where he briefly greeted Amina and noted down the names of some medicines, and the video store, outside which he now noticed a martial arts movie poster on display, before arriving back outside the mosque. The prayer was over, men were departing. Soon the area was deserted, but there was no sign of Lateef. Kamal was about to leave, but just then he heard a mysterious humming. It came from inside the mosque, an undulation so faint and low and subtly pervasive in the air, it seemed the sunlight itself had been plucked. Kamal slowly climbed up the steps, drawn by the sound as it gathered volume; but there remained that lightness to its quality, a softness to its vibrations. Kamal took off his shoes and stepped inside.

A group of about twenty men wearing pure white kanzus and caps stood in a circle towards the front of the hall, swaying back and front, chanting, *La ilaha illallah* . . . the extra-low register of the chorus filling up the hall with an insistent resonance. Outside this circle three little boys were performing the same rite, with some sense of play. Someone instructed Kamal to go out the other door and wash his feet at the taps. How could he have forgotten. He did so and returned, stood against the back wall, watching the ecstasy. The swaying became more intense, back and forth and faster, the chanting louder, keeping pace. All the time, *La ilaha illallah* . . . There is no god but God.

And Kamal watching all this in the great hall was suddenly wrenched by a sense of loss, and bewilderment at his own condition. "After such knowledge . . . ?" Is this what we mean by progress?—leaving this knowledge behind? This faith and certitude, this continuity. This connection. Is a child growing up here less happy than one in Edmonton or Toronto costing tens of thousands more per year to maintain? Did I gain or lose by being sent away?

He left the mosque, the session now winding down. He did not wait for Lateef but walked straight to the main road and took a bus back to Masoko. After a lunch of ugali and maharage—maize meal and beans—and black tea, at a small restaurant, he strolled back to his hotel.

In the driveway he bumped into Markham, who had emerged from a guest cottage grabbing a bundle of linen. They stopped together, Markham struggling to control his breath.

"Here," Kamal said and took the man's wrist, counted his pulse. "Let me give you a checkup tomorrow morning."

31

In "Town," Dar es Salaam's Asian quarter, the new arrival, Golo, the dark curly-haired half-African, was supposed to be good at football. He was. And physically strong. He was that too. When he hit a hard buyu, blocking a ball at the opponent's foot with the side of his heel, he felt nothing but triumph; the Indian went limping away. It's his African bones, they explained. Watch out for his buyu. How could this be, though, when his diet had included only a bony piece of meat on the occasional good day, and there were nights when he even went to bed hungry, while these pure-breed Indians ate three full meals and drank milk nightly before bed? As any African would tell you, it was the daal they ate that softened them. He was Golo, he did not eat daal. And he was a hero to his young cousin Azim, who once explained his prowess: "You know, you know, my brother Kamal has the blood of an African warrior—like, like, like . . . Tarzan! You should see him finish a bone—like, like, like . . . a lion!"

Strong but alone. Returning home from school in the afternoon; playing marbles outside the khano before prayer; on Sunday at the seashore; always that awareness of his distance from the others, even in their midst, and their unspoken awe of him. Often he felt the speculative gazes of the neighbourhood following him down a street.

His uncle could not relate to this half-caste nephew from Kilwa. What had made him send for the stranger to live in the family's midst? He never denied him anything, though, and Kamal never felt second class in the home, dark skin and all. No one taunted him or teased him about his background or his mother. And Auntie was simply a natural, kind and generous but crazy: stuffing a sweet into his mouth, a coin into his pocket—here, here, take it—and a pat on the head hard enough almost to dislodge it.

Of his three cousins, Azim was three years younger than Kamal, Shenaz was in between them, and the fiery Yasmin was older than him by a year. The four of them to a room, which had two bunk beds. Living on top of each other. Privacy was simply assumed when required. He knew when Shenaz got her first bra, ready-made and pointed, as she insisted, from Janmohamed's; he observed the signals among the women when Yasmin started getting her periods; he had to go across the street and buy her pads, which came in a shoe-size box wrapped in newsprint, so that everybody knew.

They fought like cat and dog, he and Yasmin. Over anything: whose turn it was to do what, who would read the paper first, who had said what against whom. There was an element in their quarrel of the fact that he was boy, she was girl, and they were not strictly brother and sister. He was an alien male and in her way as a young woman newly aware of herself. When, in a new sleeping arrangement, she took the bunk above his, to be next to the window looking down on the street, and secretly at boys, he could not be unaware of her climbing up or down and showing her knickers, tight against her ass. Black knickers, deep red knickers. Surely she knew she was exposing. He burned, pulled the blanket over his head. And then, once, only once . . . Cousins arrived from Zanzibar, Kilosa, Mwanza, or wherever, there were seven or eight to the room, adults and children, sleeping any which way. He and she shared his lower bunk, an uncle went above. And there he was, awake in the middle of the night, erected, she with her frock pulled up just, revealing the tight panties. Her bum towards him. With heart throbbing, head screaming, he squirmed, he sweated. Did he touch her? He always said no.

She reported him the next day, thankfully, perhaps prudently, only to her mother, who took Kamal aside and said, to his confusion, "Arré, you're growing up! Look at you! Chi-chi-chi, you should do it in the bathroom sometimes. Get it out, get it out!" He did not know what she meant. And why did the complainer smile?

No wonder as adults in Canada they did not talk.

"Ah Goro, what kind of Indian will you be?" Sabini would tease him. A question projected forward into the future, to be picked up eventually and taken where? Brought back here. The answer: a failed Indian.

Sabini was one of the three African tailors who sat in a row behind their sewing machines on the sidewalk of Jamat Street. A tall man, always wearing a shirt over his trousers, a kofia over his head, he was the acknowledged master, the fundi of clothes. It was he who stitched the neighbourhood boys' grey cotton school shorts, and their precious woollen trousers to wear during festivals. When the mood struck him he would intercept Kamal, who might be returning home from school or play, with, "Ah, Goro," rolling the *l* the Swahili way. Kamal would go over and stand to attention before the fundi's Pfaff machine to humour him. And Sabini would begin his act. "Eti, look at you." He would pinch the boy's arm. "You are as black as I am." And Kamal would hold up his arm and go close and say, "But there is a little of the Matumbi red there. That is the difference." Sabini would laugh. "You are a rogue, Kamalu, and a true Swahili." Which was a compliment. "Listen to this one." He would tell a story.

The lowly servants too—there were always two of them and the turnover was often fast—saw in him a fellow, the African they recognized and he did not deny, to whom they pleaded silently for understanding, and who protested as mutely in their favour. He could not yell at them, call them *boy* as others did, or *kario*, or *chhoro*, or *chhach-hundro* and so on, a long and constantly renewed list of pejoratives. They well knew he was not one to call out a burn mark on an ironed shirt and await the drastic consequences, or mention missing coins from his pants pocket, and he would rather not have seen the kitchen servant quickly put a piece of meat into his mouth from the pot of boiling curry and wince afterwards.

Only Uncle was aware of his bond with the workers: his eye would follow him as Kamal drifted in the direction of Sabini outside the shop threshold, where the two would banter; he would see through the boy's pretended distraction as a hapless servant faced the women's wrath.

The most insulting term for a servant was used by Uncle when he addressed the boy who ran odd jobs around the shop. "Weh, mtumwa," Uncle would call, You slave, do this or that. Take this chit to that shop, tell Mama upstairs to send tea, go and buy muhogo from the street vendor at the corner. Each time he heard this address, Sabini would glance up momentarily. Once he retorted, "Bwana, we thought that after independence we would not hear such terms." And Uncle replied lightly, "Well, independence has come, and I have the shop and you are still the tailor sitting outside." "You are right," Sabini agreed with a laugh. "We all bring our luck with us."

Uncle was not a bad man. Perhaps he thought calling a young servant mtumwa was appropriate. He himself did not abuse servants—that was left to Auntie and Yasmin. Uncle was the final arbiter after all the accusations of theft and misbehaviour had been heaped; when it only needed a waterboarding to draw out a confession.

Only once had Uncle beaten Kamal, severely with a stick, when the boy came home having bloodied two neighbours' kids, who themselves had fallen on him previously with a gang. Some hidden spring inside Uncle's mind released, some suppressed feeling seemed to vent, so unreasonable and uncontrollable was the retribution. He did not ask what happened, simply picked up the brass yardstick. Then, when Kamal had been rescued by Sabini, sobbing violently, he had railed, "To you I am nothing but a mtumwa, a slave . . . why have you taken me away from my mother . . . my father would have given you a good beating, he would . . ." Sabini held him, before Auntie arrived to take him away, and a servant brought him water. Azim, to whom he was a hero and a lion, held his hand, saying, "Basi, Kamalu, basi." Hush.

He would never forget the frightful look that had come over Uncle's face, a look not of trivial rage, an incontinent temper, but of a quiet and evil determination to squash him like an insect. As if some Hyde had emerged from that usually phlegmatic mien. Shocked by this outburst, at having revealed something of himself that he would not have admitted to, Kamal's defiant accusation mocking him before a dozen witnesses, Uncle never again lifted a hand to him. In fact Kamal could detect some smidgen of respect in his attitude. A respect expressed in the occasional sardonic and knowing smile, watching to see how he'd get on after all.

But why had Uncle brought him over from Kilwa?

After Kamal had been rescued from Uncle Jaffu's retribution, Zera Auntie railed against her husband. Calling him inhuman and a beast, scolding and wailing, she had finally pronounced with simple elo-quence, "If he goes away, I will die, and it will be up to you. You will answer to the children."

And Uncle, sheepish, had answered, "Look, nothing has happened to him. He's a boy. I was treated much worse."

It was on a Sunday afternoon, when Kamal had gone out with Shenaz and Azim to the seashore, that a moment of intimacy occurred between the cousins and the answer to his question was revealed to him. It was the hour when the Asians flocked to the shore every Sunday, sitting across from the cathedral, watching the odd steamer and the two tug-boats on the water, children running on the beach, rolling in the grass, vendors selling street food. At that moment, the three of them sitting on the grass in a quiet spot and sharing a picnic, the truth slipped out. "Promise you will never tell," Shenaz said quietly, flinging her head once so that her pigtails went flying. She was the quiet one, with the soft features, and an endearing way of assuming a serious, earnest, and almost adult look. "You must not tell we have told you," she repeated. Azim nodded. "Promise by God and . . . and . . ." He would have added "By your mother," but held back. "I promise," said Kamal. "By God and the Prophet." And so they told him the story—his hidden story. Their mother had become very sick, the doctor had given her only months to live. It was cancer, or TB, or some tumour, the cousins could not decide which. An Indian holy man happened to be visiting Dar and was consulted, and he told their mother and father that they should adopt a yatim, an orphan, preferably an African. The yatim was God's price for allowing her the extra years. And Uncle said,

"My cousin Amin left a child behind in Kilwa, why don't we adopt him." And so they made queries; unbeknownst to Kamal, Uncle went to Kilwa and had a look at him, and bought him from his Mama, promising to give him a bright future.

Of course none of them sitting at the beach knew how much Kamal had been bought for.

"Surely I'm not completely off track, am I"—he said to me—"in seeing a certain circularity here, history, albeit on a small scale, repeating itself? My grandmother, or her mother, was sold as a slave to some Indian; and I was also sold, to an Indian. I know, I know: I went on to become a successful doctor."

"You have a house in Canada," Markham said, and it was as if he were breaking the news to Kamal. Perhaps he was not asking but admonishing, reminding his guest of his responsibilities.

"Edmonton," Kamal replied. "Yes, I have a house there."

A big one too, designed to specs; private bathrooms, a game room, a prayer room; my study. A man comes to garden, and in the winter a team comes to clear the snow from the long, sloping driveway.

"And a medical practice?"

"Yes, I have three clinics. Doing well."

"Must be nice."

They were just the two of them in the lounge late this evening, seated at a table, John washing up at the bar to the sound of a lively music turned down very low. A cool breeze blew, leading the tide in towards the shore. The silence between them was weighted with a question. Kamal gave it time, then answered it.

"I heard a call inside me, from someone who was very close to me in the past. I had to come and find her . . ."

"An old girlfriend."

"Well, we were young then."

"Come to chase a shadow, then."

"She was real enough when I knew her."

Very casually Kamal moved his hand and touched the tawiz at his neck, to reassure himself, a secret believer before an avowed agnostic.

"Here's good luck to you, then," Markham said.

"Thanks."

It was Kamal's turn next.

"Tell me, Ed—have you left anything behind? Family? Property?"

"I've a son in England. We don't keep in touch. This hotel is all the property I possess in the world—I believe I owe you two days' rent."

That's what Markham had offered in return for a physical checkup. Now the checkup was done, whatever was possible under the circumstances, and the prognosis looked serious, even without blood results. The sample had been sent to the Kilwa hospital.

"You paid in advance, Ed. You nursed me during my illness."

"That was John."

"All right. But I'm serious, you should get a full checkup done in Dar."

"And that will help me?"

"It will."

"Seriously, tell me—how many months would you give me, Doc?"

It was a question he had asked before.

"I don't give months or years, Ed. But treatment could help you."

Nicely ducked.

The next morning Kamal arrived in Kilwa early and anxious. From the monument, where he was dropped off, he first took a brisk walk to the harbour, spent some moments looking out to the sea. The breeze was cooling, the tide was out. A few vessels were beached and receiving attention. At a kidau being loaded, he discerned the large figure of Lateef supervising the job. He had discovered that Lateef exported timber, which was cut and processed at a mill in the forest. The wood was headed for Zanzibar, and from there north to the Middle East. Kamal turned around and walked away, not wishing to be hailed.

The town was only partly awake. Outside their homes people washing their faces; two girls in uniforms, heads wrapped in scarves, striding off to school, looking rather cheerful; a woman at a porch frying vitumbua. The technology had changed from the days of Bi Kulthum: instead of a few individual small woks on the stove frying the sweet bread, there were eight smaller ones joined together in two rows of four. A bus was readying to leave for Dar as Kamal turned into the chai shop. It was busy but a table was cleared for him.

After his tea and mandazi he left to go and see Fatuma. He had resolved that he would see her alone, without the agency of Lateef; she must deal with him, and he with her. If she refused to help him, it must be straight to his face. The shop was closed. He entered the side alley and arrived at the porch in the compound behind the shop, where he saw Amina at a gas stove. "Karibu," she greeted, as though expecting him, and he responded with thanks, and before he could inquire further she indicated the room in the corner. "Mother's inside."

He went towards the room. "Hodi," he called out softly at the door, then louder.

"Karibu," came a strained reply and he walked in.

The room was small and cluttered, torn linoleum on the floor. There was a broken sofa facing the doorway, and a television on a stand against a side wall. A window, its half curtain drawn, lit up the room with sunlight. Bi Fatuma was lying on her side on the floor under the TV, wearing a khanga wrapped up to her chest. Her head was raised, supported on one hand. The wrap looked old and faded, and was likely her nightdress. He went and sat on the sofa, and they stared at each other for some moments, the look on her face an indulgent curiosity, perhaps a sour humour at his expense.

"You're still here. You like our town."

"I was born here."

Outside, Amina was talking, perhaps to her husband, Ali, saying Fatuma had a visitor. A gust wafted in a smell of cooking. His mouth watered. Barazi, he said to himself, pigeon peas cooked in coconut.

"Now this woman you're looking for . . . ," Fatuma said.

"Saida. Yes, she's your niece, didn't you tell me?"

"Enh, Saida. Now why are you looking for her?"

Patiently, he explained once again, "We were children together. We were friends. Our mothers were friends. Did you know my mother? She was called Hamida."

"So that is why you are looking for her. Because you played together."

He must seem stupid to her. Or a deceptive male, perhaps. She eyed him, the look implying, There is obviously more than childhood games involved here.

"You have any business with her?" Fatuma asked.

"It's been a long time since I saw her. I want to meet her."

"And perhaps you want to give her some money?"

"That's possible—a gift . . . Does she need it?"

"I don't know," she said flatly, putting a hand to her side.

He did not move, sat and looked at her, then around the room. There was a photo hanging next to the entrance, showing Fatuma flanked by Ali and Amina. Fatuma wore a bui-bui. He wondered what other pictures she had. She was watching him.

He turned back to her with a final plea: "Tell me what you know. I saw her last in 1970 . . ." When he had returned to Kilwa briefly, before setting off for university. And never saw her again.

She watched him reflect on his memory, then relented: "And wasn't that the time I myself got married and went to live in Lindi?"

Not a question, simply framed as such. He knew the tone.

"I hope you had a good life in Lindi, Fatuma. My mother was in Lindi. Hamida—did you know her?"

"I knew her. But they went on to Songea or Tabora."

"And Saida? What happened to her?"

"She had a child . . ."

Whose child? he wanted to scream out in English. "Boy or girl?" he asked. "Where is that child now?"

She looked away.

He sighed. "Let me know if you find out anything."

"Look at my back," she said. "It hurts me."

He went over to her and lowered himself down on his knees to examine her. "Turn the other way," he instructed and pressed her back and side, saw her wince. She was wearing nothing underneath. Women used to do that. The tenderness in her side alarmed him. Is everybody whom I see dying? He stood up and told her she must visit the hospital as soon as possible and gave her the name of an analgesic to take. She turned around, gave him a wry look of gratitude.

"If you are a doctor who was born here, why are you abroad treating foreigners?" she asked petulantly.

He had no reply, and simply smiled.

He departed, his expectations half fulfilled. He was being toyed with, of course. But he had also discovered a trail, a short one, a footstep; he had to keep pursuing. But for how long?

The town hospital was a short walk from the site of the hangman's tree, which some years ago had given up the ghost and been cut down; in its place stood a plain, whitewashed monument. There was some irony in its makeshift crudeness, compared to the century-old German memorial down the road by the taxi stand, its brass plaque intact, the names and dates exact. The inscription on this one had been hand-painted unevenly in large black letters, the awkward line breaks clearly the work of an illiterate or a lazy painter. It was an embarrassment, installed by the fiat of bureaucracy, perhaps with foreign money. No care, no loving hand had attended it.

Kamal walked over to the hospital.

The walk-in clinic was a room in the middle of the corridor facing the road; an overflow of patients sat outside on the floor; inside was packed, the air filled with the raw odour of unadorned humanity. At the far end, in a cubicle set off by a curtain, Dr. Engineer had his consulting space. Just outside it, behind a table, sat the nurse, who also registered the patients. Name? she would ask; postbox number? Do you have a cell phone? Sign here or put your thumbprint.

The doctor was a short, somewhat heavy-set man of about forty, wearing a stethoscope around his neck. "Ah, Dr. Kamal." He shook hands and led Kamal into his cubicle, walking briskly with a limp. He sat down behind an old wooden table, on which was a ledger book for recording cases; Kamal took the chair opposite him. A small shelf behind the doctor held some medicines.

"Most cases are routine," Dr. Engineer explained, after the niceties, "and the remedy is a simple painkiller. Once in a while, an antibiotic is called for, or an antimalarial. I have samples, which I distribute—and hope for the best, that they'll take them on time. Anything serious and I'm stumped—they can't afford to go to Dar. Cancer, and what do you do? Aspirin for the pain. Ditto for malaria, unless I have received a free shipment."

As he spoke, he glanced up at the curtain, and Kamal knew he was using up valuable time.

"I must apologize for the patients who drop in on me," he said. "I try to discourage them and refer them to you."

"Not at all, my friend. You are welcome to them. In fact, if you wish, I can get you authorization to practise. The DC is a friend. But you are not here for long, obviously . . ." He made a wry face. "I will send Ed Markham's blood sample to Dar. It will take time to get the results, you know."

"A formality. He has everything wrong with him. The heart condition looks severe. He had asthma as a child, and I'm positive he has diabetes. And if any of those don't kill him, there's the prostate. I've recommended immediate admission to a hospital in Dar for a checkup. Could you arrange that for me?"

Dr. Engineer eyed him thoughtfully. "I'll do that on your say-so. But if we are talking surgery, it could mean Bangalore or Johannesburg."

They said no more, and as Kamal left, his eyes briefly lingered over the waiting room, the silent, patient faces, even of the children. Life expectancy, he reminded himself, was in the fifties, if that. He recalled assisting senior doctors on their duties when he was in medical school in Kampala. The same crowded rooms then as now, the same fate-afflicted faces.

"Let's meet for a drink," Dr. Engineer said cheerfully to his back, and Kamal turned to reply, but the man was already behind his curtain.

Waiting for his taxi, Kamal couldn't get the clinic out of his mind. The crowded room, that warped shelf of inadequate medicines in the doctor's cubicle. He thought of his own clinics in Edmonton. The waiting numbers there were large too, but the expectations were different. He had returned from a pampered world, where a remedy was offered for every ailment, real and imagined. A glut of medicines and treatments. Death was an affront. But someone like Fatuma would be looked after. She would get her X-rays taken and a host of tests made and not pay a dime. Her medicine would come subsidized. Her taxi fare would be subsidized.

Curiously, he could not recall Mama ever having been sick. Tired, yes; at times sad; and angry. A whole palette of moods. But never sick in bed shivering helplessly with homa, the dreaded fever. She blamed his illnesses on his weak Indian blood; until someone else in the neighbourhood fell sick, and he would say, "See?" Children did fall sick, there were deaths, but it was all perceived as bad luck. God's indiscriminate angel Azrael out to collect souls. No question, why should children die of simple homa. There was only Allah to assist you; and the waganga, the witch doctors or traditionalists who gave roots or powders or performed more nefarious rites to keep away that angel. He himself had survived malaria on a liquor of root extracts boiled by his mother and with the prayers of Mzee Omari culled from the Quran. It had seemed the most natural thing in the world. Alternative medicine. How far would she have gone to save him? Even a human sacrifice? And then she gave him away.

· 33 ·

The making of Golo into an Indian of the Shamsi community meant that he had to learn their language and worship their gods, sing weird hymns to them. The khano was a wonderland—an alien spaceship, as he would think of it later—brilliantly lit with chandeliers; on every wall and pillar hung their imam's photos, staring at you from every angle. After the prayers a few hundred people mingled about, food offerings were auctioned in a loud, festive ambience, kids ran around screaming and playing. Khano was prayer and party combined.

Most people went every evening, some also early morning for meditation. The building itself was an imposing two-storey yellow structure topped with a tile-roofed clock tower. Late afternoon Kamal would take his bath, and wearing clean clothes stroll over to the khano. The best part of khano for boys was before and after the ceremonies, playing games and getting into mischief. Across the yard from the khano was an empty plot where they shot marbles, gambling at the ad hoc casino of marble games set up in a row: you won a marble if you hit it from a distance, and lost yours if you missed. There were sharpshooters who never missed and left with bulging pockets, and dodgy operators with false trails on the ground to waylay your piece. Just before prayer time, the session having peaked, the religious monitors would sweep in and the boys would collect their stuff, scamper off to the taps to wash their feet, and go inside.

It was easier, Kamal discovered soon enough, to conform to mischief, be among the other misfits, the poor and the half-castes, generally the darker hued. Smoking was sin and therefore a forbidden pleasure. Where else could you smoke undetected than at the cinema, where the misfits would sneak in during khano time, though at risk of painful penalty. The cinemas were the Empire, the Empress, and the Avalon. At the side of the Empress was an alley where you could hide and smoke away, and when the bell rang and the lights went out inside, as the flag came up on the screen and the national anthem played, you snuck into the theatre to watch the latest fantasy extravaganza, *Ben Hur*, *Tarzan*, *Shane*, or whatever. And try not fidgeting in case a flashlight approached and found you out, and chased you up the aisle to the lobby to receive a cuff from fat Mahesh the manager. Sometimes the religious monitors would show up while you smoked and take down your names, to report next day in school for a reckoning with the fearsome Rahim Master.

Over the religious lives of boys in Dar es Salaam ruled the great dictator Rahim Master.

"I never realized what a colourful and exciting life you Asians lived," I said to him and could have bitten off my tongue for my affront. I surely knew that the whole point of his story was what a difficult and how incomplete and unsuccessful a conversion he went through from African to Asian—more precisely, Indian.

"I didn't mean it quite that way," I apologized.

"I know." He looked around. "You know, at this moment I could do with a smoke. I gave up a long time ago."

We were sitting by candlelight at the Seacliffe, situated at the promontory of Oyster Bay, where the local nouveau riche mingle with the tourists and the foreign-aid expatriates. Before us a half-finished South African red. He'd had tilapia, I a steak. I partake in such privilege only when offered it. As I sat there I couldn't help musing how far my host had come, having undergone in his adulthood yet another unfinished conversion, into a Canadian. Was it resentment at his situation that brought out my ostensibly unintended barb?

"Tell me about this dictator—this Rahim Master."

He grinned.

"Even now," he said, "there are those who recall him fondly despite the canes and blows they received, because he taught the faith, and above all, drummed into them the holy ginans, those hymns which they will never forget. He kept the tradition alive. For me he was terror personified."

How could this Golo, with the dark chotara skin and curly hair that screamed "Unteachable!" and "Donkey!" learn to sing the Indian ginans whose ragas were stranger than the film tunes that came on the radio, which at least he learned to recognize and to like and hum to himself? "I will drum these holy ginans into you!" the teacher would thunder at him, landing a thump on his back. "Copy down all the verses fifty times in your notebook, and stand up on the table! Your mark, E!" And Kamal would join the other "donkeys," some of them punished simply because they couldn't carry a tune, and stand up on his desk, grinning back at his classmates, but humiliated nevertheless. How he dreaded those religion classes, especially on the days when a ginan had to be recited. Then Rahim Master, always in one of his two faded suits, would come in and begin the inquisition, walk down the aisles, ask each boy in turn to recite a verse from the prescribed ginan, always starting from the beginning of the first row, next to the window. He loved his ginans, there would be a smile on his face at the start, a fragile smile ready to explode at the first failure to recite. Verse after verse, the master approached, bringing judgment, and Kamal sweated; it would be over soon, but not soon enough. While he waited he would count and predict what verse would fall on him to recite; he would go over it in his mind. But the master had an antenna sensitive just to that extra heartbeat, the tingle in the nerve of the less than fully prepared; homing in, he would skip a few verses when your turn came, stand in front of you and calmly ask you to recite that impossible one. You spluttered, you failed, you shrank inside your sweaty white shirt and waited for the blow to fall. You simply had to learn all the six, or twelve, or twenty-one verses by heart.

"In Kilwa we were never religious. Rather, Islam was all around us, it was in the way we lived, even the language we spoke, the name people gave to a donkey or a boat. We lived under the benign gaze of Allah—so to speak. Mama would pray when she got up in the morning; the shopkeeper opened his store, Mzee Omari began his utenzis, always invoking His name; people went to mosque on Friday, wearing kanzu and kofia; during Eid we put on new clothes . . . It was all implicit and effortless. Now in Dar I was with a community whose faith was a musical, an ongoing Bollywood epic, with singing and food and dramatic characters, beginning with the great dictator Rahim Master. There were the preachers, who could stand up for an hour and draw tears from the congregation; the fanatics on the lookout for deviants—the stinking, foul-mouthed crazies who were tolerated and fed, the embezzlers headed for the Inferno, people with funny nicknames, men with a roving eye. All the gossip."

There was a mskiti, a simple African mosque, that Kamal would pass on his way home from school. It lay on one of several different routes he would take, in a block of African houses, and was marked only by its whitewashed outer wall, the open door, and its aura of utter serenity; the sheikh, a lean man with a stooping frame, would be standing framed by the entrance, looking out, or sitting outside on the stone bench against the wall, and Kamal would greet him, "Shikamoo, Baba." "Marahaba," would come the appropriate reply, with a pleasant smile. He would think of Mzee Omari then. On Friday afternoons a handful of people would be going in and out. One day, impulsively, when the sheikh was not around, Kamal stepped inside the mskiti, away from the raging sun, and stood in the empty hall until its stillness filled him, its air cooled him and his eyes had adjusted; without a thought he went down on his knees and began the ritual prayer he had not performed in more than a year. More than a prayer to God, this was a communion with his previous life. When he had finished and stood up and turned around, he saw the old sheikh standing at the back in the shadows, watching him. Kamal returned whenever the whim took him—when he had no one walking with him, when the street was quiet—and felt elated afterwards. After his stint inside, he would sit briefly outside on the bench with Sheikh Hemedi, who kept a bottle of water ready for him to drink, filled from a tap. He told the sheikh all about himself. Kamal asked him once why there was no azan called at this mskiti. It was too small, the sheikh replied; those who wished to come needed no reminder. However, one day as Kamal approached the mosque, he was thrilled to hear the azan being called out, just for his sake, in the sheikh's voice.

One afternoon he was observed by a schoolmate. The next day two boys watched him enter the mskiti. He was reported not to his uncle but to Rahim Master, into whose office he was called, where he received the expected bawling out for his deviancy from the true faith. But it was the pained silence at the dinner table, and schoolmates muttering behind his back, that persuaded Kamal to abandon his brief escapes into what had become his memory-life. He would pass by the mskiti and greet the sheikh when he saw him, and the old man responded pleasantly as though nothing were the matter. Soon Kamal avoided that street altogether. Zera Auntie asked him if he had asked forgiveness at the khano; he said that he had.

The boyhood games and the narrow escapes, the stolen smokes, the sneak viewings of movies, and listening to the tailor Sabini's stories while standing before his Pfaff machine and laughing till the tears came to his eyes, or receiving a whole shilling from a furtive Zera Auntie to spend in school on Coca-Cola and peanuts. Instances such as these would give a happy glow to his Dar days when he recalled them; they brought him a sense of belonging to a community, a growing comfort in his surroundings. His deviation into the austere familiarity of an African mskiti was one lapse from this new life. The pain and bitterness of that episode only highlighted how much he had been accepted by his Asian community.

Still, he was different. His features announced it plainly, spoke of provenance, posed questions. There were the reminders, the small and large ones, accidental or aimed to wound. He had his memories, his private world to turn to at night. No one could interfere with his memories, they were his solace, his hope for some future resolution in his life. They chained him to his past.

But one evening even this sanctum was violated, when any remaining wholeness he carried within him was shattered. After khano the neighbourhood streets briefly filled up in the dark—people briskly

strolling in twos and threes, and women shuffling together in ani-
mated groups with little children and all the time in the world, and
noisy youths standing around at the street vendors. On Jamat Street,
Uncle would partially open the store and sit outside, shooting the breeze
with neighbours. Sometimes the men played cards. The children and
Zera Auntie would be upstairs, drinking their milk, listening to music
on the radio, Indian filmi or British and American pop.

That fateful night Kamal brought from upstairs a pudding for his
uncle, but he did not see him sitting with his friends outside.

"Eh, Kamalu, what do you want?" one of the men asked.

"This pudding is for Jaffu Uncle, and Auntie asks if he wants tea—
but where is he?"

A man muttered under his breath and the three of them laughed
softly.

"Go, Kamalu, he is eating to his heart's content. Pudding and
everything."

"He is eating pudding already?"

"Go now."

On his way to go upstairs, however, walking through the shop,
Kamal saw a young African woman emerge from the storeroom at the
back. She was in a khanga and barefoot. As she walked out, the men
called out "Kwa heri!" just as Uncle emerged, tying up his pyjamas.
He always wore a pyjama in the evening.

"What—"

"Auntie said to bring pudding for you—"

Roars of laughter erupted behind him.

"All right. Go upstairs now."

As Kamal went out he heard one of the men say, "A total joy, isn't
she? Pudding!"

"Total joy," said Uncle. "Tonight was pudding."

Kamal understood. Excited as any teenager at this lascivious account
of a sexual encounter, and yet . . . she was a bought one; a young
African girl.

Total joy. How repugnant.

The thought kept plaguing his mind: Was this how his father had
seen Mama? Is this what she had meant to him? That couldn't have

been the case, his father had had a studio photo taken with him and his mama; acknowledging togetherness, he had left money for them in a post office account. But he had gone away. How much of what Mama had told him about his father was true, how much fanciful? And Mama herself, who had been paid for him . . . who never wrote to him—was she true?

Was there anything certain in his life to call his own?

He lay in bed that night, in tears, facing the embrace of the cool, hard brick wall, talking to his imaginary comforter.

How did he imagine her? Had she grown with him, now a teenager?

He looked embarrassed. "I imagined her as she had been, and yet older so she could understand me. I would tell her, 'Thank God I have you, Saida. Tonight I feel most miserable, and I have no one else.' And I would say other things that are too embarrassing for me to relate."

· 34 ·

Dr. Navroz Engineer had come to Tanzania as a child in the 1960s with his communist Indian parents, both of them doctors and disenchanted with India but ardent admirers of Julius Nyerere, Tanzania's president, and his brand of African socialism. Navroz's father still practised in Dar, his mother had died. He had two uncles, who also immigrated to Tanzania. He didn't know why he himself didn't go overseas for better prospects and a comfortable lifestyle, he simply got stuck practising. There was always so much to be done, day to day, he explained to Kamal.

They'd come to sit at a table in the lounge and waited to be served. A thin drizzle pattered on the roof and outside on the beach. It was cool by tropical standards, and Navroz wore a light sports sweater, of the type favoured by tennis players. How long was it since he'd had a game of tennis, Kamal wondered.

"How about your own family?" he asked Navroz.

"Two kids, boys. They are with my wife in Dar. School and so on."

"Why Kilwa?"

"Why Kilwa?" Navroz grinned. "I belong to a consortium of doctors—we have clinics in various towns across the country. We try to rotate our assignments."

"How long will you be in Kilwa, then?"

"A few more months, perhaps more. We lost a doctor recently to a more lucrative practice. Too busy to get lonely here, but there's a flight to Dar every day. And it's frustrating when you're limited by means. I try not to think too much about it . . . and avoid this"—he swirled the Scotch in his glass—"as much as possible."

They were served their dinner. The chef had finally acceded to Kamal's request for spinach on the menu, having overcome the slight that the guest should insist on peasant and servant fare instead of a culinary adventure from the local sea catch.

"Over here I'm afraid we are not very disciplined in what we eat," Navroz confessed, without sounding in the least apologetic. He put a soggy chip—the national delicacy, Kamal had decided—into his mouth. "Too tempting. Have some—though as a doctor, I wouldn't advise you to."

Kamal watched the round face, the cropped greying hair, the stooped shoulders. There was an unaffectedness in the local doctor that he rather liked. He tried to imagine Navroz's life, at home in Dar, or here in Kilwa, but couldn't. *I only have the past to cling to. I belong here, speak the language, but move around unconnected like a ghost.*

"I understand you are from Kilwa originally," Navroz said. "This is home?"

"I was born here," Kamal replied. "This is my village, I guess—my mother's place."

"But you don't belong anymore . . ."

"Is that a question?"

"Yes."

"Well. I am of here and these are my people, and yet I have a life and a family elsewhere. In Canada I've thought of myself as African—though not African Canadian or African American—attractive illusions for a while. It becomes difficult to say *precisely* what one is anymore. Isn't that a common condition nowadays?"

He sounded too anxious, too slippery, and they sat in silence together. The lounge was crowded at the bar, buzzed with the chatter and noise of one-day tourists who would depart in the morning. John had turned on dance music, though no one paid heed. Markham was not in sight.

"And what are you?" Kamal asked Navroz, more to test him.

"Me? It's difficult, as you say. I am called a Tanzanian Asian." Then he added with a chuckle, "Do you know Kilwa was settled by Persians more than a thousand years ago?"

Kamal nodded, felt somewhat slighted. This was his hometown, after all.

"My own ancestors went from Persia to India," Navroz said. "I am a Parsi, as you've no doubt guessed. A complete circle, you see. My DNA would tell you that I am ethnically related to the Swahili. Amazing world we live in, isn't it?"

Kamal agreed.

Navroz had a quiet smile on his face, his look saying, at least to Kamal's tilted interpretation, And now I am the one from here, not you. Neither of them spoke for a while. Kamal found himself still rankled by Navroz's remarks. The waiter refilled their drinks. They ordered tea. Finally Navroz said, referring to Markham, "If you don't mind my asking, why take all this trouble for the mzungu, this white man?"

At Kamal's request, Navroz had booked Markham for a checkup in Dar es Salaam. Kamal would pay the expenses.

"Why not?" Kamal said, which was no answer.

"Just wondered. For that money you could get a year's malaria medication for a dozen people. More lives saved."

"It seemed like the thing to do, I guess. I examined him. I could hardly say, Now go ahead and die."

It had turned quiet now, the music had stopped, and both turned to see that the tourists were gone. As Navroz readied to depart, he said,

"I saw another of your patients this morning. Her name is Fatuma."

"And? Her backache?"

"Cancer, I suspect. As you no doubt thought too. And long advanced. The pain is going to get worse."

They said goodbye and agreed to meet again.

· 35 ·

Markham was out in the lounge early the next morning, sober and a new man, ready to fly out to the capital for his checkup, wearing a light blue linen jacket, albeit crumpled, and a red tie. The sparse hair had been wetted and combed to one side. His shaved face looked soft and naked.

He finished instructing John, who would be in charge, and arrived at Kamal's table to join him for breakfast. He picked up his napkin, a nervous, embarrassed look on his face. Like a boy off to a new school.

"All ready?" Kamal asked.

"Ready," came the growl. "Who's paying for this examination, you said?"

"There's a welfare trust for British expatriates that Dr. Engineer has tapped into." Said with a glibness reserved normally for children to make them take medicines, and Markham bought it with a surprising naïveté.

"Damn generous."

"You British always took care of your own. Remember, I'm your physician, all queries to be referred to me. You've been booked at a small hotel on Mwinyi Road, next to the hospital."

An old Toyota taxi arrived to take the Englishman to the airstrip. He got up quickly and with a perfunctory wave of the hand departed, in his small shuffling steps, his overnight bag carried for him by John. Soon the previous night's visitors too departed, in two SUVs. The lounge was suddenly quiet.

Markham would be missed, Kamal observed, as he watched John standing idly at the entrance, looking out to the sea. That growling, rumbling presence had defined the ambience of the lounge, especially in the evenings.

"He will return soon," Kamal said a little loudly.

"Yes, bwana," the barman replied, quickly returning to his post behind the counter.

"He is a very sick man."

"I know," came the reply, with a barely perceptible inflexion in the tone, and Kamal gave a startled look at the blank face. John was not a man of visible emotion, and none had been betrayed. He was a mystery, though during Kamal's illness he was there with the others to tend to him. He was wearing the same black suit he donned daily, except on Sundays when he washed it. It did not have many days left. The shirt was remarkably white and also looked worn. I should tip him well when I leave, but when will that be? Perhaps I should just go and buy him a new shirt.

"John—where in Kenya do you come from?"

"I come from Naivasha, bwana."

"That's far. What's your full name?"

"I am called John Kariuki."

"Any family? Are you married?"

"Two children, a boy and a girl."

"Just like me—though mine must be much older. Why don't you bring them here to be with you?"

"It's far, bwana."

Kamal gave a nod to Amina at the pharmacy window, took the side alley to the back and walked into Fatuma's room like a familiar. This time she was seated on the armchair, and she looked in greater pain than before, holding one hand to her side. She gave him a curious, almost bemused look.

"You saw the other doctor—at the hospital—what did he say?"

"He gave me medicine." She pointed to a packet on the table. Then she returned her hand to her side.

Instinctively he reached out his hand to feel her pain.

"Fatuma," he said, "if the pain increases, do you have other medicines to help you? Traditional medicines?"

"There are those."

Perhaps some plant extracts, he thought. Or opium. He put some money on the table. "Use these for the medicines."

There was an awkward pause between them. Her quiet look told him that she knew she was beyond a cure, and he felt a compassion for this difficult but dying woman.

"I must know, Fatuma. About Saida and the child."

She had to tell him. He had reached her soft centre, they'd established a communion through her illness. They were intimate, if only for now. This was the moment.

"There is nothing to know."

"How can you say that? What is it that keeps her hidden? Tell me."

"You should go home. It is better for you."

"This is my home, Fatuma. This was my home. Saida—I promised her I would come."

She glared at him. "I don't know who you are, where you come from. I don't know why you come here to annoy us."

"I am not a bad man, Fatuma. You know that."

There followed that significant moment.

"You'll find her in Minazi Minne, then. But she doesn't want you to go there."

"Where is this Minazi Minne?"

"On the Lindi road."

· 36 ·

Until he could prove otherwise, for Gōlo to get top marks in the pre-dominantly Asian school was thought to be impossible, no less by him. He was African, the Indian part didn't matter. He couldn't speak the Indian language correctly, and his English sounded African, was often brutally imitated. He was the dark bonehead who could be detained in an African neighbourhood to play football or banter in Swahili, but give him a simple sum in algebra or geometry and he would put up a dumb Sambo face. His height and large head only made him look stupider. In Kilwa, he had excelled. In Dar, structured and competitive, he was beyond his depth. He could not but believe in his own innate inferiority. What hurt especially, as he entered his teens, was when the girls would take that ever so small step aside as he walked past them. What did they fear, that he would steal their virtue right there on the pavement, with the wild unpredictable blood of Africa coursing through his veins?

One day, seeing him return home, dishevelled and dirty from play-ing football after school, Sabini the tailor called out to him, "Weh Kamalu, come here!" When Kamal ambled over and asked, "What?" the fundi brought his machine to a stop and looked up from his work.

"Kamalu, I want to tell you something. Now listen carefully. When do you take time to study? It was why your mother sent you here. You know this. It broke her heart, but she wanted you to do well."

Only Sabini could have told him that. And only to Sabini could he have replied the way he did. Abrasively, though not without an edge of pain in the voice. Sabini's truth did cut him. Hadn't he struggled to do well? Didn't his twenty percents humiliate him, when others beamed at him proudly with their eighties? Wasn't he aware of the scorn in the eyes of his teachers as they threw down his test papers on his desk? Then why was Sabini, himself a tailor, sitting outside on the pavement, dressing him down?

"I can't do well, Sabini," Kamal said. "I am an African, like you. Sina bongo—I have no brains."

"So you think we Africans are stupid?"

"Yes. Which is why we were chained and taken as slaves. Africans are the most stupid and uneducated in the world. And I am a mshenzi, the most uncivilized of Africans. My grandmother was a mtumwa, a slave."

"Ah, Kamalu. You wound me. From where comes this poison in you?" He shook his head and picked up the cloth on his machine.

Uncle was watching them dourly from his chair inside the shop. It would be many years later when Kamal would realize that it might well have been Uncle who had put Sabini up to the task of speaking to him. Speak to the boy, Sabini, he listens to you.

But he had hurt Sabini, and Kamal was sorry. A few days later he went and stood in front of the tailor, silently watched him sew the seams of a dress, then turn its neckline and insert a lace border around it. Sabini ignored him.

"Sabini, you are not talking to me? Now what did I do?"

"You wounded me, Kamalu."

"I am sorry. Forgive me."

He told Sabini he had been a teacher once, had instructed Saida in arithmetic and English. He was not stupid, and from now on, he would work hard.

"Who is this Saida, eti? Your girlfriend?" Sabini smiled, laying aside the job he'd finished.

"She is my friend. Her grandfather was Mzee Omari, a great poet, a mshairi!"

"Now Kamalu, what do you know of shairi?"

"I can sing you one!"

"Go on!"

After a long moment of recollection, and a long breath, the opening words of Mzee Omari's history of the Kilwa coast came to his lips: Bismil, I begin in the name / of the Merciful the Kind / and Muhammad the Beloved . . .

He had stumbled; his breaking voice was uneven and he had strayed off-key. But when he finished singing the few lines, Sabini wiped his eyes. "You Kamalu, you really know this? It is our story, we Swahili people."

Except that I was told by my mother to be a good Indian. A Mhindi. To speak their language, to sing their songs, say their prayers. What then of the African Kamalu?

On his way upstairs through the store, he caught his uncle's eye, and went and stood before him. "Jaffu Uncle, from now on I will study, and one day you will be proud of me."

His uncle grunted a barely audible "Good."

But a teacher started coming home every Sunday afternoon to help him catch up.

When those dull Ds responded, straightened out and reformed into his proud As and Bs, when he cleared the hurdle of the bell curve and felt good about himself, he became the class target. A dumb half-caste good at football was acceptable, even admired, a smart one was an affront. The relentless campaigns against him pushed him to the edge and almost got him thrown out of school.

Mr. Sharma began to write something on the board and a boy threw a piece of chalk at him from behind. When the teacher spun around in a fury to ask, "Who was it?," all eyes were on Golo, and silly he was caught grinning and received two stinging strokes of the cane on his backside. When someone wrote *DOG=GOD* on the board, and a tearful Mr. Bandali asked who had committed the blasphemy, all eyes fell on dark Golo, who could only have the blackest soul. Six of the best from the acting principal, Mr. Haji. He was being beaten back to his former status as the class idiot.

One day Miss Kanga was at the board and the chalk gave a squeak, which she echoed with an exclamation, which some of the boys found irresistibly sweet. One of them threw a prolonged and very audible kiss at her. The teacher paused then turned around in an expression of feminine outrage, which the boys found quite erotically delightful.

Miss Kanga, fair and trim, in tight skirt and high heels, her bosom high and pointed, her bottom round and tight, and her hair done in a tall beehive, was the most beautiful woman the boys had seen. There was no doubt of that. One day she had descended like an angel among them, a refugee of the Zanzibar revolution.

"Who was it?" she said, almost in tears.

Silence. Then a voice said, sympathetic and with quiet conviction, "Own up, Kamalu."

Others followed suit, "Own up, Golo, don't be a coward!" "You made poor Miss Kanga cry!"

Miss Kanga clip-clopped off to Mr. Haji's office to report, and returned with the acting principal, who trundled in behind her wielding his cane.

"Kamalu, I am going to throw you out of the school. But first, come and bend over!"

The cane flexed in the man's two hands as Kamalu stepped forward to the front, followed by jeering tee-hees from the boys.

"Bend, you rascal!" commanded Mr. Haji.

It was the raised cane that did it to Kamal. The switch that turned the switch, he liked to say afterwards. The prospect of the sting on his buttocks, tears in the eyes, public humiliation, all over again. What did the elders sing in Kilwa—na viboko, alichapa: he whipped us with canes, the colonialist, and humiliated us.

"Thubutu!" he cried, stepped behind the tiny Miss Kanga, and put his arm around her throat. "I will break her neck, I will kill her!"

Did he know how to break a neck? He didn't think about it. He heard her whimper, smelled her perfume, felt the tickle from a strand of her brown hair on his cheek.

Utter silence in the class. The garden boy watched wide-eyed through the window. Then pleas from Mr. Haji, from one or two of the nicer boys. Be sensible. Don't do something you will regret.

Tears in his eyes, Kamal cried out, "You have been picking on me, and lying about me, and the teachers listen to you, and this buffalo Mr. Haji—"

Mr. Fernandes, the English teacher, had walked in from outside and stood beside Mr. Haji. He spoke sternly, "Now Kamal, don't be silly. Let Miss Kanga go."

Just that, no threat. Kamal released her and a boy escorted her to the staff room.

"Not only will I expel you," spluttered Mr. Haji, "but I will call the police, too. But first, your uncle. Let's see what he says to this! You, my boy, are finished! You are finished!"

"Don't you touch me!" Kamal replied. But he went with the principal to the office to await his uncle.

Kamal would never quite understand his uncle, who had brought him to his home, but not completely accepted him, and yet given him everything he gave his own children. And now, as he stood beside Kamal, facing Mr. Haji and Miss Kanga in the office in his shopkeeper's crumpled trousers and shirt hanging out and not quite shaved, he replied to the principal's charge.

"No. Kamal would never do that." He stared contemptuously at Miss Kanga and said, "You have a piece like that, dressed in this way, stand before young men, and what do you expect?"

Miss Kanga seemed to wither away behind Mr. Haji.

"Mr. Punja, I am expelling your son. And if Miss Kanga desires, I will report the attack by your son to the police."

Uncle looked at Mr. Haji and said, "I would like to speak to you in private."

"By all means," said Mr. Haji. "But don't ask for leniency. Kamal has overstepped all bounds. There will be no mercy. No mercy whatsoever. Understand this. There are rules."

Kamal went to stand outside Mr. Haji's office, and Miss Kanga went away to the staff room.

Ten minutes later, Mr. Haji told Kamal to go back to his class. And Uncle went back to sit in his store, whose confines he hated so much to leave, except to go to the khano in the evening.

When Kamal returned to class, he was a hero. Wah, you held her like that, you felt her ass. Did you dig into her, Kamal, eh, did you dig into her? You should fuck her. They like Africans with their big pricks, these educated women. You should fuck her. Just ask her. And then tell us about it!

Later they all became friends, he and his tormentors. Whenever they met, in Edmonton, or Toronto, at small reunions at the house of one or the other of them, they joked about the antics of their school days. Had bellyfuls of laughs, till the tears ran down their cheeks and the children present wondered what had happened to their fathers. And yet in his privacy when he would recall the cruelty which had been meted out to him, its crude racism, a bitter feeling would rise in him. Could the young be truly evil? Or was it all innocence? Could all be forgiven from the past? The chumminess only began when they got older and more mature, and as he began to be accepted as one of them—and indeed became one of them.

"Weh Kamalu," Sabini said to him a few days later. "What miracle did you accomplish in school that we hear about?"

"Sabini," said Kamalu, speaking forcefully but in a low voice, "I refused to be whipped like a slave." Nilikataa kuchapwa kiboko.

"So you think you are Mau Mau now?" Sabini replied, unable to keep the pleasure from his face.

And back in the shop, when one of his cronies asked Uncle, "Arré, Jaffu, what did you say to Mr. Haji that he let Kamal go?" Uncle replied, "I told him I would go to the Party office and make a report that they were harassing an African child. And they would all be deported to India, the lot of them. That took care of that stuttering, big-balled Haji."

"Was that teacher a white woman?"

"As good as white, and what a piece. So when are you sending me a girl?"

"You didn't want that Arab. The taxi driver would have brought her and picked you up. No hassle."

"No, no Arab. Bring me a Halima or a Fatuma."

One moment he was proud of his uncle, the next disgusted. He would think he deserved a father like Sabini, who worked hard and understood him, was friendly, had principles. He himself knew little about the man, but they were kinsmen, there could be little doubt of that.

———

Mr. Fernandes, who had broken that High Noon moment, the mini-hostage crisis in the classroom, as Kamal would wryly recall it, had recently taken him in hand. He was an English and history teacher of the higher forms, with a particularly haughty no-nonsense manner, because he was good and known to be so. He knew what he taught, and he could guide you to do well in the final-year national exams, which determined university entrance and therefore your future. Not the same could be said of other teachers. And so Mr. Fernandes was not one to be easily impressed or fooled, but he had been impressed by Kamal's essay on the First War of Independence, as the Maji Maji War was called after the independence of the country. In his essay Kamal had written that the Germans must have had some good in them, for they had started schools, and some Swahili poets praised them. The other boys as usual had regurgitated paragraphs from the textbook. One day Mr. Fernandes took Kamal aside in the corridor and complimented him on having taken pains with his essay, and asked him what source he had consulted regarding the Swahili poets. Kamal was dumbfounded at this close, unwanted attention. Perhaps the teacher was out to challenge him? Mr. Fernandes asked him again what book had he consulted, and if he knew any poets; did he know any poetry himself? Kamal told him about Mzee Omari and his utenzis that he had heard in Kilwa. Did they count as a source? He thought they were, for in them the old poet wrote what he remembered. Or *thought* he remembered, Mr. Fernandes corrected. Still, he admitted, Kamal's source was an important one, an original one. Not many people thought of poems as historical sources, but they were. "Keep it up!" Mr. Fernandes told him. "Keep it up, and you will go far."

Mr. Fernandes spoke to Mr. Gregory, the senior English teacher, about his discovery. Mr. Gregory had been renowned in Dar for many years as the teacher who knew Shakespeare by heart. He was essential if you wanted to understand *Julius Caesar* or *Macbeth*. Under the patronage of these two teachers Kamal became not only mainstream but also among the elite, upon whom the school's academic reputation rested. Soon he was a member of the Dramatics Society, the Literary Society and the History Society. He was made a prefect.

Mr. Fernandes practically begged Kamal to take up history or literature at university. All the bright boys pursued science, he said. But history and literature were as important. Perhaps more so, because they kept alive the soul of a nation. "Kamal," he pleaded, "you have a gift for humanities, you have sensitivity. The nation needs to learn about our poets. The *world* needs to know about our poets. We need to write our stories." But Kamal was adamant. "I want to become a daktari, I want to do something useful for the country." "History is not useless, Kamal. Literature is not useless. Think about it." "Yes, sir."

But he had already made up his mind.

I happened to go to the same school as Kamal Punja, this man who told me his story, as we sat at the Africana or the Kilimanjaro, at the A-Tea Shop or a bench on Ocean View Road watching the waves. I did not remember him from our school days, though I did try, until he mentioned the episode of the lovely Miss Kanga; only then did I recall being pointed out the large-headed African boy two grades higher who had almost strangled Miss Kanga and defied Mr. Haji.

In those heady few years following the country's independence, several slogans articulated the prevailing attitude and ideology in our country, which had taken the socialist route to development and a pro-Chinese political stand abroad. One of these slogans proclaimed, "Uhuru na kazi"—freedom and work. Another said, "Make effort, don't be a parasite." I recall myself as a young cadre marching in the streets, singing, "Who's going to build our nation, mother? Not the Americans!" Needless to say, the Americans were not our friends, because we were China's friends. And needless to say, too, that our high-minded socialism ultimately failed miserably, crippled by all sorts of inadequacies.

Kamal wanted to do something useful and practical for the country. Tend to the sick, using modern medicines. No more old women's prayers and witches digging up roots from the forest and old men writing down verses from the Quran.

Mr. Fernandes could not persuade him, but he did point me to my path. I decided to accept his encouragement and ultimately became a publisher. And now we sit facing each other, idealistic products of our time, influenced by the same teacher: one a wealthy doctor from abroad who did not tend to the sick of his own country; the other a former publisher whose vocation almost disappeared because of inept socialism, now desperately hoping to publish the doctor's story.

· 37 ·

Late one afternoon in Dar, as Kamal emerged from the shop, bathed and neatly combed and attired, on his way to khano down the road, Sabini was waiting for him outside on the pavement.

"Kamalu, kwa heri. Goodbye, I'm going away."

"Kwa heri, basi. See you tomorrow."

"There's no tomorrow, I'm going away for good."

"Don't fool around . . ." Usinitanie, sasa!

Where? Home . . . somewhere, never to return. Why? He would not say. He was just going.

First the bullying:

"You can't go, Sabini. I don't allow you to go. Your place is here."

Then the pleading:

"Nowhere else but here, Sabini. We are of one blood, Sabini. Don't abandon me! Please . . . listen to me . . ."

"Don't cry, my friend. The girls will laugh at you. I must go."

"Really?"

"Really." Mungu na mtume. By God and His Prophet.

"But you must come back. To see me . . ."

"I will, my brother."

And so he was off. Just like that.

First Mama; then Sabini.

Kamal followed him at a distance, like a stray, all the way down Mosque Street, Market Street, to Uhuru Street and the bus station crowded with workers on their way home. An average figure of a man, one to disappear easily in a crowd, not even a basket in his hand, walking at a steady, unhurried pace. Loose pants, overshirt, sandals. Only when he reached the bus stop did he look back briefly at Kamal before getting into a waiting bus.

Kamal hadn't thought to ask him for an address. He probably didn't have a concrete one, a writable one—he was going away. Kamal saw the bus lurch forward and drive out onto the main road, full to capacity, men hanging out from the door. The sun was sinking, the grey of dusk had spread all over. The khano's clock chimed seven o'clock. He would be late this evening.

Could someone disappear so easily from your life, without a trace? How did Sabini remember him afterwards? It would seem to Kamal later that unlike his ordered life in Canada, his childhood existence had been some conjuror's creation, with the ability to change shape, parts of it to disappear like smoke, leaving behind only the indelible impressions on his mind and heart, utter bewilderment and sorrow.

Sabini's departure was the last of his childhood chapters; following the fundi pathetically up to Uhuru Street until he disappeared was Kamal's last childish gesture of despair. His life was changing. He was growing up to be respected and treated like an adult, an educated one at that, with prospects. The head prefect in school. His skin colour was rarely an issue now, he had grown into the Shamsi community, he was one of them, though a dark one. What defined him were his clothes, his manners, his speech; his reputation. His Swahili intonations had gradually been smoothed away under the clamour of two Indian languages and English. He could recall Mama, but the ache of her loss was mere memory now. If she had needed him, she would have come to see him. He did not feel bitter. And Saida? What would she look like now? The tawiz belonged among his precious possessions, but he did not wear it, didn't want to explain it. He thought of her fondly, of the times they spent together. A many and a pany: she could draw a smile out of him even these many years later. But she was no longer his succour at night, to turn to when he felt unhappy.

It was a tumultuous period in the nation, in all of Africa, as Kamal entered his final years in school. One day Ethiopia's emperor, Haile Selassie, passed through the city; another day it would be Tubman of Liberia, or Nkrumah of Ghana, or the Chinese premier, Chou En-lai. A politician was assassinated in Kenya, a routine settling of scores, but the longed-for East African federation seemed to recede even further away. It was a time of action, of building the nation, a time of the maan-damano, the public demonstration. Singing slogans, student patriots marched in processions to demonstrate against the oppressors of Africa—the Portuguese, the white Rhodesians, the white South Africans—and were ready to pick up rifles to go and fight. Young and old marched in support of the new dawn of African Socialism, which would bring on a just, egalitarian society. Naive times, but proud times. The nation received aid but did not kneel for it yet.

It was then that Mr. Fernandes attempted to net Kamal Punja into the humanities, for the sake of, as he called it, the soul of the nation.

One day the Ghanaian writer Ben Assamoah came to the school, brought by the headmaster, Mr. Palangyo. Nobody knew that Palangyo himself was a closet novelist, whose only novel Kamal discovered to his amazement in the remainders bin of an Edmonton bookstore many years later. But Assamoah was world-famous even then. Mr. Fernandes and Mr. Gregory arranged a meeting of him and the senior boys, in a corner of the school hall. Mr. Gregory had deigned to wear a tie and clean shirt for the occasion.

Ben Assamoah was already sitting in the assembly hall with Palangyo when the boys entered. He was a somewhat small man with a round face and wore a coloured African shirt. Palangyo introduced the Ghanaian guest as Africa's greatest writer and an editor. Gregory mumbled something about the school's new literature program. Assamoah first spoke about his own school days, the books he had read, how they influenced him. He stressed the importance of litera-ture, of writing authentically. He concluded by holding up the samples of the boys' writing the teachers had given him to look at. "I've read these," he said, "with much interest. You will see my comments squiggled on these pages. But I have one overall comment to all budding African writers. Write about what you know. Why write about

England? What do you know about living in New York? Write about Dar es Salaam, write about Tanzania. Those are the stories we need." He looked around at the faces before him. "By all means read about London and New York, but let those in Europe and America, and indeed Nigeria and Ghana, read about your Dar es Salaam. That's what Africa needs."

Kamal would remember shaking Assamoah's hand, Mr. Fernandes having brought him forward. "What's the noose for?" the writer asked, giving a gentle pull to his red tie, and Mr. Fernandes explained, "He's our head prefect. We're encouraging him to take up history or litera- ture, but he wants to be a doctor." "Wise decision," said Assamoah. "You can be sure to do good with medicine."

Mr. Fernandes looked embarrassed.

No, Kamal was not the one who wrote about New York. He had written a sentimental story about an orphan who after many adven- tures discovers that his father is the tailor who works in the neighbour- hood. But when the boy comes to this important realization about his life, the tailor is on his deathbed. Inspired by Bollywood.

There were other writers Palangyo brought. And once a member of the Black Panthers came from America, whose message about his country seemed incomprehensible to the boys. But he did teach them the Black Power fist salute. The following week the boys went around giving the salute to each other until Palangyo announced in assembly one morning that anyone caught raising his fist would get caned on the back of his hand. But what should they see on the front page of the paper a few months later but a picture from the Olympic Games in Mexico City of two black athletes standing on the medal podium, their fists raised in the salute Palangyo had banned.

Kilwa seemed far away in the past. The future beckoned.

Kamal completed his final school year, passing the national exams with flying colours, as they said, and was admitted to study medicine at Kampala's prestigious Makerere University. Of all the boys and girls his age in the entire country, he was one of the hundred or so who was going to university. Congratulations from everybody, friends, teachers, neighbours. He was setting out on his own, to another city, another country, to be his own master. He had known only Kilwa and Dar es Salaam thus far, only the coast. His cousins with pride and excitement, and a good bit of envy, plied him with advice for his life away; Zera Auntie shed tears even as she prepared him and took him to My Tailor for his first suit; and Jaffu Uncle eyed him with a wry look that said he had done his duty by his cousin, adopted his half-caste bastard and sent him off into the world to become a doctor.

With pride in his achievement there came also a sense of being alone again. His life with his family, with whom he had spent seven years in three rooms, was over now. He was different, and adopted—what kind of relationship would there be between him and them? After he graduated he would be sent off to work somewhere by the government. He would have his own home and earn his own money. If he returned, it would be for short periods.

There was also some trepidation at leaving Dar, whose every street and gulley he knew to the last crack in the sidewalks, for a foreign place, even if it was in East Africa. They did not speak Swahili in Uganda. He knew only one other boy who would be going to Kampala that year, and a girl in the neighbourhood he had never spoken to. Kampala was not close, it took two days by bus, via Nairobi. That was the fare that came with his government scholarship.

Before he left, it occurred to him that he should visit Kilwa and see the folks there. Let them also take pride in his success. Mama, he knew, was in Lindi with her husband and new family. Would she care to hear his news? He wasn't sure. He would meet Saida. What would she be like? How would they relate? He vacillated: Maybe I shouldn't go—what's the point now, after so many years? But no. I have to go to see her.

· 38 ·

"By all means go and see your folks in Kilwa," said Jaffu Uncle. "They should see how well you have done. And in the future you could go to India and see your other folks—our folks—in Verawal."

There was a curious, almost bemused expression on Uncle's face, acknowledging more than ever before that the boy was indeed different, and yet it was not an unkind look he gave but one of concern. What lay ahead for this boy? Could he ever shed off his past?

"Will you be going to Lindi, to your mother?"

"I don't know."

His uncle did not reply, simply grunted.

Kamal would always wonder what exactly Uncle knew about his mother; what she meant to him, his absent Indian cousin's African woman, Hamida, who could never belong in the family. What did she tell him when she gave away her son to him? Were there any conditions to the transaction?

"Is my father still alive in India?" Kamal asked.

Uncle was waiting for it.

"He is, but it's been ten years since I heard from him. I can't tell you how he will receive you if you went to him."

———

Kamal returned to Kilwa by bus, speaking an Indian tongue now, and he put up with an Indian family, old acquaintances of Uncle's. As he came off the bus he was met by a man called Bandali, of the same age and manner as Uncle, who had come with a servant and escorted Kamal to his house, where he met the family and was given a large breakfast. Afterwards, as soon as was politely possible, with skipping heart Kamal stepped out. The Bandali house was one of the large white buildings on the street of the Indians, where Kamal had come wandering during Ramadan evenings when he was little with a tray of kashatas, an African street-vendor boy. And Saida came with her tray of tambi. Opposite the house was the local khano; he knew what to call that Indian prayer house now. He took a side street to the harbour and stood on the edge of the square looking out to the sea. A warm, gusty breeze lashed at his face. The tide was in and furious, the dhows had all taken to the sail. He strolled about and came to stand, musing, at the place where he would sit on the grass some evenings and listen to Mzee Omari recite his *Composition*. In the beginning, Bismil . . . It seemed so distant now.

Everything looked the same, yet it was not. Most of all, he had grown up and could stand detached from his past. He could say, This was so, and This was not so. He recalled how he had resisted leaving Kilwa.

He reached the walkway along land's edge alongside the creek, where the sea went meandering into the mangroves. Unthinkingly, a map in his head, when the walkway ended he cut diagonally in towards the old German cemetery. He idled there awhile, perused the names on the graves, and then after some hesitation—for old times' sake—he climbed down the depression back towards the creek and found the lagoon he had known as a child.

And there she was.

How did he know it was she? A young woman the right age, the right build (he guessed), wearing an orange and green khanga round her shoulders and head; and that thin face, oh still so much the same. That searching look. And how did she know he had returned? As he approached her she kept staring at him, intently.

"Saida—ni wewe." It's you. His voice breaking.

"Kamalu. You've returned? A grown man . . . ?"

Hadn't he turned cold in that world away, hardened by his loss and his fights and the taunts he suffered until he had proved himself; hadn't he emerged from his ordeals a modern, suave, successful young man? Hadn't he left the past behind—the past which had cruelly turned him out? Hadn't he stopped talking to that wall next to his bed, to which during his early days in Dar he would turn in the night, full of distress, seeing there his once closest companion? Whence this emotion now, uncontrollable; these childish tears rolling down his cheeks? All he had lost and missed and imagined in Dar, all that had been torn away from him became the burden of this sudden wave of grief. The familiar streets of Kilwa, his mama at home, the sound of the sea and the poet . . . and Saida.

"Polé, Kamalu. Why are you hurting?"

"I don't know."

They sat down a distance from each other, already aware of their transgression. You don't meet a Swahili Muslim woman on a beach in private. She was beautiful, he observed, though small; the features fine and angular, the skin a dark brown. He smiled at her. "How is your mother?" he asked.

"She's well. And your people in Dar es Salaam?"

"They are well. And you? Have you been well?"

"Well."

"And your bibi? Mwana Juma?"

"She went to Lindi."

"And my mother?"

"She went to Lindi also."

She tilted her head to gauge his reaction, and he had the urge to reach out across all the four feet of safety between them and take her delicate hand into his. Before them in the distance, a bright and clear sky rose above the wall of dark green mangroves. There was the sound of distant waves. All else was quiet and still, the shallow water at their feet, the bushes around them. This had been their hideaway, and it still protected them. He wondered what it would be like if the rest of the world did not exist, Dar es Salaam didn't exist, and he had not gone away but grown up here in Kilwa.

"What are you thinking, Kamalu?"

"Did you remember me when I went away?"

"Mm-hm." In that way of hers.

"Did you feel sad?" he persisted.

"You went away to be Indian . . ."

"I was sent away by Mama. You know how unhappy I was."

"And while you were away? In the big city?"

He gazed at her, looked away, said nothing for a long while. And then: "Every night I spoke to you . . . Couldn't you hear me?"

"I could hear you. My mother said she wanted to send me away too."

He laughed.

They sat in silence.

"Kamalu, I am happy you have come back. Now I have to go and cook."

He was surprised. "Doesn't your mother cook anymore?"

"I have to cook in my own home. For my husband when he comes back."

"You are married?"

"Mm-hm."

This is what they had done to him. Mama. Uncle. The world.

She moved closer and peered into his face. "Do you think I was given a choice?"

"What is his name?"

"Abdalla Hamisi."

"What does he do?"

Silence. She stood up and started to climb back up to the cemetery and he followed. She was lithe, he observed, and he was clumsy. When they were up, she waited until the road to the town was clear before heading off.

"Can we meet again?"

"Here, tomorrow. At this hour."

He followed her a few minutes later, when she was out of sight. As he walked back, his head drooped; he recalled with shame that he had not been sure he should return to Kilwa. Now he was here and found the connection so achingly alive. There was so much to talk about. He didn't want to think about her marriage, or the difference between them—he educated and on his way to university, an urban schoolboy, almost Indian, and she? There was so much to talk about.

Later in the afternoon he walked the small streets of the town. He greeted elders he met whom he had known, and they politely returned his greetings, but they didn't recognize him until he mentioned his mother. He went to his old home, where a government official apparently lived, for there was a flag outside. He went over and patted the old mango tree, bwana mwembe, his companion in the night, the sentry who had watched over him and his mother. Finally he went over to Bi Kulthum's house, stood on the porch where in the past he would greet Mzee Omari, and called out, "Hodi!" When there was no answer he entered the long corridor through the front door and again called out. "Karibu!" a woman's strained voice rallied from a room close by, and he entered. It was Mzee Omari's old room.

He recognized Bi Kulthum immediately. The fair features, the long face. She was sitting up on a bed, and seeing him she immediately covered her head. She was older, a little softer. The room itself bore no resemblance to what it had been; against the window stood a chair and a table with half a glass of water; the walls were bare except for a calendar. And there was the stale odour of human habitation where once he had smelled incense and stark purity.

"Who are you?" she demanded.

"Bi Kulthum, I'm Kamalu . . ."

"Kamalu who?" she shrilled, startling him.

"Hamida's son, Bi Kulthum."

"Hamida! Weh Kamalu! By God. Astaghfirullahi . . ." She looked away with a shake of her head and then turned a searching gaze back up at him. "So it's you, truly. What do you seek here?"

"I came to visit. And to pay respects."

Could this be real? Can the world change so much, people alter like this? Where was the cheerful woman who used to come to his house, always with a wisecrack or two and a sharp, knowing gleam in the eye?

"Look at my foot. It's rotting. And the doctor can do nothing."

She lifted it for him. It was purple and swollen, like an old piece of cassava, and gave off the rank odour of medication.

"I'm so glad to see you, Bi Kulthum," he said.

"Glad to see me like this?" She glared at him. "You—you seem well, Kamalu. Your mother did well to send you away."

"How is my mother?"

She did not reply. He went over and gave her some money.

"Thank you, my son. You were always a kind boy. It was a sad day when you went away . . . Saida is married," she said, looking pointedly at him.

He almost said he knew, but came out with a timely "Congratulations. I pray that she will be happy."

Her eyes twinkled and he knew that she was not fooled. She was never fooled.

"I've brought presents for her. I will give them to her when I see her."

She nodded. As he was leaving, she said,

"You, Kamalu. Your mother didn't know what to do with you . . . You should become a daktari and come and heal us poor folk."

"I am going to be a daktari, Bi Kulthum. Honestly. I am going to Uganda to become a doctor."

"All the way to Uganda?"

He had brought a smile to her face, though perhaps an ironic one, and he felt gladdened by that.

He went back to his hosts' house where he had a long nap.

With Zera Auntie he had gone to shop for gifts for her. He bought a dress; a pair of shoes; a belt; earrings, which Auntie insisted be of gold. Only kind, silly Zera Auntie had understood the emotional content of his impending journey. "You have a friend there from before, don't you?" "Yes."

He had brought his presents wrapped in a newspaper and placed the package in front of Saida. They were back at the lagoon.

"You studied all these years?" she asked in wonder. "Secondary school, and now you will go to the big school, the university? Aren't you tired of studying?"

"No, Saida. I like studying. And only by going to the university can I be something important—a doctor."

"Hm." She sounded amused. And he had picked up her hand.

He told her all about his life in Dar es Salaam. She wanted to know how the Asians lived. What they ate. How they sounded. Was it true that they ate a lot of daal? Yes, he told her, which was why they were weaker than Africans! But he had refused to eat daal. He liked chapati and bhajia. No, not all of them worshipped cows. His family ate cow meat, and they called themselves Muslims, though they were different. He mouthed a sampling of Kihindi for her and she broke into a peal of laughter, and he shushed her. "Do you want someone to find us?"

She was leaning into him. He felt the warmth of her body against his chest and he held her briefly.

"A many and a pany," he murmured. "Do you remember, Saida? Kinjikitilé? Did you really miss me when I left?"

"I cried for a few days. They said you would return."

He drew her close to him with one hand, tightly, and she released herself and picked up her presents. "I must run and hide these."

"Hide them? Why? They are for you to wear!"

"My old man will beat me if he discovers them."

They fell silent. Did it really matter if she was married? She could unmarry . . .

"Tell him some relation brought them for you."

"You have forgotten our ways, Kamalu."

She was right. What plausible reason could she have to wear a new dress, gold earrings, new shoes not given to her by her husband?

"Kesho," he said, he pleaded, as she got up. Tomorrow.

"Kesho," she replied simply and released her hand gently from his.

The next time there was no inhibition.

He had thought of nothing but her the last two days, recalling all her wonderful expressions, the new ones and those that were familiar, reminding him of the way he had known her before. He loved her thin voice and her brown complexion, her skip as she walked away when her time was up . . . a mellower Saida of softened edges but Saida all the same, there was a continuity between them, a closeness that had survived from old and become naturally this adult intimacy, this passion.

In their lovemaking was the sweet ache of the illicit, and fear of the sinful; the joy and relief of coming home to each other; the pure passion of possession and love; it was not the casualness of fucking and becoming lovers, language common where he would eventually depart to, depicting the biological and instinctual, the needful with all the brutality of the mechanical. He smothered her with kisses on her cheeks, on her body, but he could not kiss her on the lips, because she hated it. She gave herself with abandon, as did he himself, completely, so that when she said give me all you've got, he became hers in every spurt and trickle he could muster, and she became his, feeling him in the very core of her being and body.

She had married two years before, at sixteen. When he left, she had been used by her family to earn a living by practising as a mganga of the Book. Did she believe in her powers, did she believe her prescriptions worked? She said they did, for she used the Book, didn't she. And didn't he himself come to her once to ask for advice? That he did. Later she worked as an assistant to Mzee Abdalla, a powerful mganga, who married her. He was her husband. And he beat her? he asked. When she did wrong, she replied. He was very powerful. He could read your heart . . . what was in it . . .

Suddenly they heard sounds above them, and in terror they huddled closer together in their hideout, silent until the disturbance had gone away. He pushed her down and lay beside her, stroked her face.

"I will take you away. Would you like that? I will return from university and take you away."

"You can do that, eti? And I can trust you?"

"You are mine, Saida, and I am yours now. We have decided that, you and I. Haven't we? Tell me!"

"Yes."

"Then I will come for you."

She stepped aside to take a pee; he did likewise; he helped her straighten her clothes and himself felt pleasantly dishevelled.

———

One day they recalled Mzee Omari. His memory, too, had bound them together. Kamal told her that whenever he would hear a shairi recited on the radio in Dar, and whenever he read the shairi columns in the Swahili newspaper *Ngurumo*, he would hear Mzee Omari's voice in his head. He could not forget how the old man died.

"My grandpa liked you."

"Yes. And he knew I liked you. Once I heard him say, 'Anampenda.'"

She blushed, ducking her head a little.

"Sing a shairi for me, Saida. You used to."

"I have forgotten."

"How can you forget?"

"A wife forgets many things. She forgets her childhood."

"Well, I am your childhood and I am back . . ."

Mzee Omari was a troubled soul, she said. He talked in his sleep. Once the family was woken up by the old man shouting at his djinn Idris, telling him he was useless and to go away. He was sick with fever at the time. Mzee was growing more blind and Idris could no longer guide his hand. But Mwana Juma said it was his past memory that was eating him from inside. She knew all about him, all his troubles. She knew about his brother Abdelkarim, and she knew about Salemani Mkono.

"That devil!"

"The same one."

The night before Mzee died, Salemani Mkono came to see him and they sat on the porch talking. And when Salemani left, Mwana Juma gave him some money.

Watching her soft face, the nervous look she gave him, he felt a surge of tenderness towards her. He wanted to take her away, now. He would be her teacher again and teach her about the world. But he would have to wait. He was still young, he had to complete his education.

"What are you thinking?" she asked.

He recalled how helplessly she had clutched his hand and dropped her head against his shoulder at the sight of her grandfather lying dead on the ground, the telltale strangulation wound like a red ring round his neck.

"I was thinking of that day when Mzee Omari died," he said.

"Idris killed him and disappeared."

"Idris went away after that?"

"He went away. He was not seen or heard again. He went into the air where the djinns live."

"And Salemani—what happened to him?"

"He was crossing the road one day and was run over by a bus."

"Saida," he said, "I have to go back—to Dar es Salaam—"

"I know you have to go."

"But I will come back again. I will come back and take you with me."

She took his hand and put it on her breast, drawing him to her.

His hosts had become worried by his daily disappearances and his distraction. He was polite but quiet. They could not understand why he had come. He had dutifully gone to the prayer house with them, and accepted invitations at several households. Two young women had been shown to him, discreetly, but he had shown no interest. A telephone call came from Jaffu Uncle finally, reminding him that there were matters to attend to before his departure for Kampala: forms to sign at the Ministry of Education; his passport; his certificate from school. He should come home.

The night before he left he asked Bandali about the mganga Abdalla Hamisi.

"He's a powerful one," Bandali told him. "What shida do you have? Some girl you want to snare?"

Kamal acknowledged his wink with a smile.

"And we've been showing you all the beauties of Kilwa!" the man said. "My friend, it seems that some other girl has put the witchcraft into you! Tell us if you want something done about it, and we will help you."

Early the next morning as his bus drew away from the crossroads, he caught a glimpse of Saida standing at the monument, still and staring, just as she had done seven years before when he left. Clutched in her hands was something she had presumably gone to buy as an excuse to come out. The thought came to his mind, a refrain from a currently popular song: My angel, I love you; I will return and take you away. He turned around to the clamour of excited passengers settling down, the groan of the engine.

· 39 ·

To go from humble Dar es Salaam to the fabled City of the Seven Hills, Kampala, was thrilling; to study at one of Africa's foremost temples of higher learning was to be privileged beyond measure. Kamal Punja was one of a new generation sent out into the world to get the goods and serve the nation. Throughout the country, from scattered towns and villages, this chosen tiny number were setting off for university to become bureaucrats, doctors, engineers, and teachers.

The family came to drop him off at the Dar bus depot, and Uncle for once let his guard down and gave Kamal a brief hug. Zera Auntie was in tears and thrust more bills into his hands. Of his three cousins, Azim and Shenaz embraced him, the latter crying copiously, and his antagonist over the years, Yasmin, shook his hand.

He was with five other boys and two girls on the overnight bus bound for Nairobi. There he stayed with one of them at the university dorm, and only hours after their arrival they were all out watching the latest James Bond thriller, which had been banned in socialist Tanzania. The next day they went shopping on Government Road for their smarter requirements, such as blazers, and then two of them took off for Kampala and Makerere University. His co-traveller was a girl called Shamim and their fate together was sealed on that journey. He was, as expected of him under the circumstances, her protector on the bus and at the stations, sitting beside her, watching her luggage for her, so she could sleep without worry; and she smiled her feminine gratitude and ensured he ate well from the supplies she had brought.

She was sweet, she was chatty, she was a neighbour whom he had seen in the streets in Dar but never spoken to before. During those lonely Uganda late evenings after completing their assignments or on Sundays when they missed home desperately, finding the Kampala-ites too snooty or alien, they sought each other out. They remembered Dar, the likes of which surely there was no other place, and their friends and all the neighbourhood characters, even the crazies who roamed the streets. She had a wonderful way of beginning her conversations with "I say," in her high voice, and she was outspoken, but with a sense of humour, and had a subtle way of evoking a protective gesture from him. But he had told her he was committed to someone else.

"Someone I know?"

"No. No, she's in Kilwa, where I spent my younger days."

"And she was in Kilwa while you were in Dar? Is there a high school in Kilwa? I recall there is one in Lindi."

He didn't respond, but discretion was not one of her qualities.

"Don't tell me she didn't finish high school! What's her name?"

He hesitated, while she waited.

"Saida," he said. "Saida binti Ali."

"You mean . . . she's an African?"

"Yes, she's an African. Like I am, as you see."

"No, you are an Indian."

Just like that, no argument. And in the future too, she would state this belief just as flatly, regardless of what he said, how he attempted to qualify it.

And Saida—Kinjikitilé? Whom he had told to wait for him, he would take her away? His angel. He still believed he would go and rescue her, even as he continued to go out with Shamim. *Date* was not a word in use. He wished he could use Bandali's address in Kilwa to write to Saida and reassure her; but why would that shopkeeper agree to be party to something as immoral as an affair, or to cross the powerful magician Abdalla Hamisi? Kamal knew in any case that she could not write to him—even if she somehow managed the English script—without her husband finding out.

Were his thoughts about her immoral? Yes, and their passionate consummation in Kilwa had been immoral and sinful. But it had seemed natural and right. They were made for each other, were linked forever, as he had discovered. He had been removed from her, and she had been forcefully married off to an old man. Wasn't *that* immoral?

But at this remove, the promise he had made to her seemed more and more fantastic, braggadocio. A lie. Where could they run to with their sin, after all? Where would he take her to—a foreign place, far away? Saida was not made for foreign places.

His life was a tangle of impulses. There was the thrill of freedom, of discovering a new place, taking carefree excursions into the city or to the parks to view elephants and hippos, or north to watch the source of the River Nile—with Shamim. There was the pride of studying under great medical teachers and doctors, who came from Nigeria and Ghana, Britain and America. Makerere was a beautiful campus on a hill, away from the city centre. To walk along its paths and corridors clutching books and papers, to sit on its impeccable green lawns to read—or think by yourself, to hear a lecture by some visiting eminence—all this was to be vested with a sense of importance and privilege. A bright future beckoned. One of the eminences who visited the campus was the novelist Ben Assamoah, who had come to his school in Dar; Kamal went and introduced himself to the author, reminding him of their meeting. "You advised me studying medicine would be better, and I am doing just that," he said. "I told you that?" came the reply. "Literature wouldn't have been so bad!" They laughed.

And then there was the nagging guilt of betrayal, of knowing somehow that Saida had known too that he would not be able to keep his word.

Clever Shamim could read his dark moods.

"I say—still thinking of your African girlfriend? Your uncle and aunt won't let you marry her, you know. And she might get married while you are here in Kampala. They are very conservative, these Muslims."

She displayed not a qualm about inviting him to go somewhere, do something together. Nor he, about accepting. Loneliness was the strong incentive; so was the companionship of a pretty girl. In the local Shamsi community their names became linked. You didn't go out with a girl on a regular basis without commitment. Commitment was assumed, then imposed upon you. They did not return to Dar during Christmas, going on a med school excursion instead, to visit an area in the north where a severe outbreak of sleeping sickness had occurred. But they did return for a few weeks at the end of their first year—and discovered that the news about them had already spread. At home there was teasing by his cousins, remarks were made about "you two." Zera Auntie visited a few goldsmiths in anticipation and Uncle's reserve had acquired a hint of warmth. At the shop of Hassam Walji, Shamim's father, Kamal was received with as much fanfare as discretion allowed, in an atmosphere replete with plans and dates that were not mentioned. Kamal was seen to have made a catch, for he was still dark after all. On the other hand, what other qualities of a desirable young man didn't he possess?

When Kamal left for Uganda with Shamim in July to begin a new academic year, it was inconceivable to him, to anyone around him, that he would not return to walk his beloved streets for thirty-five years. He left still a boy; he returned at the brink of old age.

A brief historical digression, at a time when history itself has been deemed irrelevant. (I have in mind, of course, the recent ban on the teaching of history by our minister of education.)

We were near the end of the first decade of independence. The Cold War was at its height; the blacks of southern Africa were yet to win freedom. And as our three countries found their voices to test their own recent freedom, political life turned shrill and nerve-racking, with real and imagined dangers. Tanzania was allied with Communist China. Kenya, the neighbour and potential partner in an East African federation, was America's friend and therefore busy chasing communists. Uganda had followed Tanzania in its ideology. The Chinese sent a trade mission to Tanzania and cheap Chinese imitations of workable quality had flooded the market. The Cubans and the Russians had aided the revolution in Zanzibar a few years before and were allies. Che Guevara passed through Dar es Salaam, in disguise some said. White South Africa was the enemy, as was Portugal, which still ruled Mozambique, the neighbour to our south. The white minority in Rhodesia had unilaterally declared independence from Britain, which became an enemy because of its equivocation and because it sold arms to South Africa. The streets of Dar es Salaam therefore often throbbed with demonstrations in which emotions ran high.

Still, the sometimes runaway rhetoric and loud assertions, and the political and social experimentation, were a sign of our hope, our claim to our future. This was East Africa, not Congo. It functioned. The railways ran, the post office delivered, the high courts sat. We ran the marathons. We never thought we could slip so easily into breakdown, repression. We were not made for government overthrows.

We were deluded.

One morning in January in the second year of med school as Kamal emerged from residence on his way to breakfast, there seemed to be something distinctly different about the campus. A group of guys stood around a crackling radio in someone's hands; down the road a similar cluster was deep in discussion. Elsewhere seemed quiet and lifeless. There were no cars on the road. Kamal's first thought was that the American president, or some Kennedy, had been assassinated; perhaps the old man of Kenya, Jomo Kenyatta, had died. There were always rumours of those sorts. As he came into the dining room, which was more raucous than usual, and stood in line for his eggs, someone told him the news: there had been a coup in the country. What country? This country, Uganda—the army has taken over the government! General Idi Amin has spoken on the radio!

There came stories of celebration in Kampala streets, a show of arms by the military; the chubby giant Idi Amin was cheered when he took a tour of the city on the back of an open Land Rover. The deposed president, Milton Obote, who had been at a Commonwealth conference in Singapore, protesting British treachery, became an exile. Classes were cancelled at Makerere that day, but Kamal had hospital rounds in the afternoon assisting a professor; Shamim was upcountry with a psychiatry class under an American doctor, visiting Jinja, where the entire fourth form of a school, consisting of eighty girls, had had a fainting fit.

The coup, the coming of the "Second Republic," seemed like a good thing after the socialist rhetoric and corruption of the previous regime. The British and the Americans immediately recognized Amin's new government. Every issue of the national newspaper, the *Argus*, contained paeans in praise of Amin, beginning with "Happy Days Are Here Again!" Delegations of women, priests, elders, and others arrived from all over the country to the State House to pay homage to this saviour who promised peace and love to the nation. Schoolchildren came out for him holding up flags. All prayed for his long life. There was something of the common man about General Amin, something more African and unpretentious compared to the stiff, suited Obote. A man of humble background, who had risen through the ranks in the colonial army, this bluff heavyweight boxer and accordion player was so evidently a man of the people; he talked as straight as he punched, and he possessed a sense of humour.

It was as the days passed and "politics was suspended" by decree and the army "requested" the general to stay in power for the next five years that whispers about kidnappings and brutal murders by the soldiers slowly began to spread, and it was realized—but not by the *Argus*—that this African nationalist was not the messiah he had seemed. One night a short, sharp scream was heard in the middle of the night from one of the residences down the road from Kamal's, followed by the sound of Land Rovers grinding away. In the morning the news got around that a law professor had been taken away, the one who had protested about violations of the constitution and human rights. Soon after, a frightened Dr. Omama, gynecology professor, was escorted out of the faculty in broad daylight, to work, it was said, for the State Research Bureau, the torture factory. Thus the sanctity of the university had been violated. A satanic spirit had descended upon the city and the country, and possessed it. The *Argus*'s euphoria, however, continued unabated.

Meanwhile Tanzania, which had refused to recognize the legitimacy of Idi Amin's republic, and moreover had offered exile to former president Obote, had been declared an enemy of Uganda. The Tanzanian students at Makerere, including Kamal and Shamim, asked to be transferred to Dar es Salaam and, as the rhetoric heated up, awaited a response from their government.

One Friday evening Kamal and Shamim were returning from the main Kampala Shamsi prayer house. Prayer meetings at the university had ceased, and Shamim was one of the devout who insisted on going all the way to the city to pray. During these uncertain times special prayers were on offer every night for the well-being of the community, the nation, and Idi Amin. That evening there was no other student returning from the khano with them; perhaps those few who had come had stayed in the city. The night was thick and dark, with little traffic on the road. As the bus groaned up to the top of Makerere Hill Road, it was stopped at an army checkpoint.

Two soldiers in berets climbed up, ambled casually down the aisle, looking left and right, checking out the nervous passengers. Coming upon the Asian girl, pretty and fair at that, and dressed up, their faces lit up. They stopped.

"We are university students," Kamal said. That often carried weight. They ignored him, both pairs of eyes fixed upon the girl. Both men were tall and armed with pistols. Despite the cheerful looks beaming down from their round, Ugandan faces, the menace in the air was electric. The bus had turned quiet.

"Madam—you must come out of the bus."

"Why?" Shamim said, then looked at Kamal and stood up.

"I am with her," Kamal said proprietorially and followed her behind the two men.

"What are you doing with an Asian girl?" one of the soldiers asked Kamal as he got off the bus. "Africans not good enough for you? Are you her servant?"

"My father was Asian," he muttered. "We are Tanzanian students."

"So your Asian father likes Africans. That is good. African is good, the best. Now you, madam . . ."

The two soldiers hustled them behind the bus where it was quiet. The entire area was wooded and deeply dark. The odd car came up the hill, briefly lighting the tarmac and throwing down shadows, and was pulled over then let go at the roadblock farther up where several jeeps were parked and at least half a dozen soldiers stood around.

The soldiers were in good humour with Shamim, in the manner African men adopted with Asian girls who took themselves too seriously while being very evidently nervous. These two, joined briefly by an inquisitive third with a red bob on his beret, would have dearly wished this girl to be of the Madhvanis, the Velshis, the Mehtas, any of the wealthy Uganda Indian families they could have extorted from. I am a Tanzanian, Shamim kept insisting, finally thrusting her driver's licence at them.

That meant she was as wealthy and spoiled as she looked. Anything could have been possible that night. The few other passengers who had got off the bus were back inside; the soldiers stepped aside and conferred among themselves. There was the crackling of a radio somewhere. By this time her purse had been searched and the money removed without fuss; her neck chain had been requested for inspection—"Gold? Hmm"—and pocketed.

"Say the Nandé-ali," Shamim whispered to him, "and we will be saved."

"I don't know it!"

"Say any prayer!"

The two soldiers came over and one grabbed her hand. "Come for search, madam."

Kamal took a step forward, to what purpose he had no idea, but he had to; the gallantry and folly of the male. But the third soldier, who had returned to the scene, quickly moved up to block his way and gave him a violent push. Kamal recovered to find a pistol pointed at him. A nightmare come alive. The sheer size and strength of the man, the menace in his eyes sent a chill through Kamal. At that moment Shamim gave a blood-curdling scream. Which is what perhaps saved them, for a car or two had been stopped farther up the road, though again anything was possible. Even after her scream she was pulled away, but they brought her back very shortly. It did not occur to the soldiers that their two detainees had no relatives in town to raise a cry for them.

That scream became a legend, as did Kamal's hopeless act of gallantry, for the story would get repeated many times in their future home and among friends.

When the bus dropped them off they ran to her room, barely able to speak; she fell into her bed, shaking and in tears, clinging to him; and they found themselves lying down together like that for the night. He never asked her exactly what happened when they pulled her away, but she looked unhurt. She would tease him at having got into her bed so conveniently, and he would remind her that she had clung to him and fallen asleep. He didn't tell her that she looked attractive and helpless and he had kissed her on both eyes. They would often return at times of stress to this terrifying night that ended in an embrace that glued them together.

A few weeks after that experience General Idi Amin announced his instructions from God: the Asians of Uganda were bloodsuckers, throw them all out. He gave them three months to leave the country.

· 40 ·

"I confess that there were moments when I secretly admired Idi Amin—when I thought he couldn't be all bad, that he spoke for the common African, and the excesses belonged to those who were under him. After all, soldiers everywhere are capable of excesses."

Kamal had a point, and I recalled as a young man at university in Dar es Salaam my own reactions to Amin. There was something to Uganda's general that brought on a smile of approval, that made you want to believe and cheer. Here was an African who was utterly natural, who didn't have to assume English manners—like the Kenyan politicians in their pinstripes. Our own president was not a mimic but a scholar who had translated *Macbeth* into Swahili—laudable and exemplary, but compare that to Amin, who could jump off his jeep and join the guys in a football game. And yet he could talk back with utter insouciance to anybody in the world, including the British prime minister: if Britain was so concerned about Uganda's Asians, why was it so reluctant to take them, even when they held British passports?

Yes, I admitted to him, in Dar too some of us had cheered the general initially.

It was the Golo in him who sent up the partial cheer for Idi Amin. It was the half-caste who had identified with the house servants ("boys"), flinched at their abuse and humiliations, and suffered his own share of them in school. It was the boy who had cried for his African mother and his special friend in Kilwa. He recalled his horror and shame when he saw a young African woman coming out of his uncle's back room. He had been reminded of his mother—and wept at night because he was nothing but a half-caste bastard. He could not say all this to Shamim, of course, but he tried to explain to her why the crowds cheered Amin when he told the Asians to go.

"Are you saying you support the expulsion of Asians?"

"Of course not. I am just telling you why people support it."

She gave him a sharp look. They were sitting at an outdoor chai shop on campus, and right then they should have seen the gulf between them and backed off from each other.

But there was this other side of him that saw through the cynical reverse racism that was at work. The Asians had overnight become "aliens" and "foreigners," objects of hate and derision. Every day the *Argus* carried new vilifications of them, its language disturbingly Orwellian. When Idi Amin, speaking to Makerere students at city centre, denounced the "economic saboteurs" and the "engineers of corruption," there were loud cheers of support. Kamal was among the thousands who went to hear him; from where he stood, he saw the general at a distance, a chubby toy soldier, his voice booming over the loudspeakers, promising an economic revolution once this virus infecting the nation was gone. It looked much too easy, pointing fingers at a minority of a different colour too frightened to defend itself. He recalled that terrifying night when he and Shamim had been accosted by the soldiers, how easily they had palmed her money and her gold chain. Corruption? Who received the bribes but those Africans in power?

Many years later, after Rwanda, he would wonder, was a genocide conceivable in Uganda under slightly altered circumstances? Perhaps the Asians were protected from that fate by the fact of who they were.

He did not cheer Idi Amin that morning—though he was careful not to appear too obvious—and left thinking of his Indian great-grandfather Punja, who had made Africa his home and called himself "Sawahil," and was hanged by the Germans for supporting a resistance. *Punja was a lion.* Mzee Omari had affirmed that. And Idi Amin had served as a soldier for the British, hunting Mau Mau in Kenya. Nothing was straightforward.

They lined up, the Asians of Uganda. From Kampala, and from the small towns across the country where they ran their little shops—Mbale, Mengo, Masindi Port, Tororo, Jinja—they came and formed long queues outside the embassies of Britain, Canada, the United States, clutching their passports. Take us in. We've lost our home. Those who found even Kampala daunting, too big and sophisticated for their simple lives, were begging to be let into London, Toronto, Philadelphia. Any place would do, each foreign embassy a watering hole during a desperate drought, drawing hundreds on the basis even of a rumour of goodwill. Not every country was welcoming. Australia announced—"Let's be perfectly honest"—that its interests would be served best only with people of European background. Denmark too announced that it did not want Asians. Those who went to India had to reach Mombasa, but Kenya would allow them overland passage only in closed trains, an episode eerily reminiscent of the horrors of Europe.

Meanwhile other queues were forming, of Africans ready to take over Asian businesses.

In Kampala prayer houses became caravanserais where the communities met to discuss their futures, and people came seeking advice and comfort, among them widows, the aged, and the simple folk from upcountry, speaking no English, their only skill how to run a shop or a kitchen, their second language Luganda or Acholi. Here gathered all the bitterness, pain, and grief of a people ordered to leave their homes and life's savings behind and simply go away. Here was the heartache of families whose fate it was to be dispersed over several countries, as they devised schemes to stay in touch and ultimately reunite somewhere on the globe. Those headed for refugee camps did not know on what continent they would end up. There were horror stories to be heard, of home invasions, molestations, and abductions. The khano was raided by the army and over a million shillings were discovered hidden in sandwiches. The *Argus* gloated: here were the engineers of corruption busily devising the country's downfall. Kamal, witnessing all this at the khano where he volunteered with Shamim, was embarrassed to recall his silent cheer for Idi Amin. A half cheer from a half-caste. He came some mornings to the khano, where he helped people with their paperwork before taking some sad individual or elderly couple to a lawyer to sign an affidavit or to one of the long lines of people outside the embassies. In these long queues some fainted from shock or heat, men jostled for spaces and broke into fights like boys, old quarrels revived suddenly into vicious abuse, so that the partly trained medical student was sometimes useful as an impartial young and rational voice.

Idi Amin's three-month deadline approached but the lines were still long.

One day when Shamim and he were returning to campus, where half a long night's academic catching up awaited them, she said, "You know, when I was at the Canadian consulate something strange happened."

"What?"

"I was helping a family from Masindi Port, and this man, Mr. McDougal, said to me, 'Why don't you apply for a visa for yourself.' Can you believe that?"

"If you had been Ugandan, this would have been your day."

"Yes. But when I told him I was Tanzanian, you know what he said? He said, 'We don't ask questions!'"

"And they reject so many others."

"We could go," she said softly. Then looked intently at him: "Why don't we go?"

"Where? To Canada? You must be crazy—we are Tanzanians. We have families there. That's our country."

What a thought. To go away, kabisa—for ever. It was impossible, he would never do that. He could not imagine himself anywhere else but in the streets of Dar es Salaam; or Kilwa, though perhaps not, it would seem too small. One crazy general in Uganda didn't mean Asians had to leave Tanzania too. He had not met any Asian happy to be going away. Why should anyone volunteer? And he was an African.

"We are Tanzanians," he said.

"This McDougal said Asians have no future in Africa."

"He knew you were studying to be a doctor and they need doctors in Canada. Remember, Tanzania needs doctors more."

In the following days in her typical manner she kept up her campaign, without sulking or getting angry, and he knew a resolution had to come. "I say, there are good hospitals in Canada, you know . . . I say, we could return when things are better, what do you think?" And yet he knew she was not entirely crazy. She was an Asian, and what happened in Uganda could happen elsewhere. The Canadian could be right. And no Asian could forget how, only a few months before, some old men of the Zanzibar Revolutionary Council had forcibly married Asian teenagers, one of whom had subsequently killed herself.

And yet, you don't just go. He recalled what he had said to Mr. Fernandes about the country needing doctors—how haughty and self-assured he had sounded—and he recalled Mr. Fernandes's idealism, invoking the soul of the nation. These were vital times for his country, his place was there.

"You know, we have signed a bond," he said to Shamim. "We have promised that in return for our free schooling and university, we will serve in the country for three years."

"Oh, bonds, ponds! There must be ways around these bonds."

He could not tell her to go by herself; they were committed, now that they occasionally shared her bed, doing "things," as she coyly put it. As a lover she was manipulative, the very opposite of Saida, and always the one in charge; how far they went was up to her initiative, not his passion, for it was understood that it was she who was breaking rules, going beyond the bounds, for his sake.

When he called his folks in Dar, it was obvious to him that his uncle and aunt had been told about Shamim's proposal, but they let him bring up the subject. Zera Auntie encouraged him to go on and settle down with Shamim and be happy. "How nice!—you will be in Vilayat, among all the whites! You will become a white! All that snow!" She worked from her instincts, which was what made her kind, but it was useless to spring ideas and ideals on her, to tell her about his objections. But Jaffu Uncle, who had watched him silently over the years, understood him more than anyone else. He begged Kamal to go.

"Times will get worse, Kamal," he said. "In Tanzania, our government doesn't know where its arse is. There is no education to speak of any more. Children go to school, sweep the floors, and return not learning anything. Bribery everywhere. And blame the Asian. Kamal, I know you love this country. We all do. But they will not allow you to do what you want here. All your classmates are looking for ways to escape. And remember, if things get worse, you might not get such an opportunity again."

He would make money available to them, Uncle said. Under the socialist regime, it was impossible to send money out of the country. However, there was a certain gentleman from Tanzania who had made his fortune in Congo. He owed Uncle a good sum of money which he would be instructed to send to Kamal in Canada. Kamal could use what he needed and hold the rest for the family.

If it had been anyone else attempting to convince him, Kamal might not have listened. But it was Uncle, who always spoke straight.

"I was wrong," he said to me, these many years later in Dar. "My uncle was hiding something from me."

There was a song that National Servicemen sang during political processions in the streets of Dar es Salaam, as they marched in uniform. It was a silly-sounding song that the schoolboys who shuffled behind them in the processions put their own words to, and it went: Tanzania, I love you so much, your name is sweet and brings joy to my heart . . . This song now played punishingly in Kamal's head, its sentimental patriotism—as he would describe it later—as false and empty and saccharine as his promises to Saida. What was true was that he was taking the easy way out, abandoning his country, absconding to another world via Mr. McDougal's office in the Canadian consulate.

McDougal was a clean-shaven man in his thirties, strong-jawed and athletic, and not very tall. He shook hands and eyed the couple, and said to Shamim with a smile,

"The offer was to you, not to the both of you."

Shamim replied charmingly, "We are engaged, John. It's not allowed in our culture to be separated."

McDougal stamped their applications, gave them medical forms, and said, "Your permits should be ready in a week." He gave Shamim his address in Ottawa where he would be returning shortly.

"I say, it wasn't so bad, was it?"

"Because he likes you."

"Are you jealous?"

"Yes."

She smiled, and he put his arm around her.

She was his perfect complement. He with his easygoing Swahili ways, hakuna haraka, as they said on the coast, there's no hurry; and she with the initiatives always, and that insouciance, the courage of the innocent, as he thought of it, hiding a tender core that brought out the protective instinct in him. And his love for her. He would always recall her persistent answers to those soldiers on the road, revealing not a trace of her fear.

· 41 ·

Early one morning at his clinic in Edmonton Kamal received a phone call from his cousin Azim, who happened, he said, to be passing through. And so later that day the two of them met at a restaurant, embraced, and sat down for dinner. Shamim had taken Hanif to a tennis meet; Karima was at home from university. It was summer. After dinner, they sat with their coffees, chatting.

Kamal was ever Azim's hero and "older brother." To Azim, his cousin's African features were simply attributes, like a cool haircut or a fine physique. This open-eyed acceptance of his difference had lasted into adulthood, when others might look briefly in surprise at the woolly-haired dark Indian among them. There had grown a strong, affectionate bond between the two. Back in Dar, Kamal would hardly speak about his early years in Kilwa; he had nursed his pain in private, then gradually adjusted to his new life. But there had been a period when, while he and Azim returned together from school, he would tell stories to his cousin. They were funny anec- dotes, about the wily Sungura-rabbit, and Kamal would narrate them the Swahili way, with pauses and exclamations. Pa! Pa! Alhamdullillah! . . . Sungura akafa! Eh-he! The rabbit died. Little Azim would laugh all the way home, tears in his eyes, and Kamal would be proud and happy beside him.

First Yasmin with her husband, then Shenaz and finally Azim had all followed Kamal to Canada during the peak of socialism in Tanzania, in the 1970s. A good part of the Indian population had left, having seen the door to Canada left ajar following the Uganda Asian expulsions. But Uncle, who had griped about "them" and pleaded with Kamal to go, himself never left, saying loftily, "I was born here, I will die here." So he did, eventually, and now Zera Auntie was with Shenaz in Toronto, a shadow of her previous irrepressible self. Whenever Kamal called her, she would utter her stock refrain, "Busy-busy? How busy you must be, no, the doctor!"

Kamal was aware that his three cousins kept in close touch with each other in Toronto and thereabouts. Out in the west and away from them, he had drifted into what he thought was his natural role: belonging, yet not quite one of them. He always felt that Yasmin and he could have gotten to know each other better. Behind that animus, the cat-and-dog hostility, as Uncle would describe it, there had lurked an understanding that never got the chance to flourish. During his final year in Dar, the ice seemed to thaw between them, but then he had gone away. And pretty, delicate Shenaz, once with a ponytail, had short hair now; she was polite, still a little wonderstruck by him, but distant. He came to realize at some point what a major disruption he had caused in all their lives by his arrival at their home that morning in Jamat Street in Dar. Perhaps they still talked about it, how the strange half-caste boy from Kilwa had come into their midst, and the lives they had known had forever altered.

A tearful Azim had called him for advice some years ago from Toronto, a congenital heart disorder having been discovered in his daughter. Kamal had confirmed the options, advised that a heart procedure, however dreadful the idea, was the best among them, from a probabilistic point of view. One had to think that way, even with a child's life. And he recommended a couple of specialists. The procedure had been successful.

Now Azim was back in Edmonton, sitting across the table, the indulged little boy still present in that dapper clean-cut look; he was an accountant. They had discussed families, a little politics. Then Azim made a strange request. He had been travelling for his company and wanted to be tested for HIV. "Don't worry," he reassured Kamal, "I don't expect anything, but just in case."

"The test can be done in Toronto," Kamal said tersely, puzzled, annoyed as a big brother should be at whatever indiscretion Azim had committed.

"I need absolute secrecy, Kamal. My doctor's a community man, his wife's his secretary—they could blow the whistle. And anywhere else . . . they could call home with the results—imagine that! I can't take the chance."

"I don't have to tell you," Kamal said with some concern, "but—"

"Just a mistake, Kamal. One mistake. I don't want it to ruin me. As I said, I expect a negative result, but just in case . . ."

Kamal told him to come the next day to one of the clinics of which he was a partner.

And then Azim said, "*You* had a secret girlfriend, didn't you?"

"What on earth are you talking about? Maybe it's your head that needs checking? Not your . . . your—"

"Come on, brother. You had someone back there . . . a native . . . an African girl?"

Kamal was silenced. He couldn't know that, he thought. There is no way on earth Azim could know about her. No one but Uncle—

"What exactly are you saying? Stop making innuendoes and speak clearly."

"The African girl—she came to our shop one day asking for you when you were at Makerere. Was she your girlfriend?"

"How do you know this? What did she say—were you there?"

"Yes, I was there. Yasmin too. And it was the day of your engagement to Shamim. We were shortly to be on our way to visit Shamim's house to celebrate. She spoke to Daddy, this African girl." His eyes twinkled, and he stopped short of making a comment about her.

"And what did she say?" Kamal asked.

She asked for you: "Kamalu yupo? Nitamkuta wapi?"

"And?"

"Daddy said you were in Uganda. Then he sent me away, but I know that he gave this girl some money."

"That's all?"

"Yes. But who was this girl? What was her name? Where did you find her?"

Kamal did not reply. "What did she look like?" he asked quietly.

"She wore a khanga. I remember her clearly, because we were so surprised. And her voice—it was thin—like a . . ."

"And you've kept this from me all these years? All of you?"

"It never came up. And you were getting married, weren't you? And then we were all here. Who was she?"

They got up. "Come tomorrow to the clinic," Kamal told Azim. "And don't do silly things with your life that you need an AIDS test."

"I won't, brother."

How does one respond, Kamal asked himself driving home that night. All these years later. I am a different man now, inside and out, I have transformed, I have moulted. I have acquired an accent and an idiom, and a way of dressing and grooming, a liking for Scotch, an appreciation for wine and good food; everything that goes with wealth and standing. My world view, my faith are different. She would not know me now. Would I know her? Three decades—and more—have passed. I have worked through a marriage, wasted it, raising two children, which was for the duration the sole purpose of life besides earning.

Suppose Uncle had told me about her visit—would I be here now? Would I have come to Canada with Shamim?

Their marriage was wrong from the start. It was not meant to work. He always easygoing, she on the go, living by schedules and plans, by the dictates of form and image. She became more religious and communal over the years; and he, someone with nothing to command his loyalty or hold his attention except his practice and the children, until he wandered into a bookstore in Toronto and discovered that old book about Kilwa. Recriminations between him and Shamim had begun early on: You were always, You never, ad nauseam. What in them had seemed beautifully complementary in Kampala, in their new country became points of conflagration. It had been too easy, their union, too convenient. They were beginning to love and accommodate each other, but had never loved each other with a passion. As he saw it later, there had been no pain, no longing, no moments of sheer heartwarming ecstasy in their relationship. And so the regrets, his of the past, someone he had left behind, and hers of wanting to have been in love, of getting older without even a memory of a proper passionate romance.

They had arrived in Toronto in spring, found a small apartment, and immediately applied to medical schools to complete their training. To their delight the wait was short and both were admitted to the university in Saskatoon for the fall term. Far from people like them, they were isolated and lonely, but also excited at starting out together like pioneers, surviving in a new land, learning the rudiments of living differently from what they had been used to. They had been welcomed into Canada, and given opportunities, for which they were grateful, though it was evident that they were of an inferior status, by virtue of where they came from, their accents, their skin colour. At med school, when Kamal did the hospital rounds with the senior doctors, there had been patients who refused to be touched by "that man." Shamim would repeatedly be taken for a maid. Later they would wonder at how much the country had changed before their eyes. They had become Canadians, and, as he liked to say, Canada had become them. They carried no bitterness for past insults, because they had been so successful. Shamim was a pediatrician at Edmonton's children's hospital. He, with three other doctors, owned three private clinics, and there was ironic satisfaction in seeing the appointment books full, people clamouring for the most intimate cosmetic surgeries. That was business, though; his heart was in his general practice. His patients sat for hours waiting to see only him. He spent time with them, talked with them, which was why his manager despaired, and why his accountant—an Asian from Dar—kept reminding him he could easily bring in twice the money by seeing twice the patients in the same amount of time.

Their children had been raised by the book, according to the latest trends in child psychology. Sometimes he had pitied them for not being able to run about barefoot outside, splash in the mud, receive an occasional slap or shout from an angry parent. Eat a glob of butter. Zera Auntie would swipe up some butter with her finger and shove it into Azim's mouth as he left for school. Not Hanif and Karima, brought up with care, like creatures in a test tube, their diets, their education, their reading and entertainment strictly controlled; every childish response to be attended to thoughtfully, according to the manuals. But special attention and theories of child-rearing notwithstanding, they had turned out normal in the end, typical immigrant doctors' spoiled, bright private-school kids who would inherit a lot and earn a lot more. Here's to the next generation.

He sat for a long time that night in his study, his drink at hand. How does one respond to what Azim had revealed? He didn't know. He didn't know because the feelings that could be invoked, the nerve that could be awoken, lay well buried inside him, under layers of life lived.

Hanif had come second in the tennis tourney earlier that evening; he would be applying to prestigious colleges down south. Had Kamal shown enough excitement, as a father should? That could be a bone of conjugal contention in the morning. Karima, the older one, was hovering outside the door, waiting perhaps to pop in and bait her father on some feminist issue his generation was ignorant about. And Shamim was already in bed.

He looked up, caught his daughter's eye. "Come in, Karima," he said. "What's up? How's it going?"

The children, the children, he had heard a colleague say, wistfully eyeing a pretty nurse. And so it had been, he and Shamim inhabiting their private worlds, but keeping their home running, regrets and all—who didn't have them?—for the sake of the children. And secondly—there was no denying this—for the sake of convenience and continuity; they had memories that still occasionally tugged; they had an engaging social circle of other professionals, mostly doctors. The apple was not ready to fall yet. He liked that expression.

Over the years Shamim had identified more with her Indianness. She went to khano Friday evenings, dressed up in a shalwar-kameez or something exotic, taking the kids with her. He would wait for them, in the company of a drink, dipping into his collection of Africana in his glazed isolation. They would return from khano radiant, having met people they knew, participated in familiar rituals, and he would be envious, feeling incomplete, unfulfilled. An outcast in his own home, though it was nobody's fault. His attempts to write family history for the children, and in the process revive a secret ambition, had met with stiff resistance from all. No point harping about Africa, the children are Canadians, she said, and so are you, don't forget that. But Canadians come from somewhere? And your khano and shalwar-kameez? And your Bollywood and Shahrukh Khan? Glamorous India. What did he offer as a heritage: a dusty town in Africa, a slave ancestor, an absconded Indian grandfather. He would have embellished his history with accounts of wars and resistance, poetry and folk tales, but it all sounded so distant and destitute. What would Hanif and Karima rather claim (if anything): a hut in the bush or the glorious Taj Mahal? No choice.

They would have clung to each other this way, out of need and necessity and for the sake of the children and possible grandchildren, but for a wind of religious euphoria that rippled through the lives of the Shamsis of their generation from Africa. They were all doing well, the children grown and mostly in university, the houses were paid off, there was money to spend. A Year of Celebration was inaugurated in which like groupies they travelled the world's cities in the thousands following their imam on a tour of the faithful. It was a wave of revivalist nostalgia drawing people in their middle age, feeling spiritually empty, into a tight community network of the sort that had once existed in Africa, into which he had been adopted as a boy, but which could not engage him any longer. Once the Year of Celebration was over, alumni of the tours continued to keep up the euphoric momentum, gathering in different cities for reunions. It was during one such trip that Shamim apparently became involved with a fellow groupie, called Bhagat, who must represent all she had missed in her agnostic African husband. Bhagat was, naturally, from East Africa; more, he was from Dar. Shamim denied an affair, and perhaps the relationship was only platonic. But Kamal had observed the catch in her voice when she spoke to Bhagat on the phone, her eagerness to attend the reunions, that extra telltale touch of an accessory: a scarf, a pendant, a new Asiatic perfume. He had not observed her this way in a long time. After some months she seemed back to normal again, perhaps her infatuation was over; but that holy wave had removed all their remaining faith in the worth of their relationship, and they decided finally to separate.

That winter he attended a medical conference in the Bahamas, away from the bleak Edmonton skies and the acrimony of a broken home. It was, he had told himself, just the kind of breezy hiatus he needed before beginning life anew. As he sat with a few associates at the opening-day luncheon, under a sun umbrella atop a rock cliff, the ocean below them and scantily clad waitresses hovering around, there came the crash of a tray falling, followed by a momentary stillness. That was all he needed. As he would think of it, the clattering dissonance of the falling silverware recombined in his head to produce one resonating echo: *Kinjikitilé*. He knew he was called. He must go and find her.

It was late Sunday evening, Kamal and I among those few unable to unglue ourselves from the Africana's friendly bar. Sporadically the farther door would swing open and a frenetic hum from the casino next door would waft in, ushering out a bunch of people seeking respite from their obsessions. Women in saris and the latest European fashions, men in suits. Outside, one floor below, the streets were wet and empty from a rainfall. Stretching your neck you would see the harbour lights. Over the past eight weeks we had spoken of many things; I had apprised him of some recent history of the country: the successful though debilitating war against Idi Amin; the confounding new multiparty system; corruption scandals of such a scale and blatancy as to require a sense of the comic to live with. But all that was mere leavening, to give him the space in which to unravel. We had gone well beyond the therapeutic imperative we started with, when he had simply wished to talk about himself following his drug-induced catastrophe and I made myself available to listen. His was the story of a castaway who finally found his way home; at its heart, what drove him back, was a strange, a bizarre love story haunted by the figure—or spectre—of his childhood sweetheart, Saida, whom he believed he had deserted. That quest landed him in the hospital, at the edge of madness, where I found him, his Canadian son and daughter distraught by his side. It was at this bar that I had sat later that evening comforting the young people.

"You went to India," I said. "Your ancestral place. How was that?"

"Yes," he replied slowly. "To Gujarat, where it all began, the family odyssey on my father's side. I saw it for myself."

"What was it like—this experience? A profound one?"

"I think I've put India to rest—and come to terms with my father . . . Not an easy thing, growing up with the memory of a father who abandoned you."

It was then that I finally put to him what had been on my mind all along. What about Mama? He had insisted that he had not forgiven her, and she did not need him, and I could just believe that. But he had not broken with her, I knew that too. How vividly had I heard him recall her.

He said nothing for a long time.

"Fatuma knew her, in the 1970s. She was in Lindi, then perhaps in Songea or Tabora. She's most likely dead by now . . . I've thought of putting a notice in the Swahili papers, see if I could trace her, or her family."

I told him I knew a reporter or two who would be happy to do a story. There are six or more Swahili newspapers in the country. Not as widely read as one would like, especially in the smaller centres, but you never know.

Like other well-heeled professionals of middle age, with money to spend, Kamal and Shamim travelled frequently, "doing" different places in quick time. India was special, and they visited it with two other couples, doctors and accountants also originally from Dar. India had thrilled them and they all agreed Mumbai felt like home—meaning Dar—but multiplied a hundredfold.

Leaving Shamim and the others to shop to their hearts' content, Kamal had set off for a destination of interest only to himself, the town in Gujarat where his great-grandfather Punja Devraj had hailed from. The story of Punja the Lion had captured his imagination in Kilwa; he heard greater detail in Dar, where the story in embellished versions was well known. Jaffu Uncle, too, liked to throw off a bragging mention or two of the ancestor to impress his card-playing cronies of Jamat Street. There was such a specificity to that legend, it gave to Kamal a piece of land on the subcontinent to imagine as a place of distant—and partial—origin: Verawal, in a far-flung corner of Gujarat. It was where his father had last been heard from. It was where Jaffu Uncle had told him once a long time ago that he should visit.

He took a flight to Ahmedabad, where he checked into a hotel and spent the night. Early the next morning he departed by taxi towards the western peninsula of Kathiawad and the town of Verawal on the Arabian Sea. The day was hot and the air warm and dusty, the landscape dry and plain. This was an area prone to drought, which was why young men historically left its shores to seek their fortunes on the coast of East Africa. All the Asians Kamal had known in Dar had their origins in this peninsula. They passed women trekking along the roadside, road vendors with pushcarts, a gang of orthodox Muslim young men on their way presumably to madrassa, a troupe of transvestites on their way to a temple, according to his driver. They stopped at a roadstand for lunch. He had left the certainty of his overblown tourist's itinerary, described in the brochures as "Glorious India," back in Mumbai and as he headed deeper into this quotidian and yet alien existence he felt twinges of nervousness. Yes, he'd been impulsive. But he was in India, how could he not try to find that ancestral town, ask for the man who had fathered him, carried him in his arms, before going away completely, leaving a complex knot of feelings inside him. The baba whose photo he had always had with him, ever since Mama packed it in his bag with which she had dispatched him to his uncle.

It was late afternoon when they reached the pilgrim town of Somnath, where Kamal had made a hotel reservation. Somnath, a few miles up the coast from Verawal, was the site of an ancient temple by the sea; a beautiful new replica had been constructed in its place.

The next morning Kamal proceeded to Verawal, a small, somewhat weather-blown town, though in antiquity an important port. The driver parked the car on a main street and Kamal started strolling around; he stopped at a few places to ask if they knew a Dr. Amin Punja Devraj, or if there was a Devraj family in town. He met with blank stares and shakes of the head. Soon he was looking lost, an object of curiosity. People stepped outside their shops, others looked over balconies to stare at him, the message having gone around of a dark stranger in town from foreign parts, asking questions.

Finally a brainwave struck him. He asked at a shop if there were any people of the Shamsi community in town. Immediately he was pointed to the provision store right behind him—at which a man, perhaps in his forties and balding in front, stood behind an open serving window, staring at him. He was called Pyarali, and said yes, he was from that community. He ordered two teas from a vendor and answered Kamal's questions. The Devraj family was no longer in town, he said. The last one who had lived here, Hassanali, had died a few years before. Yes, there had been a Dr. Amin who would come to visit Verawal periodically from somewhere, when Pyarali was a boy, and would see patients. This, said so casually, to a question thrown off hopelessly. The cup in Kamal's hand shook on its saucer. This man had seen his father and remembered him. "What did he look like?" Kamal asked. "I don't recall." Pyarali smiled indulgently. "Was he related to you?" "Yes," Kamal said. "Ordinary looking," Pyarali offered. "Always polite. People lined up to consult him. Once I was taken to him for something—I forget. There was a wife, too, and some children."

A woman came inside the shop from the back and was introduced as Pyarali's wife. She took a keen interest in Kamal and quizzed him about Africa, and he answered politely. She knew of people with family members in Africa, she informed him. When he had the chance, Kamal asked the couple, "And where is Dr. Amin now?"

Pyarali answered. "Amin died five or so years ago. We had a service for him here."

There were no Devrajes in town, Pyarali repeated, and his wife told Kamal he should look for them in Rajkot. The doctor's children might be in Mumbai.

Kamal declined an invitation to stay for lunch.

He checked out of his hotel and told the driver they would return to Ahmedabad, but first he wanted to visit the shrine of Sidi Sayyad, which he understood was nearby.

"It is in the jungle," the driver told him. "There are only Sidis there—it will take us out of our way."

"Never mind. I want to see it."

The Sidis were the African Indians, and Kamal already knew the story of his great-grandfather Punja's relationship with the saint Sidi Sayyad.

They set off, taking a small road through a deeply forested area. The map called it the Gir forest. They drove for about an hour and a half, passing the occasional peasant on the road, a group of nomads with cattle, scattered huts, a chai stand. Finally they turned into a narrower road and quite suddenly it had become a different country. A few young men stood idly chatting at the turning, as you would expect to see anywhere, but these were all black. Farther on they passed a rickshaw bus full of people; everyone, including the driver, was also black and looked completely African. He knew he was approaching a Sidi village, but to see the African presence so explicit, to recognize the features as so familiar, unnerved him. He could have been in Kilwa, the young men chatting in Swahili. They parked on a side road leading into a settlement. A festive drum was beating somewhere. As Kamal walked towards the village, a young man in a Muslim cap passed him from the opposite direction and greeted him respectfully, putting his right hand on his chest, and pointed behind him, as though Kamal was expected there. The drum became loud and insistent. Kamal reached a crossroad, where he turned left, from where came the sound of the drum and human commotion. Ahead of him, behind a wall, rose the dome of a green and white building. People were removing their shoes and walking in through a gate into the compound. Kamal did likewise.

He had entered the premises of the shrine to Sidi Sayyad. The compound was packed with people watching a ritual in progress. Two men were beating on drums, one of them blind; leading them a few people danced to the beat, including an old woman and a lithe young man who leapt around collecting donations in his mouth. Not all the people present were black; the others were from out of town, having made the journey to beg a favour from the famous Sidi saint. As part of the ritual, a black goat garlanded with bright orange marigolds was being pushed towards the mausoleum. The belief was that if the goat went up the steps, the visiting supplicants' wishes would be fulfilled.

A little later, when the place was relatively quiet, most of the people having left the compound to partake in a feast, Kamal went up the marble steps of the mausoleum and entered the inner sanctum, which housed the grave. He stood in silence before the grave, which was covered with a mound of coloured cloth and flowers brought by the worshippers, the air heavy with perfume, and imagined his great-grandfather as a young man having come here with his own wish to be fulfilled. One part of my story started here, Kamal thought.

He had lost any sense of time and place, and when he emerged back into the glaring sunlight he felt faint and overcome by the spiritual experience, and by the overburdened air he had just left behind; he sat down on the steps. He was brought to by the sound of a faint shuffle and something brushing his forearm with the touch of a feather. He looked up, startled. A young woman stood before him, holding in her arms a child of perhaps one. Her head was covered by a scarf and her clothes were bedraggled, and she could have been no more than twenty. "Sahib, please," she beseeched in a soft voice, "help me," and the Gujarati words startled him, as though he expected to hear Swahili. As she turned to leave, he said, "Here," and gave her some bills. She bent down and touched his feet, and he felt a deep sense of unease.

They raced back to Ahmedabad, stopping only once for tea, and arrived at his hotel at four in the morning. Soon after he headed to the airport and caught a flight to Delhi, where he joined Shamim and their group for the last leg of their "Glorious India" tour.

That was India. The apparition at the shrine, as he would recall the young beggar woman, had shaken him. But India had held many shocks and surprises. It was much later, when he had resolved to go and find her, that he realized that it was Saida that the young woman at the shrine had reminded him of.

Before he left Canada, Kamal picked up the phone and called his older cousin and former nemesis Yasmin. He had not seen her or spoken to her in over thirty years, even though he was certain she had visited Edmonton, or at least Calgary, and he in turn had passed through Ottawa where she lived. Now when he called her, finally, he greeted her with some warmth, to which she responded in kind, and then he told her what Azim had revealed to him about Saida's visit to the shop in Dar.

"Do you remember?" he asked. "You were present."

"Yes, I remember," she replied quickly.

"Do you remember what happened? What did this girl say—this African girl?"

"She asked for you."

"And then?"

"And Daddy said you were in Kampala and were getting engaged that same day."

"That was all?"

"Yes. And she left. Daddy gave her some money."

"There must have been something more," he insisted. "Don't you remember? Why did he send Azim away? Are you hiding something from me, Yasmin?"

"I can't tell you what more was said, Kamal. By my faith. Daddy made me promise him that I would never tell you what I heard that day. It has been a long time, you should forget about it. And I am happy you called me. You are my brother, Kamal."

"What did she look like, this girl?"

"Why—like an African . . . Wait . . . she was polite. She wore a khanga."

He smiled as he recalled this. "She must have seemed so alien to them," he told me. "Yet she was so much a part of me. But I was not offended at my cousin's refusal to tell me more. I was afraid of what that might be. It was better for me to go and find out."

Four

❧

Saida

· 43 ·

Saida's whereabouts having been revealed to him by Fatuma, Kamal waited a day to gather himself. He lounged on the beach, took a long walk, then a swim. In his mind, scenes of himself with her, tomorrow. He imagined what she would look like, how she would greet him. Curiously, he did not see anyone else with her, no family. He composed in his mind fragments of speech, what he would need to speak to her—his greetings, his explanations, his life's story. And then warned himself to be prepared to expect anything, too many years had elapsed. You'll have to give it time, Kamal. In the afternoon he walked to the bus station and bought a ticket for the village—Minazi Minne—and went back and sat on the patio and read. By evening, after dinner, he was ready, he told himself. Let morning come.

It was early, still grey, but the depot was bustling with activity when he arrived. The Masoko–Lindi bus was being loaded up with all manner of luggage: suitcases, crates, baskets, and sacks of produce. One carton proclaimed a computer monitor as its contents; beside it stood a nervous-looking young man. The conductor, a young muscular fellow, stood at the door enthusiastically calling out destinations on the way, shouting friendly invectives to the loaders, greeting passersby as if on a whim they might abandon their day's plans and join him on his journey. He stopped midsentence as Kamal came up and produced his ticket, then broke into a grin. "Where to?" "Minazi Minne." "You know somebody there? Welcome, karibu, take a seat, we leave soon." He swung aside to let Kamal go past him and take his seat. The interior had been washed and smelled of wet dust and a repulsive cleaning spray. Kamal chose a seat in the third row and sat down, tentatively, by the window, his shoulder bag on his lap. No one followed him in and he realized after a while that there was still time, and went back out, telling the conductor he had left his bag on the third seat by the window. He walked over to the nearby chai shop, sat down, and ordered. The server dropped a newspaper on his table. It was a few days old.

The concerns of the world, bludgeoned into the brain by the hour and minute in the Canada he had left behind, seemed so distant and absurd from this vantage, he could be on the farthest planet; the feeling was enhanced, he realized, by the grey early hour, the woodsmoke in the air, the blue-tinged tube light hanging above him. He watched, over his tea, the Dar bus, also being loaded, and another that had recently arrived, its weary-looking passengers alighting, picking up luggage, and a taxi and a rickshaw heading out, and vitumbua being fried by the roadside, smoke rising, and a line of people walking to work—life contained and proceeding apace, there could be no other world outside. From the newspaper he gleaned bits of the local news. Yanga had won a soccer match; a man had been murdered in a village for allegedly abusing a child; a million-dollar corruption scandal involving a former minister was still being flogged. There seemed no outrage, Kamal reflected, no emotion wasted at the rampant corruption, as though after decades of socialist austerity even corruption needed its due, someone had to get rich quick. After a while he heard a call, "Minazi Minne! Minazi Minne!" and he quickly paid for his tea and ran to the bus. It lurched forward as he stepped inside, but his seat was waiting for him, with his bag.

Markham had returned from Dar the day before with a recommendation to go to Johannesburg for prostate surgery. He was going to think about it, he said petulantly. Meanwhile, Kamal observed, his chest congestion did not bode well for him. Navroz Engineer had come over in the evening for a drink and they had discussed the pros and cons of India versus South Africa as places for medical treatment.

The point was to encourage Markham, who had sat down silently to make a threesome, to take his option seriously.

Kamal had asked John if he had heard of a place called Minazi Minne. John hadn't heard of it. A kitchen hand knew of it but, strangely, said nothing more.

As he sat looking out the window, as the bus raced down the paved road past the small airport and onto the main highway south, Kamal felt numb inside, a sense of resignation. His quest was ending. What exactly did he expect? To see Saida herself, or perhaps someone who could tell him of her? Before he left Canada he had thought about what presents to bring for her. He couldn't decide what would suit her, what she would like, and so he had settled for a cologne, some handkerchiefs, and a scarf. These were with him now with his change of clothes. He recalled the gold earrings, the dress, and the blue plastic sandals with heels that he had brought for her the last time they met, which she told him she could not very well wear, for how would she explain them to her husband? She had been only a girl, and he a callow young man. Now he was on his way to see her again. What had Fatuma told him? "You'll find her in Minazi Minne." The place with the four coconut palms. "But she doesn't want you to go there." What did that mean? As if that would keep him away. She must know that.

Saida should have come to see him in Kilwa, knowing he had come a long way to look for her. Had he aroused her animus so much, by his betrayal, by her being sent away by his uncle, that she simply would rather not see him? That was not the Saida he knew. But what of Saida now, what had she become as a woman, what had life done to her? Thirty-five years is a long time. She would be about fifty-five; still young where he came from; just past the life expectancy here. You might say that Mama sent him away to give him twenty more years of life. Averagely speaking.

How he had ached for her. Were those twenty extra years of life—averagely speaking—worth it? He probably had half-brothers or sisters somewhere.

He heard someone say "Minazi Minne" and he looked up. The conductor and the driver were discussing him, the driver looking at him in the mirror. Soon after, the conductor came down the aisle with a plate of candies, and Kamal asked him if he knew Minazi Minne well. No, he replied, he did not know it. The television overhead came on with a Bugs Bunny comic and a chuckle went around. In spite of the mock airline service, this was very much a local transport. People got on and off, and in between pickups and drops the bus raced like the devil were after it, always coming abruptly, lurchingly to a stop, the conductor hanging out the door, calling out for passengers and rattling off rates. Inside, the atmosphere became progressively more stuffy, the country folk obviously not bothered with perfumes.

Finally, on a quiet patch on the road, halfway up a hill, the bus stopped. "Minazi Minne," the driver said, as casually as though in the midst of a conversation.

"Is this it?" Kamal asked, getting up. "Ndio hapo?" Outside the windows there was forest on both sides.

The conductor came over, grinning.

"Yes, here." Ndiyo hapo hapo. Nowhere else.

Kamal struggled out into the aisle. "Where is it? I can see nothing outside." He peered out on both sides.

"It is here only, baba," a woman said reassuringly, putting a fore-finger on his arm. "At the top of the hill—a road goes inside."

"Why don't you drop me there, then—at the top of the hill?" he asked the driver.

"Just here," the driver replied tonelessly, not bothering even to look up.

The woman who had touched him looked at him anxiously.

Kamal stepped off the bus and eyed the hill before him wearily.

"Do you know anyone in the village?" the conductor asked, leaning out from the steps as the bus began to inch forward.

"I know someone."

"All right, then. And in the town—you have people in Kilwa? Wait, you!" he shouted to the driver. The bus stopped.

Kamal gave Lateef's name, and Dr. Engineer's.

"All right then. The doctor will come pick you up."

"Or I will take a bus."

The conductor banged on the side of his conveyance a couple of times and it roared away. A few people inside waved to Kamal, and he waved back.

He was aware that he looked hopelessly foreign. His shoes, though dusty from walking on unpaved streets, could not hide their expensive lustre. The flak jacket was only for the comfort of not losing things— the cell phone, a pen and notebook, his passport. His shoulder bag seemed ludicrous here, but at least it carried his water and the presents and a change of clothes. The sun was hot, and even though he had kept himself fit, he found the walk uphill arduous. No traffic passed him. Panting, dripping with sweat and blistered on his feet, he arrived at the hilltop, much to his relief to see a track winding into a settlement visible from the road. As he walked in, he saw it consisted of a handful of mud houses, one of them the village store. He took a peep inside. There was no one, and it was threadbare: a few cans of food scattered on warped shelves, a closed sack of some produce, a pile of dried cassava on the ground. What do they do here? There was no farm patch in sight. But he saw a few papaya and banana trees, a single coconut tree in the distance. The cell phones don't reach here, he observed, there's no telephone line, no electricity.

He stood in the middle of a clearing, the highway behind him, and took in the scene before him. A child of about two, naked from the waist down, trotted out with a chuckle from a house to his left. A young woman followed. She was dressed in a faded khanga around her waist and a blouse and her head was close-cropped. She eyed him as if he were a ghost. "Jambo," he greeted her. "Sijambo," she replied.

"Is there a teacher here?" he asked.

It was a stupid query. But a teacher implied a school and a thriving habitation, perhaps that was in his mind, besides an attempt at familiarity.

"Teacher?" she asked, squinting from the glare.

"Yes, schoolteacher." Mwalimu wa shule.

"No."

"No school?"

"Is there something you are looking for?" she asked.

"I was told I can find a woman called Saida here," he said.

"There is no one called Saida here," she replied and abruptly ran off after the child.

"Is this Minazi Minne?" he called out.

"It is inside there, by the river." She lifted a quick hand to indicate.

He walked to the house next door; it consisted of a single room and was empty. In the third house an old man, almost naked, sat on a mat, shoving a twig into his ear, oblivious to the world. He did not respond to the intrusion. Kamal came outside and sat down on a tree trunk, and brought out a bottle of water.

What a beginning. The girl returned with the child at her waist, and an older woman emerged from the first house, the two pinning him with their stares.

"Minazi Minne is down there," the girl said, sounding more friendly than before and pointing firmly to the area behind the settlement. "But you will find no one called Saida," she added with a softer voice and a look of the slightest amusement. "Only some old people."

"Then they must know Saida," he replied.

She said nothing.

"How do I get there?"

"You go through the bushes. There is a path. Come with me, I'll take you."

As she put down the little girl, he realized that the child was wheezing, and her nose was running. He bent down to listen to her chest, then asked her mother to pick her up, and he put his hand on her chest and forehead.

"You are a doctor?"

He nodded. "Take her to the Kilwa hospital," he said. "There is another doctor there, an Indian. Tell him I sent you. I am called Kamalu."

She nodded and went into her house, appearing in a moment with an empty can.

They walked together into the bushes behind the huts.

Her name was Zara. People in her village, which was called Kilimani, she said in answer to his question, went to Kilwa and places as far as

Dar es Salaam to find work; some worked their plots behind the huts. Those who went far stayed away for months. She bounded lightly on the bush track a step ahead of him, humming snatches of a tune, beaming when she turned to speak, like a free spirit of the forest, devoid of any care. She wasn't quite sure where her husband was. He wondered if there was one. Her daughter's name was Salima.

"Eti, you have come from far?" she asked.

"Dar es Salaam," he replied.

"Not from overseas?" She eyed him slyly.

No innocent, this one, he mused to himself and did not reply. She would be about the same age he'd been when he had last come to see Saida; perhaps as old as Saida had been then. It was a strange feeling: this girl and her easy manner, these huts, this vegetation had not altered in all the years he had been away. Then they were a part of his life. Now they raised a question, Why no progress, not even electricity?

"You won't find any Saida in Minazi Minne," she said, intruding into his thoughts. "Who is this Saida?"

He hesitated. "A friend from long ago. I used to live in Kilwa then." He smiled at her.

"You will find no one who is called Saida here."

"Whom will I find?"

"Palé," she said, coming to a stop. There. She pointed.

Some hundred yards ahead, in a clearing, stood a cluster of huts. There could not have been more than six or seven, but there was about them a sense of coherence, unlike the roadstop he had just left. There was a mango tree in their midst and a baobab farther up, on the way to a shimmer that he realized was a stream. His heart lifted. This looked like a destination.

"So who lives here?" he repeated to Zara as they hurried along.

"Some people." She chuckled.

He saw no one about. She took him past a few of the huts to the farthest one, its entrance facing away towards the stream, and stopped. Saida, he whispered to himself. She is here.

"Suddenly, for a moment, I became afraid," he said to me. "Icy fingers gripped me. A gust of air, perhaps. That tingle at the back. What you feel in that second before your first high dive . . . or, more appropriately, when you say, What the heck, and walk past a baobab tree at dusk, knowing that spirits live there. What was I headed for? I should have heeded the signs. In that moment they all came back to me. Saida's—or was it Fatuma's?—injunction not to go; the strange silence of the waiter at the hotel; the amused look on the conductor's face when I told him my destination, and his later show of concern; and the giveaway—the bus driver refusing to stop at the top of the hill, where the path led inside."

"Now you were there, you couldn't escape."

"This is what I had come for. But it was not how I could ever have imagined it."

"I have brought you a guest," Zara said outside the hut, peeping in through the entrance, though her Swahili expression could have implied *your* guest.

"Let him come," croaked an ancient voice from the black hole, the interior of the hut. Zara scampered away.

He had to lower his head at the doorway to enter. As he did so, he saw a spectre standing before him, the trace of a shadow looking up at him, its eyes like glinting jewels in the dark. There was a small window somewhere at the back letting in a little light, and moments later he discerned the full, small figure of the woman. She was bent at the waist, wearing a khanga wraparound from the chest down. Her skin at the neck and arms was wrinkled and loose, her face was bony, the hair a powder-thin patch of white.

"What do you seek?"

"I was sent here by Bi Fatuma of Kilwa."

"You're deceiving me," she said in a flat undertone, with that immovable authority of the aged. "What have you come for?"

"I was told I would find Saida here."

"What is she to you?"

"I knew her."

She didn't ask him who Saida was, he would recall later, and he didn't even notice. Zara had brought him here, and his mind assumed he was in the right place. He was not frightened anymore. He answered firmly to her challenge, implying by his tone that he would say no more about that. In the moment that followed, she didn't ask him to sit, there didn't seem to be a chair around. He went and sat on the edge of her cot, which was halfway towards the back of the room and had no bedding upon it. There was a pot on the ground; across from him at the back wall were some more pots and a couple of ladles. The roof was thatched, an unlit oil lamp hung low from a crossbeam. There was an odour of wet earth in the room, and ugali, he thought. She must have had a meal recently.

"What is that you are wearing around your neck?"

Even in the dark, she had seen it at the opening in his shirt.

"It is a tawiz," he replied, holding it.

"Give it to me."

"I cannot give it. It contains a prayer."

"I want that thing."

She was toying with him.

"It belongs to this girl, Saida, whom I'm looking for."

She said nothing for a while, just stood there. Then she went to her pots and soon brought him a cup. "Drink this uji," she told him.

He took the cup, looked at the dark porridge, then handed it back. "I can't. My stomach is unsteady."

"If you want to find this Saida, you will have to drink it. It has sugar."

"If you boil it first, I will drink it," he said. "Truly, I've been sick recently."

She hastened out of the hut, faster than he would have thought possible. As he waited, all kinds of thoughts passed through his head. Should he call someone on his cell phone? He took it out of his pocket, but of course there was no reception. Who was this woman? If you want to find this Saida . . . Where was Saida? Why all the mystery? Just to find a person. The depressing thought occurred to him then that Saida was most likely dead. Then why didn't Fatuma say so? Why was he sent here?

Who was the old woman and what could she do for him?

It did not occur to him that he should leave. He waited patiently for her to return.

The old woman came back and gave him the cup. "Drink. I have heated it."

It was lukewarm and bitter to the taste. Even as he knew something was wrong, he drank it.

"Wait here," she said, and left the hut again.

He put the cup down on the ground.

He lost consciousness.

· 44 ·

He was awake, surrounded by cloying darkness, sitting on the cot.
The small porthole a dim, distant gleam of light in a corner of the
mind. And she was there sitting on a stool at a slight angle from him.
His mind was clear, yet he was weak, and sweating. Sweat pouring
from his brows, from his armpits, down his legs.

She looked the same as he had last seen her, many years ago, and
he said, "Saida, they said you were dead."

"Who said? I am here, come back to you."

"You haven't changed at all."

"And you have, Kamalu," she said. "I waited for you and you changed."

"I would have come for you, my angel, malaika, my darling."

She disappeared in the haze for a moment, and then reappeared.

"Lies only. You went away making promises, after I opened myself
to you, and you married an Indian girl. Jé, Kamalu, did she give you
much happiness? And how many children did she give you? Did you
use her as you used me by the shore, and—"

"Don't torture me, Saida. I have returned. And?" he asked anxiously. "And what?"

"And left me heavy with child." She looked down at her feet.

"No, Saida . . . It can't be . . ."

"Are you going to deny me to name the father of my child?"

"No, Saida," he whispered.

"Yes, Kamalu, you left me with child, your seed that was my destruction."

"Saida, tafadhali. Please. This can't be you, I have never seen you angry like this. You trusted Kamalu. Remember a many and a pany? And how I would comfort you? How could you know how often I thought of you, even when I . . . even when I . . . was with my wife. Do you know how you haunted my life, malaika?"

She asked slyly: "Did you always wear that tawiz?"

When he would recall that scene later he would remember her sitting in profile, wearing a white dress and a colourful khanga around her shoulders; the head bare, her hands clasped at the knees.

"How could I?" he answered. "How could she let me wear it knowing it was from you?"

"No, she couldn't. No wife would."

"Well, then. Tell me about when you went to see my uncle at the shop. I never knew that. By God and His Prophet, they didn't tell me, Saida . . . And the child?" he asked. "A boy or girl? My firstborn, my African firstborn?"

She had gone to see his uncle one afternoon, he was having his tea, and two of his children were in the shop with him, a boy and a girl. She came, with a baby at her back and he looked at her with contempt, taking her for a beggar.

"Shikamoo, Bwana Jaffu," she said respectfully, for he was an elder, and he was a wealthy man, and he was an Indian and she didn't know Indians at all.

"It's not Friday," he said, because that day was when the beggars arrived for alms.

She said, "Bwana, I'm looking for Kamalu."

"Who? Kamalu? How do you know Kamalu? What do you want from him?"

The man's face had darkened, his voice was bitter-chungu, and she knew then that he knew about her. And his scowl got darker as he observed the child tied behind her, heard it cry, for it did not seem to like his tone.

"I have come from Kilwa," she said, and heaved a little to comfort the child, and he seemed to understand that the child was Kamalu's.

The man did not say anything for a moment. He gave a great cough to clear his throat before looking at her.

"Kamalu is in Kampala," he told her in a softer voice. "He is becoming a doctor, and today he has become engaged to marry a girl. What do you want from him?"

He looked to the boy standing at the doorway leading inside and instructed him to leave. The girl remained, staring intently at Saida.

"What can you give him?" Bwana Jaffu asked her. "Have you come here to drag him down? He is an educated boy and you have barely gone to school. What standard did you study? Three? Five? He is training to be a doctor. He'll be a big man one day."

He cleared his throat again, then said flatly, "He is an Indian, and you are an African."

As she turned to leave, he came to her and said, "Here. This is for the baby." And strangely, he briefly put his hand on the child's head.

And so she returned to Kilwa and her mother and her sorcerer husband.

When her husband, Mzee Hamisi, saw her belly growing, he grew suspicious that the baby was not his. Ever since giving herself to Kamalu, she had resisted him. "My spirits inform me, my wife," he told her, "that this baby is not mine. It is Satan's." He prodded her belly, put his head to it and listened, spoke to it. He beat it with a stick. And she cried because it hurt and with every blow she imagined the child crying out inside her. And she screamed, Kamalu come and rescue your child! She ran away to live with her mother, in whose house she had her son. She called him Shabani, because it was the month of Shaban. And then she went to see Bwana Jaffu in Dar es Salaam, was rejected, and returned in terrible fear for the child.

"What happened to the child, Saida? What happened to our son?"

"He died."

"He died? How did he die? Tell me, Saida." Tears ran down his face.

"Drink this uji," she said. "It will give you strength."

"I don't want to drink any more of this uji. It is bitter."

"You will drink it if you want to know more."

"You are killing me, Saida," he said and drank some.

————

Early one morning she awoke with a start. She sensed with her body, she put out her hand beside her on the mat, then turned and looked. Her son Shabani was missing. Her mother was not in her bed, Saida found her in the backyard. "Where's my child?" she asked. "Your child was sleeping next to you, and you are asking me?" replied her mother. The child was still crawling, he couldn't have gone far. But they couldn't find him anywhere.

"Where's my child?" Saida wailed. "Who took him away?"

"Your husband's a sorcerer, what do you think? That he'll take the insult and let the child grow up?"

"My mother, what are you telling me?" She ran to her husband's home and saw the old mganga sweeping the porch. He smirked at her, continued with the chore.

"You have lost something," he remarked.

"What have you done with the child?"

"Go away. I divorce you. Talaka, talaka, talaka!"

As she ran back to her mother, he called, "And tell your mother she'll get hers."

"Forget the child," advised her mother. "You cannot defy a mganga. And he was a child of sin, anyway."

And Saida knew instantly that her mother had handed over the child to her husband.

The next morning Saida saw her mother take something out from a small bottle and put it in the tea.

"What is that, Mother?" she asked.

"A medicine to make me better. To remove my ailment completely. And it will cure your grief too."

"Who gave it to you?"

There was a look in her mother's eyes.

"And I went mad," Saida said to Kamal.

And Kamal screamed and screamed. "Don't tell me more, Saida, don't tell me that!"

————

Now he knew he was dying. He was outside under the wide open sky, sitting in the grass; his shirt had been removed. His hands were tied behind his back tightly with a rope, and his feet at the ankles in front of him. He sat by himself, awkwardly, pain shooting through his limbs, not far from three or four people who were behind him, discussing him.

An old croaking voice that sounded familiar was saying, "My heart says I cannot agree to go through with this, Bwana Ngozi. I prepared him for the rite and brought him here, therefore I have fulfilled my responsibility. But to go further and do away with him—here I balk, bwana."

"Cast aside your whimsy, Bibi Ramzani," a man's voice reprimanded. "The water is spilled, there is no going back! Long ago we made a pact with Mzee Abdalla. When the father of the child returns, he told us, ill omen is sure to follow, unless we take measures. We must spill his blood right here, and cut off his tongue. His parts shall empower us and his penis shall sheath my knife."

A breeze blew across the clearing. In the distance, a few hundred yards away in front of him, Kamal could see a few pinpricks of light, hovering like fireflies. On his left the stream glistened. An almost full moon in a clear sky gave the night a silvery sheen. He was in his senses and yet lethargic and powerless. His shouts for help produced no sound. Was he inside a dream? He was in a grotesque situation. His captors were discussing cutting him into pieces to use as medicine. And yet he knew he had asked for this. He had been reckless and irresponsible, and gone off on his search without a thought to his safety. He struggled with his hands. The bruises burned.

"Our prisoner is coming to his senses," spoke a young woman's voice. Zara.

Why can I hear you, and you not me?

"Give him some more of the uji," said Bwana Ngozi. "Let his mind abandon him completely."

"You think he will take it," croaked Bibi Ramzani. "He's a stubborn one, a mule."

I hardly resisted when you gave it to me before, did I, Kamal protested silently.

Was he still hallucinating? Had he been hallucinating? Saida, I saw you. And this is the hell you saw fit to bring me to. But if it's from you I readily accept it.

A large round sculpted face with greying hair and dull droopy eyes loomed over him, hiding the moon. "Drink," Bwana Ngozi commanded, and reached out to hold Kamal's neck with a firm grasp at the back. Kamal drank the uji. This is it, he said to himself as the eclipse before him suddenly cleared. There followed a moment of quiet, or oblivion, broken by Zara's young voice.

"I say let him be, Bwana Ngozi. I am with Bibi Ramzani there. For truly what good will the poor man's death do for us? You've already taken his child. Now why go after him?"

"It is not for you to advise your elders, young lady. You are here as a novice and await your approval. It seems that you still need time. I say the water was spilled and it is spilled again! We proceed or we perish. Do I have to explain further, Bibi Ramzani?"

"No," Bibi Ramzani conceded. "I agree. Let us proceed."

"My elders, I ask your forgiveness for being outspoken," pleaded Zara. "But let us wait one more day. Tonight is Laylatu Kadir in the month of Ramadan, and all of Allah's angels and all the spirits will be witnesses to our deed."

There followed a moment in which nobody spoke and the night made itself felt in all its eternal depth. Kamal awaited his fate. The old man coughed.

"The spirits of our ancestors are more powerful, Zara," Bwana Ngozi said. "They were here before the advent of Islam. But this night has power, and according to your wish we will be prudent and come back tomorrow night. Take our captive and hide him in the bushes. And when he stirs, pour the uji down his throat."

He awoke hot and sweating on the grass; someone had cut his ropes and he was in pain. He was sick and he couldn't move. This much he consciously knew, he had been poisoned with drugs, and unattended he could die. The moon had risen, heightening the tones on the glowing landscape. He lay on his side, resigned to a pounding head, to the mercy of whoever it was who had cut his ropes. He did not know what awaited him. He had walked into an unopened chapter of his life, so intimately connected, so tragic, one he had turned away from. The road not taken . . . he had returned and taken it. And it had joined his life and demanded consequences from a deed committed long ago in innocent youth. The evil he had discovered, this knowledge was part of him now, these forgotten people were a part of him. Mama would say some witch would take him away if he played in the dark. And Mariamu left holes in the ground to catch children . . .

A hare had come and stood before him, its jaws moving steadily, machinelike. Frightened, seeing the devil in him, Bwana Ngozi himself, Kamal groped on the ground beside him, picked up a sharp stone with mud clinging to it and hit the hare with it, and as it fell quivering, he hit it again and again with a furious energy until it was pulp. And he puked. He threw out all the contents of his stomach. Intensely thirsty, he picked up a clump of grass and started chewing it furiously, and he ran in the direction of the glittering stream.

Zara intercepted him.

She handed him his bag, from which he extracted a bottle of water and drank.

"Come," she said, "your people have come looking for you."

Dr. Engineer and Lateef hastened to him and escorted him to the waiting car.

Before getting in, Kamal turned to Zara: "You will be all right?"

"You are my witness, my shahidi. You will protect me."

"She's as old as my daughter," he said to Navroz Engineer and passed out.

Later that day Kamal was flown to the hospital in Dar es Salaam.

· 45 ·

He had to find out, he had to find out what really happened that night in Minazi Minne, if that horror in the village was real. The memory of it was raw and painful. And vague. Had he seen Saida, or was she conjured up for him with drugs? What was the truth in that experience?

Did I want to go with him to Kilwa?

I said yes, of course.

Our journey was brought forward when Dr. Engineer called to inform Kamal that Ed Markham had died, he had walked into the ocean outside his hotel and drowned himself. He was buried in the local church ground soon after Kamal and I flew in the following morning. There were not more than ten people at the funeral, some of them guests at the hotel. As we sat that night on the patio, assuming some kind of a wake, Kamal recalled how despite his initial hostility he had been gradually drawn to the man, because he could understand his loneliness. He recalled their daily encounters, their conversations late in the night over a drink. Markham had left a will, found on his dresser, leaving the property, which was heavily mortgaged, to Kamal to dispose of as he wished. All of his few papers and photographs were to be burned.

Kilwa with its history and ancient ruins has been on many a travel wish list, but few people make it here, because it happens to be in the wrong direction: south. Zanzibar and Mombasa long superseded it as romantic tourist spots. I was keen to explore it. Kamal was pleased to hear this, it was his town after all. But I had made him my charge, and I was here primarily to keep an eye on him as he came to a conclusion, some kind of resolution regarding his search. As he put it, he had walked into the past and it had almost devoured him. But in the bustle of modern Dar, away from the quiet mystery and the painful reminders of Kilwa—and no small thanks to me, he admitted—he had managed to recover somewhat. While in Dar he had couriered a letter to his cousin Yasmin, describing Saida's visit to his uncle as it was revealed to him in his drugged state in that dark hut in Minazi Minne. She had phoned him and confirmed the story with those details she could remember, in particular her father saying, "What can you give him? He is an Indian, and you are an African."

If this much of what he had heard was true, then must the rest be too? Who was Bibi Ramzani, the old woman whose revolting potion had brought Saida back for him? What to make of that bizarre experience, the evil meeting under the moonlight? What part was real, what part hallucinated? Had he really seen a hare and, in a fit of frenzy, killed it with utmost savagery, with a stone? Kamal said that after his ordeal there were indeed rope marks on him, but there was no blood from hare or rope. And I knew from inquiries made locally that the police had raided Minazi Minne but found no sign of Mzee Ngozi. Nobody had heard of him. Bibi Ramzani had disappeared too.

Fatuma had died of her cancer while in the care of Dr. Engineer the week before we arrived, and we went together to the pharmacy to pay our condolences. Amina spoke to us from her serving window while we stood outside on the street. Her mother-in-law had been in great pain, she said, and it was for the better she had departed the world. "'From Him we come and to Him we return,' isn't that so," she said, reciting the Quranic formula in a Swahili-accented Arabic, and we concurred.

"Amina, there were many things Fatuma didn't tell me," Kamal said, sounding reproachful.

Serving a customer, she asked casually, "Such as?"

"Saida's child was killed. Then what happened?"

"She lost her mind. They sent her to Dodoma." The mental hospital.

He struggled with himself and looked away for a moment.

"That's what I heard," she added hastily. "But she returned."

"Then did she go to live in that village? Minazi Minne?"

She said nothing. The answer was yes. He gazed down the street at the intersection, bus touts standing in a boisterous group. Behind them the monument to two beheaded Germans. Four young girls in headscarves hurried up to study at the madrassa next door, which was already clamouring with kids. It was eleven in the morning.

"You knew all this, and you told me nothing?" he chided, assuming the right now to such familiarity. "All those days that I came here, asking? You could have saved me so much grief by just telling me this, Amina. There was no mercy in your heart."

"I am sorry. Polé sana. Mother swore us to secrecy."

As we made to go, having thanked her, at a whim Kamal turned and asked her, "Eti, Amina. Did Fatuma leave any papers behind? In a sanduku or something? Papers written by her father, Mzee Omari?"

She replied, sounding a little guilty, "Those papers were used a long time ago to wrap things. There was shortage of paper then that you don't know about, since you had gone abroad. How could we know they had value? The government should have alerted us. We had to wait for the foreigners to tell us, by which time it was too late."

We walked back to the intersection and asked for a taxi to Minazi Minne. There was no taxi free and Kamal would not take a bus. He must have a taxi. We had to wait, and finally some businessman's Toyota Cruiser, just in from Dar, was arranged for us to rent and we took off with the driver. On our minds the same thought, I imagine: Saida had arrived at that village, then what?

At the roadstop we were met by Zara, who had seen the white SUV draw up. She looked pretty in a new dress. The child was not around.

"Daktari," she said to him, "are you well?"

"I have recovered, thank you. How are you and the child? Did you take her to the doctor?"

"Not yet . . ."

"You should." Then: "Zara, that old woman—I want to see her. Where is she? Is she hiding somewhere?"

She stared wide-eyed at him, taken aback by his tone, wondering, I suppose, How can the rich and privileged be so desperate?

"Tell me about her, Zara. Where did she go?"

"Daktari . . . she died the day after you left. She was found in the river there in Minazi Minne."

Her voice had softened out of pity. She was only a girl. It was not hard to imagine what life was like here.

Kamal was pointing at Zara's blue sandals.

"Where did you get these?"

"I found them . . . in her room."

"And the dress too?"

She looked away. "Yes. I didn't steal it. She's dead, isn't she?"

"And what else did you find?"

"Nothing. You can go and look."

He asked her, softly, "Zara, who was this woman? Did she have any people?"

"Bibi Ramzani. She was crazy. She called herself Kinjikitilé."

"What did you say?"

"Kinjikitilé."

He became still, and in those moments the girl several times looked from him to me, until I said to him, "Kamal, let's go," and reached for his elbow.

He drew a deep breath. "Yes."

We drove back to Masoko in silence.

ACKNOWLEDGEMENTS

I would like to thank Kristin Cochrane, Maya Mavjee, and Sonny Mehta for their encouragement; Lynn Henry for her perceptive reading of the manuscript, her valuable suggestions, and for seeing the book through to print; Chiki Sarkar and Somak Ghoshal for their comments; Nurjehan for a final reading. Amyn and Nargis Sunderji generously shared their memories of Kampala; Dr. Felicitas Becker was helpful with comments and references regarding Tanzania, Kilwa, and Islam. The New York Public Library's Schomburg Center for Research in Black Culture was generous with its services. I am grateful to Mohamed Sumar for his truly wonderful hospitality in Dar es Salaam, and to Iqbal Dewji for his companionship in Kilwa and for bravely sharing a memorable and lengthy visit to a mganga. And finally I would like to thank my old friend Amin Dharamsi for teaching me how to read the *Juzu*, long ago when neither of us could have imagined where this knowledge would lead.

I have consulted numerous sources on the Maji Maji War, the utenzi form of poetry, and the practice of magic in Tanzania. These are too many to name all, but I would be remiss not to mention these few: John Iliffe, *A Modern History of Tanganyika* (Cambridge UP, 1979, rpt. 1984); Gilbert Gwassa, *The Outbreak and Development of the Maji Maji War 1905–1907* (Koln: Rüdiger Köppe, 2005); Hasani bin Ismail, tr. P. Lienhardt, *The Medicine Man* (Oxford UP, 1968); Gudrun Miehe,

Katrin Bromber, Said Khamis, and Ralf Grosserhode, *Kala Shairi: German East Africa in Swahili Poems* (Koln: Rüdiger Köppe, 2002); J. W. T. Allen, *Tendi: Six Examples of a Swahili Classical Verse Form with Translation and Notes* (New York: Africana Publishing, 1971); and José Arturo Saavedra Casco, *Utenzi, War Poems, and the German Conquest of East Africa* (Trenton, NJ: Africa World Press, 2007). The excerpt on p. 28 is from *The Lake and Mountains of Eastern & Central Africa*, J. Frederic Elton (London: John Murray, 1878), p. 82; the first verse of Mwana Kupona's poem on p. 53 is from Allen, p. 58; the quote on p. 154 from Captain Wangenheim's report is from Iliffe, p. 193.

This is, however and above all, a work of fiction; any deviation from historical truth (whatever that may be) is due only to me.